THE
NIGHT
BURNS
BRIGHT

THE
NIGHT
BURNS
BRIGHT

A NOVEL

ROSS BARKAN

LAKE UNION
PUBLISHING

Text copyright © 2022 by Ross Barkan
All rights reserved.

Published by Lake Union Publishing, Seattle

www.apub.com

Amazon, the Amazon logo, and Lake Union Publishing are trademarks of Amazon.com, Inc., or its affiliates.

ISBN-13: 9781542037150
ISBN-10: 1542037158

Cover design by David Drummond

Printed in the United States of America

For Vanessa, and my mother and father

It was the nightmare of real things, the fallen wonder
of the world.

—*Don DeLillo, The Names*

THE WORST DAY

Mama watches the screen, her tears hot and blinding. The volume is low, almost a whisper, and Lucien thinks he hears Mama whispering too, her lips moving along with the trace of sound.

She is shaking. This means he should be shaking too.

"Mama?"

Two gray buildings are burning in the sky. Black smoke pours from each tower, out of a void where people should be. An image on the screen flashes, a fireball Lucien has not seen, an explosion unleashed from the steel. There are bold graphics, men and women talking, just above the pitch of static. Lucien tries not to blink.

He thinks he can hear the screams.

Jack, his mentor, sent them all home early when the news came, even if the news did not come with a lesson, an understanding phrase Lucien could nurture alone, growing his spirit. Jack had simply said, *It's time to go now—something terrible has happened*, and Mama was out on the front grass, taking his hand. He waved goodbye to Evie and Magnus, and he was in the back of Mama's car, racing down the hill home. She was murmuring, her sentences like smoke, and Lucien could only look out the window, the sky so full of blue and nothing else.

"Mama?" he asks again.

She takes his hand and holds it tightly. He wants to turn away now, to leave the TV screen and go to the front room to touch his Game Boy and feel its familiar shell on the pads of his fingertips, the small plastic buttons rising and falling below.

The screen is a whirl of smoke and fire. He decides he must read the words. Until now, this was one of his favorite tasks—transforming a written language into images in his head, whole worlds.

"Mama, what's happening—"

"Please, Lucien."

There is a north tower and a south tower. He doesn't know they are directional, one positioned above or below the other on the rounded earth. This is in the city, hundreds of miles away, and he has never gone there. He has only seen images on the TV and read about it in books. He knows the towers are there but is surprised to find them in front of him now, like a long-lost relative staggering, bloody, on their doorstep.

But there is no one but Lucien and Mama, so there would be no one at their door.

They watch together. The screen tells them planes have crashed into both towers. This is strange to Lucien as much as it is terrifying. Aren't planes guided by technology? Aren't pilots trained? Jack says planes are sinful, spraying pollutants into the sky, and Lucien nods along during instruction, agreeing so Jack can come over to him after class, place his large hand on his head, and smile.

Good child, he will say. You are growing.

The planes are being punished, then, he decides. He has secretly wanted to ride on one, to know what it is to be a body in the sky. He wants to fly. He confesses this to no one, takes this secret and buries it deep within him. There is a difference between the language of the world and the language of the mind.

"He was—" Mama begins, not looking at him. The screen shows both buildings together, vast and crackling in silence.

"Mama?"

"O. C. was right."

He follows the slow trickle of tears. Mama has cried in front of him before, but he knows this is not like that. He knows he must grip her hand tighter. The soft tremor in her right hand stirs something in him he can't name, and he's crying too, harder than Mama, the tears clouding him.

When he opens his eyes, the screen is changing. A tower is disappearing, north or south, dissolving in a fantastic cloud.

"O. C. was right," she says again.

Her hand is gripping tighter, too tight, almost like an organism independent of her. A blade of heat cuts against his throat. The screen is full of smoke, black and thick, from the vanishing tower.

"Mama, what do you mean?"

Soon both will be gone, into this colossal dust cloud. Soon it will be afternoon and then nightfall, and he will be on Mama's bed, wondering when she will move, when the screen will finally turn off and he won't have to watch the two towers crumble again and again into infinity.

Yesterday, he turned twelve.

BEFORE

When Lucien first saw House of Earth, he saw color. Each room was painted a bright shade of pink or blue, and warm sunlight always seemed to flow through the wide windows. *Happy colors*, he would later learn. There had been little color where he used to be, and Mama told him this was because he was in a good place now.

You are six and a half, she said. You deserve it.

Yes, he thought. As he grew older, he could remember little before coming here. There was no reason to, not with Jack and all the friends around him, always. And Mama too. Mama worked in the room at the very front of the building, waving to him when he walked by at lunch. Mama had a very important job, which she described as record keeping, and Lucien would proudly tell the friends and Jack about this, and they would all beam back at him, content to know of Lucien's pride in Mama.

What stood out to him was the second day: the friends and Jack, his mentor. Jack was a big, smiling man, with rounded, pale muscles under the plain green or blue T-shirts he always wore to instruction. A pair of glasses rested on his nose. Jack bent down to Lucien, small for six and a half, and asked him to say his name.

"Lucien," he said.

"Can all of our friends here welcome Lucien to House of Earth?"

"Yes!" they cried out together, surrounding him. They held hands.

"This is our place," Jack said. "And it will be your place too."

Evie and Magnus were with him that day, as well as Antonio, Cavan, and Samantha. "We are all friends now," they said to him. Lucien could see Jack, his lips spread wide. Lucien nodded.

Antonio was the tallest then, and would always be. His hair, dark and long, draped over his eyes when he laughed the hardest. Lucien would learn that Antonio was always someone the friends wanted to play with. There was a lightness they would come to recognize, one they couldn't readily explain: Antonio was where he needed to be. They circled him in conversation, his head looming over them all, like a gentle dinosaur's. Antonio liked to stand near Jack.

Cavan was almost as tall as Antonio, his nose sharp and his small brown eyes searching. He enjoyed running until his breath gave out. He was strong enough to crack large sticks in two without really trying. They knew Antonio was even stronger, but Cavan always wanted to show his strength. He would be this way as he grew.

Magnus was smaller, stouter, with red-blond hair. His eyes were a shade of hard blue, like cornflower, and he was often with the other boys, following just behind.

Though Lucien would become closer to Samantha in the years to come in ways he could not imagine, he noticed her least in the beginning. She was smaller than he was, her hair in pigtails, skinny enough that her kneecaps were like round knobs poking hard against her skin. In that first year, she spoke softly, almost in a whisper.

Half the day was for mentoring, half the day was for the outside, Jack said. Lucien loved when Jack led them on expeditions to the woods, teaching them about the types of plants, how trees aged, why bees made honey. "This is how the world should be," he would often say. "Right here. We are leading it."

The woods gave way to a small river that, Jack said, led to the mighty Hudson. Lucien had never seen the mighty Hudson, and he hoped to one day. Evie said she wanted to sail a boat down the river. Magnus wanted to surf it.

"The river doesn't belong to us," Jack said. "We must understand what we are doing to it each time with our bodies when we interact with it."

Mama started to encourage Lucien to walk to school. They lived two miles away, up a winding dirt road on a hill that overlooked town. He had learned he lived in this place called Mater, that it was a town in the state of New York, which he could pick out on the novelty map that he'd asked Mama to put up in the kitchen after he saw it selling for a dollar at the gas station one summer morning.

"Jack wants you walking to school," she told him.

"Okay, Mama."

"Even if it's cold or wet or snowy—we are going to do it together."

———

He was eight, painting a birdhouse in the instruction room, when Jack walked over to him and touched his wrist. "Lucien, what are you doing?"

"I'm painting a birdhouse. I want to give it to Mama—"

"That color, Lucien. Why?"

He hadn't realized he had been painting the birdhouse from the black in his palette. "I don't know, I just . . ."

"Why, Lucien?"

"I didn't think about it."

"Friends!" Jack said in a pitch Lucien hadn't heard before, a sharp cry that seemed to radiate from the back of his throat. All the friends wheeled around.

"Our friend Lucien here is making a mistake. Mistakes are okay, but we must learn from them."

Jack turned and slowly walked to the supplies cabinet, which was Lucien's favorite—a tall, light-purple structure of wood so smooth he hardly believed it was real. Jack leaned in, his head briefly disappearing into the dark. He came out with another wooden birdhouse. Lucien, sitting at his table next to Evie, followed Jack's hand as he lowered the birdhouse in front of him. It landed with a soft thud, light and bare next to the half-blackened birdhouse Lucien had painted for the last ten minutes.

Jack was speaking now. "Friends, what did we say about black?"

"It's, uh, it's . . . the negative," Magnus said, his arm shooting up.

"The negative," Kaitlyn echoed with more conviction.

"Yes, friends, we do not use that color. It does not represent us. Do we see it in nature? Are the trees black? The water in the creek? The grass we touch?"

"No!" they all said, except Lucien. Lucien had forgotten the lesson. Where had he been?

"We must avoid it if we are going to live in harmony with everyone. Do we remember harmony?"

"I do," Magnus said.

"Yes, yes," Kaitlyn followed.

"Harmony is about living together, sharing what we have. The world is filled with many people who do not want harmony, who want to hurt nature. This is the negative energy that comes with that. Lucien"—Jack's voice was quieter now as he turned to Lucien—"you do not want your representation for your birdhouse to be *negative*. The black paint is put in your palette as a test. Unfortunately, today, you did not pass the test. But we all fail, and failing is part of growing. Please paint your new birdhouse with different colors. Please try again."

"I will, Jack."

Lucien never wanted to let Jack down. At home, Mama told him how important it was to listen to his mentor. "You are in a special place, Lucien. Always know this."

"I do, Mama."

Mama knew about the birdhouse. She told Lucien to sit in the garden on an oak bench she had built. She told him to sit and think.

No Game Boy, no books, no time with the TV. The sun was a deep orange in the sky, robins flying overhead. He was hungry, and sitting still was more tiring than he'd thought it would be. He counted rocks, caterpillars, even ants. He did not know the time. When Mama told him to sit, there was a sun in the sky, and now it was night, the stars and moon overtaking the light of his memory. He bent over and closed his eyes. When he opened them, he hoped, he would be inside again, in his bed. Mama had told him they'd lived somewhere else before Mater, but he couldn't remember that. He had been three when they came to the cottage on the hill, their cottage, and this was his four-room world. In the darkness, he stared at the wildflowers and tried to listen to them like Jack said to, to listen for nature and hear her song. He tried hard. If he heard the song, perhaps he could go inside. He did not hear Mama. He wanted to call to her, but this might make her upset. He was sorry for the birdhouse. He tried to remember exactly why he had done it, dabbed his brush in the forbidden color and begun to paint. He wasn't thinking, that's what, and that was disobeying Jack too. Disobeying House of Earth. Hadn't Jack always said to use your mind? To open it up as wide as possible? Instead, he had closed it.

Lucien was so, so sorry.

His head dipped low and he felt the familiar pull of sleep, his knees weak on the bench. Hunger ripped at him. If he slept, he could forget it. He felt a wetness running through his hair and pinpricks of water on his forearms, and he understood, his mind drifting from his body, that it was raining. The cold drops struck him, one by one. There was the hiss of leaves, the rain simmering against him. The bench was hard against his scalp.

"Lucien," he heard, and he was on a soft surface, coughing. The front-room couch. She had carried him in. "Lucien."

"Mama."

"Do you understand now? Do you understand why we need to be better?"

"I do, Mama."

"Jack wants what's best for you, like I do. I know you will be better. I love you."

"I love you, Mama."

She held him and he saw it was morning. He would be back to instruction in a few hours. There would be many more chances to grow. His skull ached from where he had slept on the garden bench.

―――

Lucien knew his favorite time was supposed to be instruction with Jack, but it was really the lunch and recreation hour. After a morning of storytelling, woodcraft, and multiplication tables, he and the friends were allowed a whole hour on the commons. The commons was behind the building where he had instruction, leading into the woods where Jack took the collective on afternoon walks. *Collective* was a new word that had entered Lucien's awareness. Jack, during instruction, had begun to call them that more and more.

Lucien had looked up the word in the dictionary.

Done by people acting as a group.

They were a collective and soon, even, they had another name for what they were. "You are Meadows," Jack said. "This is very exciting. You've earned this. It is a symbol of your success, and the success of House of Earth."

As Meadows, the seven of them ran to the commons to play. Lucien could throw horseshoes, shoot arrows at the archery range, and toss the ball they'd made during instruction into the basketball hoop teetering at the mossy edge of the commons. The ball didn't look like a real basketball—it was softer and stuffed with tissue paper—but with bright-orange paint, Lucien could pretend it was. Though they didn't talk about professional sports at House of Earth, he could follow the leagues at home and lose himself in their myth. There were the mighty

Yankees of baseball and the Knicks of basketball. After Magnus told Lucien about something called the NFL, Lucien asked Mama and she said it was simply too violent and he wasn't allowed to watch football or play it.

Each year, more friends gathered on the commons. Lucien realized they had names for their collectives too. When he had first come to House of Earth, there had been hardly any friends beyond the Meadows, and now there were so many. This excited Lucien. He wanted more friends for play, especially for woods exploration and shooting the basketball. Instead of dribbling, they would pass the ball to each other and toss it toward the hoop. One time, Jack asked for the ball and jumped all the way up and pushed the ball through the hoop. This was called a dunk.

"One day, you will all be big enough to do the same," he said.

———

When Lucien turned ten, he was allowed to perform in the May Festival. All the Meadows except Evie were ten, and they could perform too. Every friend ten and older gathered around the maypole, where they grabbed their light-red, blue, green, pink, purple, or orange ribbons. Garlands of sunflowers and wildflowers rested in their hair. Jack and the other mentors were there, and a man Lucien did not recognize began to play the flute. Together, they bent their knees and danced in unison as Jack had taught them, moving to a tune they had never heard before but now understood had been calibrated for their movements.

Mama stood with her camera, taking pictures of him. He had not seen her so happy in a long time. Gazing at her from his position by the maypole, his feet skittering to the flute's honeyed melody, Lucien realized, for the first time, how much he looked like her. This made sense—he had come from her, after all. But this speck of knowledge, acquired from her own allusions and a science textbook about DNA and reproduction he had tried to read in the public library, had now bloomed on the May Festival, as he danced with the friends to welcome summer. He was his mama. They were one. It was like Jack said.

When she looked at him, she must see herself too.

On his way around the maypole, leading Kaitlyn and trailing Magnus, Lucien also noticed the man playing the flute. He was not dressed like any of the mentors. While they wore khakis, blue jeans, or skirts, he was clad in something else, a white robe that seemed to flow with a wind that was not there. He was tall, much taller than Jack, and his arms, legs, and chest were thinner, concave where Jack was convex. There was his hair: white blond, almost radically so, of a hue Lucien had never seen before. It rested gently on his shoulders. When he played his flute, his eyes were shut, and Lucien could see just how much the music moved this man, how it all meant more than anything else in the world at that very moment. He wanted to leave the maypole and run over to him, to ask him, somehow, for his secret.

"One more time around!" Jack called out.

They circled again and came to a rest. Lucien saw that it wasn't just Mama and the mentors who had come. A small crowd had gathered, many of them parents of the friends. Tables were set up to sell candied treats on behalf of House of Earth. Overnight, a climbing pole had been erected in the back of the commons, as well as a beanbag toss and several bull's-eyes for archery. Mama, along with the rest of the parents and mentors, clapped for them.

"It's so cool we can finally be in the May Festival," Magnus said to Lucien.

"I was waiting a long time too."

"I heard there's gonna be a relay race."

"Really?"

"Yeah."

Magnus was right. With Jack officiating, all the friends lined up for a race in two teams. When Lucien's hand was tagged and he launched himself forward with all his might, he could feel the growth Jack had talked about, the power and warmth of his body in delicious motion, one foot blurring in front of the other. He had been paired against Cavan, who was taller and stronger, and at first he was behind, trailing Cavan by several steps. He needed to reach the orange cone at the far end of the commons, halt, and then pivot to race back to his team. He could be fast too, he told himself. He could be as fast as Cavan.

When they reached the cone, they were almost tied. Lucien felt a pulse in his legs, the sunlight on his neck. He lifted his knees up and propelled himself forward, his tongue sticking out his mouth. He was tied with Cavan and then he was ahead, surging to the outstretched hand of Magnus. He smacked it and tumbled down into the grass, laughing.

"We won!"

After the race, Jack gathered the Meadows to tell them about the significance of the May Festival. "We are marking the beginning of summer, a new cycle for the planet," he said. "We must respect the gifts we have and cherish them. They might not last."

Evie asked if the planet was in trouble.

"Yes, sadly. It is under attack every day. Most people do not live as we do. They do not respect gifts from God. They cut down trees, throw trash in the river, and burn gas that destroys the atmosphere. If more lived like us, we could save the planet tomorrow."

"Why don't they?"

"It's an excellent question. Not everyone is ready yet. But they will be."

Lucien was listening to Jack but also looking past him, to the tall blond man in the robes of white. He had put his flute away and was talking to a woman who, Lucien realized, was Evie's mother. He could almost hear what they were saying. Evie's mother was shaking her head, looking down. The man was nodding. He placed a hand on her shoulder. When Lucien squinted, he saw tears in Evie's mother's eyes.

A few minutes later, when Jack told them they could go to the hall for lunch, Kaitlyn touched Lucien on the shoulder. "Hey, my mom is having people over for a pool party after school. Do you want to come?"

Lucien blinked back, his mouth not moving. No one called House of Earth *school*. And who were the people? Meadows? Other collectives? Lucien had swum in motel pools when Mama decided to go on drives for the summer, but what exactly was a party in a pool? For birthday parties at House of Earth, Lucien and the friends ate from fruit baskets and enjoyed fresh-baked cookies. Would there be fruit baskets in the pool? He could only wonder.

"I'll go."

"My mom will pick us up. Just come out to the front at three."

"Okay."

Lucien had a Pokémon digital watch that kept time. It was a gift from Mama for turning nine last year. At 2:58, he walked out to the front oval, where cars would come for pickup and a rusted flagpole rattled with an American flag. He saw Magnus, Cavan, Evie, and Antonio there already. They waved at him and didn't say anything. Antonio and Evie were locked in an intense conversation about which dinosaurs were the fastest.

A silver minivan, much larger than Mama's car, drove up to the oval. Lucien turned and saw Kaitlyn approaching from around the corner, pointing not to him but to the minivan. It slowed in front of the group just as Kaitlyn reached them.

"Hi, Sophia!" she cried out to the minivan.

A darkened window rolled down. "Come on in, kids."

Lucien waited until everyone else jumped in the minivan to enter. It was cool and dark and smelled like mint. He sat in the very back, next to Antonio, who was humming, his eyes looking out the window, while Evie and Magnus played rock, paper, scissors. Sophia asked if everyone was hungry, and Kaitlyn added that there were all kinds of snacks and would be more when they got to the party.

After a few minutes, Lucien saw that they were slowing down. The minivan rumbled through a brick entryway with two large gates swung to the sides. The roadway snaked in a wide arc to a house larger than any Lucien had seen before, sprawling enough to fit ten of Mama's cottages, maybe more. The windows were tall and wide, with sparkling glass. Long, white columns flanked a pair of doors with lion's-head door knockers. A fountain of cherubs sprayed water on a front lawn that, to Lucien, seemed almost as big as the commons.

"This is actually a party for my sister, but we are all invited," Kaitlyn said as the minivan came to a stop.

"Do you need anything else?" Sophia asked.

"Nah . . . well, maybe make sure we don't run out of orange soda."

"Yes, dear."

When they all stepped out of the minivan, Cavan yawned and stretched out his arms. "Big house!"

"My mom and dad bought it," Kaitlyn said matter-of-factly.

"Is Sophia your aunt?"

"She's our helper. She does everything for us. I love Sophia."

"I wish we had a helper."

"You can get one too. Anyone can."

"Really?"

"Yeah."

Lucien could hear the distant sound of laughter. It was coming from behind the house. He also heard what sounded like the bounce of an inflatable ball, the splash of water, and a sizzle he did not quite recognize. Kaitlyn's house, colored eggshell white and accented with gold, shot out wide in both directions, so far that Lucien couldn't imagine how people walked through it all every day. It was like the kingdoms he read about in books.

"Let's go to the back," Kaitlyn said, and they all turned to follow her. At House of Earth, she was quieter, like Lucien. But here, with her white columns and cherub fountain, she was someone new, and Lucien

14

wanted to follow her. Or someone *old*—herself at home, among what she knew best. Lucien was beginning to see that people, even adults, could be more than just themselves, that their words and feelings could depend on where and when they appeared.

This was true of everyone but Mama, who was always Mama.

They walked on a stone path around the side of the house, wedged between the siding and enormous hedgerows. Lucien noticed wild leek and red baneberry growing from the soil. He was still looking down at the array of flowers when they all walked into the backyard, a long expanse of grass that led to a swimming pool larger than any he knew existed. Plastic chairs and small tables with meat in glimmering foil and red cups and bottles of soda were set up on all sides of the pool, as well as a long table covered in a fruit-patterned tablecloth. On top sat enormous bowls of chips, fruit punch, and boxes of pizza. Children his age and older were swimming in the pool, racing outside it, readying to jump in, and then howling as they smashed through the surface of the water. He saw adults too, almost as many, reclining in chairs and holding bottles of a brown liquid. Many of them wore sunglasses.

His arm, when he wasn't looking, brushed against a statue of a pink flamingo almost as tall as he was. He stared, briefly, into its dead plastic eyes.

"What do you want to do first?" Kaitlyn asked them.

"We could play in the grass. I know a game," Evie said.

"Maybe swim?" Antonio asked.

"After the game."

A shadow passed over them. Lucien saw that it belonged to a heavy man with little hair atop his head, his tropical-themed shirt unbuttoned to reveal a soft, sagging stomach with swirling black hairs. He also held a glass bottle with brown liquid. Sunscreen congealed on his face, reminding Lucien of eggplant left too long on Mama's countertop.

He smiled down at them and placed a thick hand on Kaitlyn's shoulder.

"Hi, Dad."

"Katie! Are these your friends?"

"Yes, Dad. They came today. They are very excited to be here."

"Good, good. Whatever you want, we got. Pizza, cake, chips, kielbasa—you name it. Your mother really outdid herself. Or go take a dip! I'll probably swim a little bit."

"We can't wait, Dad."

"Good, sweetie. Good."

Kaitlyn's father stood above them for another moment, his face wrinkling in thought. He drank deeply from the bottle. Lucien did not like his smell. When he walked away, Lucien watched as the fat on his torso wiggled in rhythm with his footsteps. He was nothing like Jack and certainly nothing like the man with the flute. Lucien was glad he was walking away.

"That's my dad," Kaitlyn said.

Lucien did not recognize most of the boys and girls. They were not from House of Earth. Seemingly reading Lucien's quizzical expression, Kaitlyn turned to him. "They're my sister's friends from her school. She's two years older than me. She's pretty mean."

"Really?"

"You'll see. Let's go play."

Beyond the pool and the patio was the bright-green grass, grown long in the late spring. A red-and-blue doghouse—colors that made Lucien happy—was perched in one corner, though there didn't seem to be any dog. They all sat in a circle. Evie, who usually took the lead, opened her mouth wide.

"I like the smell here," she said. "What is that?"

"Probably the grill. My dad likes to barbecue."

"Aw yeah," Cavan said.

Barbecue. The word was familiar, but Lucien did not know quite what it meant. He wanted to ask but didn't always like asking questions out in the open. While Jack smiled and answered in his soft way—there is no such thing as a bad question, he liked to say—Lucien also sensed there were people who did not like answering questions, and if you asked too many, you showed what you didn't know. All the friends seemed to know just a little more than he did about certain things, while he knew more about other things. For example: flower names. Lucien always paid attention to Jack's lessons on flowers, while the friends didn't seem to care as much. Yet there were other facts, words, and ideas floating in the world that just seemed to elude Lucien. Mama didn't think they were important.

She did not ever say *barbecue*.

"He's making hamburgers and ribs, I think."

"I love baby back ribs."

"Cavan!" Evie jumped in. "That's *meat*."

"It is . . ."

"Do you even *listen* at instruction?"

Lucien understood now. The barbecue was a way to cook meat, the flesh of animals. He gripped his stomach. Jack and Mama had both talked often about the horror of what lay beyond House of Earth, and that included the way other people would murder and consume living animals. Jack once said that to imagine the pain of a pig or a cow going to slaughter, imagine your little brother or sister. Or if you didn't have a little brother or sister (Lucien did not), imagine, then, your mother or father. Pigs and cows *think*, Jack said. They talk to each other; they cuddle; they love. They are just like you and me. Do you like being pricked on the arm? Have you ever accidentally stepped on glass? (Lucien had, once, and it hurt like nothing before.) Now take that pain, the glass cutting through your bare skin, and multiply it (they had just finished running through the multiplication tables) by *one thousand*. Have you ever touched a flame? (Lucien's finger once darted around the tip of a candle flame.) Now take that pain and multiply it again by a thousand. We are burning living creatures. We are mutilating them. (Lucien looked up the word in the dictionary, and it was as monstrous as it sounded.) We cannot live in harmony with nature and guarantee the survival of humans if we are killing and eating the very creatures who want to live alongside us in peace, who provide balance to the world. Do we remember our lesson on balance? (Yes!) When Jack told Lucien to imagine his mother or father, he nearly cried—someone trying to kill and eat Mama! Never. Jack shook his head sadly. There is much in this world we have to fix.

"I . . . I listen," Cavan said.

Evie was shaking. "Those poor animals, they never had a chance . . ."

"My dad didn't kill them, you know," Kaitlyn said, looking away.

"It doesn't matter!"

"Let's play a game," Antonio said. "It's like Jack says: wherever you are, you can always make a positive space for yourself. We can do it too."

"Should we play O. C.?" Evie asked.

"Sure."

"Yes."

"Let's play."

"Who gets to be O. C.?"

"Let's take turns," Evie said. "Lucien, how about you? Do you want to be O. C.?"

Lucien nodded. It had been a long time since he was chosen to be O. C. Out of all the games they played, especially on the commons, this was one that held special meaning for him, as it did all the friends. It was not like shooting the basketball or tossing the horseshoe. When they were younger, Jack had taught them the game, explaining it was a way to both have fun and enjoy a healthy activity while learning about the world. We are always learning, Jack said. We must keep our minds and hearts open.

Lucien stood up. All his friends surrounded him in a circle, standing just out of arm's reach. He breathed in, breathed out, and remembered the words he had sung out so many times on the commons, the sun glinting through the sugar maple trees.

"Summon me, summon thee . . ." Lucien began. His eyes were closed and he watched the inky shapes behind his eyelids, how they called to him like the faintest of black holes. "The winds, the trees, the soil, and sun. Together, we become one. I, O. C., declare us whole, each one soul. In with the good, out with the bad, cast out those who dare attack—invite the light and not the black!"

The friends all scattered across the grass. As O. C., he had to catch each one and touch them on the skin. It was a blessing to play O. C. because everyone else in the game was a dark spirit, and dark spirits needed to be cleansed by O. C.'s light. Jack said the game was a reminder of the gifts O. C. Leroux had given them.

For one, Jack said, O. C. Leroux created House of Earth. *This is his gift to you.* Lucien remembered asking, Who is he? Can we meet him?

Jack smiled. One day, Lucien. Not today, but one day.

Did he create the world like God?

No, Jack said. O. C., like all of us, serves God, but he can have special conversations. He was told to start House of Earth to help us all live in harmony and protect the planet.

O. C. Leroux, as the man who had made House of Earth, always knew light had to triumph over dark. Darkness, sadly, was everywhere, but as long as we do what's right, Jack said, we can defeat it wherever we go. This means respecting our friends, our elders, and nature. It means always living in harmony.

Lucien sprinted after the friends, hoping to catch each one as quickly as possible. Evie ducked behind a tree. She sang out "Darkness!" and Lucien gave chase, knowing he had to get her first if he was going to cleanse the world of dark spirits and do right by O. C. Evie was quick too and kept jumping around the tree as Lucien tried to reach her. "Darkness!" she said again. He lunged at her but missed, and she pushed off the tree, running down the edge of the backyard near a long row of beautiful flowerbeds. Cavan and Antonio were closer, nearer to the adults drinking their liquid and gnawing at their awful meat. Lucien turned and gave chase, extending both hands.

"Darkness!" they cried out together.

This time, Lucien knew he could reach at least one of them, catching Antonio as he leaped away from a white plastic table. Both of his hands fell on Antonio's wide shoulders, and Antonio froze.

"Light!" Lucien cried out.

"You got me," Antonio said. "You turned darkness into light."

Lucien shook with glee. He knew, in his own small way, he was making the world a better place, just as Jack said. As he spun around to find Cavan, he heard low, throaty laughter near the pool. It was from one of the adults.

He saw Kaitlyn's father leaning over and whispering to another man. They were both laughing. Each of them clutched a glass bottle of the brown liquid. The other man was even softer and hairier than Kaitlyn's father, with a brown beard eating up his face. On a small glass table between them rested a paper plate piled high with dripping animal meat slathered in a blood-colored sauce.

"Look at them," Lucien heard Kaitlyn's father say. Cavan was still running. He wanted to chase after Cavan, but his feet would not move. From the corner of his eye, he could see Evie and Kaitlyn slipping behind an oak tree together.

"What is it? Tag?" the man with the beard answered, wiping his mouth with the back of his hand.

"To be honest? I don't fucking know. This is all Rhonda. She wanted to stick Katie in that place, help her adjust with the issues she was having . . ."

"The kids seem nice, I guess."

"Nice? They're all into this hug-the-earth granola shit. It's costing me a pretty penny too. Rhonda likes it more than Katie does, I think."

"Rhonda was always like that."

20

"You listen to these kids?" He took another drink, his head dipping back into the sun. "Shouting about light and dark? It's too weird for me. I don't know. I trust Rhonda with this and get out of the way, you know? It's a lot of weird bullshit. She thinks Katie's behavior improved with it."

"Katie's a good kid."

"Yeah. It reminds me of like, what am I thinking of—witches in the woods? Salem witches. Gives me the creeps, honestly. We send Sophia to pick her up."

"Annie is liking Penbrooke. Costs me a ton too, but you know, if you're looking elsewhere—"

"Trust me, I'd *love* to get Katie in Penbrooke. An actual private school with rules that make sense. But Rhonda likes the hippie-dippie. It ain't for me."

Lucien took off after Cavan, his head bent low like a ram's. A low wail rose from his throat, like a small radio had been tucked in his mouth. He didn't want to hear any more from the adults. They were using ugly words. He learned a lot about this ugliness, from both Mama and Jack—they told Lucien there would always be people who wanted to obstruct light with dark. Could Kaitlyn really be the daughter of someone like that? Someone who *enjoyed* swallowing the flesh of animals and drinking whatever was hidden in that bottle? He was sorry for her. He was happy to be with Mama, but not everyone was so lucky. Maybe Mama would take Kaitlyn in too. She deserved so much better. He was thinking of this as he caught up to Cavan and tapped his shoulder blade.

"Darkness," Cavan said, out of breath.

"Light!"

He chased Evie next. Again, they went around and around the tree, but this time Lucien accelerated in the same way he had in his race against Cavan at the May Festival, and he landed both hands on Evie's collarbone, coming down harder than he would have liked.

21

"Darkness," she said, looking away.

"Light."

Magnus and Kaitlyn were left. He could see Magnus inching behind a row of tall bushes. What he hated was that he could still hear the stray sounds of Kaitlyn's father, the way his voice seemed to cut open the air and land right in Lucien's ear. He was talking about something else, matters Lucien didn't understand, *securities* and the *law* and *meaningful cash flow*. A glass bottle struck the top of the table, ringing out. Kaitlyn's father exhaled, peering down at a paper plate filled with the ribs of an unidentified animal. He detached one, his large front teeth ripping at the darkened, sauce-flecked meat, brown bits standing out against the unusual whiteness of his teeth. Lucien continued to stare. Once the meat was chewed off, Kaitlyn's father sucked on the bone like a straw. Lucien felt a churning in his stomach.

"Come catch me, Lucien!" Magnus yelled.

Lucien ran. He was discovering he was the fastest of the friends. Perhaps that was because he was the smallest and lightest, his bare feet hardly making an imprint on the grass. Magnus was huffing, his arms shaking behind him. They were near the pool, not far from Kaitlyn's father, and Lucien wished Magnus would run somewhere else. As O. C., it was Lucien's duty to purge the world of darkness, and that meant following where darkness went. He could not *choose* to ignore it. He had to go after it and use his power for good. It was a game, but Jack told them games could be preparations for unexpected situations. You are all vessels of light, Jack said. This is what O. C. teaches us.

Lucien caught Magnus next to the pool, where a multicolored beach ball was being tossed back and forth.

"Darkness!"

"Light!"

"For God's sake, cut that out."

Lucien wrenched his head around. Kaitlyn's father was staring directly at them, his eyes small and black. Brown sauce filled the corners of his mouth. Lucien saw a redness in his cheeks that he had not noticed before. He heaved his large body upward, out of the chair. Lucien's hands were still on Magnus's shoulder.

"Don't run near the damn pool," Kaitlyn's father said.

"Richard!" A woman Lucien had not seen before was approaching them, moving between a walk and a run, her painted pink toes drawn close together. She wore very large, circular sunglasses and smelled like pineapples. "Don't yell at Katie's little friends."

"They were going to fall into the pool and drown. You want that?"

"You are being *very* hostile today."

"At least I know up from down."

"What's that supposed to mean?"

"Take a guess."

"Richard."

"I don't need this."

"You don't, huh? You don't?"

Lucien hadn't been aware of the background chatter and noises, the voices of conversations and clinks of glass bottles and bouncing of balls, until it all stopped. Kaitlyn's father and the woman were now the center of the party, even if they stood on one far end of the pool.

"It's one thing if you want to send her *there*—it's another to bring them *here*."

Kaitlyn's father's teeth were clenched together, as though he were trying to hide his words.

"These are our daughter's friends, Richard."

"Katie's gonna know how to build all the goddamn birdhouses in the world, but she won't be able to read—"

"We aren't talking about this here."

"I'm going inside. I can't deal with you right now."

Kaitlyn's father brushed past her, shoving aside a pair of pinkish-white doors that led to the backyard. Lucien listened for his footsteps receding into the house and breathed out when he no longer heard him at all. The woman, who Lucien guessed was Kaitlyn's mother, turned to him and Magnus and smiled in a strange way. It was neither happiness nor sadness. Kaitlyn still needed to be caught. She was at the other end of the pool, staring at them. She did not seem to be thinking about the game. Only when he sprinted in her direction did she spin around and try to evade him, jumping between trees until Lucien, his own breath almost out, tagged her on the arm.

"Darkness," she said quietly.

"Light," he answered, his task complete.

Afterward, sweat rolling down their foreheads, Kaitlyn asked if they wanted to go for a swim.

———

At instruction the next day, Jack asked them how much they'd all enjoyed the May Festival, considering it was the first one, as ten-year-olds, they could take part in. Evie said she was excited to perform next year.

"We are all excited to have you," Jack said.

"We did something cool afterward too," Antonio said, his left hand in the air, his right gripped around a yellow crayon. He liked to color continuously during instruction, and Jack said this was good for his development.

"What did you do?" Jack asked.

Kaitlyn was looking from side to side. "They came to my house for a party," she said. "It was for my sister, but everyone was invited."

"That's wonderful. And so generous of you and your sister to invite all of your friends."

"Well, it was more my mom. I don't think my sister wanted us there that bad."

Evie and Magnus snickered. Antonio was coloring again.

"You are a special person, Kaitlyn, and if your sister doesn't see that yet, she will soon."

Jack smiled and Kaitlyn smiled back. Antonio, who was making an aggressive spiral on a piece of off-white construction paper, put his hand back up.

"Yes, Antonio?"

"It was so cool. It would have been cool if *you* even came, Jack. Lucien played O. C. And then we all got to swim in the pool."

Lucien saw, at the end of Antonio's sentence, how the expression on Jack's face abruptly changed. His mouth was much smaller and drawn together.

"A pool?" Jack asked.

"Yeah! It was really big. Kaitlyn has the best pool."

"I guess," Kaitlyn said.

"Okay . . ." Jack walked slowly around the room, touching his hand to his temple. Lucien could see he was beginning to sweat. "We are going to do a new lesson today. I want you all to listen very carefully. You especially, Kaitlyn. This is going to be a message to bring home to Mom and Dad later, okay?"

"Okay."

Jack closed his eyes and then opened them again. "Friends, we talk often about being in harmony with nature and respecting the earth. We cannot live lives free of negativity if we are not respecting the earth. All of you, I know, have wonderful intentions and lively, free spirits. O. C. Leroux, when he meets you, would be extremely proud of the progress you have made. As we make progress, of course, there are still stumbles. There is still darkness. Are we all still fighting the darkness?"

They all said yes.

"To fight it means to live with light. It means we don't litter, don't eat animals, don't throw garbage in our waters. And it means we do not *waste*. The world we live in, sadly, is filled with all kinds of darkness and people who are led down the wrong path. People you know and love.

It is up to you to guide them back. This is a great responsibility. I know you are up to it."

Jack held the bridge of his nose. He appeared to be thinking deeply. Lucien gripped the edges of his table.

"We have all been in swimming pools. Some, like Kaitlyn, may even have one. Now, friends—what do you think the problem with swimming pools is?"

Lucien didn't like the silence in the room. Usually, someone like Evie or Antonio jumped to answer. Lucien didn't like to say too many words at once. He preferred others talking. Now, as he looked around, he realized no one knew the exact answer Jack wanted, and this was a new feeling. Usually, if Lucien were to answer, Jack would like the answer. But he was sure now that whatever he said, it would somehow be wrong.

"Kaitlyn?" Jack asked.

"I don't know."

"Well, this is a good time for a lesson. Swimming pools are very, very bad for our harmony with nature. They are an example of what we *cannot* do—selfishly hurt the earth for our own enjoyment. They consume a great amount of energy. They waste a great amount of water. Chemicals from swimming pools—very, very bad chemicals—can go into our atmosphere and damage it, pollute our drinking water, and poison our animal friends. Nature is under threat in so many ways. When we create more ways to threaten nature, we create an unbalanced world filled with darkness instead of light. We fail our friends. We fail the earth. Does that make sense?"

Everyone, including Lucien, nodded.

"This is not your fault. Many people who came before you made many bad mistakes. We are living with those mistakes, and we do what we can every day to bring light into the world, to save our planet. But we also have to be aware of our actions. I want all of you to think about what you have done and why you shouldn't do it again. Now, Kaitlyn, you have to be responsible too. We are all almost old enough for May Festival, so we are old enough to know the consequences of our actions. Kaitlyn, do you know what you did?"

"I think, I mean, I'm sorry . . ."

Jack stood over her, shaking his head. "Please take your chair and sit over there, Kaitlyn. You must take time now on your own to think and reflect, to go inside yourself. You need to understand your actions. We all must be better."

Jack was pointing to the far corner of the room, near their cubbies. Lucien had never been sent there, and he was afraid for Kaitlyn. It was the darkest corner, farthest from the window. Kaitlyn wordlessly lifted up her chair and walked to the corner. She turned it toward Jack and sat down, smiling.

"Kaitlyn, please turn around now."

At first, Kaitlyn didn't move. Lucien wasn't sure whether she was confused or actively ignoring Jack, which seemed impossible. A small smile held on Jack's face. He adjusted his glasses. No one else was talking. They all turned toward Kaitlyn, waiting for her to listen.

Finally, she turned around.

"Keep your eyes on the wall, Kaitlyn. Please do not close them. Think. Reflect. Understand the harm you have done to our planet but also the potential you hold to heal it. We all do. O. C. Leroux taught us."

For the rest of instruction, Kaitlyn remained turned around, staring straight into a small white patch of wall next to the cubbies. Lucien tried to focus on what Jack was saying, but he was lost in the memory of his time on the bench, the raindrops falling on his skin. Kaitlyn must be sorry. He was sorry too. He burned with embarrassment. After playing O. C., he had dipped his feet in the pool, though he did not have swimming trunks. Perhaps he should confess to Jack that he had wet his feet. He'd certainly enjoyed what it *looked* like, and that was close to the same thing. He hoped that Kaitlyn could be forgiven and he could be forgiven too. He hated when Jack and Mama were upset with him.

They had every right to be. Mistakes couldn't be made.

Jack resumed a lesson from yesterday about the Roman and Greek gods. In Rome, Zeus was Jupiter, and Ares was Mars. The gods lived on Mount Olympus. Lucien wondered how much bigger Mount Olympus was than the biggest mountain in the Catskills, and if there was a god still there, waiting to be worshipped. Jack said the Greeks and Romans had a special energy and understood the power of worship. They also lived *in communion* with nature, Jack said. Lucien didn't know what this meant and decided to ask.

"What does that mean, in com-union?"

"It means have a bond with, to be one with—it's the way we should all live."

"Wow."

In Rome, Heracles was Hercules. The gods were noble and strong but also fought each other. They weren't always so different from humans, Jack said. Zeus would get into trouble. There was his wife, Hera, and Artemis and Demeter and the nymphs and demigods, half-human, half-god. They intrigued Lucien the most. To be a god and a human—this seemed like the best way to live, to have the empathy of a human *and* the power of a god, to be able to be with your friends but also fly into the clouds.

Wisdom and heart, he thought.

Jack kept talking about the Greek and Roman gods, the shadows grew across the instruction room, and the sun, once a pale yellow, took on the deeper glow of the approaching afternoon. The teal wall clock told Lucien that instruction would be over soon, and then he would be at home for a snack of hummus and crackers with Mama and maybe cartoons, if the TV worked. Jack said the Romans and Greeks believed worshipping the gods would bring them good fortune.

"Each god had a purpose," he said.

The pulse went off and that meant instruction was over. Jack grinned and told them he was very proud of them all, despite what had happened. He didn't say more but they all knew. Lucien was standing up when he caught sight of Kaitlyn out of the corner of his eye. She was still turned around, staring at the wall. It had been many hours. She was so still, as if she had been frozen in stone. He wanted to run over and touch her, ask her if she was okay, ask Jack if she could go home too.

Jack was by the door, waving. If he was going to ask, he would have to ask now.

Lucien did not like just seeing Kaitlyn's back.

"Jack . . ."

He said it so low that Jack did not hear him. He could not even be sure he said it at all. Jack was looking away, out into the hallway.

"Jack?"

"Yes, Lucien?"

"Can Kaitlyn come too?"

Jack closed his mouth and looked directly at Lucien. Jack's fingers, so large to him, interlocked. "Kaitlyn is going to stay for a little while longer."

"She—she is sorry."

"She is."

"My feet went in the pool."

"Lucien, we all make mistakes."

"I should stay too with her. I should be punished."

Jack did not speak at first. His tongue seemed to roll behind his lips. Lucien imagined all the enormous thoughts inside Jack's head, passing through like thunderclouds heavy with summer rain.

"Lucien, it was not your pool."

"I was there."

"I understand. I very much appreciate your willingness to learn and grow from your mistakes. There is very little negativity in your wake. Kaitlyn needs to stay, however. That's the final word."

"Okay."

Lucien took one last look at Kaitlyn and walked away.

———

That night, Lucien dreamed of a ring of fire. His friends were on a footbridge. The flames were crackling below, and they all had to get over the bridge or they would be burned. Magnus went first, then Antonio and Evie and Samantha. He followed, his feet creaking on the hot wood. Kaitlyn was last, behind him. He knew the bridge would collapse once he got off and reached the other side, and he tried to tell Kaitlyn this, his words evaporating like gas. His mouth moved and nothing came out. Kaitlyn only smiled, the flames rising higher, her face lost in the heat.

———

Lucien told Mama about his dream.

"Jack said Kaitlyn invited you to a pool party. I didn't know there was a pool there, Lucien. I wouldn't have sent you."

"Mama, I'm sorry. Kaitlyn is too."

"Her family should be. That's a great waste. We didn't come to House of Earth for that. Had I known . . ."

"Will she be okay?"

"*She* will be fine. It's everyone else I'm worried about."

With that, Mama turned back to her magazine and didn't say another word about it.

———

Kaitlyn was not at instruction. After another day passed without her, Jack announced that Kaitlyn was not coming back.

"It was a decision we all reached. As a collective."

Lucien could not remember reaching such a decision, but he knew Jack meant he'd spoken with adults, maybe even O. C. Leroux. The collective could include Lucien, but it also didn't have to include him. As the year passed, his memories of Kaitlyn became less sharp. There was just so much to learn and do. A new friend joined the Meadows: Maia. When it snowed, Jack taught the friends how to survive when temperatures dropped, how to stay warm. On the commons, they all built an igloo. Lucien removed his mittens and put his bare hands on the snow, feeling the sting against his skin. They were red and hard.

He immediately drifted to Maia, who liked to talk to him about the types of flowers and explore fresh parts of the woods. He believed he would feel close to Maia for a long time, though he didn't know why yet. She wore her long dark hair in a ponytail that always flapped against her back, and her favorite color was magenta, so much so that she always had the color near her. Magenta shirts, magenta hair ties, magenta streaks on her sneakers. When she ran, she was as fast as Cavan, and she could do handstands. Her laughter was warm and deep, especially when she collapsed into the snow, her handstands or cartwheels or somersaults complete. Talking to her was different from talking to Evie or even Samantha. With Maia, there was nothing hidden. If a thought passed through her, it would be spoken soon enough. It was easy to stand next to Maia and just listen, the words tumbling forth.

Jack told them all about the Iditarod. It was a great sled race in Alaska, the greatest in the world. Alaska was like winter in New York, all year round. Lucien tried to imagine always seeing snow, the bright white of early morning, his breath hanging in the air. The racers who trained the dogs and guided the sleds were called mushers. The mushers were very special and communed with nature. They could talk to animals. Jack said the Iditarod ran almost a thousand miles from Anchorage to Nome, taking place during blizzards.

We are going to do our own race, he said.

31

At the end of February, the Meadows would face the Saplings in a sled race. The Saplings were another collective in another instruction room. Their mentor was Sebastian. Since Lucien had always been with Jack, he knew very little about Sebastian, who was younger and thinner and had dark hair that fell over his eyes when he spoke. Each collective was going to build a sled, and then one friend from each class would be the musher. The rest would be dogs.

In January and February, they cut, sanded, and painted wood. Jack sat, cross-legged, on the floor, watching and helping with the tools. Since he was little, Lucien had been taught woodshop and was proud of his ability to wield a handsaw and hammer nails. Dowels, wood screws, deck screws—in his hands, all these little pieces seemed to know where they needed to go, as if an unseen magic were guiding them. He saw in his mind what the sled would look like, how it would glide across the fresh snow. Samantha also liked building the sled, and Lucien noticed they were the two who spent most of the day assembling the wooden pieces, making an idea into something they could all see and touch. If Samantha didn't always like to talk, she could build with her hands.

"Now we just have to decide who the musher is," Jack said.

It was almost time for the race. With help from Jack, the sled was painted and sparkling, with little polished bells, ropes, and a seat for the musher. The friends still did not know who the musher would be. Lucien was hoping both to be the musher and not be the musher. The responsibility attracted and frightened him.

Could he lead a team in a race? He knew how to run. He didn't know how to guide a sled.

During instruction on the day before the race, Jack told them about the dogs. A sled in the Iditarod has a team of sixteen dogs, he said. There are Siberian huskies and Alaskan malamutes. "The dogs have been described as well-trained athletes, bred for such a competition," Jack said. "They are tied to chains at checkpoints. They must endure great pain for the glory of the Iditarod. What do we think of that?"

"I'm proud of the dogs," Samantha said. "They are doing all the work."

"Proud?" Jack seemed to especially consider this word, growing quiet. All the friends leaned in, waiting for what he might say. "That is one way to describe what is happening."

"They work very hard," Antonio said.

On the night before the race, Mama's phone rang. Lucien was hunched over the small TV in the front room, watching a show about sharks. He heard Mama's voice low in the receiver. A man with a British accent was talking about tiger sharks on the TV.

"Lucien," Mama called.

He spun away from the TV and ran to the room where Mama held the phone. "Yes?"

"That was Jack. He said you are going to be the musher in tomorrow's race."

"Oh, okay, wow. I've never done that before."

"You will do great. We all believe in you."

"Thanks, Mama."

Snowflakes swirled beyond the window. Lucien pressed a hand to the glass. Tomorrow, he would be out there, leading the friends. Jack believed in him. Mama believed in him. Now he had to prove them right.

He had to believe too.

He struggled to sleep. His eyes would close but his mind would not slow. Usually, when he was ready to sleep, his mind would melt into an image or a sensation he could not put into words, one that made sense as only his eyes closed. It never took very long to fall asleep. Now, with the news from Jack, an electricity ran up and down his limbs, his heart beating hard against his chest. He saw himself in the snow, the ropes in hand, the friends braving the cutting winds. He heard the cheers from the adults when they crossed the finish line. He wanted to raise his arms like the Olympic champions on the cereal box.

Turning his head toward the window, he watched as the snow flooded the thin pane, building in larger, wetter layers. He sensed its deepness, how it smothered the hard soil.

He sighed and waited for morning.

———

Jack raised his finger in the air. "The course will be marked. You will see orange tape on tree trunks. Those are your markers to follow. You must not leave the trail. If you do, you will be disqualified."

They were indoors, just beyond the instruction room, but Jack was already wearing a large brown parka. The friends were fastening their coats. The race would begin in the commons, he said. Lucien still wasn't sure what he needed to do, only that he would stand on the sled and be pulled along.

"The race will last several hours. Our musher, Lucien, will be given a whistle. If he feels you are in trouble or too tired to continue, he will blow the whistle, and help will arrive. Otherwise, you will need to work together to make it to the finish line. The course will take you through the woods and back to the commons. Think of it as a large loop."

"Only Lucien gets a whistle?" Antonio asked.

"Only Lucien."

Jack walked over to Lucien and handed him a silver whistle with a thread. Lucien took the small whistle in his hand and put the thread around his neck.

"Lucien, you will lead your friends today. You have it in you."

"I've never been a musher before."

"It's about leadership, Lucien. Today you will know your potential. As will all of you." Jack extended a hand toward the friends. "You all could have been the musher, but Lucien will lead you. That's how it will be."

"I'm excited," Evie said.

"Good."

The snow was falling much harder and faster than yesterday, blowing off the commons like frozen sand. Lucien held his mitten up to shield his eyes from the biting ice. Jack had brought the sled to the commons, where a series of orange cones, almost entirely covered by snow, led to a clearing in the woods. The Saplings were gathered around their sled in a loose circle, a large hooded figure next to them. Lucien guessed it was Sebastian, their mentor. Sebastian was stooped over, talking to one of them.

"Are you ready?" Lucien heard Jack say.

He realized Jack was talking to him.

"I think so."

"Trust yourself and trust your friends. They will be pulling you. Lead them, Lucien."

"Yes."

The field in front of him was like a long white mirror. Snowflakes stung his eyes. Antonio, Samantha, Evie, Cavan, Magnus, and Maia all trudged with him to the sled. He remembered the images of mushers Jack had projected onto the screen, and he tried to resemble them, how they stood straight and drew their faces together in stern, commanding expressions. His hood was pulled tight around his head, a red scarf from Mama tied around his mouth.

As he came closer to the sled, his boots sank deeper, snow crunching against his knees. Wind gusts wrapped around him. The friends were silently taking their positions, grabbing on to the ropes that would pull the sled through the course he could barely see.

Jack and Sebastian were large and dark against the white field, like shadows brought to life.

"I just want to wish you all strength," Sebastian said.

"And courage," Jack added.

"The first to the finish line will get a very special prize."

For a moment, the friends all glanced at each other, wondering what the prize would be.

"But we don't want you motivated by that. This isn't about just a prize," Jack said. "This is about you, the earth, and what it will mean to you. This is about testing your limits and understanding them. I know you will all do well."

Lucien put his right foot on the sled, wobbling up. Each second, the wind and snow seemed to gather with more ferocity. His hands shook on the reins. The friends were stumbling to the front, sliding the handmade harnesses over their jackets and taking rope in their mittens. He waited for them to line up in front of the sled.

What did the musher say?

"Mush!"

The Saplings slid ahead first, the sled rocking side to side. Lucien stood, both feet on the sled, and held on to a crossbar he and Jack had fastened together. He could barely hear the friends in the wind, and he wasn't so sure they could hear him as he cried "Mush!" a second time.

The sled, at last, began to groan forward.

"We can do it! We can do it!"

The clearing was just up ahead. Lucien saw oaks and sugar maples sagging, snow weighing down their solemn branches. Farther ahead, beyond the whipping snow that clouded his eyes, rested the faint outline of a mountain range, one he hoped to climb one day. He wished he knew exactly what he was supposed to do. At the front of the line, Evie and Antonio were pulling hardest, and he was grateful. Cavan, closest to him, kept stumbling in the snow and ice, pulling himself up with a whimper.

"You can do it, Cavan!"

When Lucien was smaller, Mama took him exploring in the snow. He had not yet started at House of Earth. They walked, hand in hand, down a narrow and icy road near the cottage, one that Mama told him never to travel alone. It was almost dark, like now. They were halfway down the hill when Lucien felt his rubber boots slip, his eyes shooting skyward. His back struck the ice and he began to roll down the hill. He cried for Mama. The world spun and shook him, the trees and sky trading places, snow and ice falling in his eyes and mouth. Behind him or ahead of him were footsteps, dull in the ground. He cried out again. His body caught against a branch and then a hand, and he was pulled upward, his boots righted on the ground again, this time flat. The sky was like dishwater.

"Lucien!"

Mama held him close as tears formed in his eyes.

"Mama."

"Lucien, you have to be careful. You have to be careful for Mama."

"I will."

"When I'm not there for you, you must be careful. Okay?"

"When will you not be there?"

"Mama will do her best."

That's all she said and Lucien was left to wonder: When *wouldn't* Mama be there for him? He now had his answer. His sled lurched into the clearing, just ahead of the Saplings'. He could make out orange flags in the snow pointing him straight. His left foot slid forward on the slick wood and he almost fell, catching his body just before he tumbled into the snow. One of the girls looked back at him—in the snowfall and darkness, he was struggling to identify who was who in their hoods and scarves—and he waved, trying to show he was okay, he was ready. He knew Maia had a magenta hood, and he strained to see the color.

"Let's go, friends. I believe in you!" he shouted.

With his cry, the sled seemed to move faster. They banked rightward, following the cones, moving more smoothly as they entered the woods. The sled reached a small slope and dipped ahead, skimming a patch of ice. Lucien gripped his reins as tight as he could. He wasn't going to fall.

"It's cold," Lucien heard Cavan moan. He knew it was Cavan only because Cavan was closest to him and his gray boot kept sliding near the sled's silver rudder. Cavan wore a lavender hat with a small ball on top. It was the bobbing of the hat that Lucien followed, even as the snow blew in more furious and blinding bursts.

The sled was not downhill anymore. They had reached a low point in the woods, a depth in the soil that made the snowdrifts only seem higher. Branches overhead sighed with falling snow. He was pulling at the reins, straining to direct the friends forward.

"Mush!"

The sled only slowed.

"Mush!"

"We're trying," Evie said.

"I believe in all of you."

When Lucien wasn't sure of what to say, he tried to think of what Jack or Mama would say. Jack would say he believed in all the friends. Mama would tell them to work harder. Lucien wished he knew what he himself would say, or that he could say what was correct, what was expected. He pulled on the reins, attempting to guide the sled left. A great wind gust blew at his back.

"Do you see the trail?" Cavan asked him, wrenching his body around to face Lucien.

Lucien squinted. They were in a part of the woods he didn't recognize—or couldn't because of how much it had frozen. No orange cones or markers waited on any trees. He didn't hear the Saplings.

The sled struck a snow-swallowed stump, and Lucien pitched forward, his knee smacking the sled's wooden frame. The bells rang out. Pain burned through his bone. The sled was still moving, the friends tugging its weight and his crumpled body.

He fought upward again, trying to balance. The rope was knotted around his wrist. It was darker now, the sky heavy with snow and wind. His familiar trees lost their form. The sun hid behind a curtain of soapy gray. When he blinked, icy flakes cut at his vision like little frozen blades. His hands and toes were hard with cold. His blood was not moving like it should.

The friends were quiet too. They were small, dark masses bent against a wave of white. He tugged at the reins one more time and then stopped.

They were deeper in snow. Lucien didn't know whether he was surrounded by trees or mountains, whether these visions of rock were moving closer to their sled, readying to crush them. He could hardly see.

"We have to find the trail," he finally said.

Evie dropped the rope and waded toward him. The snow nearly reached her waist.

Lucien stepped off the sled to hear her.

"We need to just go back," she said.

"But Jack said we had to finish."

"We don't know where the trail is, and we can't see. I'm very, very cold. Maia can't stop crying. Antonio is just chattering to himself."

"I'm cold too, Evie. But we have a mission."

"I know, Lucien, but it's too cold."

"Mind over matter . . ."

"What?"

"Jack said that—mind over matter."

"I know."

"If the mind is strong enough, the matter—all this snow—maybe it won't matter as much."

"We can try, but I don't know how much we can go after this."

"The Saplings are going to win."

"We can't find them."

Evie was right, but so was Jack. Mind over matter, mind over matter. The lesson came back to him. Jack had taught them about the *stoics*, a group of people in the ancient times who survived all types of pain with powerful minds. Nature was resilient, Jack said. Humans needed to take a lesson from nature.

"We can find the trail. I believe in what we can do."

"Lucien, we will try. I just don't know how much longer we can go."

"We can do it!"

At first, Lucien thought he was right. He was back on the sled, and the friends were pulling as a collective. There was no sign of a trail, but they were sliding forward, even as the wind howled around them. He was trying so hard to see among the snowdrifts and ghostly trees, searching for where Jack had placed the orange markers. They were struggling uphill again, into another clearing in the woods. In the summer, he would know it, touch the bark or identify a flower or catch sight of a familiar deer. When he thought of harmony, he thought of sunlight peeking through the branches, a bird faintly singing from a hollow in the tree, the leaves so full and green. He did not think of his fingers numbing, the skin of his cheeks like the surface of cold rock. His feet too. They were beyond feeling now.

"A little bit farther," he said, but no one heard him this time. The friends were still dragging the sled, slowing as the snow seemed to thicken at the top of a small hill. The sled rattled and he heard a low thud, a sound beneath the snow and wind.

What had they hit? He looked down, saw only snow and ice.

The friends had stopped.

"We have to turn around," Evie said to him.

"But the trail could be close."

"We don't know where it is. We won't ever know."

Lucien saw only Evie's pale eyes. The rest of her was covered in a blue-and-gray ski jacket, the hood pulled tightly over her head. Maia stumbled next to her. They each clutched their bodies, straining to ward off the cold. Evie's words burned at him—*we won't ever know*—and a great shame welled up, even worse than when he'd painted the bird-house black and felt the raindrops strike his body on Mama's bench. Evie was right. They weren't going to find the trail, and hadn't it been the musher's job, his job, to lead the friends where they needed to be? Jack had trusted him. What would he say? What would Mama say?

"We can try; I believe in all of you."

Magnus staggered forward now, his gloved hands outstretched. His eyes, Lucien could see, were tearing. He came close to Lucien. "I'm tired. We're tired. It's so cold it hurts."

"Then we have to go back."

"Do we take the sled?" Antonio asked.

"We have to," Lucien said. "We can pull it together."

Retracing their steps through the footprints they'd left behind was not possible any longer. New drifts of snow and ice had covered up any evidence of their presence. Lucien threw his arm up, trying to block a sudden gust that drove him backward into a tree trunk. His legs sank into snow.

At the library in town, he had read a book called *White Fang* about a brave dog in the Yukon Territory. In the wild, White Fang is mean and vicious. He is a fighter, an enemy of his kind. He is the meanest, nastiest dog, and he is solitary. Only later, when he is loved, does he become tame. Only then is he transformed. Right now, fighting through snowdrifts, Lucien could understand how White Fang acted the way he did, even though when he first read the book, he questioned how any creature could ever be so angry, so ready to attack. Mama taught him never to fight. Jack said it was a sin against humanity and a sin against the planet. But here, with the friends struggling behind him, he began to see, like a key had been turned and he was peeking into this new compartment of himself. He was hungry, he was scared, and he was angry.

Yes, that's what it was, this hot feeling in his throat, mixing with the chill below. He was angry he couldn't do more. He was angry he had failed as a musher. He was angry at the snow.

This surprised him most. Snow had always been a friend.

"It's so cold," Magnus said. "So cold."

"Where are we?" Maia asked.

Lucien squinted. It was all so alien now.

"I think we go that way," Evie said, pointing.

"Is that the way we came?" Antonio asked.

"I think."

Lucien gripped the ropes to pull the sled. They all followed Evie now, up another slope. He felt White Fang's fury, and his sadness too. He had a hard life until he found someone to take care of him. Like Mama found Lucien. But where was Mama? Where was Jack? There were only the trees shrouded in snow, the hard winds biting at the exposed skin around his eyes, the shadows long and dark. The snow blew like moondust. If it weren't so cold and it didn't hurt his skin so much, he could play in it, sprawl his body in the drifts.

Evie led them, her small elbows swinging as she trudged as quickly as she could. He was behind, the friends trailing him.

His toes were beyond feeling. It was like black magic had turned his feet into wood.

I am White Fang, he thought.

"I can't . . ."

They heard a low crunching noise. Behind them, midway up the slope, Magnus had fallen forward into the snow. He was squirming, low noises coming from his body. It was his voice, but it seemed distant, as if he had buried it deep in his body. They stumbled to him as fast as they could. Lucien bent over, putting his mitten on Magnus's back.

Magnus would not turn over. Without thinking, Lucien blew the whistle around his neck.

"Magnus?"

"Cold," he heard. "So tired."

"Magnus!"

Evie crouched low and put both her arms around him. "We have to get him back, now."

"Can he walk?" Cavan asked.

"Can you walk, Magnus?"

At first, he didn't respond. Evie shook him gently.

"So cold . . ."

"We're almost there," Lucien said. "We're so close. We just need to go a little farther."

Lucien almost believed it. They could have traveled only so far into the woods through a snowstorm. He should've counted off feet. In the summer, he would read trail markers and make some of his own to remember where he was as he trekked through the brown-and-gold woods.

"We have to help Magnus walk," Evie said.

"I can help him," Lucien replied.

"And me," Antonio said.

"Let's do it. Me and Maia can pull the sled. The rest of us, let's go."

He was White Fang. The Yukon Territory wouldn't break White Fang, and the woods wouldn't break him. Below the snow, hidden away, were the trees and grass he knew. He was still close to home. House of Earth was waiting. He just had to remember.

They staggered together. Like waves, the snowdrifts came at them, and Lucien was fighting away flakes of ice that almost froze his eyes shut. Less of his body had feeling. He sensed he had only so much time before this loss of feeling lasted beyond today or tomorrow, when it became the reality of who he was. He did not want that to happen. Magnus, one arm flung over Antonio's shoulder and the other wrapped around Lucien's, started to gain enough strength to walk at their pace. They were a six-legged creature struggling against the wind.

Evie pointed toward another clearing. He was trusting her now, whatever lay inside her. Without standing on the sled, Lucien felt how heavy it truly was and what it must have meant for the friends to pull him. How far would he have gotten? Now he had Magnus, who wasn't talking anymore.

A bolt of pain suddenly shot up his shin. He looked down and saw only snow. It felt hard, whatever he had walked into, maybe a stump buried below the drift. Tears formed in the corners of his eyes. He couldn't cry. White Fang didn't cry. He had to keep going. They all did.

"Do you see that light?"

A small light pulsed in the distance, past the trees. He heard Magnus gulp. Could it be? He gripped Magnus's arm and pulled him harder. It looked like it. He hoped. He really did.

"House of Earth!"

Home, almost home. Lucien could fall on his knees and cry. He was so thankful. In Evie's hands, the sled began to rattle as she trudged forward, picking up speed. The bells rang. She was walking, then running, snow bursting all around her.

"Magnus, we're almost there."

Magnus didn't say anything.

The snow bore down on Lucien, but he could see just enough. The light was their light, from the windows of House of Earth. It was faint, a pale yellow, and he grasped toward it, the snow spiraling around the glow. They were close, so close, yet the light wasn't as big as it could be.

He was sure they were there until they weren't there, until a wall of wind and snow closed around them.

"It's . . . it's hard to walk," he heard Cavan say.

"We're close," Evie said.

"We are," Lucien replied.

In the summer, they would be close. Lucien would run, elbows out, knees bouncing. The world could seem so small. Here, in a cold not so different from White Fang's Yukon, it was vast. Nature has two sides, Jack once said. It can nurture. It can fight back. Now it was fighting. Now it was showing them its power. It had stolen what warmth he had left. His jaw shook, his lungs hard in his chest.

They had to get to the light. He prayed for House of Earth, to be worthy and be saved. His lips moved silently.

And then his body fell toward the earth.

———

The light was everywhere. He felt his lungs filling with air. Warmer air. It was the absence of snow he noticed next. The sky was a blur, devoid of stars. He wriggled his fingers. Mittens? Gone. He began to hear voices. They formed words, muddled and then bright. This was not the woods. This was not instruction. He was gazing at the underside of a roof, incandescent bulbs hanging overhead. They twinkled like insect eyes on the slate-colored ceiling.

"We made it back."

It was Jack. Lucien struggled up. Below him was a sky-blue sleeping bag. He looked right and left. The friends were here too, also on sleeping bags. Some rose like him. Others were on their backs, eyes closed. He was closest to Magnus and Maia. Maia was waking. Magnus's eyes were shut, his cheeks raw and red.

"We're in the back," Evie said suddenly.

Lucien turned to look at her.

"That's right, Evie," Jack said.

Jack was dressed in the same parka as before. As the fuzziness around Lucien's vision began to melt away, he saw they were all in a large equipment or storage room. Lawn mowers, hoes, bags of seed, and wood were piled against one wall. There was other machinery with winding tubes and spokes that Lucien didn't recognize. He was still cold. Even indoors, no heat was pumping through the walls, and through slit-shaped windows, he could watch a band of snow thickening on the glass.

Against a far wall, tilted upright, was their sled.

"What happened?" Lucien finally asked. It was the only question now hanging in his mind.

Jack crossed his arms. "No one finished the race. No one won."

"It was very cold and snowy," Antonio said.

"Yes," Lucien added quietly.

"If we didn't turn back, we were—we were going to freeze to death," Evie said.

Jack was smiling. He uncrossed his arms and walked closer to them, his boots crunching on the shards of ice left on the concrete floor. In that moment, he looked enormous to Lucien, like a deity from a storybook.

"The weather forecast said this was the worst blizzard to hit this area in fifteen, twenty years," Jack said. "It's only getting worse. The roads are all closed. It's two, three feet deep outside now."

Maia sat up. Most of them were awake, wet snow soaking their bodies. Lucien felt a jolt in his stomach. It was hunger of a degree he hadn't known in a long time. He was desperate for food. His body was remembering how little he had eaten. More than anything, he longed for Mama's hummus and crackers, the sweet crunch in his teeth.

He touched his stomach.

"Did the Saplings make it to the end of the race?" Evie asked.

"No one did, I said. You were farther in. But no one won. No one was able to reach their destination."

"We really tried."

Jack clapped his hands together. The echo was sharp in the open room, hurting Lucien's ears.

"You all tried. But you couldn't make it. Why?"

The friends looked at one another, waiting for one to answer for them all. As musher, Lucien had an obligation to guide the friends and he'd failed—there was no arguing that.

He deserved punishment. Hunger devolved into shame. No, he didn't deserve to eat either.

"I didn't mush like I should. I didn't lead us," Lucien said.

"It's not your fault," Evie jumped in. "It's no one's fault."

"Tell me, Evie," Jack said. "How did it feel pulling the sled?"

"Feel?"

"Yes. How did it make you feel?"

"I don't know . . . It was hard. But we had to make it."

"How do you think it made, oh, Magnus feel?"

They collectively turned to Magnus, who was quiet and not moving. His eyes remained closed on his ruddy face.

"Magnus struggled," Evie said. "We all did."

"You all struggled."

"Yes."

"You all struggled . . ."

Jack held his hands behind his back. He seemed to be thinking again. Lucien always tried, and failed, to guess what Jack was thinking.

"Do you think the dogs tethered and chained to their sleds, forced to traverse Alaska, all *enjoy* what they do?"

Traverse and *tethered* were words Lucien didn't know but could guess at, based on how Jack used them. He waited for Evie to answer. Together, they all were looking to Evie now. She should have been musher all along.

"I don't think so," she said.

"Were you cold outside? Hungry? Fearful for your lives?"

"We were cold and hungry."

"We were afraid," Cavan jumped in.

Jack's smile widened. "We assume, because animals do not speak like we do, that they do not deserve the same rights. They walk on four legs instead of two. They live outside. They eat what we do not eat. They don't drive cars, play basketball, or watch movies. They should be pushed beyond their capabilities for our amusement. Do we think that's true?"

The friends shook their heads, Lucien following along.

"We don't. But sometimes, we need to truly learn. I chose this day for you to race because I knew it would be particularly challenging. Did you wonder why you couldn't follow the trail markers?"

Evie opened her mouth to answer and then closed it. Lucien had a guess. He didn't want to say it out loud. He hoped he wasn't right.

"You couldn't find them because they weren't there for the entire trail. I only placed them there in the beginning. This was frightening,

I know. But a lesson needed to be taught. In your disorientation, you would work together. You would be tested. Pushed to your limits. Now—did you really have a choice in the matter? No. I told you to do it. You did it. The dogs who must pull the sleds in the brutal races across Alaska do not get a choice either. They are forced to compete and suffer for our amusement. At House of Earth, you are all learning empathy for your environment, for all living creatures. This is how you live in harmony with what is around you. This is how you destroy negative energy. This is how you live in the light of O. C. Leroux and, ultimately, God. But, as you will learn as you grow, it's not always easy to live in this light. You must learn its power."

Magnus had begun to sit up. His arms were wrapped around his body, and he was gently rocking, clutching himself. A line of clear snot dripped out of one nostril. In his stare, Lucien saw only a lack of feeling, his eyes like white marbles buried in his head.

"Magnus, I'm glad to see you," Jack said.

Magnus continued to shake.

"You are all going to spend the night here. All your parents have been notified that you're spending the night. In the morning, we will have a hot meal for you. Sleep tight, my Meadows."

Jack flicked off the lights and they were plunged into darkness.

SPRING

In the spring before Lucien watched the towers fall, House of Earth started to grow. Flatbed trucks rolled onto the gravel, carrying steel beams and cement blocks. Men in hard hats walked in black boots across the grass, taking measurements. In instruction, Lucien heard the sounds of hammering and drilling, a structure coming to life.

"House of Earth is growing," Jack said. "You should all be proud."

A new collective, the Sunflowers, joined the Saplings and the Meadows. Lucien didn't know exactly what the new building would be for, but he could guess it was very important, based on how the men with hard hats worked. Every day, he ventured onto the commons to watch them. Their skin was deeply tanned, their forearms covered in hair. They spoke in English and a language he didn't recognize.

"What's going on there, you think?" Antonio asked him one day during free play. They were on the basketball court, passing the ball back and forth. Evie was with them too.

"I don't know. It could be more collectives are going there."

"My mom heard something else," Evie said.

"What?"

"She heard"—Evie drew closer, her mouth nearly to their ears—"they may be dormitories."

"What's that?"

"Housing for people."

"They want us to leave our homes?"

"Maybe."

"Nah," Antonio said, waving his hand. "It's probably something else. Like a bigger nutritional hall."

"Maybe," Lucien said.

As spring melted into summer, Mama was home less and less. She had errands to run, she said. She would walk him home, set out a plate of hummus and crackers, and then walk away, down the path that led to their cottage. At nightfall, she would return. Usually, Lucien had strict instructions to stay inside while she was gone. He obeyed, watching the TV or reading his books on animals. The hours would grow long in the cottage alone, the shadows creeping across the floor.

When summer break began, Mama started to take him into town. "You stay at the library until I come back," she said.

"Okay, Mama."

The library was a small redbrick building at the end of Superior Street, standing next to a duck pond. It smelled like old newspaper, and the light overhead was dim. A woman with a purpled face like a prune sat at the front desk, trying to solve crossword puzzles. She smiled faintly when Lucien and Mama entered.

"You wait here, Lucien, until I come back. I will meet you by the front in a few hours."

The library rarely had many people. Occasionally, he would see someone around his age. When he tried to talk to one of them, the woman with the face like a prune, looking up from her crosswords, would make a shushing noise. No talking allowed. He sat at the computer terminal, but he didn't have a library card to go on the internet.

After watching the screensaver, a rotating labyrinth of brick, he would walk over to the books. The sections were dizzying, in many topics he knew so little about. Jack said reading was good but to be careful, always careful, because the mind is a temple and you want to show it proper reverence. Your mind must be clear, free of pollution, Jack said. When Mama first left Lucien at the library in June, he read a guide to North American wildflowers and then an illustrated compendium of African and Asian

50

reptiles. When he read these books, he sat on the library's carpeted floor, his small legs crossed. The images were vivid and lush, and they occupied him until he heard Mama's soft voice from across the room and ran to her. The woman with the prune face said, "No running."

At the end of the month, Lucien walked into the fiction section. Other than the fact that fiction was pretend, he didn't know what else he would find. *White Fang* would be there. He could read that again. He wasn't sure he was supposed to after his experience with the sled race. They had suffered in the cold, learning just how the dogs felt. The memories of that night still clung to him. Not just fighting through the snow and wind and the way the cold burned at him, from the inside and outside. It was the time after, with Jack and the friends in the equipment shed, that night they all slept on a hard cement floor with just their sleeping bags and whatever they could feel from Jack's space heaters. He'd been so cold he dreamed he was in a coffin made of ice. He was to be buried at dawn, in a field of snow, crying into the permafrost.

He woke up whimpering. No one heard him.

There were too many books to ever read. He stared at their spines, reading titles, touching the fabric. His watch told him it was the last day of June. Mama had just left him, and it would be a few hours at least before she returned. He was hungry. Sometimes, Mama forgot to bring him hummus and crackers. Sometimes, she was in a hurry. He would never just ask Mama. She knew what was best. This afternoon, he would have to make do.

That was that.

His stomach churned. He ignored it, moving his finger like a wand over the spines of the books.

His finger hovered over another book he had never heard of before. The title called to him. He read it twice.

The Natural.

It was a title Jack would approve of.

"*The Natural*," he said out loud. No one was with him in the stacks. It was a flimsy light-blue paperback, with a bolt of dull white running across the cover. The white wasn't part of the design. It was a very old book, Lucien realized. It was in a state of decay. At the top was a large baseball with the words *Bernard Malamud The Natural* printed between the seams, and Lucien took the frail book in his hand, weighing it.

He turned to the first page.

Roy Hobbs pawed at the glass before thinking to prick a match with his thumbnail . . .

The book, Lucien guessed, was about baseball, but there were no games played in the opening pages. Roy Hobbs was riding on a train. It was dark out, almost dawn, and Lucien thought about the nights he had stayed up watching the sky, the transition from bruised black to watery orange, the excitement in his heart rising as the sun, as promised, arrived again. Many of the words were big for Lucien. *Appraised* and *pygmy* and *fried kippers*. He kept reading, the world building in his head. This was one of his favorite aspects of books: how these little black squiggles could create so much behind his eyes. He inhaled the scent of the yellowed pages, thin in his fingers, turning each one carefully. Roy was with a man named Sam. Sam was something called a "scout," which seemed to mean he traveled across the country, to towns like Mater, looking for boys and girls who played baseball. Roy, Sam said, was the "coming pitcher of the century."

House of Earth did not have a baseball field. Lucien knew about the Yankees and the Mets and had seen, in passing, a few games played on the TV. He had heard of the Cubs, the team that Roy was going to pitch for. There was a pretty woman Roy liked named Harriet Bird. Lucien kept reading.

What Lucien noticed about the library was how cold it got, despite the heat from outside. The temperature was beyond ninety degrees, and on the walk into town, his hand was very sweaty in Mama's. Inside the library, a breeze from no direction he could see struck his face. He gripped his elbows. "It's air-conditioning," Mama said. "Very wasteful. We don't do that at home and at House of Earth." She didn't say any more. There must be a machine generating the air. Machines ran on electricity, and electricity ran on the burning of coal, which also created negative energy.

Mama never told him how to take books out of the library. She left him here and picked him up. She never took a book of her own. *White Fang* was in the cottage. If Lucien wanted to read *The Natural* at home, he would have to leave with the book. He decided, with the time he had left, to ask the woman who was always doing her crosswords. At the front desk, she was talking to a man, who was asking about where he could find a certain cookbook.

"Excuse me," Lucien said.

The woman kept talking to the man.

"Excuse me."

She continued to talk. It was as if Lucien hadn't said anything at all. He had read a scary story about a man who didn't realize he was a ghost and still tried to talk to living people. He would wave his arms, jump up and down, and even scream. The people never talked back.

"Excuse me . . ."

The woman cleared her throat. She was smiling at the man, who thanked her for the cookbook suggestions. Her purpled face turned toward Lucien at last. "Yes?"

"I'd, um, I'd like to take out a book."

"Do you have a library card?"

"No."

"Then I can't help you right now. Ask Mommy."

"Mama isn't here."

"Wait until she comes back."

"I can check it out for him."

Behind him was a girl holding out a piece of moss-green plastic. Her eyes were large and dark, her hair, the same dusky color, pulled into a long ponytail that hung over her shoulder. The woman behind the desk took her card and grunted.

"Thank you," Lucien said.

"Don't worry about it."

The woman stamped his book hard. She squinted down at Lucien. "Due back in two weeks. If he's late, Gabrielle, it's on you."

"That's okay, Mrs. Yelich. He won't be."

The woman turned away, dipping back into an unfinished crossword. Lucien held his book.

"I've seen you here lately. You from around town?"

"I don't live far away. On Darling Drive."

"Darling Drive?" Gabrielle shook her head. "That's one of the back roads up near the mountains?"

"Yes. We walk to town, though, me and Mama. I'm waiting for Mama right now."

"I'm right off Superior. Gabrielle," she said, holding out her hand. Lucien stared at it for a moment, forgetting exactly what to do. He hugged the friends and Jack and Mama, but none of them held out their hands to shake. From TV, he knew this was something adults would do to show appreciation for one another. He lifted his own right hand and held Gabrielle's, enjoying the feeling of her skin on his own. She released. He followed.

"I'm Lucien."

"That's an interesting name. What type is it?"

"Type?"

"Like, I don't know, Italian or Greek or whatever?"

"I don't know."

"Oh. Well, it's a cool name anyway. Didn't your mom or someone sign you up for a library card?"

"No. No one ever did. I usually sit here and look at the books."

"It's a library! Borrow them. Next time I'll sign you up. I gotta run back home soon. How come I don't see you at Mater Middle School?"

"I don't go there. I go to . . ." Lucien stopped for a moment to think. This was one of the only times he could remember explaining House of

Earth to someone who did not already know all that it was. It was like explaining the changing of the seasons to someone who lived only in a desert. "House of Earth."

"Oh, that private school up in the hills? You're the first person I've met who goes there."

"I've never met anyone from Mater Middle School."

"Really? Like, everyone in town goes there. I'm in eighth grade. Then it's Mater High School! The school district is so creative, I know."

"What's the school like—"

"Lucien!"

Lucien wrenched his head around. It was Mama, calling him from the door. The woman at the desk, Mrs. Yelich, went to make a shushing sound but stopped when she saw who had called out. She returned to her crossword, the yellow pencil dancing over newsprint.

"Mama."

"Come over here now!"

Lucien bit his lower lip. "Sorry, Gabrielle, I have to go."

"It was nice to meet you, Lucien. See you soon."

Lucien ran over to Mama, who took his hand hard and walked him out of the library, past the duck pond, and up a sun-drenched Superior Street. Lucien liked how daylight lingered into the evening.

"Who was that, Lucien?"

"Just this girl."

"Who?"

"She's from town."

"You need to be careful around strangers. Libraries are for reading books, not talking. What book is that?"

"It's called *The Natural*."

"I don't know much about it. I will look at it later. Let's go home, Lucien."

As the summer continued, Mama would leave for longer periods of time. Most of the friends were at camps in the Catskills, but Mama said he wouldn't be going to camp—there was no point. He would stay at the cottage or go to the library. Mama told him to watch out for strangers. That seemed to apply to Gabrielle, whom he saw once a week, maybe more. Since they couldn't talk too much in the library—Mrs. Yelich was always ready to shush them—they sat on a bench by the duck pond. Gabrielle liked to talk and Lucien liked to listen. She had much to say, and Lucien, unused to someone speaking to him for such a long amount of time, could only sit in mild awe of someone caring so much, or at least regarding him as worthy of all these words.

"I come here a lot because my parents yell too much, and they don't notice when I'm gone," she said one day, her legs swinging from the bench.

Lucien was watching one duck, a puddle duck with luminous wing patches, gnaw at the wet soil on the pond's bank. "Why do they yell?"

"It's everything. Mom and Dad always fight. Dad hasn't worked in a while, Mom works a lot; he's home too much, but he's also out too much. I wake up in the morning to them shouting. It's like an alarm clock. But then the quiet is worse."

"How?"

"You know it's building. Mom and Dad will be incredibly mad but not say a word. We have a small house, and they are always walking near each other, brushing elbows. Not saying anything. You know it's building. The explosion. The *rage*, Lucien. My dad is like, 'Serena, you're judging me.'" She lowered her voice like a man's, and Lucien giggled—Gabrielle did almost sound like an adult male, her face bent and stretched to match her dad's girth. "And then my mom is like, 'No I'm not, Miles.' And he walks around and stares, and he's like, 'Those eyes, those eyes,' and then they scream and curse. They don't actually hit each other, though. Not like other parents."

"You know parents who . . . hit each other?"

"Here? Duh. Sorry, Lucien; I guess all you House of Earth rich kids have it easy, everyone living out their country fantasy or whatever. Half of my school is like, drunk dads and battered moms. It just is. My dad is something else. He's got problems, but he's not going to go out and beat someone up. My mom did throw a broom at him once. That was crazy. I actually laughed. Noah didn't."

Gabrielle had this habit of introducing names and places he hadn't heard of before. He was sure this was the first time the name *Noah* had appeared in a conversation, and he was caught between not acknowledging it and letting Gabrielle continue or interrupting her to ask about Noah. With Jack and Mama, he preferred not to ask, even if they said it was okay to. He was worried about what he didn't or couldn't know.

"Mama doesn't raise her voice," Lucien said.

"*Mama*, right. She's your mom, not mine. You're a single-parent household, right?"

"Yes."

"If you don't mind me asking—sorry if I'm going into dangerous territory—was your dad around ever?"

"I don't know."

"You don't know?"

"It's always been me and my mom."

Around Gabrielle, Mama would have to be *my mom*.

"So you never met him?"

"No."

"Name?"

"I don't know."

"Wow, okay. One of those, then. No problem. Dads take off all the time. My mom *wishes* my dad would take off. She works for the county, so she says she's gonna get a small pension, and my dad won't do a divorce because he wants a piece. Seriously. My mom told me this when she drove me to soccer practice. What does your mama do?"

"She works at House of Earth."

"Cool. You must see her all the time."

"It depends on the day. She will say hi sometimes after instruction or during free play. A lot of times she is busy. She does a lot."

"You must get awesome grades, having your mom there," Gabrielle said with a smile.

"Grades?"

Gabrielle was shaking her head. "Oh c'mon."

"We, um, when you say *grades*—"

"A, B, C, D. You don't get grades on your assignments? To tell you how good you did?"

"Jack tells us."

"Jack?"

"Our mentor. We don't have any letters for what we do."

"Jack gives, what, constructive feedback or something? So you don't get a GPA?"

"No . . ."

"Well, okay, then. Private school is really different. You'll probably still get into a better college than me."

"My mom never talks about that."

"My mom always reminds my dad he barely got out of high school."

Gabrielle lived only a few miles from him. Her life, however, was entirely different, and Lucien began to think more about how this was possible. Everyone in House of Earth was more similar than different. No one acted surprised that there was no such thing as a GPA. It made him want to tell her both more and less. What would she think about the birdhouse? The sled race? Where Gabrielle went to school, *mentors* were *teachers*, and they were called by their last names, not first. This created a distance that was acceptable where she came from. Lucien didn't even know if Jack *had* a last name or what it would be. The same was true for Sebastian.

Gabrielle knew of TV shows he'd never watched, sports figures he didn't recognize, politicians who held office, and even books that he hadn't read or that weren't in the library. It was as if she were her own library, a counter vessel of knowledge, and here he didn't need a card and wouldn't be shushed by Mrs. Yelich. She told him *The Natural* was a movie too; her dad had shown it to her once, and they wore old-fashioned uniforms.

Lucien had watched some movies on TV, but Mama hadn't taken him to the movie theater. Gabrielle said it was one town over and the air-conditioning blasted you in the summer. In the dark, she said, boys and girls did all kinds of things.

"Like what?" Lucien asked.

Gabrielle could only roll her eyes. "You don't know much, do you?"

"I guess not."

"You're like the mountain boy. Do they smoke weed up there?"

"Weed."

"Really? I need to explain weed too?"

"There are *weeds*, I guess. I never saw a fire."

"Marijuana. Grass. That funky stuff. A bunch of kids in my school smoke. I don't really like the stoners. You're lucky, then, if you never heard of it. Means you'll never fall asleep in your mom's car at two in the afternoon, cutting class, like all those people."

"I won't, no."

"I've never been high. I think my mom used to smoke a lot of weed, sometime, when she was like, my age, before I was born."

"I don't know what my mom did before I was born."

"Yeah, she doesn't tell you anything. Probably something secret and illegal, if she doesn't talk about it."

"Mama, I mean, my *mom*, she wouldn't."

"Lucien, you're great and all, really, don't change, but you gotta understand—these adults, they're as messed up as we are. They're just older."

———

One August afternoon, Lucien saw Gabrielle on their usual bench next to the pond. Her arms were crossed over her stomach. She was staring at the ground.

"Hi, Gabrielle."

"Hey, Lucien."

Her voice was lower, almost at a whisper. When she turned toward him, he could see her eyes were damp. Her hair hung long down her shoulders, unbraided and shimmering in the heavy orange sun above them. He sat next to her. He had never seen her this way.

"Mama dropped you off again?" she asked, rubbing her nose with her fist.

"She had errands to do."

She smiled at him, wiping her left eye. A few tears glimmered off the back of her hand. "Errands, Lucien. Don't you ask where she goes?"

"She doesn't tell me."

"But you can *ask*."

It was true. Lucien could ask. He dreamed once that he did and Mama stared at him for a very long time, her eyes turning as black as coal. She told him she didn't love him and walked out of the cottage. When he woke, he was shuddering, sweat covering his whole body. Mama's errands were her errands. They were for her.

"I could, yes."

"Life is strange sometimes," she said.

"Gabrielle, I just wanted, to, um—"

"Ask what's going on? Why I'm here, like, cleaning my eyes out in front of this *shitty* duck pond."

The word slashed at him. No one used it—not Mama, not Jack, not the friends—and he only knew of it from TV, when he once accidentally heard it late at night when he wasn't supposed to. These were *curse* words, Mama said, and they were never to be uttered. Curse words were unspoken words. They bore only pain and destruction. They were the negativity that Jack warned of, the dark energy that any strong person must be prepared to combat always, everywhere. How could Gabrielle say it? She wasn't much older than he was. Was this what happened when you were not sent to House of Earth? He didn't imagine she was that type of person.

"Gabrielle, why did you say that?"

"I was just mad."

60

"You should never say it."

"Mom and Dad say it all the time . . ." She was clenching her right hand into a small fist again, this time bobbing it up and down. "They say it a lot. So I hear it. And it describes what I feel. That's the truth. I won't say sorry for that."

"Did something bad happen?"

"Noah is going away. My brother is going away. It's my parents' fault, of course."

"Where is he going?"

"The army! He's eighteen in a month. He enlisted. Can you believe it?"

He didn't know whether to believe it or not since Noah had been only a passing figure in their conversations, a reference point with little meaning beyond a name and a relationship. Now he was fully formed: an older brother, nearly eighteen, about to take up weapons to kill.

Jack had taught several lessons about war. Humans are capable of great and terrible things, he said, and it's important you understand that now. At House of Earth, we are building a peaceful future, for the environment and the survival of our people. But there are humans filled with negative energy, with darkness, who use machines to take lives. You may even know people who own guns. It is important that you never go near a gun. It is important, if you ever see one, to tell one of us. The American *military*, the army—they are filled with these people who are trying to kill in the name of our country, Jack said.

"Why does he want to go kill people?"

Gabrielle turned to him, her mouth closed. Her eyes were now dry. Both of her hands gripped the bench. "There are people in this town who would call him a hero."

"Oh."

"But he *is* going to kill people. Or get killed. He told me first and then my mom. My dad is up north for the weekend. He'll find out soon enough. My mom doesn't want him going, but you know what? They made him. Every day. See, I don't know how you are, Lucien, since you never ask your mom anything and she seems to just drop you wherever, but I can handle stuff. I can take people yelling around me and even throwing a broom here or there. I know what my parents are. They are two people who shouldn't be together. My mom is better. She could do better with someone else. My dad is drinking now. He thinks I don't know. He passes out on the couch. But you know what? At least they aren't hitting *me*. A friend of mine, her uncle tried to make out with her. No one did that to me. I know how to survive. Noah, Noah . . . he's not like that. Maybe he's like you, I don't know. He's sensitive; he's quiet; he's reading about the space program in his room. He's playing *SimCity*, managing budgets. He's getting chocolate fudge ice cream all over his face. He could go to college, but I don't think that's enough anymore. It's not enough to dorm at a SUNY. He needs to be *away*. And they did it."

"Gabrielle, I wish it wasn't happening. I want to help, if I can."

"You can't. No one can. He decided. He enlisted. It's done. He's going to boot camp. And I've known you like, two months, so I'll tell you. It wasn't just a broom. My dad has hit my mom. And she hit back. It sucks. All of it. I want him dead, my dad."

"You shouldn't ask for someone to be dead."

"But I can! And I told Noah, just go away for four years, it doesn't have to be the army. They're gonna ship you to boot camp, and you might end up in a war. He says there isn't one right now and it will be good for him, to go and train. But another war always comes, Lucien. I read my history too. I pay attention enough. Noah can feel something. He's smart. He chose this."

Droplets swelled in the corners of her eyes. She was smiling hard now, her face scrunching up. "I just need a minute."

She turned away. He placed his hand on her back. She said she had to go to the bathroom and stood up, walking over to the library.

He would do anything to get Noah out of going to war.

If Noah wanted to get away, why not go live in the woods? There were no guns there. Would House of Earth look out for him? If he listened to Jack, then yes. When Gabrielle came back, he would tell her. If Noah simply wanted to get away, then he could be with Lucien, Jack, and all the friends.

He watched three puddle ducks resting on the pond. There was a sign that said not to feed them, but people still came with bread crumbs, tossing them at the ducks. Lucien knew it wasn't natural to throw bread at the ducks. Beyond the pond and the treetops was the jagged mountain line, fading against the approaching nightfall. He checked his watch. Mama would be back soon. She always came back around this time.

"Sorry, Lucien," Gabrielle said, sitting back down. She was blowing her nose in a tissue.

"There's nothing to be sorry for."

"I don't cry around people. I don't like to. Girls cry and they get a reputation."

"A reputation?"

"Like, as whiny or weak. My mom cries. I hate it. I need to be a lot stronger than that."

"It's okay to cry from time to time."

"I dunno. I suppose. Anyway, it's getting late. My mom probably ordered pizza again and is wondering where I am. You know, the Domino's on Ember Street."

He nodded slowly in the way others did to show they agreed or knew of something they didn't really know. From the TV commercials, he knew Domino's was a place that made pizza, but Mama never bought it for him. You have to be careful about food, she once told him. Certain food can be poison. Especially fast food.

Poison, Mama?

Yes.

Do they mean to hurt people?

Those who eat it don't think so. But I think they do.

"Yes, Ember Street."

"Anyway, I'll be seeing you around."

Gabrielle stood up. With a jolt, Lucien remembered his idea. "Instead of the army, I was thinking—can Noah go to House of Earth?"

"Huh?"

"He wants to get away. House of Earth could help him. He would not have to go to war and kill."

A wide grin spread across Gabrielle's face, her small, bright-white front teeth peeking out from under her lips. She put her hands on her hips. Lucien saw, for the first time today, she was laughing. "Noah is *not* going there, I can promise you that."

She touched him on the shoulder and walked away.

———

On the first day of September, they gathered in the assembly hall, a large white-walled room with an oval skylight above and cherrywood pews below. Lucien had not gone there much, but this was a new instruction year, and he was almost twelve. At eleven, once-a-week assembly was mandatory. There were many friends he didn't recognize, new faces that belonged to collectives with new names.

Jack was right. They were growing.

He sat between Evie and Samantha, the hall swelling with chatter. Samantha spoke more than she used to, when she was younger and skinnier with her hair still in pigtails. He remembered how they'd built the sled together, her hands so steady and assured.

"I wonder what this will be," Samantha said to him.

"I do too."

"It might be wondrous."

So many people were talking to each other. He saw Sebastian and the Saplings. Jack sat on the end of the row, speaking with another mentor.

Antonio was playing a furious match of rock, paper, scissors with Cavan. They each kept picking rock. Lucien was looking for Mama.

"Welcome back, welcome back."

At the front of the room, behind a small lectern, stood a woman Lucien hadn't seen. She was younger than Mama and younger than Jack. Her hair was pulled into a bun behind her head, and the sleeves of her light-blue button-down were rolled up to her elbows. Everyone began to grow quiet.

"Friends, let's lower our voices."

She held up her right hand. The room, including Lucien, held up their right hand in reply. The chatter ended.

"It is so wonderful to see you all again. For those who don't know me, I'm Natasha. I work with O. C. Leroux, so I am not here in front of you as much as I like. O. C. would like to be here today, but important business has called him away. For my growing collectives, including the Saplings and the Meadows, you will all be meeting O. C. soon."

That meant Lucien. He had played O. C. for so many years, both chasing out dark energy and being chased. It seemed almost impossible they would actually meet. What would he say? He felt a whirl of nervous energy. He wished he could tell O. C. he had been a successful musher. Had he been different, somehow, he would have guided his friends through the woods. Snow and wind were not an excuse if you believed strongly enough. He hadn't inspired the friends, and O. C. would know. The shame slowly crept back.

"This is a very important year, as you all are aware. House of Earth, not too long ago, was little more than a hope and a dream, a vision of one man. O. C. saw our planet dying. And he decided he could no longer live the way he used to. He drove a fast car, lived in a large house, and burned energy without a second thought. He threw garbage in the ocean. He ate meat, so much of it—rare steaks and hamburgers and venison. His energy was dark. He was not just like you all were—once. He was *worse*. Much worse. I tell you this as a reminder that change is possible, that we are not fated to be who we are. Humans are a fallen species, yes, but when you are fallen, you are not beyond redemption. For our children here, this is especially important to remember. God loves you. O. C. loves you. We all love you. What we are building here is a future, a *real* future, especially as the world grows more dangerous and unstable."

Natasha paused, smiling at them all. Lucien was hunting among the heads and faces for Mama, who must surely be at the assembly too.

"We are bigger than ever before. Five new collectives this year. Instruction rooms are full. The nutritional hall is full. Our new habitation facility is nearly complete. All of it wouldn't be possible without you. What you contribute, what your families contribute, it makes this all possible. For the children, thank-you letters have been sent to parents. Your dollars have taken us so far. The word is spreading, frankly. More people are understanding that living in harmony with nature is our only chance at survival. We are a planet of great dark and great light. The dark must not unbalance that light. All of you create light, and all of you are going to save us. This is going to be a very special year."

"I wonder how special," Samantha whispered to Lucien.

"I don't know."

"You the mentors—you are also driving this change. I want to give you all a hand. Everyone, please applaud our mentors."

Natasha clapped, and all in the assembly followed her. Jack, along with the other mentors, waved.

"You are all undergoing great growth here, and I have no doubt you are ready for the challenges ahead. The people outside of here"—Natasha gestured to a far wall, indicating the chaos that festered just beyond it—"are going to want to tell us we are wrong. That the planet is not important enough. That we must abandon our ways for sin, for lives of easy destruction. Sin is tempting, I know. O. C. knows. We have fought it. In the future, we need to be ready for a confrontation, especially as we grow. You are all old enough to hear this: not everyone wants House of

Earth here. That's why your commitment is all the more important and why we are here to celebrate how far you've come."

Lucien considered the gravity of what Natasha had said. There were people, perhaps many, who did not want House of Earth to have a future. There was going to be a clash. Would he have to fight? Jack and Mama had said fighting was wrong. But now, Natasha was saying something very different. He remembered how Gabrielle had laughed when he'd said Noah could run away to House of Earth. Why had it been so funny? Would the army Noah was joining threaten House of Earth? Or would Noah come to defend them?

"We are building a real future. The only future!"

Jack suddenly stood up. Other mentors joined him, their backs straight, their chins pointing outward.

"The only future!" they cried out together.

Hands began to clap. Samantha and Evie glanced in Lucien's direction and clapped too. He followed, his hands stinging together, the sound taking him away. Natasha waved her hand. The clapping grew louder as she left the lectern.

Jack turned to them, his mouth moving. Lucien didn't hear what he said, but Evie, who was closer, did. Assembly was over. Instruction would begin.

When they sat down in that familiar room, Lucien saw that there were even more friends he didn't know. Boys and girls. Excitement built within him. More were joining their collective. This meant they were stronger, more filled with light, ready for whatever came their way. Jack took out a piece of clean white chalk and began to write on the board. Lucien watched his right hand in motion, how it created such neat, bright lines on the dark board.

"Today, we are going to talk about war," he said.

AFTER

Since the TV was showing only what he had seen and didn't want to see anymore, he stopped turning it on. Mama would watch alone. And then she stopped watching too.

"I will be gone two days, Lucien," she told him on Friday, three days after the towers were destroyed on TV.

"Where are you going, Mama?"

"It's very important. It has to do with family."

"Family?"

Lucien knew of no family other than Mama. The friends had brothers, sisters, fathers, cousins, and grandparents. He had Mama, but it had never bothered him he didn't have more. It was like asking for a third arm—he had what he needed. But now she was leaving. Panic gripped him.

"You'll understand soon, Lucien. There's enough food in the cupboard and the fridge. You be good. Stay by the cottage. If you wander into town, stay away from strangers."

"If we are attacked, if the war comes, what should I do, Mama? What should—"

"Don't talk anymore about what you saw. We are safe here, and that's all you should think about. On Monday, Jack and O. C. will speak to you at assembly. I will be there too."

"Really?"

"Listen to them. Listen to me. Listen to House of Earth. Now, more than ever, listen, Lucien."

Mama walked away Friday night. He was growing more accustomed to the layers of silence in the cottage, how the absence of some sound gave way to new sound he hadn't considered before. Tires crushing gravel around a distant bend. Birdsong in darkness. The branches of a great oak trembling. When he closed his eyes, he saw fire turn the black sky white. He slept with his knees near his chin. Sweat crawled on his chest.

Saturday arrived, enormous and bright. The cupboard had Cheerios, but three-quarters of the box was gone, and Mama hadn't bought a new one. He filled his bowl carefully, pouring only a trickle of milk. The expiration date had passed. He didn't mind, though, and Mama had said you could always go a few days beyond the date, at least. The fridge held several yogurt cups, stalks of celery, three red apples, and a plastic container of baby carrots. He spotted rye bread in tin foil. The crust was cold and hard. He took one bite and stepped away.

He had returned *The Natural* to the library without finishing it. He wanted to read it all, but time was up and he didn't want to make Gabrielle have a late book. Now was a good day to read it. He strapped on his sandals, changed into a fresh T-shirt, and began the walk down Darling Drive, away from the cottage and into town. The sun burned at the back of his neck, and the heat simmered on the dirt road. Sweat dappled his eyelids. He tried not to rub them. Town was only a few miles down and away, and he had time, all of it like a coil stretched out, flattened almost to his liking.

But he missed Mama and hoped the family, whoever they were, would be okay.

Downtown Mater had flags. This he noticed first. American flags, freshly cleaned, flying from almost every storefront, hanging over the empty sidewalks. Storefronts without flags had stickers in the window. He saw only an elderly man pushing a blue cart and a police officer checking his watch. A flag fluttered next to the clock tower too, which chimed now for noon. He could hear a black fly buzzing in his ear, following him down the sidewalk. The parking meters were not in service.

A dog barked, but no dog appeared. It barked again and then it was silent.

He saw the towers in the middle of the street, burning with the bones of the dead. He blinked once and they were gone.

He was afraid to blink again.

The library's windows were dark. On the door, however, were the hours of operation, and Saturday before three p.m. meant he could check out books. He pulled at the handle. The door still opened.

"Hello?" he asked.

No one answered. At the front desk, where Mrs. Yelich normally sat, waited another woman, even older, her white hair knotted into a bun. She was reading a paperback book instead of finishing the crosswords. She didn't look up as Lucien passed. He whispered hello and waved. She looked up, nodded, and returned to her book.

He found *The Natural* where he had left it, under fiction and the letter *M*. He held the book and waited.

Gabrielle wasn't here and Mama wasn't here. He walked back up to the desk.

"Excuse me?"

The woman looked up, staring at him without emotion. "Yes?"

"Can I get a library card?"

"Yes. Just fill out these forms and return them to me."

The woman passed the forms to Lucien and included a yellow pencil. There were basic questions: his name, date of birth, where he lived. Until Gabrielle had told him over the summer, he didn't think one could simply *have* a library card. It was reserved for others, people who moved through the world knowing always where they were going to be. But anyone can get one, Gabrielle said. Just return your books on time.

He wondered, for just a passing moment, why Mama had never signed him up.

"Thank you," the woman said when he handed his forms back. She glanced at them and typed into her computer. After a few minutes, she handed him a green plastic yard with the yellow words *Mater Public Library* printed across the front.

He gripped the card tight, holding it up to the fluorescent lighting overhead. It was his. He placed it carefully in his pocket. "Thank you!"

"Anytime, dear."

At the duck pond, he read. Roy Hobbs had been shot, he last remembered, and he reread that harrowing scene, how a woman filled with darkness tried to kill him because he was a great ballplayer. Why would she do this? He couldn't understand. Roy had done nothing to her. Yet his dream was dead. No pitching for the Cubs, no superstardom. The yellowing pages were still smooth under his fingers. He turned slowly, afraid he would tear a page that did not belong to him. Roy would come back. He was a hitter, not a pitcher. He was older. He was damaged, but he wasn't finished.

Lucien clutched the book tightly.

Why did people shoot other people?

"Lucien!"

His head shot up. It was Gabrielle, walking alone toward him. He felt a swelling in his chest. It had been several weeks since they last saw each other. That was well before the worst day.

"Hi, Gabrielle." He was grinning, and his hand, with hardly any command from him, was touching the library card, holding it up proudly.

Gabrielle squinted one eye, like a prospector appraising gold dust. "I do declare you got yourself a library card."

"I did."

"Same old book."

"I need to finish it."

"We all need to do stuff these days."

They grew silent. A green-and-white duck fidgeted on the lip of the pond, joining a rare swan, the two next to each other. The swan hissed and the duck flew away, a dark parenthesis against the hard blue sky. On the far side of the pond sat a man and a girl. Though they were too far to see clearly, Lucien thought he could recognize both, if only they came closer. He leaned forward. They were standing up and walking away.

"Is school as lame for you as it is for me?"

"*Lame*, you mean—"

"Oh, you know, boring garbage. Teachers don't know anything. Class goes on forever. The best part of the day is when you finally go home. I had an algebra teacher talk to the class for like, fifteen minutes about how her boyfriend left her. I swear to God."

"Jack doesn't talk about any of that."

"Jack, right, what your only teacher—"

"Mentor."

"*Mentor*. How many years has it been with this one dude? Seriously?"

Lucien bit lightly on his lower lip. These kinds of questions weren't settling easily within him. At first, there had been a silent thrill to Gabrielle's inquiries, how every question built on the next toward what was undeniable and new: a person outside House of Earth caring about what he said and did. But he could also see his ways were nothing like hers, that she came from a place that did not value what he valued and perhaps never would. He still liked her. He liked her a lot. He liked how it felt to sit beside her, the way her mouth moved, how sunlight shone off her dark hair, and the dull gold of the bangle around her wrist. He was afraid, yet he wanted to draw closer. He would not know how to say any of this out loud. It was a wordless, colorless churn within, and he could only follow it like the current down a river.

"As long as I can remember."

"And that isn't strange to you? I have like, six different teachers this semester alone. The idea of being stuck with one . . . I don't know."

"Jack knows a lot."

"I bet he does."

"Gabrielle . . ." He would try out a question of his own. He liked how her name fell, syllable by syllable, from his mouth. "How is your brother?"

"Noah shipped off. He was excited. My mom bawled. I did too, but like, I can't cry if she's gonna cry. She will do all the crying. And now this terrorist attack. I have the worst feeling. I don't even want to say it."

"It was scary and horrible to watch."

"My mom keeps the news on now all the time. I hate it. It's Twin Towers twenty-four seven—I want to just smash the TV screen. I almost did. I hear what they're talking about. A war is coming, Lucien. A big . . . a big *fucking* war."

Another word that landed like a bomb in his stomach. Once, when he was little, Mama had said it, and only under her breath. She had found red spray paint on a tree trunk near their cottage. After the worst word, Mama didn't say anything more.

"I hope there isn't a war. Our harmony is really threatened then."

"Harmony? Try *lives*, Lucien. My brother's."

"Unnatural death disrupts harmony." Jack had said this once.

"Let's go for a walk. This bench is hurting me."

He followed her away from the pond, through a back alley, and onto Superior Street, where the American flags waited.

"There weren't this many flags last time," he said.

"War flags," she answered.

They came to a stop in front of the Walgreens along the corner.

"I want to get a drink in here," she said.

Inside, as Gabrielle ran her fingers along the coolers of iced tea, soda, and beer, she asked Lucien if he was thirsty.

"No."

"You sure?"

"Mama—my mom, she left me a—"

"This is one of her errands, right? And she never tells you where she goes."

"She doesn't."

"See, my mom and dad leave me too, but it isn't like, a mystery. My dad goes to bars and goes up north, maybe to see girlfriends, and my mom doesn't stop working. Or she stays home and watches the towers keep collapsing on TV and practically begs me to leave the house, like today. You need to find out what's going on, Lucien."

"Maybe next time I will ask her."

Gabrielle reached for a light-blue Gatorade. She waved it in front of him. "This is refreshing stuff."

"It's a lot of sugar."

"House of Earth tell you to say that?"

Before he could answer, she jumped in again. "Come to think of it, there's word going around Mater High that like, a few kids dropped out to go to House of Earth. So you may be getting new recruits or whatever."

New friends were always showing up. It was the growth Jack had talked about. Until now, Lucien never considered where they had come from. It was as if they descended from the sky or grew from the ground. Gabrielle offered a new reality: children stepping out of her world and into his.

"It has been getting bigger."

"One day, you take me on a tour."

At the checkout line, Lucien watched Gabrielle pay for the drink on her own. Mama always bought him food and drinks. He could tell Gabrielle had done this many times. In the back pocket of her jeans was a small leather wallet. She flicked it open, ran her finger across a smooth dollar bill, and slid it to the man behind the counter. He took it and nodded at her.

"Bag?" he asked.

"Yeah," she answered.

"Gabrielle, plastic bags are really bad for the environment."

"I heard that. But I could use one today. Look right here." She held up her wallet to show him. It was weather-beaten in her hand, with deep creases and a faded, amoeba-shaped stain. "Noah's. He left it for me."

"Wow, that was nice to do."

"Something like that. So if I feel like a plastic bag on a week that couldn't get any worse, then yeah, I'll take the plastic."

The automatic doors of Walgreens slid open, revealing a man and a girl. At first, they were only familiar splotches out of the corner of his eye as he watched Gabrielle put her wallet away. He turned to see them both, walking into the shampoo-and-body-lotions aisle.

It was Evie, her white-blonde hair bright in the pharmacy's soft light. Just a few weeks ago, she had turned twelve. Her hand was being held, Sebastian leading her. Lucien had never seen Evie or Sebastian or anyone from House of Earth in the outside world, except for that pool party at Kaitlyn's several years ago. A pool party that should not have happened.

Gabrielle touched him on the shoulder. "What are you looking at?"

"It's one of my friends."

"Oh yeah, let's say hi."

"We could."

Gabrielle led him now. Sebastian was searching the shelves, his eyes roving up and down. Evie looked like a doll next to him, her hand gripped tight and lifted into the air. Lucien tried to figure out why, on a Saturday, Sebastian and Evie would be together at Walgreens. Of course, *he* was in a Walgreens too, with a girl they wouldn't know when she walked up to greet them.

Evie saw them first. Sebastian was scrutinizing several types of sunscreen.

"Hi," Evie said.

"Hi, Evie. This is my friend Gabrielle."

"Nice to meet you, Evie," Gabrielle said.

Sebastian, turning from his sunscreen, appeared to frown. "Lucien?"

He could only nod in reply. "Hi, Sebastian."

"I'll see you on Monday."

Lucien could never articulate it fully, but he was always glad that Jack, and not Sebastian, was his mentor. He remembered Sebastian from the day of the sled race, how he'd huddled with the Saplings. All mentors were supposed to radiate light and not dark energy, and Sebastian, surely, was not the exception. Yet Lucien never enjoyed the energy he could feel in Sebastian's presence, whether he was passing Lucien in the nutritional hall or watching him as he played on the commons. Evie's smile was almost flat, like a line chiseled painstakingly into stone. Lucien wanted to ask her what she was feeling.

"It was nice to meet you," Gabrielle said, clearly looking at Evie and not Sebastian.

"It was nice to meet you as well," Sebastian said. "I apologize, but we must get going."

"Sorry," Evie said.

"That's okay."

Lucien was about to turn to leave the aisle when he saw Gabrielle's mouth open again.

"I like your daughter's shoes," she said.

Evie stared, saying nothing. Sebastian's eyes fell to Evie's pink-and-white sneakers. Long, dark hairs dangled over his brow.

"She appreciates the compliment," Sebastian said.

"Does she? Do you?"

"I do," Evie said.

"Good to hear from the source! Seriously, I need to pick up sneakers like that."

"Only the best for my Evie," Sebastian said.

"I'll see you Monday," Evie said.

Sebastian spun around first, walking quickly out of the aisle. Evie, her hand still held, followed him, her feet close together. Gabrielle opened her Gatorade and began to drink. She and Lucien left Walgreens together, coming to a stop on a stretch of empty sun-scorched pavement in the middle of town. Several robins fluttered overhead. Lucien looked right and left for Evie and Sebastian. They hadn't left Walgreens yet.

"I didn't know Sebastian spent time with Evie," Lucien said.

"She's your friend and she didn't tell you?"

"Evie doesn't talk about that stuff much."

"I like her. I get strange vibes from her, though. And that Sebastian? I don't know about him."

"Jack is better."

"Yeah, let's go with that."

"I wonder where Evie went to school before House of Earth," Gabrielle said, her voice airy and rising. "And where Sebastian worked."

"Evie was there when I started. I remember her. Sebastian, I think, came a few years ago."

"I don't like how he held her hand. I'll say that much. Every dad who gripped skin that hard was up to something else. People have layers, Lucien. If you don't learn that yet, you'll learn it soon."

"I see it more and more."

"Keep *seeing*, Lucien. Now, what else do you want to do on this fine Saturday, after the worst week of all our lives?"

———

They came at sunset, when the grass stretched deep into the dark. A bonfire swirled at the center, in a cavity of land none of them had noticed in daylight. All day the friends had chopped wood. Now they could watch their labor take its truest form: an explosion of white flame on the commons.

They all asked what it was for.

You'll see soon, Jack said.

This was a night for friends, for mentors, for parents. This was a night to draw bodies into the grass, ringing the rising fire. As the sun disappeared, Lucien saw Mama. She waved gently. Antonio said his mother and father were coming too. And Cavan's, Maia's, Samantha's, Magnus's, and every other friend's parent in the Meadows would come, as would parents of every other member of a collective.

This is a big night for our family, Jack said. We will witness the power of a real and lasting community.

Everyone had grown. Sometimes Lucien had to remind himself how long he had known the friends, these six years, and the ways they had changed since he'd first met them all. Antonio was even taller, his dark hair hanging down past the nape of his neck, his limbs now long and bony, arms swinging like vines at his sides. He was someone, as he had always been, to be followed, whether in a game on the commons or a hike in the woods. Cavan and Magnus were closer to Antonio now, closer than Lucien would be, but that was okay with him. When Magnus smiled or laughed, his face scrunched up so his blue eyes disappeared, and he was the only one of the friends who had rolls of thick skin on his belly. Still, he tried to keep up with Antonio, who walked and ran much faster, and Cavan, who strained to be the very fastest of them all. None of them liked slow walks through the woods as much as Lucien or sitting quietly in grass. They shouted and raced and tossed balls back and forth. They maintained, he could see, a rolling conversation that could extend from one day into the next, like a train speeding through one continuous tunnel.

Lucien drew closer to the girls. Maia was the most excitable, her voice bounding off the walls whenever she had a story she needed to tell. Magenta would always be her favorite color, but she didn't need it to be so ever-present. One bracelet or pencil or hair tie would do. If Antonio was one locus, she was another, smaller but no less crackling. Samantha, it seemed to him, had followed Maia's lead, no longer so shy, her pigtails undone and her hair grown out so it flowed far down her back, nearly to her waist. She was not as skinny as she used to be either. Lucien noticed how she was becoming more like Mama: she had small breasts on her chest now, what all the girls would soon have. And there was Evie. Why had she been with Sebastian? To have that kind of time with a mentor was special. Out of all the friends, it was Evie, with her large and trembling eyes, who could be worthy of such attention. He knew it even when she was littler, when her hair was like the white part of a flame. She understood more than they ever would, as if she had already lived through this life and was experiencing it for a second or third or fourth time. Sometimes Lucien felt that whatever he said to her could not surprise her because she knew, somehow, what he would say. If there was a rainstorm, Evie could know when it would end. In her state alone, there were answers. He wasn't sure whether the other friends felt this way about Evie.

It was now Monday, six days after the two towers collapsed. Sometimes Lucien saw them looming out of the woods or in the street, burning bright, smoke howling from the blasted craters within. They would stand tall and dark like tombstones against a cloudless sky.

———

He felt a pair of hands on his shoulders. He spun around.

Mama.

She was behind him, smiling into the fire. He was between Antonio and Magnus. Their parents were with them too. He was proud to have chopped the wood to make the fire possible. Instead of instruction, they had chopped. Instead of playing on the commons, they had chopped. His shoulders ached. The calluses on his hands stung. The late-summer sun had burned his neck a shade of reddish gold. Jack only told them it was an important fire for an important meeting and to do what he said.

And then Lucien saw Evie and Sebastian.

They were together again, like on Saturday. Sebastian's hand rested on Evie's shoulder. She was looking down and away, toward a patch of grass. He tried to wave to get her attention, but she didn't see him. The friends knew Mama worked at House of Earth, like Sebastian. From her office door, she would occasionally greet them. Had Mama decided to be a mentor, Lucien certainly would've told everyone. He was proud. Gabrielle had said she didn't like how Sebastian gripped Evie's hand. Perhaps this was just the way fathers held daughters.

He waved again. Evie still didn't see him.

The bodies grew. They stood in concentric semicircles around the fire, talking to one another, the mass taking on the low, continuous hum of expectant conversation. Words to fill gaps in time until the moment of true attention arrived. Lucien saw a sharp crescent moon in the sky, so defined it was almost as if one of the friends had stood on a ladder to paint it there. Last year, they'd learned that astronauts had gone to the moon. Jack said this was a moment of pride for America, men reaching another world.

But we can't turn our backs on the earth. Can we?

We can't, the friends said.

We only have one planet. And we aren't getting another one. We will only save this one with sacrifice, here and now.

Yes, Jack, they said together.

Lucien heard a low horn. He turned right and left to see where it came from. Eyes swung to the source of the sound. Coming around them was Natasha, holding a gleaming brass horn. She smiled and put it down.

The fire roared, higher than Lucien's head. He couldn't help but gaze into the glowing flame. How beautiful it was, but how painful it could be.

Fire builds and fire destroys.

"Good evening, everyone!"

"Good evening," the crowd chanted back.

"For those who don't know me, my name is Natasha, and I help keep the ship afloat here at House of Earth. And for those that do, it's good to see you all again. First, I want to thank all of you for being here. Notices went out only over the weekend that this was a mandatory nighttime assembly for parents, mentors, and friends alike. We think it's important, in times like these, that we come together as a *whole* community. I also am going to introduce a very, very special guest. He is so thrilled to be here tonight."

Natasha paused, breathing in and briefly closing her eyes.

"These are undoubtedly very trying times for you and your families. We all saw what happened last week. We all understand the enormity of this tragedy. And we understand the sickness that's in the world. What's important, especially as we move forward with another successful year at House of Earth—we have more collectives than ever before—is that we don't allow this sickness and negativity to overtake what we've built together. There are going to be many who try to divide us. Who try to convince us that a planet-first approach to education and spiritual development is not what we should be doing. Now, more than ever, we need to stay focused—to fight for the future of this world and do it together. Our very special guest will have *a lot* more to say on this topic. Now, should I introduce him?"

A hush fell over the crowd. Some could guess at what was coming next, but they were too worried to hazard it out loud for fear that a vocal wish could somehow scuttle what was going to be. They would not be in the business of altering realities. They would not test Natasha. Waiting was easier.

Lucien sucked in his breath.

A tall man ambled through a clearing in the woods. To Lucien, he was little more than a shadow, the darkness cloaking his body. The friends around him tipped forward, straining to see what the whispers were building toward. They all wanted to be the first to see. Natasha was turning toward the man now, an arm outstretched. The fire licked at the night sky, the warm air a blanket on Lucien's soft skin. His sandals dug into the soil, his toes cooling in the grass. He was waiting. He was ready.

The towers came to him once more in a flash, twins at the height of death. He was ready to cry.

Where was this man?

"That's him," Evie said.

The figure emerged from the darkness of the trees, firelight flickering on his long, thin body, covered in white. He walked deliberately, one foot guiding the other, his smooth face shrouded in a beard the color of grain. He was tall, very tall. His sharp knees, Lucien saw, poked the cloth of his tunic.

He had a face that Lucien, somehow, knew. Where? When? His brain, on fire with this realization, battled to remember. He had to know. The friends would know.

The mass leaned in, all pulling closer to the tall man in front of the fire. Antonio gripped Lucien's elbow. They turned to each other.

"Hello," the man said simply.

Natasha drifted backward and away. "Introducing a man you all know so well," she said. "O. C. Leroux!"

The whispers rose in unison, the hushed words tickling Lucien. Antonio's father placed his hand over his mouth. Parents were turning to each other. Magnus and Samantha had wide-open mouths. *This is him*, Lucien heard again and again. *This is really him.* As the man, O. C. Leroux, stepped forward, Lucien noticed the color of his blond hair, how it took on the golden-white brightness of the firelight.

A garland of wildflowers rested in his hair.

"Thank you all for coming here tonight," he said. "You are all what makes our success possible."

His hands floated at his sides as he spoke. They were far larger than any Lucien had seen, the fingers bony and spidery, pale in the light of the flame. His voice calmed Lucien. It was like a whisper, though it wasn't—he heard each word perfectly. He was sure he had never met O.

C. Leroux, yet the face and body were somehow a memory of his, like an early dream he was now recalling without even knowing why. Jack had spoken about him enough, and maybe that was why, Jack's words conjuring an image in his head.

He had been waiting for O. C. Leroux all this time. That was it.

"I came here tonight to address all of you as one. As Natasha said, community is so important, and what we have achieved at House of Earth, already, is remarkable. It is profound. Our young friends here are the new generation, a generation without sin, a group of boys and girls who will go out into the world to cleanse it. I couldn't be more thrilled by their progress. And I know that takes hard work from not just our mentors but parents too, parents who understand that education doesn't end at the last chime of instruction. Education continues in the home. I truly believe that."

O. C. Leroux held one finger in the air, his lips closing in thought. He was so tall, Lucien thought. And his bones—were they hollow like a bird's? Could he fly? Was he like a wind spirit, able to slip between trees?

The voice was like the low rustle of leaves in his ear.

"What I came here to talk to you about tonight, however, is not just what we have done. It's what we are going to do. It's what we must do. Our planet, tragically, is in a crisis. We have known this for a long time. We have seen a sickness in the land. We have touched it, felt it, observed it in our friends. Modern life has brought many wonders. We use electricity here at House of Earth. Automobiles have entered our land. We understand. We know. But the sickness grows. None of it is sustainable. Our young friends are our future, but they must make it there first—and that depends on the actions of all of us."

He was walking slowly now, approaching different sides of the crowd. No one spoke. The fire, improbably, was gaining strength.

"Last week, the nation endured a tragedy. Thousands of lives were lost. We are now seeing a war machine of the modern world mobilized, ready for bloodshed. Even as the planet dies, a war must be waged.

Why? For what purpose? We know we cannot live this way any longer. We know we are committing murder, against nature and ourselves. The earth will not stand it. The earth will reject it. And we have to be prepared. Right here, in our little community, we have been preparing for what we knew would happen eventually. If not these towers in New York City, then another cataclysm. Another explosion, another mass death. You are going to be very afraid in these next few weeks and months. That is natural. Fear is a part of who we are. Fear came with us in the womb. But fear can be defeated."

O. C. stopped again. He peered up and down, his hands drawn behind his back. Lucien was close to him now, only a few paces away. He heard O. C.'s feet on the grass. They were bare, he saw. They were enormous and he wore nothing on or over them. Grass flattened in their wake.

"We all grieve. I can say love is the answer, and love *is* the answer—but, you my friends, know you will ask for more than a recitation of the word *love*. We can profess love for a person or a reality while simultaneously destroying it. You can feel love in your heart, real love, and still power the machines that will bring about our eradication. But we do have an answer—all of you do—through the work you've been doing here for many years. For our friends, learning from our mentors, and for the parents, and an increasing number of you who are dedicated to the future—you are seeking answers. You are seeking solutions. You are not just hoping but building the reality we must have to guarantee harmony between human beings, the most ruthless species to ever grace the planet's surface, and nature, which welcomed us here and was rewarded, for its generosity, with murder. Each hour, another species goes extinct. Each day, another world lost. The tragedy last week, two airplanes obliterating two office towers in New York City—that is nature's reality, each minute of each day."

A body rustled near Lucien, pushing through the mass to step closer to O. C. A thick elbow brushed Lucien's own. It was Antonio's father, clear mucus running from his nostrils, his eyes soft and pinkish. He ran a finger under his nose. Tears, sparkling from the light of the fire, dotted his cheeks. Antonio reached out to his father, but he didn't see him, walking instead toward O. C. The tears passed his jawline.

O. C. landed both hands gently on Antonio's father's shoulders. "My friend, what troubles you?"

"My, my—"

Antonio's father bent his head, trying to hide more tears. He couldn't speak. His right hand pinched the bridge of his nose, his eyes on the grass below. Lucien could see tears, like dewdrops, landing on blades of grass.

"It's all right. We are all here with you. We are here to help you."

"My—my brother, he's dead . . ."

Antonio suddenly looked straight at Lucien. They were left to watch and wait, for O. C. Leroux and Antonio's father to come to an understanding.

"Your brother?"

"Last week."

"I am very sorry to hear this. Your name, my friend?"

"Anders."

"Anders, you must know you are loved, and you are now joined in a special community that is going to make sure deaths like these don't happen again. You are exactly, *exactly* where you need to be."

"He was declared missing and—and I didn't even tell my son, because he was *missing*, but it's been a week, and Darius, if he was around, he would come home and he's not coming home and I didn't even tell my son and I realized this, here, with you, with you, oh, my brother, he's gone and I don't know what to do, I don't know . . ."

"Anders," O. C. said once more, his voice softer, his gaze now meeting the eyes of Antonio's father.

"Yes?"

85

"You are strong. And you are not alone. You will never be alone. You belong to House of Earth."

O. C. looked up toward the mass, silent in the light of the fire. Lucien could hear only the sobbing and, behind them all, a wall of crickets in the woods.

"Does Anders here belong to House of Earth? Does he belong to us?"

"Yes!" they chanted back. Lucien joined in, his voice high in the night, the word so light yet powerful off his teeth. Antonio's father was smiling. Antonio was too.

"Do you see?" O. C.'s hand was outstretched, pointing to all of them.

"I see," Antonio's father said.

"You are exactly where you need to be."

"Thank you."

Antonio's father had not stopped crying. O. C. returned a hand to his shoulder. Another half of Antonio's father would have equaled one O. C. It was as if a tree had become a man, Lucien thought. Our tree.

When Antonio's father returned to Antonio's side, O. C. began to speak again.

"What you saw just now is the power of a community built on values that will save us—on harmony, on love, on trust for one another. We will need every last ounce of commitment to this world we have built when the war comes. Not just the war we are seeing now, this mobilization for Afghanistan, more innocents set to die. No—we're looking at a much greater war. One that will envelop the planet and all those who are living the lifestyle of war, of destruction. That isn't us, but this is people we know. For those that can be saved, they must be saved. You all once led lives different than the lives you are living now. If you know someone who is ready for House of Earth, who *believes* in the planet, bring them to us. There are those out there, those who want help, those who want to be saved. By being here, you will be saved. For this planet, in the end, will know justice. And it will cull those who have sought to harm it. At House of Earth, we are ready for the future. All of us, together."

Lucien saw that Antonio's father was looking deeply into O. C.'s eyes, not moving.

"Now, let's join hands."

Everyone seemed to know what to do. Antonio and Magnus held Lucien's right and left hands. Sebastian gripped Evie's left hand, along with Samantha's right. They formed a chain of flesh, circling around the fire. O. C. stood still, his own hands at his sides. At first, they moved gradually, shuffling through grass. Lucien passed O. C., almost close enough to touch. What if he did? What would he feel? He could not imagine O. C. talking directly to him. He was not an adult and he was not special. He had not even been the best musher. He was proud, though, to have passed so close, to know that, as part of a collective, he was seen by O. C., who could recognize them all. Lucien wasn't afraid.

He was exactly where he was supposed to be.

And then Lucien remembered. The image returned, lighting up his mind. The May Festival. The tall man with the flute. Lucien looked into his eyes. The man playing the flute, that was, he was—yes, it had to be. He *had* seen O. C. Leroux before.

They continued to circle the fire, their speed now increasing. Some adults around him hummed. Others closed their eyes. Lucien decided to do the same, to see what kind of power he could draw from following them. His thoughts slowed, the blackness behind his eyelids overtaking him. He listened for the hums, the crickets layered beneath them, the crackle of fire on wood, feet pressing grass. He heard his own breath, easy now.

He was exactly where he was supposed to be.

"Keep your friends close," O. C. said. "Always keep them close."

They circled again. Lucien opened his eyes, the night soft and smudged in his recovering vision. The fire was beginning to weaken.

Lucien saw Antonio's father ahead of him, his head lolling to the side. He was smiling. O. C. had stopped his tears.

"Let's lie down now," O. C. said.

Hundreds fell to the grass, their eyes trained on the night sky. Lucien knew the constellations because Jack had taught them to him. He spotted Taurus and Gemini, as well as the North Star. *Gemini* was Latin for *twins*. Taurus was a bull. Gazing upward, he imagined he was on a craft floating to the stars, darkness all around him. He would travel into the cold for the human race. He would be alone, without even Mama, his only comfort his belief in the mission.

Who lived up there?

"Breathe in, breathe out."

O. C. walked among them, his head bowed. Lucien watched for his feet, how they carefully rose and fell with each gentle step forward. Lucien breathed, hearing the air sucking in and out, the expansion and contraction of his chest.

"Watch the sky. What do you see? You see stars, of course. You see what is beyond us. We know we are but a speck, a grain, nothing against a universe so vast it will take countless lifetimes to begin to understand it all. Do you see another planet? You might. But we are not going there. Not today. We are here. We are destined to stay, to save it or die as it destroys itself. The choice will lie with us, what we decide to do. I see great determination in all of you. Together, we will build the world that must be built. We will survive the destruction to come—if we do what needs to be done. Now, breathe in and breathe out one more time. Stand."

Together, they stood. Lucien straightened his back. O. C. was walking again, his head bent toward the faces in front of him.

He was coming closer to Lucien.

"Many changes are in store. Follow our wonderful mentors, who have been instructed to guide you where you need to be. They will speak to your mind and your soul. As long as you are on the side of light, of harmony, of protecting what is around you, you will survive and inherit the future. This I believe."

Lucien felt a pressure on the top of his skull. He looked up, unable to speak.

Gazing down, his hand on Lucien's head, was O. C. Leroux.

"Friend, what is your name?"

Lucien's jaw was like jelly. He struggled to make it solid, to form words into language and answer to the giant in front of him. He bit the inside of his cheek. Anything, anything, he just had to say—

"Lucien."

"Lucien! And how old are you, Lucien?"

"Twelve."

"That's a very special age. Lucien, you've been with us for a long time?"

"Yes."

"That's wonderful."

O. C. released his hand from Lucien's skull and continued his loping walk, his long body taking on the glow of the firelight. Lucien still felt the impression of O. C.'s hand on him, how it continued to radiate through his bones. Magnus and Antonio stared at him, their eyes wide and trembling. Even Evie seemed amazed. Sebastian's expression, a slight upturn of the lips, had not changed.

"Boys and girls like Lucien are our best hope," O. C. said, coming to rest near the fire. "They deliver new energy, new light, and will come from here unpolluted by a world *out there* that seeks to annihilate all around it. Boys and girls like Lucien, yes—they are our future."

I am the future, Lucien thought, understanding this was the first time such a thought had ever materialized within him. He had a purpose, a reason for being, and they all did, Antonio and Magnus and Evie and Cavan and Samantha and Maia and every other friend—all of them together in a chosen place. Lucien wanted to sing. His heart beat faster.

"O. C. Leroux chose you," Antonio whispered in his ear.

"I know."

"Lucien, wow . . ."

Lucien felt a tap on his shoulder. It was Mama behind him again. She no longer gazed down at him. He realized they were almost the same height. Until now, until this night with O. C. Leroux, he hadn't considered this. Mama touched his head, not far from where O. C.'s own hand had been just moments ago.

"Remember this night."

"I will."

By the fire, O. C. extended both arms, the light beginning to die around him.

"Our future, then, is right with us. If we do what we are supposed to do—if we respect what we've built at House of Earth—it's possible to triumph over the darkness you all witnessed last week. It's possible to undo that damage, that horror. All of it . . . all of it is within reach."

O. C. turned away from the fire. His long white back faced all of them, his blond hair touching the bottom of his neck. He walked on, away from them all.

Lucien watched him enter the clearing, the shadows overtaking him. He was a white streak against the trees, moving deeper into the woods he had once emerged from. Where was he going? Where would he rest? When would he come again?

Lucien touched his own head. Here, just moments ago, a part of him had been sacred.

———

On Tuesday night, one week after the towers fell, Mama came to him as he was watching TV. She walked to the TV, bent down, and turned it off.

"I was watching," Lucien said about the show, a National Geographic special on the Sahara Desert.

"We are not watching TV anymore."

"We aren't?"

"I am getting rid of it tomorrow."

"Why, Mama?"

"It's like O. C. Leroux said: changes are coming. You don't want to disobey him, right?"

"No, of course not."

"We are not to watch TV anymore. There is nothing good there anyway."

Mama left the TV at the side of the road. Outside the cottage, it looked smaller than he had remembered it, a meek black box perched next to several bags of trash.

At instruction, Jack asked if all the TVs had been thrown out. Everyone nodded except for Maia. Usually, she smiled when the friends' attention turned to her. Today was different.

"My dad's getting rid of it tomorrow," she said.

Jack placed a hand on Maia's desk, his finger nudging the pencil she had painted magenta. Lucien could see the curve of Jack's biceps in his short-sleeve shirt, how it flexed as his fingers grew white from the pressure being applied to the desk.

"Tonight, Maia."

Lucien also noticed that Evie, usually one of the friends most likely to answer Jack's questions, stopped asking and answering questions. When Jack called on her to ask if she knew what the inner bark layer of a tree does for the tree, she shrugged and shook her head.

"We talked about this earlier, Evie. You must remember."

"I don't know."

The inner bark, Jack said, transports sugars produced by photosynthesis through the tree. And what is photosynthesis?

Evie shrugged.

Later, Lucien found Evie on the edge of the commons, sitting near the large construction site. She was picking at the grass, her hand on her chin.

"Hi, Evie," he said, walking up.

"Lucien."

He sat next to her. "It was pretty cool, how we all met O. C. Leroux. Right?"

"Yeah."

"And how we get to learn all new stuff in instruction. The types of bark, why trees grow . . ." Evie, he saw, was not looking in his direction. She was focused on the blades of grass she kept pulling out of the ground. "I don't think you should just pull grass out like that. It's living, like everything else—"

"I *know*, Lucien."

"You know what photosynthesis is."

"What?"

"You know what it is, Evie. When Jack asked you. You knew, didn't you? You know everything."

"I don't know about that . . ."

"You did!"

"Lucien, I'd rather be alone right now."

"Why?"

She swiveled her head, peering past him, over toward the woods. "Sometimes people need to be alone."

"Is everything okay?"

"Everything is what it is."

"I don't know what that means."

"Just forget it, Lucien."

"It was cool to see you and Sebastian too, that one time. Both my mom and your dad work here. And I didn't even know until recently he was your dad—"

"Lucien." Evie was standing now, her hands balled into fists. "Please shut up."

No one at House of Earth had ever told him, or anyone else, to shut up. It was another phrase that existed only in the TV he used to watch. Gabrielle's curse words had cut at him, but he knew they were never aimed his way. They could hurt only so much. Here was Evie, one of the friends, using dark language against *him*, just shortly after O. C. Leroux had talked about the importance of living in harmony with others. His breath grew short. He put one hand in the grass, steadying himself. How could she? Who was she?

This was not the Evie he knew.

"Evie, I just—"

But she was walking away, back toward the main building. He stared at the small spots in the soil where the grass had been before Evie ripped it out.

———

On the following Monday, Lucien went to eat lunch in the nutritional hall. Serving him beets and barley behind the counter was Antonio's father.

"Hi!" Lucien said with surprise, holding out his tray.

"Yes, you're Antonio's friend. How are you? Today's my first day."

"That's great, I mean, Mister . . ."

"Just call me Anders."

"Okay, I will. Thank you for the food, Anders."

Antonio sat down next to Lucien to eat.

"That's pretty cool. Your dad works here now."

"Yeah, it's good to have him here. Like your mom. It just makes you feel a bit more safe."

"Definitely. He said he just started."

Antonio leaned over. "I heard him on the phone with my mom. He told her he quit his job. They aren't together anymore, but they still talk a lot. I didn't see him as much with his old job, so having him here now, I get to see him every day. My mom may come too."

Antonio waved to his father. After a moment of shoveling more beets onto a plate, his father waved back.

"It must be hard, what he's going through," Lucien said.

"It's hard for all of us. Uncle Darius . . . he was nice. I didn't see him that much. He lived down in the city. I didn't even know he worked in the towers."

"I just don't know why it had to happen."

"You heard O. C. He said it was bound to, one way or the other."

"I just wish it was different."

"I do too."

"This year is definitely . . . well, things are already changing," Lucien said, thinking back to Mama throwing out the TV.

"Jack is getting more serious."

"No TV."

"My dad pulled out the internet too."

"We just had TV. My mom, she didn't want us on the internet."

"I liked the internet. My dad went up and threw out the cord we put into the phone. He said no more. It's not good anymore. And yeah, our TV was trashed too."

"I guess it's for the best."

"It has to be. Why else do it?"

Samantha and Maia sat down next to them, their plates filled with identical portions of beets and barley. Maia wore a magenta bracelet on her wrist. Lucien liked how the sunlight glinted off its surface.

"I met your dad," Samantha said.

"Yup, first day," Maia said.

"That's so great."

"We'll be seeing him every day, probably," Maia said.

"I think so," Antonio said.

"Hey, Lucien," Samantha said. "How much do you get to see your mom during the day?"

Lucien had to think. Mama was here every day in the office, and there were times he would walk by and see her. She had stepped out to wave at the friends. But these were *times*, not every day. He didn't see Mama every day. At night, he could see her while she was awake. If Antonio's father, Anders, was in the nutritional hall, they would come to see him all the time, every day. They would see Anders much more than Mama.

"I see her. I don't know if it's exactly every day."

"Your mom is pretty busy, right? I heard she gets to work with the mentors and even O. C. Leroux."

Lucien hadn't heard that. Mama never talked about working with O. C. Leroux. She never said much about the day, only that she had been good and productive, and then she asked Lucien how his instruction was progressing. He could only guess that she was busy. What the busyness amounted to, he could not quite imagine.

"I don't know."

"That's what I heard."

"My mom is busy, I know that. But she doesn't talk too much about it."

"Oh, okay. My mom is starting here next week, actually."

"Really? That's great."

"My dad supports it. He's still an accountant. He wants to have her or himself work at House of Earth, and my mom said she'll do it. Last night she said at dinner she was going to work at the new habitation facilities. Those are getting built fast."

The construction that had started before the towers were destroyed was now accelerating. Men in orange vests and hard hats walked the commons each day. Trucks continued to pull into the oval, crunching over the gravel. Skeletons of steel were rising in the grass. On some days, Lucien would sit nearby and listen to the pinging and crashing, how machines were wielded for the creation of new things. Was this natural? One day, he would ask Jack. Jack talked about how the way men and women lived was hurting the planet, with their houses and cars and big buildings spewing pollution and extracting energy from nature. But even House of Earth had construction. The habitation facilities were on grass fields that had to be dug up, turned into dirt pits, and then filled in. This confused Lucien. How to justify it with all he had been taught.

"When are they done?" Antonio asked.

"I don't know. My mom thinks soon. She says she heard the schedule is definitely getting speeded up."

"That's good."

"It'll be fun when everything is built."

Antonio finished his beets, leaving a purplish smear on his white plate. "Things definitely change every year, so it's never boring," he said.

"People change too," Maia said.

"What do you mean?" Lucien asked.

"Well, look who's over there, eating with no one." Maia gestured to a table in the far corner, near the window. It was Evie, her fork picking at a plate of beets without bringing any up to eat.

"She has been different," Lucien said, thinking back to the horrible words she'd aimed at him. He didn't want to repeat them here because he still liked Evie, and if anyone else knew what she had said, there would be punishment. Certainly from Jack. They had all been very good lately, and it had to stay that way.

"Evie and I used to talk a lot. Now, she hardly looks at me," Maia said.

"I've noticed that too," Antonio said.

"Something must have happened," Lucien said.

"But what?"

"I don't know. I know sometimes, back when I watched TV, if I saw something bad, something hateful, a show that really had negative ideas and energy, it could make me . . . I don't know. Maybe she watched a show."

"The show must have been really bad, if so."

"We should try to find a way to cheer her up."

"Yeah."

"I saw her with Sebastian in the summer when I was in town," Lucien said.

"My parents avoid town now. They say it's a bad place. We used to go a lot. I liked the pond by the library and the candy store."

"I love the pond," Lucien said, remembering how he would sit there with Gabrielle.

"They just told me not to go, though. I go home and then I come here and then I go home. It's for the best."

"That's probably for the best," Antonio said.

"My mom still takes me to town sometimes," Maia said. "She also didn't love getting rid of our TV. She was like, 'How am I gonna watch the news?' and my dad said it didn't matter anymore. House of Earth matters."

"That's true."

"My mom was pretty upset, and my dad actually had to sit down and talk to her. My dad was like, 'We didn't have House of Earth as kids, and what good is the news if you're getting lied to and poisoned?' and my mom was saying how it still had 'value,' and then they yelled for a bit before my mom got quiet and went to bed."

"I hope it's okay now."

"It's a little better. But I mean, Evie is so lucky to have a mentor for a dad because then stuff like that never happens."

"I just wonder why she never told us," Antonio said.

"She didn't look happy when I saw her in the store. It was a Walgreens and Sebastian was holding her hand. She didn't say much. I don't know. I was always glad we had Jack, not Sebastian," Lucien said.

"I agree."

"And then he kind of pulled her away. It wasn't like how I would hold hands with my mom. Maybe they were in a hurry."

"Should we go over to Evie's table?"

"Maybe tomorrow."

Lucien hoped the old Evie would come back soon, wherever she was. In all their instruction and games, she had always been willing to lead, to show them exactly what they needed to do. Outside of Mama and Jack, Evie was the person Lucien trusted the most to guide him and the friends. That's why it hurt so much that she had said what she said. He thought back to the night with O. C. Leroux, how he had spoken about the wars to come and being prepared for darkness before light. That it wasn't always going to be easy. Perhaps this was a part of that. Evie, herself, was a kind of test. She could be battling her own darkness. Would she then need help? Should Lucien go over there as soon as possible?

When he looked over his shoulder, he saw Evie still sitting there, the beets cold on her plate.

———

Mama was not running errands on weekends as much, so Lucien didn't go to the library on his own. Soon, he would have to go there to return his book. Without the TV, he read more of *The Natural*, which was nearing its end. He wanted Roy to win, to beat everyone, to prove his enemies wrong and deliver the Knights the pennant. Roy was a slugger now, one of the very best. He was always hitting home runs. The Knights, once a team no one thought could ever be good again, were on the cusp of greatness.

On the first Friday in October, Mama said she would be gone for the night and into early tomorrow.

"It's a very important trip, Lucien."

"Okay, Mama."

"Now, this is important. I want you staying in the cottage. Do not wander away. I know you've liked to go to town. Don't go there anymore."

"Oh, okay. I didn't know it was bad. I wouldn't have gone—"

"Lucien, things are changing. You've heard your mentor; you've heard O. C. Leroux. The world is changing and not for the better. We have to be prepared for that. Here, it's safe. And at House of Earth. I don't want you in that town."

"Okay, Mama. I'll stay right here."

"Good boy."

She kissed him on the top of the head and walked away, down the slope of Darling Drive. One day, he would ask her where she went. Gabrielle had told him to. If he couldn't go into town, he couldn't see her again. She was there, with the library and the pond and Walgreens and American flags flying from every storefront. Mama was forbidding him from all that. As she disappeared around the curve of the road, he began to fully consider what her new dictate meant. This was not just getting rid of a TV. He could read his book instead or walk in the forest. TV, ultimately, was not his friend, would not talk back to him. But Gabrielle . . .

He thought about her more and more and always assumed he would see her again. It would happen. The summer had ended and she was back at school. If he found his way to the library on the weekend, she could be there too because she didn't like to be at home. He wondered about Noah. There was more talk of war, and he would be taking up arms, going to the distant land Lucien was hearing about now, one he'd found in the old atlas he kept under his bed. *Afghanistan.* Why did people have to be killed there? Jack didn't talk about it much, and neither did Mama. Only that there was a war, people would die, and he would be safe as long as he was at House of Earth. More war was coming, more death, but none of it would be here—as long as he listened.

Mama said not to go to town.

It was Friday afternoon and the sun was going to set. He went inside and sat on the couch. About now, he would like to walk down Darling Drive into town. He didn't want to be here inside the cottage.

His toes were curling, his legs restless. He flexed his fingers. Energy coursed through him. He walked around the living room, bent his knees, stretched his legs.

He decided to find his sketch pad and draw.

Clouds smothered the sun and soon it was raining, the window chattering with drops. He was hunched over the kitchen table, his pencil sketching tentative lines. On the side of the silver toaster, he caught a warped reflection of his face and decided, for the first time, to attempt a self-portrait. Usually he liked to draw animals, plants, and objects in the cottage. Attempting to capture the likenesses of human faces was not a usual desire. Today, with the rain falling hard and Mama gone, he would try.

A nose, two eyes, a mouth. The face, when he thought about it, was a strange creation, a bony palette of curvatures, sudden openings, and subtle slopes. His pencil wobbled on the paper. The drawing that took shape in front of him was not the resemblance he wanted. It was a face he hardly recognized. What he had drawn was narrower, more severe, almost birdlike. He looked to be in a rage. He flipped his pencil over and began erasing.

The rain beat harder on the windowpane. He hoped Mama was okay.

He tried again. The next face was not his either. He squinted harder at his own reflection, bent and stretched in the toaster. He could also draw from memory, but that too produced only a face that was rounder, weirder, nothing like what he showed the world each day. The pencil was growing hot in his hand. His index finger pressed hard against the wood. When he looked up at the rain and down again at the paper, he saw he had poked a hole through it.

Even though it was raining, he wished he could walk to town.

A new feeling overtook him. His hand, now on the toaster, gradually shook. He wanted to pick up the toaster and throw it. Throw it very hard. He wanted to see how it smashed against the glass, if it would blow apart the window and tumble across the grass, rain smacking its shattered silver hull. This was rage—he could identify it with a word, but what was it, really? It was new and unexpected and he had to sit down, his mind a brackish whirl. When Mama told him to do things, he always accepted her words, content in the knowledge that what Mama told him was absolutely what was needed because she knew. She never had to explain. But why couldn't he go to town? He only wanted to go to the library and look for Gabrielle. It would not interfere with his instruction. Jack had praised him recently for his knowledge of plant species. At instruction, he was always sure to listen and respond in a way that would grow his mind and soul. He was always listening, always ready.

Trust me, Mama, he wanted to cry out.

He sat in the kitchen chair, his forehead against the table, listening to the rain. The swell of rage slowly disappeared. When it was dark outside, he felt shame for the thoughts that had appeared in his mind. He was never going to break anything. Mama loved him. He loved her. If Mama made a decision, she always made it knowing it would be best for him, and if he didn't understand now, one day he would.

He pushed through the back door and stood in the backyard, near the bench where Mama had punished him all those years ago. The rain was not so hard. Now it merely tickled him, and he sat on the bench, feeling pools of rainwater on his haunches. At night, the trees and bushes could be like fantastical figures, taking on new forms in the shadows. At any moment, one would come to life. He stared upward, at a sky obscured by clouds, the stars tucked away. What came after House of Earth? Mama had never discussed this with him. It was possible there would be no *after*. He could become a mentor or work there, like Mama. Mama, though, had not been raised at House of Earth because there wasn't a House of Earth when she was a child. This was a sad truth, she said. She had grown up elsewhere, in the city.

Once, he had asked: Where are you from, Mama?

New York City. You don't want to be from there, honey.

Why?

There are none of the precious gifts you enjoy every day. People don't live with the forest in their backyard, the deer in the road. They can't see the stars. They are stacked like the carcasses of rodents, one on top of the other. It is a dirty, destructive way to live, and there is much more darkness than light in a place like that.

So you came to Mater to live a better way?

Yes, Lucien.

We're so lucky, then.

You're lucky, Lucien.

I'm lucky, he thought. He had always believed this. When O. C. touched his head, that certainly confirmed it—he was living a chosen life. And that meant he needed to live the values worthy of that life.

He had to listen to Mama. He had to stay at the cottage.

That night, he slept deeply, hardly dreaming at all. The towers never came to him. In the morning light, he read *The Natural*, his nostrils filled with the rich scent of aged paper. Roy was in a slump now, which meant he couldn't hit the baseball. A woman named Memo could be to blame. In Chicago, the Knights were playing the Cubs. A woman in the crowd stood up for Roy. Roy saw her and was filled with new strength. He smacked an amazing home run.

Lucien imagined himself, for a moment, in the Chicago ballpark, his hands clenched tightly around the wooden bat. He would swing mightily and hit a long home run like Roy. Standing for him, cheering for him, would be Gabrielle.

He read faster now, comprehending more of the words tumbling to him from the page. This was a city like the one Mama said was so dirty, where people lived like dead rodents. Yet there was liveliness to this place as described, and it was so full of people. Why would so many people be attracted to a bad place? Why would so many choose to suffer?

The woman was named Iris Lemon. She was everything Memo was not. Roy told Iris, finally, the great shame of his life—that he'd been shot fifteen years ago and it had ruined his career. He wanted to be the greatest ballplayer but never could be now. "If you leave all those records that nobody else can beat—they'll always remember you. You sorta never die."

"Are you afraid of death?"

It was a question for Roy, but it could have been for him. Was he? What would he have done if he somehow, instead of being at House of Earth, were living in the towers, living and then dying, the fire of an exploding airplane incinerating his flesh and bones, all that he had ever been?

Yes, he was afraid, because he didn't know where he would go next. Mama and House of Earth wouldn't be waiting.

The book said Roy and Iris had sex.

At noon, Lucien heard the doorknob jiggling. He turned from his book. The door opened and there was Mama, smiling at him. He had been reading at the kitchen table, right near where he had tried to draw his own face yesterday.

"Mama!"

"There's my Lucien."

He put the book down on the table and ran over to hug her. She was warm, and he threw both arms around her body. He could feel her patting him on the head. He was grateful she was home and grateful he had listened to her. No trips to town had been made.

"I was here the whole time," he said.

"Yes, honey."

He could feel Mama releasing him and walking away. She was bent over the kitchen table, her eyes narrowed at *The Natural*, which had been turned over, the pages splayed outward so Lucien could remember where he was in the book. Her finger touched the blue cover.

"What is this?" she asked.

"It's the book I've been reading since this summer. I got it at the library."

"Yes . . ." She had picked it up and Lucien knew his page was lost. It was 160-something, he remembered, and he would have to go back and page through to where he had been.

She looked up from the cover, which she had been reading. "The *library*—Jack did not approve this book."

"I didn't ask. I thought it was okay, though."

She was close to him now, the book dropped on the table. He could meet her fully at eye level. His chest began to hurt.

"We talked before about the changes that are happening, didn't we? We are not living in the same world we used to, and this means, in order to keep doing what we do—for us to be strong, for House of Earth to grow—we need to be better. Now, what are you learning from this book?"

"I don't know . . . certain words. I enjoy it—"

"Lucien, you never asked me or Jack about this book. I realize now I might have been too lenient in letting you go to town because you never told me everything you did. How did you come by this book?"

"Come by?"

"Did you take it from the library? Steal it? Did someone give it to you?"

"Someone first checked it out, and then I got my own library card."

"Who?"

"A girl, Mama. She goes to the school in Mater—"

Mama's hand shot through the air and slammed, open-palmed, onto the kitchen table. The legs rattled on impact. He felt like she had just hit him, and not the table, with the full force of her palm. He stepped back, his knees shaking. Tears filled the rims of his eyes.

"You are *not* to talk to people at the high school, do you hear me, Lucien? Am I clear?"

"Yes, Mama, yes."

"You do not *know* what they are learning at that school. You do not know the poison, the sin, the hate in that school, in all places, especially now—you do not know what kind of trouble you can be in. You cannot wander around God knows where without my permission."

"Mama, I'm sorry."

"Sorry is one thing. I can accept an apology. But you cannot be going out and talking to people who could hurt you and hurt us and then take their books from a library that do not have the approval of Jack, of myself—you cannot do that, Lucien. You must change."

"I'll be good, I'll be better, Mama, I will."

He could hardly see through the blur of warm tears dripping down his cheeks.

"Let this be a lesson. And you promise you went nowhere when I was gone? You were not back in that town?"

"I wasn't, no, I was here, at the table and in the backyard. I tried to draw and sat outside, and then I read the book."

"This book is going in the trash. You are not reading this book anymore. The books you will read will be provided to you by Jack. Is that understood?"

"Yes."

"You are twelve now, Lucien. Next year, you will be a teenager. There is tremendous responsibility for you. You will be a leader at House of Earth. You were one of the first boys, and the collectives will look to you. You are already the leader of the Meadows. Leaders lead by example."

"I know, Mama. I'm very sorry."

"This book . . ." It was pinched between her fingers, like the very rat carcasses she said people lived like in the big cities that cheered on Roy Hobbs. She walked with the book to a trash bin she kept under a cupboard near the front door. The book thudded in the black bag. Lucien could see the faded blue peeking out before Mama shoved the bin back out of the light and straightened up again, her eyes still small and hard. "I am trying, Lucien, and you have to understand we will not be perfect. We will make mistakes. For a long time, we lived with the TV. I let you watch so much. And I watched too. Now I know what a mistake that was. We can learn from our mistakes. We can grow."

"I know," he said, trying to keep himself from crying further. He was running the back of his hand over his eyes, squinted shut with new tears.

"I don't know what's in that book. Perhaps, someday, Jack will approve it. He is your mentor. He knows. He is guided by O. C. Leroux. We live in a wonderful place. We are very lucky. You will see this now, especially with the war coming."

"I'm afraid of the war, Mama. I don't want to fight. I don't want anyone to fight, anyone to get hurt."

"As long as you listen to me and listen to Jack, you won't."

He sat down at the kitchen table, his gaze on the spot where the book had been. His bones ached from crying. He was done now, and the shame he knew too well had hardened inside him. He was the boy on the bench again, lying in the rain, begging quietly for Mama to take him inside. He knew when painting a birdhouse black became bad because Jack and Mama told him. He knew when TV became bad because Mama threw it out. And now *The Natural* was bad too. It belonged to the library, and now it lay in the garbage. The library would never get its book back, and he would never know what happened to Roy Hobbs, and this could not be his concern anymore. Mama said so. He would have to forget.

———

Autumn was Lucien's favorite season. There were obvious reasons, like the turning of the leaves, and more subtle ones, like how the sunlight bent and played through the thinning canopies in his backyard. By October, he was prepared for the drop in temperature, how the air would grow heavy with a chill. There was a gravity he couldn't describe. He armored himself in sweaters, blew on his hands, and accepted the darkening afternoons.

On the commons in the second week of October, Magnus pointed to the construction site, now filled with the structure of the habitation facility. Lucien could see it taking shape. Magnus was not pointing to show him what he knew, that progress was being made. He was pointing to a man carrying a plank of wood over his shoulder.

"That's my dad," he said.

"Your dad is working here too, like Antonio's dad."

"Yup."

"What about your mom?"

"She says she will be coming soon."

Samantha walked up, holding a basketball. "Everybody's joining here," she said. "All the parents."

"Do you think any of them will become mentors?" Lucien asked.

"It's hard, that's what I heard," Magnus said. "My dad, I think he was interested and he had to wait or something. So they put him on construction. He's happy, though. He had a contracting business, but he says this is much more important, and my uncle is gonna take it over, for now at least."

"My parents say the same thing. This is the most important thing we can do right now," Samantha said.

"Yes."

"Do you wanna play?" Samantha asked.

"I'm in," Magnus said. "What about you, Lucien?"

"I will in a little. I want to look at the foliage."

"Look at the foliage? Okay."

Magnus and Samantha might think he was avoiding them, but he was being honest. He wanted to walk to the edge of the commons and look up at the majestic autumn trees, their golden-and-ruby leaves floating off the branches he knew so well. He had the sudden urge to climb a tree. He had scaled a tree in his backyard when Mama wasn't home, but never here, at House of Earth. Now he wanted to press his feet into the bark and climb high in the air, feeling the surge of power through his muscles as he reached into the sky. He walked away from the area of play to a secluded part of the commons, far from both the construction site and the friends.

This morning, at instruction, Evie hadn't been there. She was rarely missing. Jack didn't say anything about where she was. Instruction continued without her. Lucien wondered where she was and whether it was related to how she had changed. Each day, she seemed quieter, darker, more withdrawn into whatever thoughts swelled in her head. He longed to know what he could say to her to make her like she used to be. Each time he thought of a word, a phrase, a way to make it better, he quickly lost courage. She walked away when the friends tried to ask her questions or make an observation. When instruction ended for the day, she was gone before anyone could speak to her.

Lucien was alone now, where the commons met the deep woods. His eyes fell on a thick birch tree, one he had run by many times before. There was a hollow in the tree he could slide his foot in to propel his body upward, and a branch not far above, perfect for a perch. He lifted his leg and jumped to the hollow, his feet catching in the bark. Both hands held the trunk.

The tree was not a tree anymore. He was clutching a dark and smoldering monolith, black fire and smoke filling his eyes and ears, flaming glass sparkling from the sky. The tower was here. The other had already collapsed. He was the last person, man or boy, to be here, to be holding on. Flames curled around his skin. He was shouting, but no sound came from his mouth. There were others too, hundreds of voices, each crying out to him as a wall of flame rose up from the glass, eating away skin and bone. The tower would be gone. He could feel his fingers slipping, a choice between heat death or a plunge backward. When had the plane hit? It didn't matter, only that he was choosing between the fire and the air, his body's ragged tumble down. He shut his eyes. It was hotter and hotter.

He wanted to stop thinking about the towers.

At a long branch hanging above the clearing, he sat. The tower was gone. It had never been here. He needed to stop seeing them, dreaming of them. He had to think. With *The Natural*, he'd had a book to guide his mind elsewhere, but the book was gone now. He couldn't talk to Evie either. Mama had a good reason for throwing the book out but never told him exactly what was so poisonous about it, just as Jack could not explain more about the coming war, the inevitability of two towers destroyed. He would have to trust them.

Lucien climbed higher. His fingers dug into bark, and he steadied himself on another branch, elevated enough now to glimpse the top of the coming habitation facility. It had risen so fast. He was glad for the change, he really was, and Mama was right that he was becoming a teenager, a leader, and he needed to act that way. Up here, away from Mama, Jack, and the friends, he could also admit something else, what he would never say out loud, what he hated to even think: he was unsure about some of this change. He wanted to read his book. He wanted TV. He wanted to go to town. He wanted to see Gabrielle. None of these wants were dissipating. Would they in time? He could ask Jack. House of Earth was more important than all that, of course, more important than all that put together.

No, he would wait for them to go away.

"Lucien!"

He turned his head around. It was a male's voice and he knew it immediately. There was a sinking feeling in his stomach.

"Lucien!"

It was Jack, waving from below. "It's time to come down."

How had Jack known he was up in the tree? Jack hadn't followed him here. Jack was inside for most of their play on the commons. One of the friends could have told him. Magnus or Samantha. But he hadn't told them he was climbing the tree.

He'd told no one.

"I'm coming!"

"Good."

When he slid down the trunk and his sneakers smacked against a bed of leaves on the ground, the small smile on Jack's face vanished. Jack strode forward and touched Lucien on the shoulder. "We don't want you climbing on trees."

"Okay, I understand."

"You could hurt yourself. And you could hurt this tree. It's a living creature. We taught you that."

"Yes, Jack."

His fingers were now digging into Lucien's collarbone, almost like a pinch. He felt a sharp blade of pain. Jack walked forward and Lucien followed, Jack's hand still on him, digging like a pincer. They were back out on the commons, in the sunlight.

"No more trees. Do you understand?"

"I understand."

"Good, Lucien. Good. We expect so much from you."

Jack would not let go. The friends were going inside, along with other collectives, and a few turned to see Lucien being marched through the grass, the pain shooting down his arm and chest. Please let go, he thought. Please. I'm so sorry.

"I'm sorry."

"Yes, Lucien, I know."

Jack released him when they were inside. By now, several of the friends had gathered around him. Lucien was wincing from the pain still flaring in his bone.

"What happened?" Cavan asked.

"It was nothing."

"Didn't look like nothing," Antonio said.

"What made Jack upset?" Samantha asked.

"I said I was sorry and that was it."

"What was it?"

Lucien wanted to return to his desk and not speak. But the friends were not moving. They needed answers from him. Normally, he would like to help, to give them what they wanted. Now he felt differently, a sour sensation taking hold. He didn't want to talk. He wanted to be away from them, at the top of the tree or in his backyard. His small hands, without him realizing, were balled into fists.

"I want to talk to you all about something very important," Jack said, standing now at the front of the room. "It's about the future."

Lucien swallowed hard. It was about him, wasn't it? Jack was now going to tell all of them how he had climbed a tree without anyone's permission. They would all turn to him and stare. He wanted very badly to hide.

"I wanted to tell you this first, before assembly and before you speak with your parents. You deserve to hear it."

Jack came closer, standing near the front row of desks. Lucien tried to look happy. Not like someone who had climbed a tree to be alone.

"We are changing. You are changing. This community grows stronger every day. House of Earth would be nothing if not for your efforts, for the learning you do, how you support one another. That's first. If the world beyond us followed our example, we would be living in peace. We would be living in balance. If they could only *listen*—and, well, they will. Now we focus on our community, on preserving it and growing it. That will only happen when we can be together *all the time*, to focus on this growth."

The friends nodded slowly.

"The habitation facilities, as you've noticed, are almost finished. When they are, they will be available for you and your families to live in. Your parents and guardians have been notified as well. For most of you, this will be no great change. Your parents and guardians are already integral to this community. Many work here. It will simply mean the end of an unnecessary commute."

"We will have to live there?" Samantha asked.

Jack's head tilted to the side, his lips scrunching. He appeared to be digesting, in all parts, this simple question. "No one *has* to live there. But O. C. Leroux only wants those who are committed to our community, to House of Earth, living there. If you are not committed to the future, you don't live there."

"Oh, okay."

"Are you committed to the future, Samantha?"

"Yes!"

They all murmured their assent after Samantha, Lucien included, his forehead now damp with sweat. Another change. The cottage—this meant he could not stay there. The backyard trees, Mama's bench, the rain on the windowpane, Darling Drive. This meant he could not stay there. The sinking was now a sickness. He fought the urge to keel over, to turn into a ball of flesh on the floor. He should have known all along.

"When are we moving?" Lucien heard himself ask.

"In two weeks," Jack said. "It's very exciting. I will be living there too, as well as all the mentors."

After instruction, Mama told him to go home first and she would meet him there. Tonight, she said, she would make him a big bowl of salad because he was such a good boy.

"Am I?" he asked.

"Of course."

Lucien went home to wait. With no book and no TV, he decided to draw again. He would try to capture the likeness of his face—again. This time, he entered Mama's room. He was rarely there without her. On her dresser was a rectangular mirror perched next to loose papers, partially folded clothing, and a picture of himself as a baby. He sat at the foot of the bed, glancing toward the mirror, the drawing pad balancing on his knee.

His face wasn't as soft as it used to be, no longer as rounded. He noticed small black hairs sprouting from his upper lip. What he began to sketch, diffidently at first, was the new definition in his cheekbone, the way a gentle valley of shadow now played across one side of his face. His left hand inched deliberately, as if he were extracting blood from the paper. He needed to get this right.

All of it, right now, mattered.

This time, he was also listening for footsteps. Mama was not going to catch him here. On the paper, the lines were coalescing into a cheek, a jaw, the birth of a being in ghostly pencil. He looked up, looked down. He still wasn't sure what to make of the face he saw in the mirror. It was his own, yes, but it was also like a relative's he had only recently met, familiarity mingling with the alien, the uncanny. That's Lucien's face, he thought. My face. That is what the friends see every day—Jack, Mama, even O. C. Leroux—this is who I really am. He would draw that.

His pencil dropped when he heard the footsteps on the gravel. The pad was under his arm and then on the kitchen table when the door swung open, and Mama, a paper bag in her hand, walked into the cottage. He was sitting at the table, smiling at her. The paper bag appeared to be filled with fruits and vegetables.

"There you are," she said, setting the bag down.

"Hi, Mama."

Mama opened the cupboard to take out her wooden salad bowl. "So how was your day today?"

"It was okay."

"Just okay? That doesn't sound like my Lucien."

"It was good, really."

Mama put the bowl down and sat across from Lucien, her fingers interlocked on the table. "I heard Jack told you something very important. Would you like to talk about it?"

"I think so."

"Let's talk about it, then."

"He said it was happening."

"What is?"

"That . . . that we're leaving."

"I wanted you to hear it from your mentor first. That was very important."

"I know it's for the best, I'm excited, but I like it here. This is our home. I don't know—"

"This is a big change, Lucien." She put her hand on his shoulder. "Are you concerned?"

"I'm a little bit."

"It's okay to be nervous. These can be scary times. There are a lot of bad people in the world who want to hurt us. But we can be safe from them. This is the next step toward making sure we are safe. Do you understand?"

"Can't we be safe here too, though, Mama? That's what I'm wondering."

"Not as safe as at House of Earth, surrounded by those who care most about us. You do know how much O. C. Leroux cares about you? And all of us?"

"I do, Mama."

He remembered the enormous hand descending from above, resting on his small head.

"So there's nothing to worry about."

"It's just a lot of change, that's all. I like it here. This is our home, too."

"House of Earth is our home, Lucien."

"Yes."

"I want to tell you a story." Mama stood up and opened up the fridge, removing a carton of orange juice. She opened the cupboard and took down one of the good drinking glasses. "Would you like some juice, Lucien?"

"No, Mama, I'm okay."

She poured herself a glass, drank a sip, and then sat back down in front of him.

"There was a time, before you were born, when I didn't have so much. Even that glass of orange juice—to have a kitchen with a cup made of glass and cartons of orange juice and *food*... it was all unimaginable. I was very poor, Lucien. I had very little. I don't like to talk about this because I don't want to fill your head with bad thoughts, because there was a time when negative energy was all around me. When I had so little and didn't know what to do. It was my mother and father's fault, for being controlled by bad things, and mine because I didn't understand that I could only fix my life if I found the right path. I did bad things too, Lucien. I drank things I should not have drank. There were substances you will never use that I used. I was very, very bad."

"But now you're good."

"I am. When you were very little, I found House of Earth. I moved up to this town. I needed to be away from the city, and they were here for us. O. C. Leroux himself welcomed me in. He saw you as a baby. You, of course, don't remember. He didn't have to accept you and me, but he did. He took us in, and look where we are."

"Yes, I do see how lucky we are."

"O. C. has done so much for us. Now, when someone has done so much for us and asks something of us—as simple as going to live somewhere nearby—we have to listen to them, don't we?"

"We do."

"If for a moment we feel nervous, how can that compare to the great meaning of living among the people who care for us most? You're going to do great things, Lucien. It starts at House of Earth."

"I know, Mama."

She held him, both arms around his body, and he wished this was how it could always be, Mama's warmth surrounding him. All he had to do was listen. She was only mad when he did something wrong, and all he needed to do was stop doing wrong things. Stop reading the wrong books; stop going places without permission; stop using the wrong colors. He was getting better. He would be better.

"When we move, what will happen to the cottage?"

"It will be sold, honey. We don't need it anymore."

"Okay."

"Now, we have a lot of packing to do."

———

Lucien started to fill the wall.

On eight-by-ten construction paper, he drew what he saw in his head. Wilderness, water buffalo, soaring eagles, the sun hanging golden and enormous over the land. He began in pencil and colored with crayon, a yellow Crayola box with more than thirty varieties of color. At night, when Mama slept, he drew by the miniature lamp, the dim light wavering over the paper he pressed to the new desk. Samantha and her mother would be asleep as well. He was careful to draw quietly, the desk hardly shifting under the weight of his left hand.

He taped his drawings on the sliver of white wall between the bars of the bunk bed and the window. He liked the cottage window more, but this would do, he resolved, a view of the lavender siding of the second habitation facility, the one rising next to their own. With increased instruction hours, assembly, mornings and nights at the nutrition hall, and play on the commons, there wasn't much time for the view anyway. When he sat down to draw, night had fallen and he could see little. So he closed his eyes and drew.

He liked to draw Roy Hobbs too, swatting baseballs deep into the sky.

By November, he had taped five drawings to the wall, one on top of another. Dead leaves, crisp blood-reds and pear-yellows, gathered on the sill, and one night Lucien counted them all. He tried to sleep as deeply as he used to in the cottage, when his mattress was large and soft, his body always settling into the imprint he had left behind over so many years.

There was no TV now and no front room here.

Sometimes, Jack would walk down the hallway and knock on the door just after nine p.m. He peeked his head in and smiled. "All set?" he would ask.

"All set," Samantha's mother or Mama would reply.

It was important, he was told, to be in the habitation room by nine p.m. This was a rule that must not be broken. When they'd first arrived, Mama had put her hands on Lucien's shoulders and looked directly into his eyes. "We must all be here by nine p.m. Okay, Lucien?"

"Okay, Mama."

Where else would he be at nine p.m.? Jack didn't always check. Natasha could come by. Or Sebastian.

The habitation facility had three floors. Lucien, Mama, Samantha, and Samantha's mother were in Room 8 on the first floor. All the walls of the hallway were painted so brightly. That was very different from the cottage. He didn't have his own backyard anymore, and the mattress, hard and stiff, groaned on springs each time he rolled over. A silver pipe in the far corner hissed with heat, but the walls at night were still cold. When the wind battered the window, he could feel it through the glass, a stray chill touching his face. Each morning, his bare feet would press the ground for the first time after a dream, and he would shudder from the shock of the chill against his skin. As November blended into December, the cold hung in the room, never leaving, day or night. His breath was a white cloud in front of his face. His fingers wriggled—with, and then without, feeling.

The cottage had a rug. There were no rugs here.

On other floors were other friends—Maia, Antonio, Cavan, Magnus—as well as their parents. On the third floor, in Room 27, lived Evie and Sebastian. Unlike the others, Evie and Sebastian were rarely

Ross Barkan

seen at the habitation facility. Occasionally, Lucien could see Sebastian clutching her hand. There were times when Evie missed instruction too, but Jack never commented on it. Whether she participated or not, instruction continued, Jack teaching them about bird migrations or the periodic table of elements.

Evie sat alone at lunch or didn't sit at all. There were days she didn't seem to eat.

Two other buildings were filled with collectives too. One day, as Lucien saw Jack leaving their building, he decided to ask a question. It was one that had been growing within him like a small parasite, insisting on being fed, even if he still didn't want to ask too many questions of Jack.

"I have a question," he said to Jack, both of them standing in the dirt patch just beyond the habitation facility.

"Yes, Lucien?"

"Does O. C. Leroux live in the habitation facilities too? I never see him."

Jack began scratching his chin, a small frown on his face. "O. C. Leroux lives elsewhere."

"Okay."

Jack said nothing more. He walked away, leaving Lucien to wonder where *elsewhere* could be, and why no one could know.

In the nutritional hall, when Lucien mentioned this, the friends had theories.

"I heard," Antonio said, brushing his long hair out of his eyes, "O. C. lives on a *spaceship*."

"No, he doesn't," Cavan said.

"Like, not a spaceship, but a ship that can hover in the sky and go anyplace at super speeds."

"He lives underground, probably," Samantha said.

"You think?"

"My mom thinks so. There's some special place. No one is supposed to talk about it."

"A big compound?" Maia asked.

"I don't know."

"The spaceship has a docking bay," Antonio said.

"I just don't know," Lucien said.

"Jack didn't say anything else?"

"No. He didn't like being asked."

"My dad says he'll go talk to O. C. in the woods sometimes," Antonio said. "O. C. comforts him about his brother."

"When does he go?"

"At night. He will meet him and they will talk around a little fire. My dad says they're the best talks of his life."

"I'm worried about the war," Lucien said.

"Me too," Samantha said.

"I'm glad there just aren't any battles here," Maia said.

"They're going to be everywhere else. We're safe at House of Earth. We're lucky," Antonio said.

"We are."

"Can a plane bomb the habitation facility?" Samantha asked.

"The plane has to find us. And they wouldn't mess with O. C., let's be real."

"Yeah."

Lucien continued to think about where O. C. might be and when he would appear again. Since the night on the commons with the fire, no one had seen him.

When O. C. didn't enter his mind, Gabrielle did. Where was she now? Did she still go to the library, looking for him? He would never be at the library again, and when he considered this reality, that it was unchanging, a somberness gripped him that was deeper and harder than any he had known. It was not like the shame of disappointing Mama or the fear of punishment from Jack. It was bound to the passage of time, to the looming realization that there were moments in his life that could not be reclaimed, that were imprisoned solely in memory. He would not relive them.

Gabrielle was not underground and she was not on a spaceship. She was home or in school, somewhere in Mater. House of Earth was technically in Mater, but neither Jack nor anyone else used the town name. It was as if it didn't exist at all.

He caught sight of the new Meadows sitting at a table across from them. They all had come in the last month and still ate together, though he hoped these divisions would soon melt away. There was Leon and Jayson and Colt and Carlina and Elizabeth and Rylie and Jacinda and Madison and Gerrit and Micah and Karthik and Samuel. Jack had welcomed them all. All were there because they, and their parents, had agreed to live at the habitation facilities.

Antonio, whose father seemed to tell him what he knew, said House of Earth was only accepting those who would agree to live there.

Would Gabrielle come one day? Would she want to live here?

Everyone, Lucien thought, should want to be here.

NEW YEAR

House of Earth had never had a wall. But by January—Jack told them this year was a *palindrome*, which meant it was the same forward and backward—it did. Or at least the front of the property, where automobiles would occasionally enter on the gravel road, gained one. The wall was ten feet high, made of cement and granite blocks, and it was paired with a booth for a guard. The guard, who wore a bright-blue shirt, was Maia's father.

"You may have noticed this small change," Jack said during instruction. "A wall ensures our protection, in case the war comes close."

"The war is coming close?" Samantha asked.

"We don't know. It's all possible. Unfortunately, there is a great deal of chaos outside of here. The earth is in peril. But we are safe. We only want to take precautions with a wall."

"No one can climb over?"

"We will know *who* tries to climb over. That's very important."

"Why would they come here?" Cavan asked.

"We can't know. People who live like that are very unpredictable. Think of how an animal acts when he or she is wounded. Unfortunately, a desperation sets in, a hunger. We are focusing on life, on the future. When your society is steeped in death, bad things can happen. And we have to be prepared."

In the late afternoon, Lucien stood at the base of the wall, shadows consuming his body. He thought about what Jack had said about a palindrome and began, in his head, to draw the year: 2002. Frontward and backward, forever and ever. Maia's father stood in the small booth, staring straight ahead. No one was coming or going. Dinner was in thirty minutes. Lucien had permission to run on the commons, play by the maypole, shoot the basketball, toss horseshoes, or go to the archery range. Antonio and Cavan had told him they were doing archery. What he wanted to do was be near the woods, to listen for the sounds the creatures in the trees made. He would not climb a tree, of course.

Waving to Antonio and Cavan, he walked to a clearing, the very same one he'd once entered in the dead of winter as the musher. He knew it now. There was no snow on the ground, though the wind bit and reddened the skin of his ears. He had forgotten his hat.

It was a short stroll, the dead leaves underfoot, the sun like an ancient coin in the fading sky. This was his time. The sounds of the commons receded as the woods, the rustle of branches and the crackle of leaves, overtook them. He wanted to stay, to not go to dinner, to feel the cold and the coming night washing over him.

He wanted to be in a place where he wouldn't stop to stare at his reflection.

"It's beautiful," he said out loud.

A branch or stick cracked. Leaves crunched in rapid succession. He spun around. Someone was here; someone was close. From behind, from the commons, there was no one. He had to look the other way. Deeper in the woods, he saw the shape of a figure, a shadow taking on human form. He moved toward it. Now it was coming his way, taking on the form of someone he knew. Those eyes, that hair, that mouth.

It couldn't be.

It could be.

"Gabrielle!" he cried, louder than he expected, too loud. But she kept coming. She was wearing a dark down jacket, a heavy bluish-black that Jack would say conjured negative energy. He didn't care. He broke in a run toward it, and she ran to him, and they were standing face-to-face on a slope tilting deeper into the woods.

"Lucien, that *is* you."

"You're here."

"It's winter break and I went for a walk."

"Up here?"

He was surprised to find he was out of breath.

"You grew a little," she said, smiling. "An inch or two since I last saw you."

"I did?"

"Don't act surprised."

"I didn't know, I mean—I'm glad to see you."

"I'm glad to see you too. How far up is your school?"

"It's a little bit just up that hill. It's good you came this way. There's a wall at the front."

"Well, if they want to secure it better, they should be doing walls everywhere, no?"

"Maybe that's next."

"Hmm . . ." She put her hands in her pockets. "It's something else, running into you. You know, I knew I was getting close, and I remember thinking, 'Maybe I'll see that wacko Lucien up there,' and wow, you just popped up."

"*You* just popped up."

"You don't come to the library anymore."

Lucien turned away, looking down at his shoe tops. His tongue rolled in his mouth, and he hated, suddenly, the taste of what was there, whatever flavored the inside of his cheek. He tried to remember what he had eaten.

"I'm not allowed to."

"Allowed? What?"

"My mom says I can't."

"That's ridiculous."

"I had to throw the book out. I live here now."

"At your school? At the House of Earth?"

"We all do. It's for the best."

"So much for the best you can't go to a freakin' library?"

"We avoid town."

"Oh, because it's filled with people like *me*?"

"No, it's not that exactly."

"I never liked this school when you described it. It seems worse now."

He wanted to interrupt that it wasn't a school, that she was rejecting his life from morning to night, everything he had been and would be, but he also didn't want to argue with her. He wanted to keep her in front of him for as long as possible.

"How is your school?" he asked. "How is your brother?"

"Noah writes home once in a while. He was in boot camp, and they're, well, sending him away. But he's excited. I don't get it, but he's excited. School is whatever. I can't wait until it's over. When I graduate in a few years, I'm just gonna travel the country."

"Where will you go?"

"Everywhere. It's a huge country, Lucien. Have you traveled at all?"

"A little bit, we traveled . . ."

"Outside of New York?"

"I think—yes . . . or no, maybe not quite."

"You really need to. Life is more than House of Earth and your mom. But I can't talk either, really. We don't go anywhere. My parents don't have money for that. It's the same crap. My dad is trying to get into God now."

"He's in church a lot?"

"When he's around, he prays, he quotes Jesus. He says it will help his drinking. Who knows? The less I see of him, the better. But you, Lucien—do you like it where you are?"

It was a question he had hardly been asked. Did he have an opinion on air, water, or sunlight? *Where you are.* What else was there? He dug his toe into the soil, his eyes rising to a sparrow dancing off a tree branch.

"Of course," he said, because he didn't know what else to say.

"Your school transformed into boarding school, I guess. I mean, there is that prep boarding school like twenty miles north of here. A bunch of rich, weird white kids. So it's like that. My mom wants me to start thinking about college applications. *You'll be fifteen soon, start thinking about it.* I'm not going. I just need to see the country, go on a real trip, get away from here. I bet your mom has started talking college, huh? Since you guys are a sleepaway boarding school/prep school in the woods."

"College?" He knew what it was, comprehended the concept, but it was no different, to him, from knowing the theory behind space travel. Jack never talked about college. Mama never talked about college. From TV, he knew they were out there, places you traveled to after school was done. Going there implied you had a place you needed to *leave*. And no one had ever mentioned the idea of leaving House of Earth, of moving to a different community. With the war coming, that was not possible. They had each other, the strength and power of their bond, and a way of being that would save the planet. None of that had to do with college.

"Well, you're still twelve, right? So probably not on your radar."

"I don't think so."

"I'll say this, Lucien—you're not like the kids in Mater. That's refreshing."

Gabrielle reached into the pocket of her coat and pulled out a small device, which he recognized from a TV show. Mama didn't have one, and neither did Jack. It was a small portable phone, and he had never seen one up close. On one of the trips to town, he remembered there was a person talking on one. Mama only used a phone connected to the wall.

"I should be getting back soon," she said, looking at the phone. "But hey. We shouldn't go like six months between meeting, right?"

"No. I did want to see you again, I really did. I do think it would be okay if I went to town, that it wouldn't be so harmful, but my mom and Jack don't—"

"It's okay. Look, life gets complicated, right? My dad can't hold a job and talks to Jesus at 7-Eleven. My brother is in Afghanistan. I don't plan to apply to college. My friend Tara smokes way too much weed already. But if you can't go down there, I can come up here. It's not too bad a walk, just a few miles, and I like walking. You can get to this spot?"

"Yes, I like to come here after instruction, before dinner. It's a nice part of the woods."

"Well, good. Today's what, Thursday? And let's see . . . it's five forty-five now. So you think you can get here around five thirty on Thursdays? I'm gonna try to get here too. If one of us misses a week, that's okay. If you or I miss *two* weeks in a row, then let's worry and check on each other, okay?"

"That's a good plan, Gabrielle. I like that plan."

"So they threw out your book, huh? I remember, the blue one, they made it into a movie—"

"*The Natural.*"

"Yeah, that was it. I could see if maybe I could get another copy. Library probably won't have another, but there's a little bookstore a few miles north, and maybe I can get my mom to drive there and we can order it, or *I'll* drive because I basically taught myself and know what to do."

"You would do that? I don't know; it's a lot to go through, and if you brought it here, I don't know if I could keep it. There could be a problem."

"Read it in secret, Lucien. What adults don't know won't hurt them. A golden rule to life."

She stepped forward, spreading her arms wide. He hesitated, unsure what he should do, and she hugged him, her arms folding all the way around his back. "It was good to see you," she said.

"I missed you," he said quietly.

"Me too."

"Until next week," she said, letting go.

"I'll be here."

He watched her disappear down the slope, her back slipping behind the tree trunks. His fingers bent into a slight wave, and he sighed, backing up the hill, toward dinner. He remembered what she had said—it was five forty-five, which meant he was going to be late. He sped up, his elbows pumping out as he walked quickly out of the woods and back onto the commons, where the collectives had all left for dinner.

The nutritional hall was teeming with friends and mentors, voices ricocheting off the freshly painted lime-green walls, bounding to him in sharp, familiar fragments. Antonio's father, Anders, was serving corn, broccoli, and kale, and Lucien happily allowed him to fill his plate.

"How's everything, Lucien?"

"It's good. How are you?"

"I'm great. Hey, next time, don't be late, okay?"

"I won't."

He was late, this was true, but it wasn't the first time he or any of the friends had come to the nutritional hall a few minutes after they were due. Sometimes, they fell into a long conversation and arrived slightly later, or there was the time Cavan had a card trick he wanted to show everyone. He didn't like Anders reminding him of his lateness, but perhaps that was another change he would have to get used to.

At the Meadows table, several of the new friends—Colt, Madison, and Jacinda—had joined them, and this made Lucien feel better.

"There you are," Antonio said. "I'm almost done with my broccoli."

"I was walking in the woods and lost track of time."

"That does happen to you! You love the woods. Colt here was actually telling us about the city where he grew up. It's nothing like here."

"I'm from Queens," Colt said.

"What's Queens?" Lucien asked.

"A part of New York City. One of the big parts, a borough."

"Oh, okay."

"Colt's parents moved up to Mater recently," Antonio said.

"They're in finance, and they didn't like me in public schools anymore. My dad was very into the sixties, I think, and that never really changed, so here I am."

"The sixties?" Samantha asked.

"You know, hippies and stuff, tie-dye, peace and love, man."

"I like tie-dye," Cavan said.

"They're studying to be mentors. They're working with, what's his name, the guy with the black hair that sometimes falls over his eyes—"

"Sebastian," Lucien said.

"Yeah, Sebastian. I'm still getting used to all of this. It's way quieter than the city. You guys need a real basketball court, at least, and a real ball."

"What do you mean?"

"C'mon, you're serious?"

Lucien stared at Colt, whose smile resembled a precise mathematical graph Jack once drew on the board.

"We play basketball."

"You don't even dribble. The hoop is too low, but that's whatever. The curriculum is also super different than in the school I previously went to, which was also a private school."

"It's cool your parents could be mentors," Antonio said.

"They want that. Look, I mean, they talked about getting out of the city, and then the attacks happened and we all freaked. House of Earth—you guys got an interesting reputation. Not bad. So here I am. The no-TV thing isn't fun. I also wish the dorms had more heat."

"Habitation facility," Samantha said.

"Right, yeah."

Jacinda was chewing her broccoli, speaking between bites. "I'm used to this because I grew up in Ghent, which isn't that far away."

"I've heard of that town, I think," Antonio said.

"I was in another school where they also had a maypole so, like, this one is better, I think, more *involved*."

"We're safe here," Cavan said.

"That's true. My mom calls it a self-sustaining community, so that's why she wanted to come and put me in. My sister is in one of the lower collectives, one of the new ones. My mom is going to move into a dorm next month—"

"Habitation facility," Samantha said again.

"Right."

"She'll like it here," Samantha said.

When Lucien was finished eating, he stood up and saw Jack standing by the entrance to the nutritional hall. Jack waved to Lucien and motioned for him to come closer. The friends were going back to the habitation facility to do the readings Jack had assigned during instruction. Lucien would have to do them too. Earlier today, Jack had passed out a spiral-bound book with thinner pages that were not as glossy as those found in a textbook. "These are important teachings you are now ready to learn," he said. "Read the first verse and we will discuss tomorrow." Lucien had yet to open his own book. He planned to retrieve it from his cubby before walking to his room in the habitation facility, where Mama would join him.

Now he stood in front of Jack, who had crossed his arms in front of his chest.

"You didn't come on time today," he said.

"Oh, you mean to dinner? I know, I'm really sorry. I was walking in the woods, and I lost track of the time."

"Lost track? Dinner is at the same time every day."

"I know. It was an accident."

"An accident . . . Lucien, I know you are good, that you nurture light inside of you, not dark. Yet I don't know yet if you appreciate how much we all love you here, how much we all care about you."

"I do, of course."

"Then you wouldn't disappoint us with being late for dinner."

"I'm very sorry."

"*Sorry* cannot undo time, Lucien. You're old enough to see this now."

"I know it can't, Jack, and I won't be late again."

"This is an important lesson to learn. You are old enough to know the world is not an ideal place, that there is a war, that there are bad people and bad things and they want to hurt us, Lucien. They want to take from us what we have because what we have is special. What we have is *community*. What we have is the future. It may seem small, lateness at dinner, but we all need to do our part here. We all need to listen, to try our hardest, to be our best individual selves. Now, House of Earth can survive without those who aren't putting in the full effort to be a part of this community. In fact, House of Earth could even *thrive* without these people."

"I really won't be late again, I promise."

"I want to believe you. Please come with me."

Lucien fought the burst of nausea within him, the sense that all that was below was now above, and he was hurtling deeper into a hole that had opened up to swallow him whole. As Jack walked, Lucien touched the wall, seeking balance. He wasn't going to cry. Jack told him to follow, to keep up, we're going outside.

They exited onto an expanse of grass away from the commons, between the main building and the habitation facilities. Jack walked around the buildings, to a far side near the woods where Lucien usually didn't venture. They came to a stop in front of a rectangular wooden structure that was only slightly taller than Jack. It was dark brown and windowless, with rusted hinges holding a door in place.

"Go inside, Lucien."

Jack opened the door. Inside was bare, with dead leaves strewn on the planks making up a floor. It was like an outhouse, but there was no hole for him, just a bench and four walls that closed in hard. He could make out a stack of firewood in one corner. It was, he thought, a very small storage shed.

"You're going to stay here until I come back, okay? I want you to think about what you've done. I believe in you and I know you have light inside you, not darkness. I know you have good intentions, Lucien. What I want you to think about, while I'm gone, is how we can't afford to simply have good intentions anymore, that what we *intend* to do is not enough without actions to back it up. It's going to get harder and harder to make mistakes like these, to not listen to what I say, as the war gets closer and closer to our doorstep. That's the sad truth. I am going to lock this door, okay, and I will come back for you at a later time."

"When?"

Jack's smile disappeared. "When I return, Lucien."

The door closed and Lucien heard a lock click into place. This was not a punishment he had known existed. No friend had discussed it. Perhaps this was because he was the first person to be here, his crime deemed egregious enough. The nausea held and he bent over to feel a rush of blood to his head. He could hear Jack's footsteps fading away, the soft crunch of grass and leaves that would now not be his.

When I return. The words were looping within him, on a circuit that trailed his spiraling nausea. Despite the cold, he was sweating, and each time he reached out a hand, he immediately touched wall. He hardly had a foot of room to each side of him.

The darkness was nearly total. He held his hand up and strained to see its trace. The only proof he had of its existence was the feeling of his knuckle rapping the wood, hoping someone would hear.

What he hated most about darkness was the possibility. Within the absence of light, anything and everything could ferment, could be given life. His imagination had its greatest and most terrifying power. Any creature could emerge from the dark. From when he first arrived at House of Earth, he had been taught to fear the dark, to combat it with all his might, to welcome light into his existence. He had played O. C., casting darkness out. He had always tried his hardest.

Now he was trapped here, unable to see. He gripped the side of his stomach, confirming he had not lost his body to the darkness. His heart slammed his chest. With each passing second, he was sure the space between the walls and his skin would only shrink, closing him in. There was no difference between opening and closing his eyes.

He could only stare into the dark.

Time was only what Jack said it was. Lucien had no clock, no way to measure seconds, minutes, hours. He had left his watch in his room. He had only Jack's word. He heard himself cry, a low whine from his throat, but he felt so little, only what unseen skin he could press with his nail. Time was the death of sight, the death of light, the unchanging curtain of black that hung over the eyes that, if the present alone were to be believed, no longer existed. He couldn't say anything. His mouth wasn't producing sounds anymore. Through the slits in the wood, he could try to determine what was outside and what was not, what belonged to nature and what was caged in here, within him. He didn't know the difference anymore. He didn't know if minutes had stretched past him, or hours.

From his cheek, he tasted a tear. From his finger, he knew there was still a cheek, the soft flesh that layered his skull.

He was sure, through the infinite black, he could see them.

The dream came. They were tombstones in a graveyard, the only two, the ground surrounding them a wasteland of gray ash. The sky was not deep blue like the day. With the night, with *his* night, it had transformed, bleeding all color. The two tombstones stood against the dark. As he approached, they grew higher and higher, reaching to the very top of the sky. He saw the stone was glass and the glass held people, people like Antonio's uncle, and they were without faces. He called out to them. *They're coming. You need to watch out. You need to get out.* He cupped his hands to his mouth. No one could hear him. His feet began to sink into the soil, the ash swirling at his ankles. *You need to get out.* The towers were so tall, so high, and he bent his neck as far backward as it would go to stare straight up. He knew what was coming, but he could only draw closer, his feet sinking into the planet. He was swimming in soil, thrashing as near to the glass as he could, reaching out one hand. He needed to touch it. His arm burned, his fingers fluttering in dead air. *You need to get out.* But why was he coming closer?

All the people, locked in a tombstone.

He heard it first, the howling through the sky, the long metallic body disappearing into the tower with a flash. The airplane. He was neck-deep in soil, breathing the crackling air. A small speck was falling toward him. *A blackbird.* He was happy to see a bird.

The blackbird had arms, legs, a head, and a face that came screaming down, straight for him, a mouth filled with fire and blood—

Lucien jolted forward. He tasted his own saliva, a staleness like old milk. It was lightless, but he was where Jack had locked him up, back here. He looked right and left, from one pit of blackness to another. His eyes had been closed. Now he was awake, his body recomposing itself.

He had been sleeping. For how long?

He was suddenly certain he was going to die. If no one came, if they didn't open the door, the darkness would take him. A cracked sound escaped his throat. He still had a throat; he still could make noise; he still could swing his arm around and touch the walls that held him. His hands slammed the wood, the pain of impact burning the flesh of his shaking palms. He reared back, balling his left hand into a fist.

He could rattle the walls, but he could not break them. He could not cut open the darkness. Broken breaths escaped him. He felt the rivulets of sweat rolling down his forehead, stinging his eyes, dribbling into his mouth. Bitter milk and salt. He bit down on his tongue, tasting the rush of blood. The right fist smashed the walls, and then the left fist followed, and still only darkness, the light no closer than when he had dreamed of the towers in the sky. He beat at the wooden planks, crying out.

He could feel his mouth stretching, the tendons in his tongue and the flesh in his cheek straining with the force of the scream that wouldn't stop, not with his fists rattling the wood or his feet thrashing whatever lay below him. The dark was eating him. It would never be morning or night again, only this, the taste of unseen blood in his mouth and the remnant of a dream inside him that could have been real, because there was no way to know here if he had really watched, from the soil at his neck, the plane hit the towers.

He punched and kicked and punched and kicked and the blackness would not change. It had him now. His hands and feet slowed, fatigued from the effort. Mama floated to him and then Jack, and they both told him to rest, just rest, and he said he couldn't, it was dark, and now, he realized, very cold, because he could focus on this instead of the absence of light. The cold was deeper. He gasped. His toes were hard and unmoving in his shoes.

There would be no daylight. Daylight was for those who deserved daylight. A hot urge shot through him, and he trembled in his own urine, feeling the trickle from his thigh to his calf to the ground. He sagged, the punching and kicking done. His head drifted forward, into the wall of darkness.

If his eyes opened or closed, it did not matter. He saw nothing. The soil rose to meet him, as cold as it should have been.

———

He sipped from a bright tin cup, the water cool on his lips. He drank gradually, unsure of how much he should take. When Jack nodded, his teeth flashing white, he tilted the cup back and the water rushed down his throat. It took a drink like this to remind him how thirsty he was.

"Drink up, Lucien," Jack said, resting his hand on Lucien's shoulder.

The sunlight was a caul over his eyes, almost blinding. He was in a cushioned chair facing a large window in a white-walled room he did not recognize. His teeth, he realized, were chattering. Jack was sitting next to him, on a small bench.

"You will feel the heat very soon."

Lucien slowly turned his head. His fingers were reddened and stiff, chilled to the tips. He pressed his hand to his cheek, feeling the cold burning the flesh of his face. He was remembering his body, the physical architecture of a life. He could see.

He was out of the darkness.

"When is it—what time is it?"

"It's morning, Lucien."

He'd never noticed before how often Jack said his name. They were the only two people in the room, and he did not need to say his name. Yet he always did, his front teeth hissing on the soft *c*, the *n* almost lost on his tongue.

He did not want to hear Jack say his name.

"Morning, okay."

"You were sleeping on the ground. You should have stayed sitting."

Sleeping on the ground. He remembered now, all the night, his infinity in darkness. The urine on his pants had dried, though he could still smell and feel where it had been.

Jack had locked him behind the door, and Lucien had punched the wooden walls as hard as he could until he cried and no one came, no one heard him, and at some stretch of uncountable time, he had fallen down, his head resting on the grassy floor.

Before he fell, he saw the tombstones become the towers and the people dropping through the clouds, screaming.

He shivered and retched and tasted his own blood. He tried to see his own hand in front of his face, but he could not.

Jack had put him there. Lucien was sorry, he was afraid, and he wished Jack hadn't done it, that he loved him enough to not lock him in the dark.

"It was hard to sit up."

"How do you feel?"

"I'm cold. I think I'm hungry."

"Don't worry about that."

A door swung open and Lucien saw it was Mama, carrying a plate of bread rolls. The blood rushed to his legs and he stood up, his knees shaking. Mama rested the plate on the windowsill, and he ran to her, burying himself in her chest. She took him without speaking, holding him to her and rocking gently as his body convulsed.

"Mama, you're here."

"How was your night?"

Lucien could not answer. Each time he attempted to form a word, a sob swallowed it, thick tears rolling down his cheeks. He moaned softly into Mama. She continued to rock side to side, holding him.

"Do you understand what you did?"

He struggled to turn his cries into language, into the words he wanted to say. Jack was sitting on the bench, his arms crossed.

"I do, Mama."

"Good."

Jack stood up. He touched Lucien's hair. "It's important to listen," he said.

Lucien, his eyes a muddy pink, nodded, trying to look at Jack.

"He's learning," Mama said.

"We don't want to send you there again," Jack said.

"I won't be late, I won't . . ."

"We know you won't, Lucien."

Lucien was so grateful to be with Mama, to be in the light, to be able to see her and see himself and know time could be counted again. He was never going back to the pit. He would be good. Mama and Jack were forgiving him. Light was not a guarantee and darkness loomed and House of Earth was a blessing, always a blessing, and he would have to be much better for House of Earth, to be what Jack and Mama wanted him to be. He hugged her again, his tears mingling with the warmth of her sweater, sunlight dappling the skin of her neck.

"I'm so happy to be here," he said.

"We are always happy to have you," Jack said. "You are a very important part of this community."

A shard of memory cut him. He was at the pool, with the girl named Kaitlyn he would never see again. The pool was a sin against the planet. He understood now that Kaitlyn and her family were asked to leave House of Earth. They were not worthy of the community. If Kaitlyn could be asked to leave, so could others, and so could Lucien. Nothing was guaranteed. If he was cast out, he would die. That he was sure of, just as he knew the darkness could have consumed him had he stayed longer, had Jack decided he did not need to be saved.

Death meant he could hold up his hand to his face and never be able to see it, never again for all days and nights.

"Have a roll, Lucien," Mama said.

He ate, the roll disappearing in his mouth before he could even enjoy its taste. The water reminded him of his thirst, and the roll reminded him of his hunger. He knew now how empty his body had been, warring against the dark with so little inside him. There were two more rolls, and he ate them both, crumbs spraying from his lips. Mama smiled at him.

"I know this can all seem hard," Jack said. "We don't like this. O. C. doesn't like this. But all of you Meadows are so important now, especially as you grow into teenagers. These are the years that will shape your life. Mistakes become harder to fix. As a boy, you make a mistake like spilling your juice, and all it means is you have to clean it up. As an adult, Lucien, a mistake can cost lives."

"I won't make any," Lucien said, sniffling.

"The war is coming closer. We all have to be ready. We have to be at our best."

"How close is it?"

"We can't say. We just have to be prepared. The planet is sick right now. We can heal it, but it's very sick."

"I won't fail the planet."

"We care about you," Mama said.

"Now, instruction starts in a half hour. Why don't you run over to the habitation facility, get a fresh pair of clothes, and get ready?"

Mama took Lucien home. He walked with a fresh pair of clothes to the shower at the end of the hall. Everyone shared the bathroom and the shower. Hot water sizzled through his hair. After one minute, he had to stop showering because there was a rule against wasting water. Once he had broken it, but he was not going to break rules anymore because he was not going back to the dark.

He rubbed his head with a towel and sat on the bed, feeling the water dry on his body. In a few minutes, he would go back to instruction. Snowflakes were melting on the window. He looked up into the sky, a watery gray today, with gratitude. He could have this sky again. He would only have to be better.

At instruction, he sat among the friends again. They were quieter around him, their eyes not quite meeting his own. Cavan opened his mouth to say something, and then Jack walked in and Cavan was quiet.

"Hello, friends," Jack said.

"Hello, Jack."

"Before we begin, can everyone give a special greeting to Lucien?"

They all turned to him now. Everyone knew. He shifted in his chair, his head bowing. He somehow wished they did not know.

"Hello, Lucien!"

Jack clasped his hands. The friends grew quiet again.

"Lucien here has learned a great deal in the past day, and you should all feel proud to know him. He is a part of our future, just as all of you are, and I want us to recognize those who make special efforts in our community. Lucien, thank you."

He did not know what to say. Jack was looking to him, waiting. The friends were leaning forward, waiting too.

"Thank you—to all of you," Lucien said, his voice cracking.

Jack stood above him. He touched the back of Lucien's neck. "We are all happy to have you. Now, let's go on to today's lesson."

On the commons after instruction, Antonio found Lucien standing alone, a light snow flaking his hair. Antonio wore his bright-red beanie. Many of the friends were playing O. C. Today Samantha was O. C., racing across the grass to catch as many friends as she could. Antonio had been in the game but was taking a break, his breath hanging in the chilled air.

"How're you doing?"

At first, Lucien did not want to answer at all. Antonio was standing in front of him, concern etched into his face. What else could he say? He was grateful, and he did not want to consider what his existence had been, one night ago.

"I'm okay. I'm glad to be here."

"We were all worried. My dad told me they are getting a bit more strict with stuff. They have to, of course. But Jack seems okay now. Right?"

"He is."

"I walked by there. Jack told us we couldn't say anything to you until he let you out. That was the rule."

"It's okay."

Antonio looked down, twisting the toe of his boot in the shallow layer of snow. "You were only late. Jack didn't have to put you there."

"I learned my lesson."

"You know, if something happens again, you can just—my dad is getting closer with O. C., I think. He will go to see him for talks in the woods, and maybe if you need something and Jack is being hard, my dad can tell O. C.—"

"You don't have to do that, Antonio."

"Okay, I just wanted to let you know."

Antonio continued to stand next to Lucien, not saying anything more. Lucien wondered if he wanted a description of what it was like. They all must want to know. The words would not come, or they did not want to come, and Lucien scratched the back of his head, saying nothing.

"Everyone still likes you," Antonio said.

"I know."

With that, Antonio took off running, back to the game. He turned to see if Lucien was following him, and Lucien shook his head. Today he wasn't going to play. He would sit and watch and think about what he was going to do next. He hoped no one else would have to go where Jack had sent him.

And then there was Gabrielle. He wanted to meet her again. She was the reason he'd been late, and he would have to ensure, in the future, he could talk to her and not lose track of time. That was all. He didn't have to stop seeing her. Jack had never said that. He'd been mad about dinner. Even if dinner lateness, on its own, could not greatly alter dinner, it was a lesson that had to be learned, especially if there was a war coming closer, because a war, above all else, meant listening to others.

He could still look forward to seeing her again.

Meanwhile, he watched the friends. They darted across the commons, fleeing Cavan, who had now become O. C. Cavan pursued them with great vigor, his tongue peeking out the side of his mouth like the basketball player Lucien had once seen on TV, when he was allowed to watch TV. He did miss the comfort of the screen. He missed the shows about safari animals and sharks, as well as the glimpses of organized sports.

He missed his book. He wanted to know whether Roy Hobbs saved the Knights, but he could never know—it would be an unsolved mystery of his life. It was not a question he could ask of Jack. He could ask

Gabrielle to read the book *for* him and tell him what happened. But that would not be the same as reading it himself, and he knew that too, that Mama had deprived him of this, and he could not quite understand why. The book had not made him late for dinner or made him not respect the planet. It was a way to infuse pleasure into the hours of his day when he was not at instruction, with the friends, or asleep.

He was thinking about his book when Evie sat down next to him.

Where had she come from? She was at instruction today but not playing on the commons, and there were moments when she seemed to simply disappear, only to reemerge hours or days later. She hardly spoke out loud. Whether she was at instruction or not, Jack no longer asked her questions or even noted her presence. It was as if she had become a ghost visible only to Lucien and the friends who still asked what became of her, their former leader floating silently and glumly through these changing days and nights. He used to think the old Evie would return, that it was inevitable.

He had no reason to believe it now. There was no evidence. Jack had taught them the scientific method, and evidence was very much a part of that.

Evie turned her head, as if readying to speak to him. He waited. Her mouth remained closed. Instead, her hand touched his and he looked down to see a crumpled piece of paper. He took it.

"Look at it later," she said, standing up to walk away.

She was letting him decide when later would be.

———

In the morning, the water ran brown into the sink. Lucien was trying to brush his teeth when the water changed color. It had a strange scent, like a spoiled vegetable, and he immediately backed away. Samantha was behind him, waiting to brush her teeth. They used this sink because the other one no longer worked.

"Uh-oh, that does not look good," Samantha said. "I'll tell my mom."

"Okay."

Lucien waited. The brown water pooled in the sink like a miniature lake of mud. Pinching his nose, he shut off the faucet.

In the cottage, the water never ran brown. He tried not to compare his life then to his life now because he was actually living at House of Earth now, and he needed to remember how grateful he should be to be living among those who looked out for each other and the planet that would have to carry the human race into the future.

"The earth was once very strong without human beings," Jack said during instruction. "It can be very strong without them again."

Lucien tried not to compare because there were ways the life he once knew in the cottage could be considered better. He could shower for a long time, the water was always warm when he wanted it to be warm, heat came through the walls, he had his own room, and there was TV and books and the backyard with Mama's bench. He had not seen Darling Drive since they moved into the habitation facility. He was afraid to ask Mama if they would see it again, even once, because he feared what she would say.

She would say that there was no need to.

He stood in the bathroom, observing himself in the mirror. There were more small black hairs appearing over his upper lip. Gabrielle had said he had grown taller, and she was right—he *was* taller.

He ached to see her again. When he thought about it, her presence before him, there was a stirring inside him he had never felt before, not for any other person. It was new, this feeling. He did not have a name for it. No one had given him one.

He only knew he liked it.

Samantha returned, shaking her head. "My mom is gone. I could knock on other doors and see who's around."

"Let me see if the water has changed back."

Lucien turned on the faucet again, hoping for clear water. It was a dark brown now. Samantha gasped and he shut it off.

"I can see if anyone else is around also."

"Sounds like a plan."

They tried Room 6, where Cavan and Cavan's mom and dad lived. Cavan's dad answered, rubbing his eye. He was not wearing a shirt, and Lucien glimpsed his expansive, fleshy belly, dark hairs swirling on his chest. It seemed too cold for anyone to sleep without a shirt on.

"What's up, kids?"

"The water is all brown. It smells funny too."

"Better tell, uh, Jack."

He did not answer his door often, and their knocks brought no one out.

"Do you know where your mom is?" Samantha asked after they stopped knocking on Jack's door.

"No. Where is your mom?"

"Honestly, not sure. She wakes up early and goes out with the other adults. They talk with O. C., I think. She never says."

"My mom never says either."

"Let's just go back to our room and wait."

Lucien still had not read what Evie wrote on the paper for him. He went to bed last night wondering what it said and woke up forgetting about it at all until he saw the paper crumpled with his sketch pad, where he had slid it yesterday. Was it *later* now? He would have to determine. Evie had said nothing else. He did not know what he hoped it would say.

While Samantha peered into her drawer to search for her socks, Lucien grabbed the paper and unfurled it.

He read the words, scrawled in crisp dark-blue ink.

I was there too.

The paper shook in his hand. He rolled it up and jammed it in his pocket, fearing it would somehow catch fire and burn away, taking him with it.

Samantha found her peach-colored socks and slid them on her bare feet. "I hope they fix the water," she said.

Lucien was touching his pocket, feeling for the paper. Snow, he saw, was beginning to build on the windowsill.

"Lucien?"

"Yes."

"I said, I hope they fix it."

"I hope so too."

Soon they would go to the nutritional hall for breakfast. He hoped to see Evie there. If she was there, she would eat without speaking, and Lucien, more than anything, wanted this morning to be different. He wanted her to talk to him.

He wanted to know why she had been sent to the pit of darkness too.

Samantha went to the bathroom one more time to see if the water was no longer brown. She reported that it was the same shade of brown, and the odor made her gag. After, they walked across the grass to the nutritional hall, their feet sliding over a fresh layer of snow. Inside, Lucien's eyes hunted for any sign of Evie. Most of the tables were full, but he did not see her. Antonio's father, Anders, served him porridge with cinnamon and placed a small grapefruit on his tray. He sat down with the Meadows, feeling disappointed that Evie had not come again.

Was she punished each time she missed breakfast, lunch, or dinner?

Did this mean she went to the pit many, many times?

The new Meadows now mixed with the old. Colt and Cavan sat next to each other, along with Magnus and Jayson. Karthik and Samuel were at the table too. Antonio sat down soon after, immediately gobbling his porridge. Cavan was telling Colt about the maypole. Colt said his parents would be certified as mentors soon.

"O. C. Leroux will lead a ceremony for them. That's what they told me," Colt said.

"Wow, I wish my parents would become mentors," Cavan said.

"My mom too. That would be really cool," Samantha said.

Lucien was searching for Evie. He kept his eyes trained on the front doors, spooning porridge into his mouth slowly. He needed to make it last as long as he could.

"My dad does like his job," Antonio said.

"Nutritional hall is super important," Samantha said. "By the way, did you see all the brown water this morning?"

"I had problems with the water in my facility too," Karthik said. He lived in Habitation Facility Building B. Lucien and Samantha were in A.

"Was it brown?"

"It wasn't coming out at first, and then it was brown. We haven't been getting as much heat lately also. The pipe hisses for a bit and then stops, and I have to sleep with extra blankets wrapped around me."

"It does happen," Cavan said. "I guess it will be easier in the spring."

Lucien was glad that none of the friends were talking about him or his punishment. It was over now, and there would not be a need to make it a part of the conversation again. He could focus on the future, whatever the future held. Spring, summer, more lessons from Jack. A war, of course, but perhaps it would not come after all. He had not seen it yet. He knew he had to be ready, that they all did, but the weather forecast did not always come to pass when he still could see the TV weather report. Although he knew Jack was right, he hoped events could somehow unfold in such a way where they remained safe at House of Earth.

"The colors of all the rooms here are so bright, though," Karthik said. "It's very nice to see, to look at."

"Colors are very important," Antonio said. "We use good colors, not bad colors."

"I see what Jack means by the energy they create. I can really see it."

Lucien's spoon dropped on the plate. He saw her, walking between a few Saplings, going to get her tray. He almost shouted her name.

Nothing mattered more than hearing her. He stood up, the friends eyeing him strangely, and hurried to the line as Evie held out her bowl for Antonio's father to pour hot porridge into.

She was late again.

"Lucien," she said without feeling, when she saw him standing next to her.

"Are you coming to eat with us?"

"I'm not."

"Then where are you eating?"

"Elsewhere. Listen, Lucien, it was good to talk, but I can't—"

"You *can't* eat anywhere else, Evie . . ."

"Maybe *you* can't . . ." He saw she was gently shaking, biting down on her lower lip. "But I can."

She held up the underside of her right wrist. On her pale stretch of skin, he saw two letters, small and black.

O. C.

"What?"

"I can go anywhere."

Her voice had dropped to a whisper, her eyes small and dark and far from him. She put her hand down at her side.

"I don't understand."

"You will someday."

"You were in the pit too. You were in the darkness. When? For how long?"

"I need to go."

"You gave me the note."

"That's all you'll have."

"Please."

"This isn't a place to talk."

"Then where?"

She drew close to him, her lips nearly touching the shell of his ear. "There is no place. You will learn that soon enough."

"Evie."

"I have to go."

"Just tell me—was it the same? Was it as dark?"

Evie was staring at her tray, not looking at him anymore. Her hands had steadied. He wanted to know who or what had made the mark, if it was O. C. himself, if it was ink or a tattoo or something else. He missed Evie, and this seemed like the only way to get her back—to keep her near him, to keep asking questions.

"It was worse," she said.

He watched her push through the doors of the nutritional hall, leaving alone.

———

At first, he feared that Gabrielle would not come. They had promised to meet at the same place at the same time, but what did it really mean? They had never written it down. There was no oath. They had exchanged words, but words, without being committed to a page, were easily forgotten. He knew the story of Roy Hobbs only because it had been written in a book—placed into a library—that he could access years later.

No one else knew of Gabrielle. She existed to him but not to anyone else at House of Earth. This was the reality he had to accept. If she never showed up again, it would be as if she never lived at all.

He just had to make sure not to be late for dinner.

It was almost dark, the sun disappearing behind the mountain line. A harsh wind blew through the woods, wrapping around his bundled torso, ruffling the orange scarf he'd slung around his mouth. Ice cracked under his boots. He descended the slope, glancing at his watch after a few steps downward. He no longer had the Pokémon watch. Now it was a Casio digital watch, purchased by Mama last year. Dinner would start in thirty-two minutes.

He saw her, little more than a dark blotch among the snow-lined branches, coming toward him.

There was only so much time. He took off running downhill.

"Lucien," he heard her call, his feet sliding on the ice, his head pitching forward. His right hand flew out to brace himself against a tree trunk. Old snow flecked his shoulders. Between breaths, he waved at her.

"No need to kill yourself like that. Jesus. I was coming right up."

"Not much, not much time today . . ."

"What?"

He caught his breath, standing upright. She was now in front of him, laughing, her smile brighter than anything else around him.

"For next time, let's meet a bit earlier."

"A bit earlier? Okay."

"I can't be late for dinner."

"I didn't know you had such an appetite."

He wondered whether he should tell her. Although he was satisfied that the friends were no longer interested in his night in the pit, he could not just forget it either. Like the towers, the night came back to him, and he would find himself sweating in the early morning, fear burrowing into him.

A morning ago, he'd woken up moaning. Mama had asked him what happened, and he'd said he was having bad dreams.

"Positive energy will bring better dreams," she said.

The night would not leave him. He could see this now, as the days rolled into each other, and still he could find the darkness and feel his hands burning from the pain of punching wooden walls that would not give him light. He thought it would be gone by now, that he would not have to think about it anymore, especially after Jack forgave him. He was free. He was not going back.

Yet as Jack spoke at instruction today, teaching the friends about the number of species that went extinct after industrialization in the nineteenth century—this was the time to learn of the "modern sickness," Jack had said—Lucien could not rip the memory of the night out of his head. He wanted to, begged to, shut his eyes and opened them and began drumming his fingers on the desk, a pulsing in his chest. The walls of the room were dark, and they were closing in on him.

Gabrielle was now waiting. Several seconds of silence had passed without him realizing, and his head jerked to his watch, which melted time no matter what he did.

"I don't, I just . . . I need to be on time next time. I will get in trouble. So for the future, if we can meet earlier—"

"Of course we can. Are you okay? Your hands, they're shaking a little. If it's too cold out here . . ."

"It's not too cold out here, no. I'm happy to see you."

"When can you get off, I don't know, whatever you call it here, the campus? Do you take day trips out of the House of Earth?"

"We're here. We're always here."

"Right. The ban on going to town. That new, shining wall. How could I forget? I feel like it'd be easier if we could meet somewhere like the library—you'd be less nervous, I think, less in a rush."

"I can't meet there. It has to be here."

"Are they doing anything to you, Lucien?"

"They're teaching me."

"What do they do if you're late? Tell me. You don't look well."

He began to open his mouth, stopping only when he realized he had told no one out loud, that he would have to form these fears into language to communicate to her. He wished he could rest his head against hers and transmute the images, to show her what it meant to stare into the blackest night and feel death so close to him. What it meant to see the tombstones, the towers, to hear the people screaming from the sky.

"Jack was mad at me when I was late."

"Jack, that's your teacher, right?"

"Mentor."

"Mentor, yeah. I need to keep up with the terminology. My crappy teachers would love it if we called them *mentor*. It would make them feel much more special than they deserve to feel."

"Jack, he was mad at me."

"You said that already."

"I'm just trying—it's hard to say."

"Take your time."

"But I *can't* take my time. Don't you get it?"

His voice had jumped sharply, the back of his throat enflamed. It was a pitch he had never reached before, never with Jack or Mama or any friend. He closed his mouth. There was a strange broil in his chest.

"Lucien, seriously. Let's calm down. Please."

She rested both of her hands on his shoulders. He was breathing deeply, the broil receding into his stomach. He was ashamed for sounding this way in front of Gabrielle, especially since he had looked forward to seeing her all week. She did not have to see him. There were other people who wanted to be her friend, people who did not live at House of Earth and did not have to be at dinner in twelve minutes. She had to choose to come to him. He could never seek her out, never walk through the woods and find, across many roads, her house. Once she chose not to come, that was the end.

She might as well not exist then.

"I'm sorry, I'm really sorry."

"It's okay, really. Just let it out. Tell me what happened. Maybe I can help."

"No, I deserved it."

"Whatever happened, I don't think you deserved it."

"I was late and—"

"So? I'm late to dinner like, every night. All my mom does is leave the spaghetti in the bowl, and I get to heat it up on my own."

"But we have to listen—it's important. If we disobey what Jack says, it means we will disobey more things in the future when it gets a lot worse, when, well . . ."

Gabrielle knew about the war because her brother was in it. Maybe she would understand. Maybe Mater High School was preparing too, in its own way. When Jack said the war could come to House of Earth, that the planet was in danger and sick, did that mean Gabrielle's brother would be fighting *against* House of Earth? Or fighting *with* them, for the planet? He was afraid to ask.

"I don't really understand what you're saying. This sounds like boot camp, honestly, with drill sergeants making you follow orders because they're all angry, insecure assholes. Noah likes that, I think, because Mom and Dad gave me so little discipline at home, but he's going to get over it real fast and come back. But you, Lucien—what did they do to you? Five hundred push-ups? Fifty laps around the quad? Did they tie you up? I can't stand this shit, honestly."

"They put me in the pit, Gabrielle."

"The pit?"

"It was dark and I couldn't see."

"Okay, so a dark place. In the night? Why couldn't you see?"

"Jack locked the door and I wanted to get out, I couldn't see anything, I was afraid I was going to die because there was no light, and when I put my hand up to my face, I couldn't even see anything. I didn't know my hand was there, and then I was cold, I was hungry, it was the darkest night, and if I don't get to dinner and I'm late again, Jack will put me back, and I don't want to go back but I don't have time, Gabrielle. I don't have time."

"This is really awful. I want to get you out of here. Like, would you go to public school? Is your mom into this private-school-woods thing so much? Maybe I could talk to her. You don't have a cell phone, right?"

"A cell phone? No."

"Yeah, I figured. I'd text you. Listen, if things get rough and you miss a week here, that's okay. I will be coming every week. I have the time. School gets out by three. My mom doesn't give a shit where I am after that. She's got work, and my dad—you know the story with him by now. I am going to keep coming. And we'll figure out some way. We can get you out of here."

"I don't want to leave, though."

"Lucien, okay, let's just take it slow, then. I can get here earlier next week."

Lucien glanced down at his watch. He had five, almost four minutes. "I need to run to dinner."

"You can't be late. I know."

"I will see you next week."

"I'll be here."

Lucien dashed as fast he could go, up the slope and out of the woods. He was not going to slip on the ice, not with the threat of another punishment hanging over him. He had no time to look back to see if Gabrielle was still there. By the time he turned around, he was inside, the smell of tonight's vegetables already reaching his nose.

He was not hungry, but he would try to be.

SPRING

The friends began to turn thirteen. First Cavan, then Magnus. For instruction, Antonio's father, who worked in the nutritional hall, brought a baked chocolate cake. It was, Jack reminded them, dairy-free, which meant no animals were harmed to make the cake yummy.

"Let's all thank Antonio's father," he said.

Jack said that there were religions where thirteen connoted manhood, and thirteen was an important age for House of Earth, an age for discovering knowledge and finding out who you are.

"When he was thirteen, O. C. Leroux learned who he was."

In late March, after the water stopped turning brown but before the lights started to flicker on and off, Jack told them to take out pieces of drawing paper.

"I want to tell you a story about O. C. Leroux. Afterward, we will do a project."

The friends walked to the art-supply closet, where they pulled out their colored pencils. When Lucien was younger, the black pencil was always there, in the plastic case. He used to think it was a test, to prove that the black pencil could be ignored for brighter colors. Since they all moved to House of Earth, the black had been removed altogether. The option was gone.

Perhaps Jack thought they had passed the test.

Colored pencils in hand, Lucien sat back down. The sun was bright today, and he could feel its warmth through the window. Winter was ending. He liked springtime, when the winds could not cut at him and the grass was free of ice. The habitation facility would be warmer too. It would have to be. When he woke up in the morning, his feet would no longer shiver on the hard, cold floor.

"House of Earth wasn't always here," Jack began. "This land sat here, unused. As a younger man, O. C. visited it and saw what it could be. He saw all of you in his future. He was only thirteen and lived not very far from here. At the time, there were many people who wanted to chop down more trees, dig up more earth, and hunt as many animals as possible. Automobiles had become very popular, and that meant more gasoline to make them run, which meant more oil. Pollution entered the sky. Some of you have come from the city. You know the city encourages this—the consumption of resources, the bleeding of the earth. The suburbs, built around the car, do as well. We all live together so there is no need to enter an automobile. We are sustainable. We are ready for the future. And O. C. saw this all."

"He was thirteen when he knew he wanted to build House of Earth?" Magnus asked.

"Yes. It was one night around this time, in March. He had what we call a vision. He looked upon the land and saw this, saw us. He understood the possibility and promised, one day, to make House of Earth."

"House of Earth was new when we first came?" Samantha asked.

"You were among our very first collectives," Jack said. "Though O. C. had his vision at thirteen, it took many years to make it a reality. It took planning. He needed to find the right people to follow him. He found me, Sebastian, and Natasha. We followed him because we saw the light in him immediately. Before I met O. C. Leroux, I wasn't living my best life. I wasn't so lucky, to have grown up in House of Earth like you."

The friends nodded. Lucien was looking at his blank piece of paper, wondering what he was going to draw. He had heard Mama say this too—how lucky he was to have what they did not have. What had Mama's childhood been like? She would never say. Perhaps it was a school like Gabrielle's. Gabrielle did not like her school. But *she* was a good person, despite that. Not having House of Earth did not make her any worse than he was. He perceived strength in her that he did not possess. She had somehow fostered it within herself without the House of Earth's teachings, without a mentor like Jack, without a habitation facility or coloring with the right colors.

What would Jack say about Gabrielle? Lucien hoped he would accept her. He hoped she would never have to go to the pit.

"I remember, when I was your age, wishing I could have a place like this. A real community, where we all loved one another and we cared not for ourselves but for everyone around us, the whole planet. Not just the fleeting present we all lived in, but the future. I wanted that, and when I met O. C., I knew it would be possible."

"Where did you meet him for the first time?" Samantha asked.

"It was many years ago, not far from here. He was giving a speech and I heard it. It was incredible. It's hard to describe. As I said, when he was just thirteen, O. C. had his first vision of House of Earth, and you are all of that age now. You've already seen that this is a year of great change. Many years ago, O. C. spoke of a coming war, and he was right. But he didn't speak of it to simply scare us. That was not his intention. He wants to prepare us. You should all feel confident because you have been preparing. We are not just physically prepared—we have a wall and a guard booth, and the wall will get bigger with time. We are prepared in all ways. You have rejected the poison of those who are killing the planet. You are living in a way that will guarantee your survival and therefore the world you will inherit. You are living as O. C. says you should live. For that, you should all be proud."

When Jack paused, a question took shape inside Lucien. It was one that had existed more as a feeling, dim and unrealized, in the back of his head for longer than he could remember. The question had been embryonic until now. In this proto-state, it had not been a concrete set of words he would pose to someone else.

Now he knew what it was.

He opened his mouth. "Jack?"

"Yes, Lucien."

"Do we ever leave House of Earth?"

"Leave?"

"Well, you know—"

"When is graduation?" Karthik jumped in. "At what point, I assume, in a few years, it just wasn't clear."

"Is that what you are asking, Lucien? When graduation is?"

The left side of Jack's mouth was inching upward, a half smile that disguised an emotion Lucien could not quite recognize.

"Yes, I think."

"Do you want to leave?"

"No, no, of course not."

"I never heard about a graduation," Samantha said.

"I was just wondering," Karthik said.

"Now, when O. C. Leroux had his vision of House of Earth, it was nothing like your typical school," Jack said, walking slowly from the chalkboard to where Lucien sat, his gaze wandering across the room. "A school out there"—he pointed to the window—"does what schools typically do, which is stop educating children at a certain arbitrary point. Do we know what *arbitrary* means?"

There were diffident murmurs and nods.

"*Arbitrary* is something that is done for not any reason at all. Performed without logic. Without meaning. Some of the new Meadows here came from schools like that. You left them and came here because your parents and guardians probably recognized that the education there was, in some ways, falling short. It was not what education was supposed to be, or what we imagined it to be. In most of these schools, it ends at eighteen. And then you go to a college or a university, which you surely have heard of. I attended college myself. There are several problems with a system like this. One, it does not teach you proper *reverence* for the world around you. That's another big word. You are at an age to understand words like these. So you have no appreciation or respect—you are jumping from place to place, using up resources, moving on. When O. C. Leroux first spoke to me, he said he wanted to create a true and lasting community. These kinds of schools can't be communities like we have. Lucien asked a question before: Can you leave? Karthik asked about graduation. Both questions come from a mindset that we must get rid of, for the sake of our survival. It's very important."

"I'm sorry, I didn't mean to ask it like that," Karthik said.

"It's all right, Karthik. You see, when O. C. spoke to me and Sebastian and Natasha about House of Earth, he said he wanted it to be a place where we could live in harmony for a lifetime, where learning and living and work and play could all exist in one special place. In the very old days, small towns were like this. But we've lost our way. Even the town here, Mater. Mater does not live by the values it should. It's why we must exist beyond it. And the schools and colleges of the world outside of here, they don't build any kind of community. People come and people go. It's temporary. There is the rush to go elsewhere. Lucien asked when we leave—anyone, at any time, can leave or be asked to leave. But think of how well you know each other, how well you know your mentors, the parents of your friends, everyone here at House of Earth. This is a family."

"I am proud to be part of a family," Karthik said.

"Good! I know you are. And you too, Lucien."

"I am."

"O. C. Leroux hopes you stay with us for a long time. He wants you all a part of this family. He, and all of us, want you all to be here, to build your lives here."

Lucien told himself that nothing about the answer should have surprised him. He was here, and would always be here. It was wonderful that O. C. Leroux wanted him to remain, that he had a family and a community when so many people never would. There would be no graduation when he would be wrenched away from his family and forced to build a community among strangers. This—his present, seated in the instruction room with Jack and the friends—would be his future. Mama was never going to let him go.

This was the answer he was always seeking. It was. He gripped his pencil tighter.

Would Gabrielle always come to see him?

Would he ever see Darling Drive, the library, or the duck pond again?

He did not have the courage to ask these questions.

"Now, let's draw," Jack said.

———

In the evening, Antonio said that his father had gone out to buy supplies, in town.

"He can go to town?" Lucien asked.

"Some adults can. I think it depends."

Lucien remembered what Evie had said. "Does he have anything on his wrist? Your dad? Letters?"

"Uh, I don't think so. Haven't seen any."

That afternoon, they had all been told to draw O. C. Leroux's face. If they had not seen him yet—there were Meadows who had arrived at House of Earth after his talk in front of the bonfire—they would work from their imagination. Jack said to take one hour.

"I want to see your drawings infused with love," he said.

Lucien drew O. C.'s flowing golden hair, his beard hanging like a cloud around his high face. For eyes, he imagined two cerulean gems, mixing colors to achieve the needed hue. On paper, O. C. rested flat against a pale sky. Lucien wanted to give him life, to come as close to the real face as he could.

None of it looked right to him.

When they were done, Jack taped each drawing to the far wall so light from the windows would be cast directly onto them. He said he would invite O. C. to instruction one day to look at the drawings himself.

"These have love."

After dinner and before their nine p.m. bedtime, Lucien planned to meet Antonio on the commons. They were going to look at stars. He had time, his vegetable soup finished, to go back to his room. He decided he would nap for ten or twenty minutes. Last night, he had slept fitfully, waking up from a dream in which the sun, for reasons never explained, had been extinguished.

They were calling it the black sun.

When he entered the hallway of his habitation facility, the lights were out. Mama had said there were small electrical problems but not to worry about that—Jack or Sebastian would have it fixed soon. Though he slept in the bunk bed above Mama, he saw her only in the early morning and at night. During the day, he rarely caught sight of her. She was doing important work for O. C. Leroux, he guessed. She was running errands.

His heart beat quickly when he had to walk through the darkened hallway.

Room 8's door was closed, as always. In his old room, at the cottage, he'd had a lock on his door. There were no locks at the habitation facility. He never had to worry about carrying around keys.

As he pressed his hand to the door, he heard an unfamiliar sound. It was a muffled voice, sniffling or whimpering, faint behind the door. His hand fell away. He knew it wasn't Samantha because he had just seen her by the commons. He could walk away and come back and hope it was gone. That was easiest to do.

He pushed the door open. The hinges groaned. He was sorry, prepared to back away and stumble out of the room. His hand, meanwhile, continued to push.

Bent over on the bed across from his, her head falling into her cupped hands, was Samantha's mother.

Samantha's mother was crying.

The door had swung fully open. He could still ease himself away, into the hallway's cool darkness. Samantha's mother was always quiet, rarely saying more than hello or goodbye to Mama, and only nodding and smiling at him. She, like Mama, slept on a bottom bunk.

He closed the door. He was in the room, alone with her.

Her hands dropped from her face, and she looked up at him, blinking between tears. Without the flickering of the overhead bulb, the room was filled with a crepuscular darkness, an oceanic shade that left him uneasy, his feet shifting beneath him. It was like sinking farther into the deep, great waves folding over the last light from the sky. Samantha's mother had drawn the curtains.

He walked closer. Her eyes widened, her hands now resting on her knees, just below the fabric of her indigo skirt. New tears were falling down her thin cheeks.

"I—I can go," Lucien said.

Samantha's mother shook her head. "It's fine, Lucien, it's fine, just . . . everything is okay. You can stay or go. It's okay."

"I can get you water."

"I don't need any. I really don't."

She held her hands in her lap. He'd never known her to be somber quite like this. For a moment, her right wrist turned and he saw, on its underside, the two letters printed dark against her skin.

O. C.

He decided he would not tell Samantha what he had seen.

"I'm sorry I came in. I can go now."

She ran a hand across her eyes, wiping them slowly. He saw, through a slit in the blinds, a crescent moon had risen in the sky.

"It's okay. I'm good now. It was just—long day, that's all. A lot of changes, right?"

"Yes."

"And it's all so good and everything is good and everyone is good and we all need to be thankful, right? Thankful every day."

"We do, yes."

"Sometimes I wish this room was larger."

"I can get that, for sure. More room would be . . ."

"Just larger. But everything—I don't know. It's good. Samantha will be here soon. Just tell her everything is okay, Lucien. Will you do that?"

"I will."

"Don't tell her that her mother was like this. She doesn't need it right now."

Samantha's mother stood up from the bed, shaking her head slowly. For the first time, Lucien realized she was older than Mama, with small wrinkles etched into the corners of her mouth and eyes. He did not know how old Mama was.

"I need some air, I think. I really wish you didn't see me like this, but it's okay. I know I—we—did the right thing in coming here. It can just seem hard sometimes. The way they touch—the way they treat you."

All Lucien could do was mumble, "Yes."

"Do you ever miss Christmas? Or, I don't know, Hanukkah?"

These were holidays he knew from TV. Both real-live actors and cartoon characters celebrated them. Once, he had watched a *Rugrats* Christmas and Hanukkah special, the babies enjoying both holidays in different episodes. He understood there were people who followed religions, Christian and Jewish and Muslim. They were as abstract and remote to him as the physics that powered rocket flight. Mama never had a Christmas, so he never had a Christmas. House of Earth did not have a tree, a menorah, or an iftar. If asked, he could not guess what religion Gabrielle followed. Only that her father had started becoming a Christian. If asked, he could not explain the purpose of following through with such rituals, especially if there was someone like O. C.

Leroux already watching over the community. What did O. C. have to do with Christmas? Why was Samantha's mother asking him about it at all?

It was a question, though, that ate deeper into him as he struggled to reply. She had lived a life he would never know, one that took form far beyond the reaches of House of Earth, like Mama and Jack and all the adults. Had she been celebrating these holidays with Samantha before she moved with her to House of Earth last year? Had she tried to celebrate it this past December? He could not know.

All he deciphered was her longing for a place that was not this one. There was a town and there was the vast elsewhere. There was the coming war.

He could not think of anywhere else.

"I never celebrated them," was all he said.

She smiled.

"Of course."

In April, Lucien waited for Gabrielle. She was never late. Each minute that passed beyond the minute she was supposed to appear at the bottom of the slope in the woods, he stole a panicked glance at his digital watch, hoping that somehow the rigid digits would conjure Gabrielle for him. It was lighter now, the weather warming, and he could roll the sleeves on the eggshell-white button-down shirt Mama had brought to him recently, bring them all the way to the elbows.

His sleeves were tight on his skin. In the space between the fabric and his flesh, a sheen of sweat formed.

In eleven minutes, he needed to be at dinner. If Gabrielle came, they would hardly have any time to talk. Each week, he learned a little bit more about her. How she had two friends in school, Nina and Rama, and Rama wore something called a hijab, which meant she followed the

Muslim faith. Lucien had never seen one, but Gabrielle described it to him, the vibrant colors wrapping around her head. Rama was called a terrorist at school. This confused Lucien greatly.

"It's racist. Because there were Muslim people who flew the planes, all the assholes are blaming her for it. It's fucked."

It was like asking him about Christmas or about the planets he had never visited, and never would. For Gabrielle, he wanted to understand, to give her the answer that would satisfy her, that would part her lips and show him her teeth as she broke into another wave of laughter. He'd wanted nothing more in that moment, one week ago, but he could not unearth words that were not within him.

He felt confused and weak.

"Well, that's okay."

And now she wasn't coming at all. He had six minutes. It was time to run. Each week, he improved his sprint to the nutritional hall, remembering the branches, trunks, and concavities of the terrain like words on a page, like the sentences of *The Natural* that still came to him when he least expected them.

He was no longer afraid to stumble.

His right foot was in front of his left when he heard her cry across the woods, his name at that singsong pitch he knew all too well.

"Lucien!"

He spun.

"Lucien, wait!"

Gabrielle was running up the hill, breathing heavily. She bent over, both hands on her knees, huffing air. He fought the urge to keep looking at his watch.

"I just wanted . . ."

"It's okay, Gabrielle."

"I knew I'd be . . ." She was catching her breath, her face flushed with exhaustion. "I knew I'd be late, and I didn't want you to think I forgot. Go to dinner, okay? I'll tell you what happened next week."

"Tell me, please."

"It's okay. Just know I didn't forget."

"What happened?"

"Go to dinner."

"Please tell me."

"I'll tell you. Then you go."

"Yes."

"I came from Noah's service, Lucien. It was a service for him. I just wanted you to know."

"A service? That means—"

"Listen, I'll be all right. I'm getting through it. I didn't want to talk about it until now. They shipped him home. We can talk more about it next week. You can't be late. They will put you in the pit."

This was true. He was not so certain he could survive another night within total darkness. His dreams were finally beginning to fade, of the walls without light and the tombstones rising from the ash. He was no longer waking up in a sweat, his hands clawing the air. He was recovering.

"I just wanted you to know, Lucien, okay?"

What he didn't expect were the tears pushing out of his own eyes, these small, compressed drops that stung as he fought them away. He turned from her. He never knew Noah, only that he wanted to fight in a war.

"Please don't, okay? Go to dinner. I just wanted you to know it happened and I'll get through it. I wanted you to know."

"It's not right," he said.

"Nothing's right. Nothing is. You being here, Noah being . . . none of it is. But we'll talk more later, okay? I don't really have the energy for much more right now. I just wanted you to know. Go to dinner. Come next week. I'm sure you'll have stuff to tell me too."

After Gabrielle left, he ran faster than he ever had to the nutritional hall. He no longer cared whether he was late. He no longer cared

The Night Burns Bright

whether Jack locked the door on him and doomed him to the darkness, because whatever darkness he faced would not be the same as what Noah saw now. He knew nothing. What Noah looked like, sounded like, what it meant to carry a gun around Afghanistan—it was a void inside him, one that triggered a fresh electric rage that seized him, throttled him, launched him through the door and into the hall where the friends were not friends and the mentors were not mentors, only props he could erase with the flick of his trembling wrist. He did not remember holding his tray out and accepting the food. He did not remember sitting down, Antonio and Cavan greeting him, the fork shoveling peas into his mouth. He had felt none of this before. He could howl like a bloodthirsty coyote, gnash his teeth, beat his fists against the glass, and demand—demand what? And this was where the electricity began to leave him because his fury would always crash against the limits of what he knew, the vast worlds hidden from him, all occluded by these bright walls, the faces swimming to his right and left.

Gabrielle's words returned. *Nothing's right. Nothing is. You being here . . .*

But he always wanted to be here! And if he didn't, if somehow Gabrielle was right, where would he go? Outside was no better. The town didn't want him. There was no Mama in town.

Noah lived outside. Noah was dead.

Colt nudged him, asked if they had always drawn pictures of O. C. Leroux and what it was like to actually meet him. Lucien continued to eat. Antonio, who had been there the night of the bonfire, readily told the whole story.

He needed more time with Gabrielle. He needed her, and she, now, needed him. Why did being on time for dinner—not being late by a single minute—affect the outcome of the war that had killed Noah and would be coming to kill them all, according to Jack, unless they acted appropriately? Why must he eat his peas at the appointed time?

Jack had made him leave her.

165

Had Jack ever known someone like Gabrielle?

When he returned to his room, an hour before he was required to go to sleep, he saw Mama taking his drawings off the wall.

"Hi, Mama. What are you doing?"

"We aren't putting up drawings anymore, honey."

"Why?"

Her back had been to him, removing his favorite drawing with both colored and graphite pencil: Roy Hobbs, swinging his mighty bat, Wonderboy. She was looking at him now, the paper, like her face, suddenly crumpling. "What do you mean?"

"Why are you doing it?"

"Lucien, Lucien . . ." She moved toward him, her smile beginning to return. "What has gotten into you of late?"

"I just wanted to know."

"Don't I always do what's best for you?"

"Yes, Mama."

He watched as her hand closed around the drawing, crushing the paper like a white, dying star. When they first moved here, he had spent hours meticulously rendering Roy's face, the shadow under his chin, the pulse of muscle in his forearms. He wanted to make him as powerful as he imagined him to be, the savior of the downtrodden Knights. Every night, he glanced at the drawing before he went to sleep, proud that his pencil had made Roy real.

The paper was smaller and smaller in her hand.

"You know, I have another picture of yours to put up."

"You do?"

"Jack gave it to me."

She reached into a small green bag near her feet. Inside was a folder, and within the folder, now in her hand, was Lucien's drawing of O. C. Leroux. She applied clear tape to the back of the paper and placed it where Roy Hobbs had been.

He saw that all his drawings were now gone.

"Thanks, Mama."

"Of course. We just need to make sure we have the right drawings in front of us, the *important* ones. O. C. Leroux loves us. Your drawing is filled with that love, I can see it. And I want us to see that love every day."

Jack had said this too, that the face had been drawn with love. He understood what they meant, and he wanted, fully, to feel it. Love is the highest of all feelings, Jack said. We all must love one another.

Love was what you longed for when you were in the deepest of the dark, hoping for a way out. Love was what he begged for, his hands stinging from the lightless walls he struck in his mind, again and again, with the full force of his flesh.

Love, too, was the pit.

"I do see it."

"Good. Then we have nothing more to discuss. Are you ready for bed?"

"I'm going to go to bed early."

"That's a good boy. I'll be outside for a few minutes, and then I'll see you soon, right when you're ready to sleep."

"Mama," he said, his voice weaker. She was nearly out the door, past him with a quickness that still surprised him, even after a lifetime of her appearing and disappearing from rooms.

"Yes?"

"I have a question."

"Okay, Lucien. If it's about the drawing, we've already decided what to do."

"No, it's not. It's about something I saw."

"What did you see?"

"How come there was a mark on Samantha's mom's wrist and Evie's wrist but not other wrists? You don't have it. I don't have it. Is this something we should get? What does it mean?"

"A *mark*. That's a good question. Why do you want to know?"

"I only saw and I didn't know. I wasn't sure who to ask."

When he was younger, Mama could always stoop down to him, her hands falling softly on his shoulders as she brought her eyes down to meet his own. Now, when she wanted to stare into his eyes, she no longer had to move. He stood as tall as she did. He felt no larger in her presence than when he was five or six years old, tugged by her hand through the sun-dappled mornings and afternoons of the cottage.

She was now close to him. She smelled, faintly, like pine. "Lucien, there's nothing to worry about, certainly with us."

"Evie said she could go anywhere with it."

"Evie is . . . How can I say this, Lucien? She is a good girl and a good friend to you, and I am glad she was in the Meadows for so long. But Evie is not who you should be thinking about, okay, honey?"

"The mark, it had the letters *O. C.* Like O. C. Leroux."

"We all have important roles in this community. Me, you, Evie, Samantha's mother, Jack, and everyone else. That's all you need to know."

She leaned in, kissing him firmly on the forehead. "I want you to understand we are all doing what's best for you, always. Never forget that."

"I won't, Mama."

"I don't want you thinking about all this anymore. It's not important. Focus on the future."

"I will."

That night, he went to sleep in the room alone. At some point later, Mama came back, creaking on the bottom bunk. Samantha and her mother had not come back. When he woke up, his dreams blank, he saw that the bunk bed across from him was still empty. Mama was below him, asleep.

It was April, which meant a month until the maypole, and another month after that until summer. It had been a long time since he had last visited the library and the duck pond. In the bathroom, he leaned in to see himself in the mirror, saw more hairs overtaking his upper lip and chin, his eyes hazy from sleep. Usually, Samantha would be awake too, and he would go into the bathroom shortly before or after her. This was strange, going in alone. He heard a knock. He told the knocker to come in.

Magnus entered, holding his toothbrush. Lucien turned the faucet on for him.

Brown water, the color of his feces, spilled out.

"Again? Wow," Magnus said.

"The water is bad."

"It was bad like this before. They'll fix it."

"They probably will."

Magnus frowned. "Probably? *Of course* they will."

"They will."

"Yes."

The dark water pooled in the sink.

"Did your parents put your O. C. Leroux picture up on the wall in your room?" Lucien asked.

"They did. Just last night. I was really excited. I had no idea Jack liked it so much. He gave it to them and they put it right up."

"Mine went up too."

"Yours was really good. I'm not so great at drawing."

"Thanks."

Lucien turned the water off. He glanced down at Magnus's wrists to see if a mark was on either one. They were both clear. Whatever the marks meant, they had not come for Magnus.

———

Samantha was not at instruction or in the nutritional hall. Lucien could not find her on the commons. Jack did not say where she had gone. At dinner, he asked the friends if they knew anything.

"I don't know. I haven't seen her," Antonio said.

"She's gone today, I suppose," Maia said.

He remembered how Evie had changed, the way she'd yelled at him, the darkening of her face when he asked her a question. No one else seemed to care that Evie was seen less and that, when she did appear, she hardly talked to them. Didn't the friends miss her like he missed her? Didn't they see her wrist? Mama had not answered him. This was either because she did not know the answer or she was concealing what she had learned.

He wished he knew which was true.

"Samantha? I don't know either," Cavan said, shoveling string beans into his mouth. "We'll see her tomorrow, probably. Wherever she is, it must be pretty important. Maybe she gets to meet with O. C. Leroux too."

"She was there every night, and now her and her mom aren't. I just wonder," Lucien said.

"They'll be back," Antonio said.

"I hope they don't change, like Evie."

"I was told Evie was real bad and that's why."

"Bad, how?"

"I don't know. But that's what my dad heard."

When Lucien walked the commons after instruction, Antonio's words looping through him—*Evie was real bad*—he noticed men in hard hats were building new portions of the wall. A foundation had been laid many feet beyond the front, halfway around the perimeter of House of Earth itself. The foundation reached close to his favorite entry point in the woods, the clearing where he bounded down to meet Gabrielle each week.

Once the wall was done, he would have nowhere to wander to, no woods to reach. He placed his hand on the cool cement, looking up to the top. It was at least several times his own height. He pressed his shoulder to it, to see if it would give. The wall was strong, and why wouldn't it be? A war was there, somewhere, beyond it.

He tried to imagine what it would be like when the ends of the wall touched each other, like a snake kissing its own tail.

At nightfall, he walked to the habitation facility, alone. He was getting used to Mama coming in as he slept. Without a book to read or TV to watch, he could try to talk to Samantha, Samantha's mother, or simply fall asleep. This time, when he pushed the door to Room 8 open, he heard no one. No laughter and no tears. Forcing the door fully open, he saw that their bunk beds were empty. Usually, Samantha left her sheets and blanket unmade, waiting until she was about to go to sleep to straighten them. Both beds were now tightly made.

When he was much younger, Mama would take him on vacation to motels. The way Samantha and her mother's beds were made up, the sheets crisp and untouched, reminded him of those long-ago beds. He glided his fingertip over the blankets, folded tightly across the sheets. At some point during the day, when he was at instruction or on the commons or in the nutritional hall, this was done.

He lay on his top bunk, his eyes squeezed tight, and tried to sleep.

What made Evie bad? Why had Samantha's mother been crying? If he could just answer these questions, he could ease this low hum growing inside him, a hum that he now perceived as a new strain of fear, unlike what had seized him in the pit, when he'd believed the darkness would be all he ever saw again. If he could just *know*, the hum would fade away. He could go back to how he was before Evie yelled at him and he saw the mark on her wrist and Mama ripped his drawings from the wall. Before, even, this habitation facility, which he wanted to love like the cottage but never could. He could never say this to anyone. It hurt even to consider it and what it meant for his future, that the past would always be something he grasped toward, unconsciously or not.

Samantha and her mother were not back in the morning. Mama was awake before him, looking through her drawer for a top to wear.

He rubbed his eyes and rolled over toward the edge of the bed, looking out to the sunlight, almost white between the curtains. She heard him and looked up.

"Good morning."

"Good morning, Mama."

He sat on the edge of the bed, his feet dangling. When he'd first moved here, the bunk bed had seemed impossibly high. Now, with spring's approach, he could jump down from it easily and climb right back.

"How was your sleep?"

"It was good."

"You seemed peaceful. Nothing fitful."

"I hardly remember what I dreamed."

"Good."

Bent over the small oval mirror that adorned their drawer, Mama was applying a light cream to her face. He watched her, as he always had, and considered how little she had changed while he, since she gave birth to him, had grown so much larger, from a baby into a boy—a boy about to become a *teenager*, as Jack said.

Did the way she saw him account for all this change?

"Mama?"

"Yes, Lucien."

"Are Samantha and Samantha's mother coming back?"

"Oh, honey, let's not talk about that. You need to focus on instruction today. Jack, I hear, has a very important lesson for you."

"Where have they gone?"

Mama stopped rubbing cream on her face and turned to face him. She looked up at him, from where he sat on the bunk bed, and something about this asymmetry shook him, urged him to leave the bed and jump down to look at her as he should. He did this, his bare feet smacking the floor, the impact stinging his soles more than he believed it would.

Mama stood, unmoving. "Sometimes people have to leave. You shouldn't worry about it."

"I'm not worried, Mama."

"Now that you're old enough, you will understand things sometimes happen and they're for the best. House of Earth is protecting us from many bad things."

"I know it is."

"They happen for a reason, Lucien. They happen because O. C. Leroux loves us and is watching out for us. You especially. This picture . . ." She gestured to his drawing of O. C. Leroux's face, now taped to the wall alone. "I can see the love that radiates from it. I can see *your* love, Lucien, and his."

"Yes, I know."

"Everything—it always happens for a reason, honey. Okay? They had to go."

He nodded silently and she took him in her arms. It was almost breakfast, then instruction, then play, then instruction, then dinner. In a few days, he could see Gabrielle again. Mama held him close, his face muzzled in her shoulder.

At breakfast, he saw Evie eating alone as he was getting his tray of porridge from Anders, Antonio's father. He hurried for his spoon and then for her, not sure exactly what he could say. He wanted to ask her about what Mama had said. He wanted to ask her about the mark on her wrist and tell her he had seen the same one on Samantha's mother and now she was gone.

He could warn Evie.

Warn her of what?

He didn't speak to Evie. When they reached instruction, Jack said today was going to be a very special instruction day, on the commons.

"It's such a beautiful day, isn't it?"

They all agreed.

"Lucien, Maia, you can come with me. We're going to need you to carry the *equipment*."

They looked at each other and then back at Jack. Jack pointed to them and they stood, following him out of the room.

"Everyone, wait for me to return. Maia and Lucien will meet you on the commons."

They walked behind Jack in silence, out of the instruction building and around on the grass, toward the woods and the habitation facilities. Jack stopped in front of a large, sunken shed that Lucien knew well.

They all did. It was where they'd slept the night of the sled race, when the cold had punished him, his hands and feet beyond feeling. Jack had turned out the light and he'd trembled in the dark, his teeth rattling in his mouth. He remembered hugging himself for warmth, rocking on hard cement, the cold closing his throat.

They all froze. And then it was morning.

"We're getting those two big old vinyl sacks inside. You see them, the mint-green color?"

Jack pointed again and he saw. This was the first time Lucien had entered the shed since that night, and he was surprised to see how much smaller it really was, the ceiling not much higher than his head. When Jack had brought them there in the snowstorm, it had seemed immense, like sleeping inside the belly of a whale. The absence of light only enlarged it further, lending it the dimension of myth. Now, on a warm April day, he was walking through it, grabbing a vinyl sack.

The sack was heavy in his hands, slung over his shoulder. Maia seemed to be struggling with hers as well.

"Nice and easy, friends. Take these over to the commons, and we'll meet you there."

Jack walked away and they were alone, tugging the bags over their shoulders to the commons, which was only a few minutes away but would be much farther with the pounds of equipment. Jack had never

said what it was for, only a lesson, and they had to trust in its importance and their own for being asked to ferry it there.

Maia exhaled, her forehead caking with sweat. "He's got us carrying
rocks?"

"I don't know."

"I'm excited, but these are very heavy."

"They are."

He could hear the rattling of objects, the shifting of larger and
smaller pieces within the bag. Near the commons, they stopped to rest,
setting the bags down at their feet. A monarch butterfly flew past them,
weaving between the trees and disappearing behind them.

"Beautiful," Maia said.

"It is."

"My dad sees them a lot, over by the booth."

Maia's father stood in the guard booth now, at the front of House
of Earth. He heard the wall's construction each day.

"I like monarchs a lot," Lucien said.

Maia glanced right, then left. "I wanted to ask you—you're in
Samantha's room, right? Room 8?"

"Yes."

"She's really gone."

"I haven't seen her in a while."

"She never told me where she was going. She would've told me. I
thought she would've, if she was leaving . . ."

"My mom says it all happens for a reason, that O. C. Leroux does
it for a reason."

"What did he do, do you think?"

"I don't know. I wish I knew. I wish harder every day I knew more."

"I know the feeling, Lucien."

"Her mom is gone too. The beds are empty. They were made like
they were in a motel room, like no one had ever been there."

"It could be like when Kaitlyn left, except I know Samantha didn't do anything wrong. I know her. She was always so good in instruction. She respected the planet. She told me how she looked out for any ant she might step on—she didn't want to step on any, and we all do, by accident, it just happens, but it never happened with her."

"I get worried sometimes."

"I do too."

"Samantha and Samantha's mom, and Evie."

"I see her so little."

"Have you seen what's on her wrist?"

"Her wrist? No."

"She had a mark. And Samantha's mom had the same one."

"I didn't, no."

"It was small and in black. It said *O. C.*, like O. C. Leroux."

"He marked them, maybe, but why?"

"I'm realizing, every day, how much more there is to know. But my mom doesn't want us worrying about it. She said to focus on the lesson today."

"I'm not worried. I'd just like to know too. If Samantha and her mom left, why didn't they tell me?"

"They probably wanted to."

Lucien didn't know this, but it sounded better when he said it out loud. He could hope they chose to leave and would return when they also chose, like taking a long, lazy hike in the woods. Deep in the woods was a river, and they could have gone there. Once, Jack had taken the Meadows to the river, pointing out the striped bass that swam in the clear, rushing waters. He said there were people, bad people, who caught and ate the fish, disregarding their souls and causing them great pain. Samantha and Samantha's mother weren't doing that. They were there, he hoped, just kneeling at the riverbank, the water glittering around their fingers.

"Yes," Maia replied.

They were walking again, heaving the bags over their shoulders. The friends were gathering on the commons with Jack, who was standing over them, his hands on his hips. Lucien was as tall as Mama, but he was not nearly as tall as Jack. It was possible he never would be. He considered, briefly, what this meant, then let the thought slide out of him.

"Samantha would like this," Maia whispered in his ear.

"She would."

Out of breath, they lowered the bags to the grass near the friends, flinching at the thud the unknown objects made when they collided with one another inside. The friends huddled around the bags, hoping for a glimpse of what was within.

"Thank you, Maia. Thank you, Lucien," Jack said. "You may now unpack the bags."

Lucien reached into his bag, and Maia reached into hers. First he felt a long wooden object, and he pulled at it, realizing there were, in fact, several of the same variety. In the light, he saw they were large wooden sticks, rounded at the top, a white handle at the bottom. Feeling along the stick, his finger glided over several slats and leather strips. There were at least six of these sticks in his bag. All of it was puzzling to him. He could not guess what Jack wanted them to do.

"Oh, I know what that is. I've seen these when I used to watch TV," Colt said. "These, uh, Japanese swords, what are they called—"

"Kendo," Jack said. "A traditional martial art, native to Japan. We're going to be training ourselves physically."

"All right, I'm ready," Antonio said.

The other friends eyed their swords excitedly. Jack said they were made from bamboo and were very special.

"We're going to learn how to sword fight?" Jacinda asked.

"We are going to train ourselves," Jack said again. "Kendo strengthens the mind, body, and spirit. You're going to be wielding your swords, or *shinai*, as they are known, to prepare yourselves."

"For the war?" Magnus asked.

"Yes. Unfortunately, O. C. Leroux has told me we need to be ready at any moment. There has been a great deal of chaos beyond House of Earth, and the war gets closer every day. Outside these walls, in the town and elsewhere, they know we are a powerful community. They are learning about what we've built. Since they are committed to killing the earth, they must hurt us to do that. So while we enjoy ourselves here, we must be increasingly serious and aware of the threats. O. C. wants us to be thinking about them all the time. By being always ready, we are physically and mentally ready—today, this is training."

"How close is the war now?" Antonio asked. "I try to listen for it at night."

"You won't hear it yet, Antonio. But you might soon."

Gabrielle lived in the town, and she had never mentioned a war there, unless Jack was referring to the Afghanistan war, the one where Noah went to die. He did not know how far Afghanistan really was, only that it lay across the ocean, which he'd seen in the atlas he'd kept at the cottage. He assumed it was many thousands of miles away. So the war was now moving here, to this land? To Mater? Gabrielle would tell him if that was true. In a few days, he would ask her.

Jack took the shinai in his two hands. He held the long bamboo sword in front of him, perpendicular to the ground, then pointed it diagonally, in the direction of the friends. They took this as his signal to grab their own shinai. Lucien gripped the bamboo, which was heavier than he expected it to be, and mirrored Jack's stance. The others were doing the same.

"I want you all to practice striking. Like this." Jack stepped forward, swinging the shinai over his head and then down hard, slicing the air.

Lucien and the friends raised the shinai and sliced as hard as they could.

"Good. Now, keep going for a few minutes. Then we'll pair up."

Lucien swung and swung and swung. The action lulled him as much as it tired him, a repetitive strain of the muscles in his biceps he was not used to feeling. His body was metronomic, set to a rhythm that Jack, now holding his shinai at his side, had devised. Maia was to the right of him, Antonio to the left, and their shinai crashed through the space in front of them like the war had surged from the grass to meet them right there, where they bellowed into the air.

"Keep going," Jack said. "Keep it up."

The sun was high in the sky, beams of light exploding out, and Lucien understood why it was a star, the titanic power it held. He kept peeking at the sun as he swung. His breaths were short, sweat pooling on his back. Jack was still watching them.

"Let's go. Almost done."

Magnus had to stop first. Colt was next. They were breathing heavily, the shinai at their feet. Lucien, his arms ignoring the fire in his muscles, continued to swing.

"Now, we will pair up."

Jack began pointing with his left hand, his right still clutching the shinai. He told Lucien to pair with Magnus. Maia was with Antonio. The rest of the friends, whom Jack had singled out with his gesture, found those nearby.

"I want you all to practice striking your friend's shinai. You go one at a time, ten times. Hold your shinai, like so, at a diagonal. At ten strikes, you will switch."

"Do you want to go first?" Magnus asked Lucien.

"Sure."

Just as before, Lucien held the shinai over his head, his slick hands trembling with its weight and pressure. He grunted when the bamboo struck Magnus's shinai, the impact reverberating in his bones, the crack loud in his ears. Magnus shuffled in place, staying upright. Lucien reared back and struck again. All around him were the cracks of bamboo, the cries of the friends as they made contact. Jack was surveying them, his shinai still at his side.

"A few more," Jack said.

As Lucien swung his arms up and back for his seventh strike, he saw a shadow flitting across the commons. It was moving quickly, a shadow attached to a body, one with flailing arms and thin legs and light hair splayed at the shoulders, whipping with the strain of flight. His shinai falling, he turned to catch who this was running as fast as he had ever seen across the commons, straight for the new wall that guarded House of Earth's entryway.

His head had turned completely by the time his shinai smacked against Magnus's bamboo, the sound fading in his mind, receding in the wake of what was, undeniably, in front of him: Evie, running as fast as she could.

Evie, her lips crooked, one arm outstretched, a light cry from her mouth. She was close now, almost past them, not looking their way or any way other than at the wall that lay just beyond the oval. Lucien's shinai was pointed to the grass, unwilling to rise for the eighth strike.

When he opened his mouth to call for her, he saw the side of her face, a tendril of blood dripping from her brow to her chin, fresh and bright.

"Evie!"

She did not turn around and could not turn around because she was running from someone, another body larger and faster than her own. Sebastian was across the commons, his feet thudding on the soil, the corners of his mouth upturned. Evie was dashing on the oval, gravel spraying from her shoes.

The blood had rolled beyond her chin, to her cotton shirt twisting in the wind. One drop, then two, stars of shining red on white, her legs near the wall now, Maia's father sleepily turning from his booth.

Sebastian was faster. He was close to her, his arms spreading wide. Jack was watching too, the shinai leaning against his leg. The friends began to turn, trying to see what he saw, drawn as much to his own cry of her name as the two bodies converging, the large prepared to swallow the small.

Lucien began running toward her. "Evie!"

Sebastian seized her, both arms tightening around her stomach, lifting her into the air. He was carrying her across the oval, his feet sliding on gravel. Lucien saw the blood dripping from her chin to her shirt to Sebastian's hair-lined forearms, shining with sweat. Sebastian was bigger and Jack was bigger and House of Earth was bigger, and even if he grew beyond Mama's height, what could he do but stand here, in this grass with his bamboo sword and call her name, again and again?

Evie. Evie. Evie. Evie. Evie. Evie.

"Evie!"

He felt an enormous pressure around his mouth, his head wrenched downward. His breath caught in his throat and would not escape. There was an arm around him, a hand and an arm, and he was being pulled down and away. The shinai fell to the grass.

"You will not yell," Jack said.

Lucien's eyes hurried above, to the hand that belonged to Jack now smothering what was left of his face. Soon he would stop breathing. Soon he would meet the darkness.

"You will not yell. Understood?"

There was a release, and Lucien's head pitched forward, the ground rising to meet him. He heaved, pressing both hands to the grass, trying to regain his balance and vision.

Magnus was blinking at him, not saying anything. The other friends had stopped their practice.

Sebastian held Evie to his chest, his mouth in her hair. He carried her back to the habitation facility. He ignored the blood pooling in the crook of his arm. Evie's legs kicked right and left, into the air and nowhere.

Lucien saw that Jack was looking straight at him.

A scream broke open the silence. It came from Evie's mouth, the blood dripping at her upper lip, Sebastian clutching her tighter as he pulled her away from the commons, into the shadows. Lucien was on his knees, his hands clawing at grass, tearing at it. A door opened in the habitation facility, a building he did not live in, and they were gone.

He closed his eyes.

"Everyone, please line up, single file, with your shinai," Jack said. "Except you, Lucien."

He could only think of Evie running across the commons, the blood dripping down her face. The scream was locked within him. He could feel its reverberations still, a sound to shake bone. He was struggling to breathe, as if Jack's hands were still around his mouth.

The friends lined up as Jack commanded. Jack stood between Lucien and all the friends. "Lucien, please put down your shinai."

He did as he was told. He could hardly hear Jack's voice, the memory of Evie's scream still loud in his ears. The bamboo sword fell at his feet.

"The war, every day, gets closer. I say this a lot. But what does it mean? What does it really mean?"

Jack was addressing all the friends, the shinai in his hand. He smiled at Lucien and turned away again.

"We have to be ready," Cavan said hesitantly, the last syllable swallowed in his mouth.

"What we have here—this community, this harmony—none of it is guaranteed to survive. You are old enough to see this now. The world is filled with a growing darkness. Wars, famine, disease. A new war coming for us, with the planet itself at stake. It's all very fragile, and if we aren't doing all we can—if we are living in darkness instead of light, if we choose to ignore what O. C. Leroux has shown us—we will suffer. There is a reason our community has thrived as much as it has. It's because most of you have lived in this light, have put the planet first, have put *harmony* first over your own individual needs. This, in the end, will be what saves us and saves everyone else. O. C. Leroux understands this, and it's why he built House of Earth."

Jack paused, his hand raised in the air. "Part of this struggle to build a future, a sustainable future, is ensuring the darkness doesn't infect us. It's casting it out wherever we see it. What you saw before—I want you to forget it. That's a person who has been bad. Sebastian will help her and guide her, as will O. C. Leroux. Bad people can be good. But sometimes, the badness—this darkness—is stronger. Much stronger. And when it is, we have to think about the community too. We have to weigh our survival, the planet's survival, against this darkness. You are not to say her name anymore, okay? Not without my permission. Is that understood?"

The friends all replied with loud, clear yeses. Lucien's lips moved, but no sound came out of them.

"I do not want this to happen more, because it makes me very sad. It makes O. C. Leroux very sad. You have all grown here and made such wonderful strides. I see it every day, in your answers at instruction, your artwork, even your play. So many of you are on the right path. So many of you are an example O. C. Leroux is so proud of. His vision for House of Earth was like this, and it's up to us to fully *realize* it, to be the very best we can be. Because if we aren't, we will be hurt. We will suffer. I say this word a lot, *suffer*, but sometimes we forget what it means. It means hurt and pain, of course. It means losing everything that matters to you. It means the darkness is winning, has won."

Jack pivoted now, back to Lucien. He pointed a finger straight at his heart. "There is great light in you, Lucien. And, it hurts me to say this, darkness in you too. We saw how drawn you were today to what we saw, how you called out for another friend of ours consumed by what seeks to destroy us. You are not yet her. We do not want to forget your name. Do we?"

The friends murmured a medley of noes and unidentifiable sighs.

"We want to save Lucien. We want him with us for a long time. He, like you, is very important to the future of House of Earth. But we also can't let dark energy grow. If the war comes to our wall, if the war comes *over* the wall and you are all in the fight for your survival, if the very future of House of Earth is threatened and therefore the *planet's* future—if all of this comes to pass, our worst fears"—Jack paused for a moment, hunting for the words he wanted, those with the proper weight—"and you still have not conquered the darkness within and walked in the path of O. C. Leroux's light, the only outcome is destruction. Death. You are old enough to hear this now. You know life can be cut very short. Naturally. And unnaturally. We can't allow this to happen. *Lucien*"—Jack was staring directly at him, both hands curling around his shinai—"please approach here. I want you to face your partner, Magnus, at the front of the line. Look into Magnus's eyes. And you, Magnus, look into Lucien's."

Lucien inched forward, standing several feet from Magnus. Magnus's gaze wandered up and down, avoiding Lucien. His eyes moved back briefly, and Lucien saw they were a shade that blended gray and blue, a pale color that reminded him of the smooth rock below the river's surface.

"Lucien, we saw how you called out before to a person with a dark, destructive energy, a person who has, sadly, resisted help from Sebastian. We saw how you were *drawn* to such an energy. That is not good, and it means that energy is within you too. It means you are threatened, and we are as well. You can change. But it won't be easy."

Jack strode to Magnus's side, touching him on his back. "Magnus, I want you to strike Lucien. I want you to do as you were doing before, but this time you must strike his body. Lucien, you must keep your hands at your sides."

"I have to—I have to hit him?"

"Yes, Magnus. We are helping Lucien."

"Okay."

Magnus held the shinai in front of him. He no longer could look anywhere near Lucien's face. His right hand, just above his left, was trembling on the bamboo. Lucien tensed, awaiting the impact of whatever was to come. He could still hear Evie's scream, how it cut inside him, like an incision into bare flesh. He wondered whether the friends felt like he did.

"Magnus, now. I don't want to see darkness in you too."

Magnus raised his shinai and swung it down on Lucien's left shoulder, the bamboo making a low, sick thud against his bone. The pain was strange and immediate, a wildfire through his body. His knees buckled, one crashing to the grass. He looked up at Magnus. Jack, unlike Magnus, was smiling.

"One more time."

As Lucien stood, Magnus swung again, crushing Lucien's right shoulder. He gasped from the impact, his mouth flailing open. Both knees dug into the grass. His hands shook in front of him, as if they were straining to escape the body on fire.

"Antonio, you're next."

He saw Antonio shake his head—or almost shake his head—before he raised his shinai and smashed Lucien on the plane of his back, missing his spine by inches.

"Stand, Lucien."

Somehow he stood.

"Now, Cavan."

The shinai smashed him on the right side again, rolling down the front of his body. Once more he fell. He was shaking. He was beginning to taste blood.

"Jacinda."

He threw his hands up to block the bamboo, feeling the crack of bone just below the skin of his forearms. Reeling backward, he collapsed again to one knee. The air had been torn from him, and he could only stare into the grass, the pain driving him deeper into himself.

"Lucien! You are not supposed to move your hands."

He felt Jack's hand on his neck, tugging him upward. He did not know how much longer he could stand. Each second burned him. He tasted blood and tried to focus there, on the flow of his own blood through his teeth.

"Jacinda, one more time. Lucien, do *not* move."

The bamboo blasted the side of his body, driving into his rib cage. He could see Jacinda as he fell away, her expressionless face fading into the sunlight. He heard Jack tell him to stand, but he could not, the command beyond him, the pain scorching him. There was no part of him that did not hurt. Jack was calling more names, Jayson and Carlina and Karthik, and the bamboo fell hard again on a body curled like a shattered embryo on the flattened grass. He heard Colt, and the bamboo came from the sky and crushed the top of his skull. He was wrong. *This* was the last part of him that still needed to hurt, the head that held his galaxy of thought and memory. Roy Hobbs had been shot, a bullet to his stomach, and this was like that, he reasoned, each strike from above a bullet to his body. He heard Maia, Jack uttering her name, and Maia making a sound that was not like the other sounds. Jack said she had to do it. Maia was shaking, the shinai hardly held at all. Another shadow marched across the grass, across time, and Lucien could see a man much larger than him. Dad, Maia said, and the man was cupping Maia's face, telling her this was *right* and she had to do *what was best* and Lucien could hear the words *light* and *dark* and knew both pertained to him, that he was very sick now, that he would not escape this and if the pit was the absence of all, this was its opposite, burning bright, too much of everything, his lips wet with blood.

"Do it, Maia."

He heard her begin to cry and saw, through the broken light, her body still suspended above his. Her father was pointing. Jack had crossed his arms. *We are trying to help him. By doing this, you are helping your friend—you are saving him.* Jack's voice was distant, like it was underwater or locked behind glass. *Help Lucien.*

He did not see the bamboo smack his back, the lightest blow so far. He still felt the pain of other strikes, Maia's a pale echo of what came from Colt and Carlina and everyone else.

"Again!"

It was the familiar sound of sobbing. Someone, somewhere, always seemed to be crying. The bamboo came hard now, and he seized with fresh pain, a bolt across his spine. That was two from Maia.

"Again!"

She was crying as she struck him a third time, hitting the convexity of flesh where hip met thigh. He would be thankful for this, her relatively safe choice on his body, had the other blows not come, the dozen from the friends already.

Jack seemed to understand what she had done. "Again! You are *saving* Lucien."

The bamboo drove into the other side of his rib cage. He could not comprehend standing up again, telling the annihilated skeleton to move up or down, right or left. The blood was pooling in his mouth, inching down a chin now dug into the grass.

It all hurt so much. He did not have the strength to cry.

"Again, Maia! *Save* Lucien."

He was sure this time he felt her tears. That was all he knew, the tickle of her teardrop on his open skin. The rest was lost in the crashing against his skull, where Maia had finally struck, and the blackness behind his eyes.

———

The light, like everything else, hurt him. He was swimming upward, from the well of a swollen dark, reconstructing what he had been, the pieces of self like shards of glass trying to fit together.

One eye was open, then the other.

He felt the coolness on the infinite plane of his forehead.

"There you go, honey. There you go."

His fingers inched in place, as did his toes. He turned his neck slightly to the right, to the voice above him.

"Easy now."

His mind formed the word before his mouth, aching shut, could make the sound. *Mama.* His arms burned and his shoulder burned and his back burned and he remembered why and he wanted to go back to wherever he just was, the time beyond memory. He wanted to go back to sleep. His lips cracked open, the taste of blood dulled. A soft cry left him.

"Easy, Lucien. Don't move too much now."

Mama was above him. The coolness, he saw, was some kind of ice. There was light from the window, so it must be day. He didn't know what day. Pain gripped him. It came with each breath, each tick forward of time. He began to roll over and stopped, a shooting sensation in his shoulder pushing him back onto his back.

Every time he inhaled, it hurt him more.

"It's good to see you awake. You had a long night."

"Night?" he groaned. The word felt brittle and alien in his teeth.

"You've been asleep since yesterday. It was hard to see you like that. But Jack loves you very much. We all do."

"Jack . . ."

He saw the bamboo sword, the shinai, falling against him again and again, Jack crying out for another strike. The blood had dried in his mouth, but he tasted it again, how it rolled through his teeth as each friend reared back to beat him. Maia. He remembered her too, Jack urging her to hit him, telling her she would save him. And Maia's father. The memory was an assault on a mind still reassembling itself in the sickly light from outside.

The bunk beds across from him were still empty. Samantha and her mother were really gone.

"Jack loves you, okay? And I do too. You shouldn't have called out like that. You need to listen to him."

The words were a soup in his mouth. His jaw was like wet cement. He had too much to say, and all of it could not become real, no matter how hard he strained.

"Evie," he said.

Mama's expression began to change.

"Lucien, you do *not* say that name. Do you understand? Jack told you not to say it, and you are choosing now not to listen. That's not how I raised you. It's not what House of Earth expects from you. Nothing here is guaranteed. You are old enough to know that. This place, all we have, our blessings, our place in a community that will survive the war and build the future this planet needs—none of it, Lucien, is guaranteed."

It occurred to him, even in his daze, that Mama sounded just like Jack. That they had sounded alike for a long time. That whatever he heard from Jack, he heard from Mama, and that the reverse was true too. They could be speaking as one person to him. This had always strengthened his conviction that they were right, had to be right.

Evie was screaming in his head.

Evie was bleeding. Evie was hurt. Whatever was going to happen, Evie didn't want it to happen.

"Evie . . ."

He felt a pinching around his lips, the tender skin crushed shut. Mama was holding them closed, her eyes small and dark. Despite his effort, he looked directly into them.

"You do not say that name. She's a bad girl and she could not accept the love and help offered to her. Sebastian loved her very much, as a father would, and she could not love him back. Isn't that terrible? Are you going to yell out for her now? Imagine if you loved me so much and I hardly loved you back at all. O. C. loved her too. She was filled with too much darkness, that one—I knew it from early on. I knew it from when you two were little. She is the type of person who is hurting our planet. Its survival, and ours, means nothing to her. She is the type of person who could grow up to destroy House of Earth."

Mama still held his lips shut. He watched her, how the dimensions of her face, once so familiar to him, seemed to shift each time he blinked.

He was ever more aware of how little he knew.

"You rest now, Lucien. Know I still love you and I'm still proud of you, despite what happened yesterday. Jack loves you too. We want to help you. You must keep following him, because that means you are following O. C. He loves you most of all."

Mama released his lips. He gasped for air, his nostrils too crusted with mucus or dried blood to breathe as he normally would. She was smiling at him again. "Now you rest. Tomorrow, you can go back to instruction."

"Tomorrow . . ."

"Yes."

He remembered—today he was supposed to meet Gabrielle. He needed to find a way to the woods. On his back he squirmed, trying to force himself upward. He nearly sat up, feeling the deep bruises that had formed all over him, both visible and hidden.

"Lie back down. You need more rest. I will come for you later."

"I want to—I want to go out."

"Tomorrow. You need to rest. I will be back for you later, okay?"

"Okay."

"Put the ice back on your head."

He heard the door close and Mama was gone. From the light in the window, he could discern it was sometime in the late morning or early afternoon. He wanted to know the time, and his watch was no longer on his wrist. Turning his head, the cables of pain pulled taut within his neck, he saw that Mama had laid his watch out on the drawer. The digits were hidden in the reflection the light created from the window. He was, for the moment, timeless.

All he wanted to do was see Gabrielle. He didn't even know exactly what he would tell her, how much or how little. She would know enough by looking at him.

That he could do, with the unknowable time he had. He would look in the mirror.

Easing one foot toward the ladder of his bunk bed, he gingerly turned over, lying on his stomach. His body felt like it had been compressed between two enormous plates of metal, every part of him crushed together. The throbbing in his skull increased as his feet reached the ladder and he began the once-familiar descent to the floor. He took stock of what he had: no bone, somehow, had been broken. Everywhere bruises, aches, flares of pain that emerged by the second, but no breaks. He had thought, before, that there had been one. One foot followed the other down the ladder.

On the flat surface, he groaned. The throb in his skull had consumed his forehead, making it hard to concentrate. He teetered, gripping the frame of the bunk bed. He decided he needed to be in the bathroom, where he could run water on his face. Turning, he shuffled slowly. His hand felt the doorknob and turned.

The hallway was empty and he was thankful. The friends were probably at instruction. The adults, elsewhere. With one hand on the wall, he inched along, reaching the empty bathroom. He flicked the light switch, but the light would not turn on. The electricity was gone again. From a foggy back window, enough sunlight slanted into the bathroom for him to make his way to the sink. Without looking up, he turned on the faucet and breathed out when clear water emerged.

He would have that. They would let him have that.

Washing his face and slurping water—he hadn't realized, until now, how thirsty he was—he still wouldn't look up. He could feel how his face changed, where the bamboo had struck and where the swelling and bruising begun. Seeing himself in the mirror would be a confirmation of all that had happened yesterday, hardening the terror into an unshakable reality, a memory he would never lose. Once he saw his face, there was no going back.

The water was cold and clear. He continued to drink, in big gulps now, the water dripping through his fingers. The throbbing eased. He began to splash water on his face, feeling how the droplets rolled down his skin, mingling with stale sweat. Soon he would have to look.

Questions trilled through him. Why was Evie bleeding? Where had Sebastian taken her? What had he done to her?

Where was Samantha? Samantha's mother?

Why were they bad? Why was he bad?

He watched water slip between his fingers. For so long, he had been sure that all that Jack and Mama told him, collectively, was true, that they had learned the essence of the world to pass on to him and the friends. O. C. Leroux could not be wrong. Outside, there was violence and war and destruction of the planet. Inside, peace. He was protected. He was loved. But he was struggling, the water still slipping through his fingers and the pain in his limbs flaring from where each friend had struck him, to see it all as they saw it, light against darkness. He did once see, or thought he did—now, curled over the sink in the semi-dark, he was having a harder time making their vision his own, as he always did. It was like slipping on a mask that became his face, or slipping on a mask before he had ever even formed a face to hide. The mask was slipping in his fingers. A face had taken shape. The face was not fitting.

He looked up in the mirror and saw himself.

His right eye was blackened, his nose and lips swollen, patches of his skin reddened. On his cheek, he would have a scar. Still, it was all him, and he was less horrified than he'd thought he would be. He recognized what he saw. The beating had not taken away who he was.

Now he would have to find out the time.

The walk back was quicker as he adjusted to the new limitations of his body, the way he held his hip to avoid pain, the barking of muscle in his back. He was less dizzy, sturdy enough to stand upright as he opened the door. His watch waited on the drawer.

He saw it was 4:41.

If he left now, at the pace he moved, he could just make it. In that moment, with the excitement coursing through him, there was nothing that mattered more than seeing her. He pushed his body away from the desk and back out into the hallway, heading toward the light of the building's front door.

Clouds were rolling across the sky. He guessed rain was coming, a late-afternoon shower. Looking out to the commons, he saw it was empty, the collectives at instruction. He would have only a few minutes before they came out because he usually met Gabrielle just after the lesson ended. He did not want to see anyone else. Not Antonio, not Magnus, not Cavan. Not even Maia. Maia, who he remembered last, the sword cracking his skull. He had to remember she thought she was doing what was best for him or was striking him because her father and Jack were standing there, urging her on. One part of himself told him not to blame Maia, that were he put in her position—Mama and Jack telling him to swing the shinai—he would have to listen. This was inarguable.

Yet there was the rage, dull now, that he couldn't ignore, that seemed to grow with each step he took through the grass. He had been beaten. All he had done was call out a name. This fact, the fact of her name, her life, kept looping through him, and he would not forget, no matter what Mama or Jack told him.

Evie. He had called her name.

He needed to know where she had gone.

When he reached the clearing in the woods, he heard the friends spilling out onto the commons. If he didn't move quickly, they would see him. He grabbed at a tree trunk and pulled himself into the woods, pushing off again for extra momentum. At the slope, he picked up speed, his legs aching from the effort. The throbbing in his forehead, which had begun to dissipate minutes earlier, returned with a vicious-ness he didn't expect. Halfway down the slope, he fell to the leaves, sitting in their coolness. Gabrielle would be here soon. He could wait and she would see him. He tried to catch his breath.

Gabrielle knew now not to call his name when she saw him. She was more furtive, understanding, through his language, their meetings carried a significance beyond what either of them quite understood. She emerged as a patch of color against the trees, gaining size as she approached. From his seated position, he waved. He watched as her smile melted away. She was jogging now, the leaves flying up around her white sneakers.

"Gabrielle."

"What the hell happened to you?"

She was kneeling beside him, staring furiously into his face.

"It was . . . we were practicing martial arts and—"

"I'll kill them, whoever did this."

"You can't."

"I can and I will. Tell me. One week I'm gone and you look like you were boxing with Mike Tyson."

"Mike Ty-sun?"

"Forget it. Another reference that's meaningless in your school. You look bad. Does your mom care? Did your mom beat you?"

"No."

"Your teachers? Who? I had a friend who got beat at home. Her strung-out fucking dad, who else? Dug his knuckles into her face when-ever he felt like it. We can call the police."

"House of Earth would be threatened."

"It *needs* to be threatened."

"My mentor didn't beat me."

"Who? A bully?"

How to tell her? How to explain Evie? In his head, before he saw her, it all had seemed easy: the truth would unspool from him and she would see. What he still couldn't imagine, what he still couldn't conceive, was what came *after*, when Gabrielle understood and he decided that Mama and Jack could be wrong.

There was no next. It was a bridge that ended halfway across the gulf.

"Jack wanted to train us. He says the war is close. Gabrielle, what is happening with the war? Is it in town? Is it close? We are building the wall around House of Earth. They want to close off the woods."

"Lucien, the war is in fucking Afghanistan, where my brother got blown to pieces. It's there."

"But it's in town too. It must be, it's coming close, that's why we are training—"

"No! Lucien, don't you understand? Town is the same. Town isn't changing. There's a war thousands of miles away where we are going to blow up people for 9/11. For freedom, for whatever. It's insane and my brother is dead!"

He realized he was shaking.

"I'm sorry, Lucien. But you have to know the truth." She leaned in, her eyes on his bruised face. "Someone horrible beat you up. There's no war in town, Lucien, no war in New York. No one is coming for me. My house is safe. Town is safe. All of these people are lying to you."

He felt like a candle melting in heat, his throat tight, his hands limp at his sides. Gabrielle was his friend, and Gabrielle wouldn't lie to him, but Jack couldn't lie to him, and Mama had talked to him about the war, and she couldn't lie to him either. He began to bite on his lip, so hard there was a droplet of blood he could taste. He knew this taste now. If Gabrielle was somehow right, there was no reason for kendo, no reason for the pit, no reason to be where he was, who he was. His eyes shot upward toward the maze of branches above, the birds as they were, a squirrel leaping into shadow. He remembered learning that water evaporated into the sky, only to return to the earth as cold rain. He always wondered why people couldn't evaporate as well, why flesh and blood weren't allowed the same privilege of rising into the sky to change form and cleanse the planet.

His body was a failure. That he knew. If there was a person who could do such a thing, it wouldn't be him.

He felt a rising terror, Gabrielle's words sinking deeper into him.

"I don't know what to do. Jack said it. Mama said it. And Noah, he . . ."

"Far away from here, Lucien. But I don't want to talk about him. Not right now. Focus!"

"Noah deserves focus."

"What he *deserves* doesn't matter anymore, because he's dead, because my mom is wailing and can't get out of bed and my dad is around more now and it's worse and I have to just think about school and other shit because, yeah, if I focus on Noah, I'll be crying in bed twenty hours a day and I'm not going to live like that, no one is. He chose to go. I told him not to. I hate myself every day for not forcing him to stay home, for not trying harder. I could've. We all could've. But I'm not here to talk about Noah anymore. I can't, Lucien. I talk about him enough with myself, in conversations throughout the day and night that never end. I hear his voice every day. I hear his voice right now. I *can't*. You—you have a problem. The war is overseas, okay? Mater is fucking Mater. It hasn't changed. It's Superior Street and the library and the pond and Walgreens and a bunch of dudes who chew way too much tobacco, and we sing 'God Bless America' at the baseball and football games now. It's Mater. Jack is a fucking liar."

"Jack, he—Jack can't lie."

"Everyone can lie. He's not God. And even God can lie."

"Gabrielle," he said, the last syllable trailing off his lips like dust. He could only say her name now. Instead of the tree canopy, he found the soil, blackened at his feet. A recent rain had turned it the dark, rich brown that was so familiar, soft enough to dig out with his bare hands. He had the shreds of memory to gather and hold, ghosts of himself kneeling in soil. He had his terror, so close now it could choke him. The soil blurred. An earthworm flickered and vanished.

He began to speak, low and quietly.

"Jack had us practice kendo, a Japanese martial art with swords, to get stronger. He said we needed to be stronger. Then I saw a friend, Evie, running across the commons. She was bleeding. Sebastian came out and grabbed her, and I called out her name."

"That was the girl we saw with that creepy dude in Walgreens that one time. I remember, Lucien."

"Sebastian was grabbing her and she was struggling and I wanted to help her. I didn't know what to do. I wish I would've done something. All I ended up doing was yelling out her name. And then Jack punished me."

"So he did beat you?"

"The friends did. Jack told them to. I had to stand there as they hit me with their shinai, their bamboo swords."

"Lucien, that's horrible. We have to do something."

"I don't know what to do."

"I can tell the police."

"The police. But House of Earth. What will happen?"

"You've been beaten nearly to death and you care?"

"It's my home."

"You can find a new home. Maybe my mom will let you stay for a bit. We can figure it out."

"I can't leave my mom."

"Yes, you can."

"She's done everything for me."

"No, she hasn't. You do things for *you*. If my mom let people beat me like they beat you, if she lied to *me* about a war, I'd walk out tomorrow. I'd sleep at bus stations. I'd get the hell out of that place."

He wished he could make her understand. Without Mama, he could not even begin to explain his future. There were no words, let alone images. He didn't know what a bus station looked like. He didn't know how to ask for food that wasn't in a nutritional hall. Only Mama touched money, and he had seen it so rarely, even in the cottage.

He could only sit there. The new rain was falling now, light drops whispering through the leaves. It was almost time for dinner. He didn't think he was expected there, given his injuries, but someone would probably be back to check on him in his room. Gabrielle touched him on the shoulder. The terror, slowly, began to release him.

"Be strong, okay? I'm gonna figure this one out. We'll find a way."

"We can, I think."

"Look, I know you don't have a phone, but remember my house number, okay? My mom or me usually picks up."

She recited her number to him and he chanted it back to himself, hoping to remember it later. He made it a song as he left her.

He knew she was watching him limp up the hill, how he was determined, against the pain now strangling his legs and head, to pretend he was what he'd been before.

———

No one was in the room when he returned. He felt hunger and ignored it. He would sleep early, sleep through the night, and figure out tomorrow.

The phrase was new—*figure out*. He had never had to *figure out* a day, a time. It simply came and he accepted it.

Soon he would be thirteen.

As his eyes closed, there was a knock on the door. He lay flat on his back, and the effort to raise himself again, to be a body in motion, was too much. It wasn't Mama because Mama didn't have to knock. Jack didn't knock either, nor did Natasha. He tried to think, through the pain in his head, who it would be. His curiosity warred with the desire to stay on his back, to find sleep.

Gabrielle told him it was all a lie. He dug his fingernails, one by one, into the skin of his palms, the points of pain like white-hot stars exploding in cold space. Gabrielle told him.

She told him there was no war coming for them, for Mama and Jack and him—

"You can come in!" he yelled, the sound louder than he expected it to be.

The door creaked open. It was Maia, holding a tray from the nutritional hall. He saw a plate of steamed carrots, string beans, and corn. It was one of three dinners Antonio's father served to them.

"I thought you might be hungry," she said, setting the tray down on top of the drawer.

"Thank you."

She looked away from him. "I wanted to say, I wanted to—I never wanted to do it, I begged them not to."

"I know."

"My dad was there, and Jack, and they said they were helping you. I don't think they were helping you."

"I don't know."

"How are you feeling?"

"It hurts in a lot of places. I'm okay. I will be at instruction tomorrow, I think."

"That's good."

She came closer to the bed where he lay, standing on her toes. Her voice dropped to a whisper. "Samantha and Evie—I want to know what happened to them too. I'm worried."

"No one is going to tell us."

"I know. I'm just worried. I hope everything is okay soon."

"I hope so too."

"That mark you mentioned, I did see it. On Evie's wrist as she was being pulled away. The letters *O. C.* It means something, if his name is there. It should be a good thing."

"But it might not be."

"Yes."

His eyes began to close. Sleep was coming to him.

"I'll see you soon, okay, Lucien? Feel better."

"I'll see you soon. Thanks for the food."

In sleep, he barely heard Mama when she came back to the room to tell him what a nice girl Maia was for bringing him his dinner.

"I'm so glad Jack told her to do it," she said.

———

Throughout April, he slowly recovered. Each week, his bruises hurt less and less. The headaches came and went and came again and went again. He spoke less at instruction, but this worked for him and Jack. When he was called upon, he could provide answers. The friends still sat next to him at dinner. They said fewer words to him, sensing he knew things they did not, but there was always a place for him when he came with the plate Antonio's father had filled with vegetables.

On the last Monday in April, he saw more men with construction equipment than he had ever seen before. The wall was growing, cinder blocks hardened into place, the foundation now gobbling up his path to the woods. Meeting Gabrielle would mean weaving between the men and their cement.

Soon meeting her would mean climbing a wall. Or not meeting her at all.

After lunch, before afternoon instruction, he walked along this wall. It was an intrusion of stark gray on what was once his view of the sturdy oaks and their verdant colors.

If Gabrielle was right and there was no war close by, then the wall was simply a wall, to keep him from going where he used to go.

"Where is the wall going?" Lucien asked one of the men as he mopped his brow.

"Going? All around."

He considered this, a ring around everything he knew. He backed away from the construction pit, the men fidgeting over their tools like oversize insects. When he came to House of Earth, he remembered the brightness, how the walls had exploded with fresh color. How did this wall of cinder block fit in with that idea of color? Jack had never explained.

Would the wall get a new coat of paint?

If he couldn't get past it to see Gabrielle, it wouldn't matter anyway.

He told Gabrielle about the wall, how he was leaping over pits of mud and planks of wood and the foundation of a new barrier that, on any given day, would cut him off from the woods.

"We can find a way," Gabrielle said. "Even if it takes some time. You'll see. Every prison has its vulnerabilities."

It was not a prison, he said. Not as a stern rebuke, but as a statement of fact. Prison was where criminals went.

"Innocent people go to prison too," she said simply.

April dissolved into May, the weather warming. Maia turned thirteen, along with Colt. In two days, it would be Samantha's birthday too. After Evie's appearance on the commons, no one asked about Samantha. They had learned the lesson of Lucien's body, how he had curled on the grass to take the beatings.

No one had seen Evie since the day Sebastian took her, bleeding and screaming, away. Lucien had looked every day: in and around the habitation facilities, the nutritional hall, even the shed where Jack stored the kendo equipment.

There was no longer evidence of them having lived here. All he had were his memories of them both, what he could trust in his head.

Jack said neither of their names out loud. Their drawings of O. C. Leroux vanished too.

Lucien looked up, and there was the maypole. It was time again for the festivities. He remembered when he was ten and he was told he was old enough to participate and how wonderful this made him feel, the hope inside him. Had it been just two years? He had only recently begun considering full years for what they were: great self-contained bubbles of time designated for assessing change.

He had not been doing this in the past, recounting the evolution of his life. It was all at once an endless spool of identical thread, trailing off to the horizon line. He would follow it dutifully. He would follow it wherever it took him.

He heard Gabrielle's words as much as he heard Evie's scream. *Innocent people go to prison too.* He didn't know what good it would do against the maypole, as they danced again, and he heard the flute player who was not O. C. Leroux, as he was all those years ago, golden in the afternoon. The flute player was Colt's father now, much shorter than O. C., his wire-rimmed glasses glinting in the sun. The pitch was not right, too high or too low, and Lucien's feet couldn't dance along in the same way. In front of him was Antonio, behind him Cavan. More than a hundred people, all the collectives and mentors and parents, had gathered to clap as they spun around the pole.

Mama was there too.

Jack whispered in Colt's father's ear. The flute continued to play, weak on his lips.

Lucien was looking in the crowd for O. C. Leroux. Wherever he was, like Evie and Samantha, he was not here.

After the maypole dance, Antonio's father presented treats: sliced watermelon for each of them.

"This is so juicy," Cavan said, the pale-red liquid dripping down his chin.

"Uh-huh," Antonio said.

Lucien couldn't think about the sweet taste in his mouth. His mind was unable to focus on the filmy red surface of the watermelon, the dark seeds sliding between his teeth. He hurt less, less than he ever had since the beating, the pain receding within him. He thought again about the spool of thread, how it was tangling now in his fingers, threatening to snap. When it did, what could he do? Where would he go? Here. Home. Mama, Jack, the friends. They were talking about playing O. C. again. Karthik and Jayson each wanted to be O. C. Jacinda did too. Antonio, appointing himself referee, asked them each to guess a number.

Lucien drifted away, toward the window that held his instruction room, the same place he had learned almost everything he knew for as long as he could remember. The room where he wrote and drew and sang and answered Jack's questions. The room where he met Evie and Samantha. He was nearer now, gazing through the window into the empty classroom. Everyone was on the commons. Who would he expect to find?

He found his body, moving independent of his mind, near the adults. They were parents of his collective and parents of others, mothers and fathers who were familiar and new. Magnus's mother was speaking to Karthik's father. Colt's mother, Maia's father, Antonio's mother, and Cavan's father were in a small semicircle, engaged in a conversation that mentioned O. C.'s name. Lucien drew closer, their larger words wrapping around his ear.

Colt's mother began to laugh. She drew her hand up to cover her mouth.

Lucien saw the markings on the underside of her wrist. Two letters, black, the same he had already seen on the people he saw no more.

Colt's mother, he remembered, was named Kara. She was going to be a mentor.

"We needed the departure to the rustic," she said to the other parents, who nodded along with her. "The city had failed us."

"Yes."

"We have much less here, but that means we have so much more. We used to worry about Edmund's Roth IRA, paying for Colt's college, how much money to send for a wedding for a couple we didn't even like. And then we heard about this, and it was every dream we ever had and Colt is just thriving here."

"So is Karthik."

"Maia too."

"Cavan's moral fiber is just so much stronger."

They smiled at each other.

"Occasionally, O. C. invites me for conversations," Colt's mother said.

"That's great."

"He says he can sense the strength of my soul, how much stronger I'm getting. It's flattering. What's more important, though, is that we are building a *real* sustainable future here."

"How much longer, do you think?"

"With everything?"

"Yes. The country. All of it."

"Two years. I'm more aggressive than O. C. on that, even. Edmund and I watched the towers explode in front of us. We were both downtown, on Church Street. One was an accident, two was war. I turned to him then and told him, 'None of this will last.' He fought it at first and then we agreed. Colt agreed. We had to go."

"That's terrible."

"I know you've had your son here much longer"—Colt's mother had turned to Antonio's father—"so it was less an adjustment, especially after that day."

"We always talked about what it would be like to live here, and once we saw the facilities go up, we knew it was happening. After my brother, I was ready to go. He didn't have to die like that. It's such a sick world, and at least O. C. recognizes that. He's the only person trying to make it better. I used to be into politics, volunteered for a few campaigns myself, and it was all lies, all short-term thinking—O. C. is the only one I know who is long-term *first*."

"Exactly."

"Maia just has to stay in line," Maia's father said. "I want to make sure she's listening to what's being taught, that she does the right thing."

"You don't think she's doing the right thing?"

"She *is*—you just worry, right? She's at that rebellious stage. Thirteen is a tough age."

"Absolutely."

"Colt complains sometimes," Colt's mother said. "There's been a small adjustment period. He needs to be less encultured, which is Edmund and mine's doing, from the way we used to live. Part of coming here was breaking him from all that. I'll hear him fret about a night without electricity or if the water isn't perfect one day."

"Yes, Karthik has complained."

"I looked at Colt. I said, 'Listen, baby, this is for the best. You don't need the things you think you need. Modern society has entrapped us. It's a fact. Would you rather be outside, in your old, crumbling school, in your old, crumbling society?' Two years, I really do give it. Environmental devastation, a war, and where do you want to be? On Queens Boulevard? No. Not us."

"We were on the Upper West Side," Karthik's father said.

"I used to like it there."

"We sold our apartment to come here. My wife wanted to leave the city. I did too."

"I feel my energy just growing here, every day," Colt's mother said. "It is, quite literally, the only place to be."

Lucien, standing as close as he could without the parents noticing him, kept trying to catch glimpses of the two letters on the wrist of Colt's mother. He didn't see them on any other parents, as far as he could tell. Evie's words came back to him, how she'd said she could go anywhere, and at the time Lucien had assumed this was a kind of strength, a freedom she was able to enjoy, even if she seemed changed by it.

The mark clearly meant more than the power to eat dinner whenever you wanted to or not show up to instruction. It meant whatever Jack and Mama didn't want to tell him.

It was like the darkness he once saw, filled with possibility. The letters could deliver hope, freedom.

They could also make you disappear.

Colt's mother didn't seem to be afraid of that. Her wrist flipped almost casually as she went to scratch the side of her nose. No parent acknowledged the mark, how dark the letters appeared on the light-starved underside of her wrist. Lucien edged closer. He almost wanted to ask her.

He understood now there was danger in doing that.

The parents walked back toward the center of the commons. There were games of horseshoes and archery in addition to the friends who were running through the grass—Jacinda today chosen as O. C. He told himself he wanted to be a part of the game, racing up and down, shouting *darkness* and *light*. He told himself, more aggressively now, he *had* to be a part of the game. This was festivities day, the May Festival. This was always a favorite day. The sun always found a way to shine.

He sat on the grass, cross-legged, and waited to want to be there.

"Hey there, Lucien."

It was a voice he didn't hear very much, lighter in pitch, almost tickling his neck. He spun and looked up.

"Hi, Natasha," he said, widening his lips for a smile she would recognize.

Natasha was not like Jack or Sebastian, though she also led a collective, the Sunflowers, who were instructed in a room on the other side of the building. Many of them were several years younger than Lucien, and he never talked to them very much. They lived in a different habitation facility and ate lunch earlier than he did. At dinner, they congregated at their own tables. He would talk to them when he would see one—there was a Sunflower boy, Harrison, who was running at the outer rim of the woods, near the clearing where Lucien went to meet Gabrielle—and he was sure, had he grown up with them, they could be another version of the friends, Harrison or Miles or Chloe worthy substitutes for Antonio or Cavan or Maia. Natasha seemed to teach like Jack taught. Unlike Jack, she spoke more whenever all of House of Earth came together at assembly. She had the voice to give a speech.

"What're you doing there?"

"I'm just resting, enjoying the grass. I like the smell."

"That's great. Do you think you want to play?"

"I will play. Very soon."

"Good. O. C. wants to see you play and have fun."

"O. C.? He's here?"

Natasha raised her eyebrow. "He's always here."

"Of course."

Jogging up behind Natasha, a glimmer of perspiration on his forehead, was Jack. Lucien last saw him near the maypole but didn't know where he had gone since.

"Lucien sitting all alone here?"

"I'm about to go play," Lucien said.

"Good. Good. Natasha, thanks for looking out. You ready for tonight?"

"I am. I'm very excited."

"Me too."

"There will be a big night for you too, Lucien," Jack said, looking down at him. "Kara, Colt's mother, will be taking you and all the Meadows on a hike through the woods. I know how much you love the woods. In a number of days."

"That's very exciting."

"You'll enjoy it."

The word *love* sank deeper into Lucien, settling like a stone at his core. He didn't like how Jack had said the word, the way his front teeth dug into his lower lip, as if biting off an invisible piece of meat. Did

207

Jack know he loved the woods because he watched Lucien enter them each week to meet Gabrielle? Lucien was always careful to slide into the clearing when he didn't see Jack nearby. He was breaking no rule, but he sensed the more he met her, the closer he was to violating an orthodoxy that would soon leave Jack's lips, becoming law. He had to meet her without asking, preserve her as a secret within him. He couldn't predict what Jack would do if he ever followed him into the woods and down the slope to where Gabrielle waited. He couldn't predict how Jack would react if, somehow, he heard everything Gabrielle said about her life, Lucien's life, and House of Earth, which so fully enveloped what constituted Lucien's life, in Gabrielle's view, that there was hardly a way to distinguish the two.

Whatever happened, Jack couldn't know about Gabrielle.

After the festivities, the friends were allowed special treats at the nutritional hall. Antonio's father served blueberry muffins with natural sugar, and everyone was allowed one. They were large and fluffy and Lucien ate his quickly. Crumbs rained down from his lips onto the plate. There were conversations all around him, but none with him. He wiped his mouth, folded the muffin lining, and sat.

Jack approached their table, laying both palms on the flat, cool surface. The conversations came to an abrupt end.

"Meadows, what a wonderful performance at the maypole today, and a great day overall. I'm very proud. I just wanted to say, tonight we are going to be in our rooms with the lights off at *seven*, not nine. Okay? The adults are going to have a special time, and they need all the focus they can get. Your parents and guardians are going to have fun too."

"Okay, so it's just for them, the special time?" Cavan asked.

"Just for them. It's one night where they will need to really focus with O. C. Leroux. You'll be back at the habitation facilities, and your parents will join you soon after. Sound good?"

They bobbed their heads and Jack pushed his palms off the table, leaning back. "Good."

There was no afternoon instruction because of the festivities. They were free to play for the final few hours before their early return to the habitation facility. The day had left a strange taste in Lucien's mouth, overpowering whatever was left from the watermelon and the blueberry muffin. No games appealed to him. The maypole, seen through the window of the nutritional hall, was like the colorful ruin of another world he had left behind.

In a moment like this, with no one to speak to, he would find a piece of paper and draw. Mama liked most when he drew a picture of O. C. Leroux. He wanted to draw the trees he saw, Roy Hobbs, even Gabrielle. He wanted to trace the contours of the ground and sky, how they could bend toward him as he drifted off to dream.

He did not want to draw O. C. Leroux.

On the walk to the habitation facility, he heard footsteps behind him. It was Maia, who had spent most of the blueberry-muffin lunch talking to Jayson, Cavan, and Carlina. He hadn't paid attention to what they were saying.

"My dad is excited about tonight," she said to him.

"My mom hasn't said anything. I haven't seen her."

"He doesn't like the guard booth much, but he says he's glad to have something important to do. I heard they're doing a ceremony with O. C."

"What type of ceremony?"

"I don't know. He doesn't know much. He just told me to relax in our room."

"Jack doesn't want us out there."

"No, he doesn't."

"They don't want us to know so much."

"Maybe it's for the best?"

"Maybe."

"If we knew too much, maybe we'd be scared."

"I've been scared."

He meant to emphasize the past tense, how he was *once* scared and no longer was, a survivor of the pit and a survivor of the beating and a boy Mama would be proud to say was her own. Looking at Maia, her face darkening, he knew he had failed to communicate any of that. He realized how fast the sentence had left him, instinct as much as thought, and how it must have sounded to her—I *am* scared. I will *be* scared. And he had been. He saw the tombstones in the pit, their transmogrification, the airplanes burning through the sky and then the bodies falling from the blasted-out windows, their limbs tumbling through the air.

"I know you have. I have been too."

If Maia was scared and he had been scared and Evie, before she disappeared, told him that she, too, had gone to the pit, then how many others were scared too? Half the friends? All of them? Parents? Mentors? He didn't know. Jack was never scared. Those who bore enough knowledge of what lay around the corner, behind the curtain, in the dark— they couldn't be. Jack understood the pit. Darkness had no possibility for him.

It was an absence of light, for the punishment of others.

"I'd like to see what they're doing tonight," she said.

"How?"

"Maybe we sneak out and watch."

"Where will it be?"

"It will be on the commons. We'd have to hide somehow."

"I can't get punished again."

"I'll say it's my idea."

"I can't."

"I'm afraid to do it alone."

"I just can't."

"I'm hoping, somehow, I can figure out how to get Samantha and Evie back. Can we?"

He looked at her and how her eyes, an aqueous brown, seemed to take on a depth he had not seen before, a new and unsettling despair.

He could feel it too. They hadn't disappeared because they wanted to. He was sure of that much.

"I don't know how we do it."

"Maybe tonight we can get an idea. It seems special, different, I don't know, whatever our parents are doing and everyone else. If they don't want us to see it, maybe we have to."

"I have to think about it."

"I'll knock on your door. If you want to go, come out. There's a hiding place in the woods I can think of."

When he got back to his empty room, his own drawing of O. C. Leroux staring at him, he wished he could find a way to answer Maia's question. He didn't believe he ever could. It was no different from raising Noah from the dead, no easier, no more fraught.

But he couldn't think of it that way. Evie and Samantha weren't dead. They were just somewhere else. Somewhere he couldn't go.

What was the difference between that and death?

The afternoon light bled across Mama's drawer, showing him a stagnant cloud of dust hovering just above the wood. He heard horseshoes rattling on the commons, arrows finding their targets at the archery range. Events increasingly played on without him. This was new too, to be hardening into an observer, a body removed. He touched his chest and felt where one of the last bruises had yet to fully heal, a tenderness from the bamboo that once smashed him there. He lay down and closed his eyes.

If only he could know what Samantha and Evie had done. He could admit it to himself now, alone here, that he was not just afraid for them, where they had gone, Evie screaming as the blood trickled down her face.

He could disappear too.

Lucien ignored the first knock. He knew it was Maia, from the diffident way it reverberated on the door, mirroring how she'd first come to him with the tray of food after he had been beaten. He waited for a second knock, for the familiar thud, and rose from bed.

There was no way forward. He only knew he could not ignore her, that she was a friend, and if Evie was gone and Samantha was gone and Gabrielle would never live here, he needed someone who could at least understand the faint hum of fear inside him. If the night yielded an answer—if, somehow, it was revealed to them as they hid away—he would not have any concept of how to transform this answer into anything more than knowledge inside his head. It would sit there and rot.

If Jack and Mama didn't want Evie and Samantha and Samantha's mother found, they would not be. If Jack and Mama did, if O. C. Leroux told them to, then the reality would still be unchanged, power where it always was.

Jack had said, earlier in the year, they would become House of Earth's very first teenagers.

"Maia," he said when he opened the door.

"I'm glad you answered."

"I was always going to. I just don't know about what comes next."

"I don't really know either. I just have this feeling."

"Jack said intuition can be powerful."

"It is, whether Jack said it or not."

The hallway was empty. This habitation facility was Meadows only, and the friends would all be in their rooms, doing as Jack said. Lucien and Maia walked the grass at sunset, a violent orange above them. Maia was in front, leading him into the woods, an area he knew well. He recognized the types of trees, the large sugar maples and eastern hemlocks, as well as the bloodroot and bunchberry springing from the soil. When he was younger, he would categorize all the flowers in his head, allow their names to spill out of him as he walked on. Nature was to be named, and the knowledge, cradled inside him, lent strength and power. Today, he could still do it, summon these names from the well of his mind and recite them all to Maia.

He began to name them. His days would proceed here, unchanged, no matter what he did, no matter what new names he added to his memory. Maia turned around.

"I thought I saw a cardinal. They are one of my favorites," he said.

"Oh."

It wasn't true. He didn't see a cardinal, a rose-breasted grosbeak, or any other bird that would cause him to stop. He only hoped to. He was walking side by side with her, deeper into the woods. Just a few minutes away, along another path, was the slope where he would run down to meet Gabrielle. Today wasn't their appointed day, and he wished it were, feeling the tug in his stomach, hope that went nowhere. Not far beyond them he spotted the wall, rising by the day, gobbling up more grass he once ran across. They were walking through the woods on a diagonal, so soon they would be parallel to the commons, visible to all unless they went farther into the trees.

"They might see us," Lucien said.

"I'll show you where we'll hide."

This was the first time all the collectives had been told to stay inside so the adults could be on their own. It seemed that there were an increasing number of *first times* in his life. The first time Mama said he couldn't watch TV anymore, the first time Mama said he couldn't read *The Natural*, the first time Jack said Evie's name wasn't to be spoken out loud. Today was just another one, to be piled up in his memory and absorbed into who he was.

"It's right over here."

She was weaving between several thick tree trunks, putting a hand out to feel the bark. They were on another slope, just out of view of the commons. He heard voices there now, the building of a crowd. The sun was nearly gone. Maia stuck out her hand against another tree and jumped. "This is it."

It was an enormous sugar maple, Lucien saw, one he had walked by many times. Within the trunk was a large indentation, a hollow he had never seen before. It was large enough for Maia to slide her body in sideways. He was as thin as her and could do the same.

"We can slide in here and then peek out, one at a time. You can see a good stretch of the commons."

It was true. From the hollow, he could see and hear the gathering, the parents amassing as the last glimmer of daylight vanished. Among them, somewhere, was Mama.

"You can look first. I'll go in behind you. Then we'll switch."

"Okay," Lucien replied.

"I wonder what we'll see. We can tell the friends what we saw."

"We won't tell them anything."

"Nothing?"

"No one can know we were here."

He understood more than she did because he had seen the pit, the violence in Jack's eyes. He could admit to himself, in this moment of stillness, that's what it was. If Jack loved them, he could hurt them too, and even if it was for the future of House of Earth and therefore their own, the pain was devouring. If a friend knew, Jack would know. He'd once told Jack so much.

He reigned, like Mama, over all, from sunup to sundown and into his dreams.

"Okay, Lucien."

"No one can know."

The commons was nearly full. More than a hundred bodies were clustering near the maypole, their voices meshing, words bouncing off words like the atoms Jack said made up all things. Maia folded her body sideways into the tree, and Lucien followed, his head and neck still visible. The cluster grew larger, the voices louder, and suddenly, with the appearance of one more figure, they were quiet.

Lucien didn't have to see his face to know. The height gave him away.

O. C. Leroux stood by the maypole, spreading his arms wide, as if he were preparing to fly away. The voices fell to a whisper. Another body, which appeared to belong to Natasha, with her long brown hair tied behind her back in a ponytail, carried several long wooden sticks under her arm. When she planted them in the ground, he saw that they were not just sticks and not swords either, though the wood could have been bamboo, the color and texture belonging to the weapons that had beaten him. There were ten of them, planted in a horseshoe pattern on the grass, and another man emerged with a device in his hand.

A lighter. The man was Jack. Flames burst from their rounded tops.

"Torches," he whispered to Maia.

"What?"

"They have torches on the commons."

"I wonder why."

"I don't know."

The torches were unlike any Lucien had seen before. On TV, many years ago, a certain show had torches on a tropical island. He understood such technology was rudimentary, wood and flame, but since no torch ever burned at the cottage or House of Earth, it was a creation for the pretend world of TV. Mama said most of TV was make-believe. He knew this to be true, people called actors staging events for the screen.

The torchlight danced through the dark.

"Welcome," O. C. Leroux said. "It's good to see you all again."

Lucien could only see him from behind, as a flowing, cream-colored robe with arms and legs, the fabric extending nearly to his ankles. The adults were like toy figurines next to him, all of them so small and unreal.

"Tonight is a very special night. We wanted the children to be here, but we thought it best if they witnessed tomorrow what happened. It could be a special surprise."

"What did he say?" Maia asked, her elbow jamming against his forearm.

"O. C. said it could *be a special surprise.*"

"Oh, I thought he said *sunrise.*"

"No."

O. C. lowered his arms, beginning a slow walk toward the adults. They were silent now. Lucien thought he saw the faces of Antonio's father and mother, as well as Colt's parents. There were others he didn't know as well, parents from other collectives, and faces that might have been familiar but were increasingly lost in the darkness.

"The community grows stronger every day. I'm so proud of the progress you've all been making. I'm so proud of the progress your children, by following *your* example, have been making too. Last time, I told you that as well. It's true. The war may be gathering at our border, but we are stronger than ever. That doesn't mean, however, we are guaranteed survival. Sadly, far from it."

Lucien had heard this turn in O. C.'s speech before, how praise would wither into warning. It still unsettled him, even if he could predict it now, home in on the soothing cadence of his voice. He could never stop thinking about his height. From Lucien's vantage point in the tree, that's what mattered most: O. C. as the lone enormity on the sprawl of grass, his shadow stretching in torchlight. O. C.'s words were momentarily lost to him. He heard a wall of crickets behind him and the jittery crunch of leaves. He recognized the sound. A deer had wandered near them and scampered away.

"To survive, we draw closer. We commit to one another. Think of tonight as a promise and a vow. Think of it as a way to show what you mean to each other, to all we've built. When the planet rebels to purge all those who've been harming her, the men and women with their societies of sickness, who will be spared? Who will be allowed to be a part of the new future, to be there when the planet heals? *You.* You have shown yourselves worthy. Tonight, there will be evidence of that."

Lucien twisted his neck around to where Maia was breathing deeply in the tree. "Do you want to look now?"

"I can look for a little."

He edged forward so she could push past and then folded his body sideways, disappearing as far as he could into the tree. The bark was rougher on his skin, but he enjoyed the coolness of the hollow, the way he could tuck himself so deeply into the space. He could not see anything except the side of Maia's body, her stiff left arm, and the darkness of the tree.

———

"Please, Lucien, I want to switch now. Answer me."

"Switch?"

"I can't—I can't watch."

"What's happening?"

"Please switch."

He slid past her, angling himself so he could see out from the hollow. In the time he had been tucked into the tree, there had been a shift. The torchlight seemed to burn brighter. Natasha was now standing next to O. C., their difference in height making her seem like a child in his wake. She held in her hand a small prong-like device Lucien recognized from a TV show about a farm he had watched many years ago. Her hand wrapped around a smooth wooden handle, a cylindrical metal piece extending beyond the handle several more inches. At the top of the small, thin cylinder was another flattened piece of metal, shaped like a square. Natasha held it up. The square piece appeared to be blackened and steaming.

"Those who are marked tonight have demonstrated their commitment to light over darkness," O. C. said. "Their flesh will be a reminder of that, a testament to that. May *your* flesh testify your love for House of Earth. Some have struggled with this gift. I know you will not."

Jack appeared at O. C.'s other side, a small piece of paper in his hands. He stared down into it and looked back up at the crowd, lost to Lucien now in the encroaching dark. Only the shapes of O. C., Natasha, and Jack were familiar to him. He focused on the device in Natasha's right hand. From the memory of the TV show, he could guess what it might be.

He didn't want to be right.

"Now, let's begin," O. C. said.

Jack looked down again at the piece of paper. Lucien imagined Jack wheeling around to find him in the tree, the paper printed with his own name. He would read it out loud over and over, and the adults would come for him, tearing his body from the hollow and marching him into the darkness.

Jack cleared his throat. "Theresa and Jonathan."

Lucien heard a murmur from the formless crowd. Two figures emerged, taking shape as they walked into the torchlight. He knew them now. They were Cavan's mother and father. Cavan's mother walked slightly ahead, approaching Natasha first. He saw the glint of light, like a small spark, off the glasses Colt's father wore.

"Approach," Jack said.

Cavan's mother was first. Instead of advancing to Jack, she moved next to Natasha. The murmuring died. Without being told, Cavan's mother held out the underside of her wrist for Natasha. O. C. had turned his neck toward her. At that moment, before Natasha lowered what Lucien knew to be a branding iron, he felt Maia's elbow in his back. It was an accident, he realized, and she meant nothing by it.

He tried to focus on Maia's elbow as the iron pressed against skin of the open wrist, hissing as Natasha held it there. A trace of smoke floated off the blackened metal. Cavan's mother's lips, suddenly visible in the light cast from the nearby torch, contorted into a strange shape, her shriek cutting through the night. He knew Maia had heard it too because there was a shuddering behind him, the elbow digging deeper.

"We should go," she whispered.

But now he had to see. Cavan's mother backed away, her knees weak. She was looking down at her wrist. Lucien thought, though he couldn't be sure, he saw her smiling.

"Approach," Jack said.

Cavan's father was next. He held his wrist out for Natasha, and the branding iron burned against his wrist. He strained to contain his scream, to make it like another bodily function. Lucien could hear the fear joining the pain. He knew what it sounded like.

Cavan's father was kneeling on the grass. Again, Lucien believed he could see a smile.

"Anders and Yolanda. Approach."

Antonio's parents were next. His father came first, his wrist out-stretched, as if Natasha were offering a sugary treat. The branding iron seemed to come harder for him. His scream was the loudest, the smoke rising off where the metal had charred him. Antonio's mother was quieter, her pain more remote. They looked at each other when they were done, wisps of smoke rising from their skin.

"Jasper and Leah. Approach."

Maia tugged at his arm. "Those are my parents!"

"Do you want to see?"

"I want to leave, please."

"I don't want them to see us if we run out of the tree."

"We'll be careful."

Maia's father was standing straight, much like he did in the guard booth each day. Lucien didn't see Maia's mother as much. She was much smaller than her husband, trailing him as they waited for Natasha to lower the branding iron.

Maia pushed behind Lucien, and he slid out and around the tree, out of view of the commons. He could hear the press of the branding iron, another cry, this one masculine. It was Jasper, clutching his arm.

"I bet it's the letters," Maia said, stepping out in front of him and hurrying ahead.

"I think so too."

"O. C."

Each time Natasha branded a new wrist, she raised the iron to the sky. It was an image that was now burned into Lucien as they dashed through the woods, back to the habitation facility. What he struggled to understand was how so many people could welcome pain like that, a hot piece of metal searing the skin.

Perhaps they all believed they could finally belong to O. C.

"We'll say we were asleep the whole time," Maia said.

"Yes."

The hallway echoed with their footsteps. Maia was in Room 6 and opened her door first. It was empty, her mother and father, of course, still gone. She peered in, as if expecting them to materialize on their beds.

"I hope no one saw us," she said.

"I hope so too."

She stared at the empty room. "What do we do?"

"With what we saw?"

"Yes."

"I don't know. I wish I knew. I guess I'm figuring it out."

"If they like it . . ."

"Samantha's mom had the mark. She was branded. I saw her crying before she disappeared."

"And Evie . . . but tonight, they all wanted it."

"Maybe it was because they were all together."

It was a power Lucien had observed an uncountable number of times, at instruction and in assembly and wherever House of Earth came together, children and adults alike. It was the power of the crowd, of many minds and hearts uniting as one. They could gather behind a person, like Jack, or an idea, untouchable and unknowable until the moment they were amassed, and any reality, in that burning moment, was possible. He had learned to love this feeling, to anticipate it like he would a fiery sunset or a summer downpour, and now he could understand that there were other possibilities too, like the shapes and sounds that hid in the dark. The friends had united to beat him. The parents had united to accept scalding metal on flesh. He could only hope the mark was different somehow, not what he had seen on Evie or Samantha's mother.

His hand trembled over the doorknob of Room 8. Inside, as always, was no one. He hadn't seen Mama on the commons, but she was likely there, among the faces the torchlight didn't pass over. Soon enough, she would be back.

He wanted to be asleep when the door opened again.

LATE SPRING

When morning came, he was still alone. Mama hadn't come back. He tussled under the sheets, rolling his body around to make sure his eyes, wide open now, were not failing him. Mama's bed was empty.

Whatever had happened last night, she was not back.

It was nearly breakfast time and he had slept late. The light eyes of O. C. Leroux that he had once sketched and colored stared down at him from the wall, and an impulse seized him to reach up and tear the paper down. He was out of bed, his arms tense at his sides.

He could not remember the last time he'd been alone in this room in the morning.

When he stepped out of the room, several of the friends were in the hallway, walking to breakfast. Magnus was talking to Cavan. Antonio was behind them, wiping toothpaste from the corner of his mouth. He waved to them, saying nothing. Magnus and Cavan passed. Antonio stopped.

"Good morning," he said.

"Good morning, Antonio."

"Breakfast time soon. I heard today is the cinnamon porridge. I'm excited."

"That sounds tasty."

"Definitely."

The cinnamon porridge was a favorite, and on another day, at another time, he could share Antonio's enthusiasm and forget what he had seen last night. But Mama wasn't here. The panic was a small blade flaying him from within. Each minute that passed was another minute Mama wasn't accounted for. Of course, Mama was often gone during the day, even in the evening. She had run overnight errands when they lived at the cottage. She always told him if she wasn't going to come back, if the errand would take more time, or if she hadn't, he could always expect her back soon.

He was beyond expectation now. Outside again, on the familiar walk to the nutritional hall, he could no longer count on people to be exactly where he thought that they would be.

In the distance, he spotted Maia pushing the doors, disappearing into the hall.

A new energy pulsed in the air, of an intensity and degree he could not immediately classify. The collectives were at their usual tables, the friends settling in over their porridge. Antonio's father was in position, doling out breakfast from his ladle. Jack and Natasha and Sebastian at one table, Colt's mother and father joining them. Lucien lifted his tray and approached Antonio's father.

The two black letters shone from his wrist as Lucien turned to take the porridge. Antonio's father smiled at him.

"Good morning," Lucien said, the words sounding hoarser than he thought they would.

"Morning, Lucien. It's good porridge today."

Lucien only nodded. The letters were larger and darker, the *O* more rounded, the *C* curved like a hungry serpent. From the way he turned the underside of his wrist outward, Lucien could almost believe he was showing him the mark on purpose, making his night as clear as possible to him. *I was there, I was chosen.* Lucien, looking down, hurried on, over to the table he knew so well.

He joined the friends with the conversation already in progress, speeding to a conclusion without him.

"Did your parents get them?" Colt asked.

"Mine did," Jacinda said.

223

"We know, of course, Antonio's parents did," Cavan said.

"I think my dad and mom got them too," Maia said.

She found Lucien's eyes and then looked away.

"What about you, Lucien?" Colt asked.

"I don't think so."

"You either see it or you don't," Magnus said. "My parents got them. It's very clear."

"I haven't seen my mom yet."

"She didn't come back at night?"

"No."

"Oh, okay. I'm sure everything is good."

"Jack doesn't have it," Cavan said.

"That is true," Karthik said. "Why would some of our parents— mine included—get it but not Jack?"

"You all noticed them this morning, right? My parents definitely didn't have them yesterday," Colt said.

"I didn't notice them before now."

"Evie and Samantha's mom had them before. That's it," Maia said.

The friends all turned to stare directly at Maia. Several spoons dropped against the bowls, ringing out in the sudden silence.

"You don't say those names, okay," Magnus said.

"Right. Jack said. You can't say those names," Cavan said.

"You really can't," Antonio said.

"They aren't here, so why say them at all?"

Maia's gaze had dipped, her eyes wandering to her cooling porridge. "I just said what I saw."

"Right, of course," Antonio said. "But you heard Jack. These just aren't names we say."

"We don't. Ever," Magnus said.

"I think she understands. She won't say them again," Jacinda said.

"She *better* understand."

Maia's eyes were now locked on her bowl.

"She does," Antonio said, smiling now, his hand finding Maia's. "We've forgotten those names, right?"

"Right," Maia said, her voice low.

"We aren't going to the pit," Magnus said.

"Yeah," Cavan said.

"She understands now," Antonio said.

"The names forgotten," Karthik said.

"Forgotten."

Lucien knew they would all look his way soon enough. He had been to the darkness. He had suffered the beating. He was still the boy who painted his birdhouse black all those years ago. He was still the boy on the bench waiting for Mama, hoping he could come inside. Turning slightly away, he ate his porridge quietly, hoping time could crawl forward enough for breakfast to end and instruction to begin.

It was supposed to be wrong to keep thinking about Evie. She had once been so courageous, leading them out of the woods in a blizzard. He couldn't forget that day or how she always seemed to know what to do. Even now she would know, whether to tell him to be quiet and let the friends agree or to challenge them directly.

But to challenge them would be to challenge Jack, who told them what to say and do. Challenging Jack meant challenging Mama. Challenging both meant challenging House of Earth.

Life itself, challenged.

His porridge was done. The friends were talking again about the marks, as if Maia's words about Evie and Samantha's mother had never been uttered.

"My mom is really proud," Karthik said.

"It was a very important night. I do wish we could've been there or seen it happen," Magnus said.

"Our parents needed to focus. They needed to be alone."

"Yes."

"They got to meet O. C. Leroux again."

"I hope we see him soon."

Lucien stood up to leave. Maia followed, and they were together in the hallway, a few minutes early to instruction.

"I guess I shouldn't have said their names like that," Maia said.

"I'm glad you did."

"You are?"

"Yes."

"My dad was so happy this morning. He actually showed me the mark. My mom, I think it hurt her more. But she was happy too."

"I don't know where my mom is."

"She'll be back."

"Yes."

"How can a mark like that make someone so happy? I could see how much it hurt. I never would—"

"They feel like they belong. We used to."

Jack was sitting at his desk when they entered the room. He was writing with a pen, bent over a piece of paper Lucien and Maia couldn't see. When he heard them, he stopped, showing them a warm smile.

"Good morning, Lucien and Maia."

"Good morning, Jack."

"Maia, do you mind if I have a private word with Lucien outside the room? Lucien, do you want to come with me? It will only be a moment."

"Yes."

His heart froze in his chest. He was certain soon he would stop breathing. Jack led him through the door and down the hallway from the opposite direction they came. The friends were filing into the room, some craning their necks to see where he was going with Jack. After a few more feet of walking, Jack stopped.

"How are you doing?" Jack asked him.

"I'm doing well."

"Very good. I know these last few months haven't always been the easiest. The thirteenth year can be a difficult one. You have a birthday coming in September."

"Yes."

"That's wonderful and exciting, I can imagine. So many of your friends have enjoyed turning thirteen."

"They have."

"We take on responsibility—as we age, and as we grow more deeply entwined into our community. Your mother is an example of that, Lucien."

"She is, yes."

"She is so very important. Last night, you might have noticed she did not come back to your room. I don't want you to be alarmed. She is going to be gone. She will come back when the time is right. She has many very important responsibilities that she is fulfilling for us. When she does, we will be even stronger as a community."

"I understand."

"Good. She loves you very much. She wanted me to tell you that. She is very proud of you."

"When is she coming back?"

"Soon, Lucien. When the work is done. There is nothing to worry about. She is exactly where she needs to be. As are you."

Is Evie where she needs to be? Samantha? But he knew. The capacity for punishment could be so much greater if he asked. Other than Maia, he knew no one who was even willing to speak their names out loud. He had no plan and no means to execute it, even if it came to him. He could only maintain his existence, in its once pleasant loop, until one came. All he could think now was that he needed to find them all. Evie, Samantha, Mama.

If Jack was right, he had nothing to worry about.

"Okay," he said, because there was nothing more to say. Jack led him back to the instruction room. He sat in his seat, two desks from

Maia. He tried to listen as Jack began to speak, a lesson about plant species found in the Pacific Northwest versus those found in the Northeast, where they lived. Jack pressed a piece of chalk to the board and wrote names. These names once meant so much. Lucien could write them down and memorize them and recite them, but what did it matter if Mama was gone? He wanted to believe she was doing what was best for him. She always had, hadn't she? Even if she was angry, it was always meant to encourage him to be better, to be the best son and member of House of Earth he could ever be. That was the purpose.

He never did see her last night. He had assumed she was there, believed it because if she wasn't in her room and she wasn't with every other parent, there was no third possibility, no reason that made sense to him. She was not hiding in the ether. Even if she was missing during the day, she always came to the habitation facility at night.

Where was she sleeping? Was she comfortable? Did she miss him?

When he went outside, he could see the wall growing. The perimeter would soon swallow his favorite clearing in the woods, where he met Gabrielle. She said she would still find a way to meet him after the wall rose. She was the most determined person he knew, but what would determination matter against cinder block? He could ask himself questions or focus on Jack.

Neither would tell him what he needed to know.

He was pulled toward the wall, as if the cinder block throbbed with its own alien gravity. A man stood near where the wall blocked the portion of woods he knew so well. The man, tall and thick, was one of the workers, and his face was deeply sunburned. He was dipping a brush into a bucket and applying a coat of white paint. Lucien stood and watched him, the rhythm of his right arm up and down, the paint gleaming in sunlight. A small ladder was propped next to him. It seemed he had already painted the upper portions of the wall, and now he was done, focusing on the sections he could reach.

Did the workers still think there was a war coming for House of Earth? Did they live in town with Gabrielle? From where did they spring, and how had O. C. Leroux found them? Lucien imagined they grew like flowers for O. C. to pluck from his secret garden. He could do anything he wanted to. He could, like Mama, bring people into this world.

He could take them away.

"You enjoying the work?"

The man was speaking to him. He stood much taller than Lucien, his eyes suddenly wide, one large hand curled around the brush. Lucien, not knowing what else to do, began to approach.

"The work?" Lucien asked, looking toward his own shoes.

"My painting here. You've been staring, kid."

"No, I mean—it's . . . I like paint. I like the smell."

"Me too."

"It's a large wall."

"We're wrapping up very soon."

"Oh, okay. How soon?"

"Soon, right on schedule."

"Okay. Then it's all done, for good, the wall all around?"

"Don't look so down. It'll be for the best. That's what I'm told, anyway. And you kids will get some nice security from those big bad wolves or whatever."

"Wolves?"

"Oh, you know, the wilderness. I'm a city boy myself. I came up here for a job, latched on with a company where a buddy of mine had a nice position, set me up. It's peaceful up here. Cheap too."

"Peaceful . . ." Lucien considered the full weight of the word, how many times it had been used by Jack, Mama—the images that sprang up in his head. The opposite of war is peace. This man was telling him, then, what Gabrielle had also told him. Perhaps Lucien had always sensed it, like a deer in the darkest woodland knows it is being watched

229

by a human eye and scurries onward. He couldn't imagine the war anymore, the scope and the blood, the unnamed and faceless people behind this fresh wall, their weapons poised. He could see only hushed forest.

He walked closer toward the man.

"My name is Roseboro, by the way. What do they call you?" He held out an enormous hand, his fingers spreading wide. Lucien had seen adults do this. Not at House of Earth, but on his old TV, the one Mama threw in the garbage. "This hand doesn't have any fangs, I promise. At least I don't think."

Lucien reached out and placed his hand in his, curling his fingers around the meat and bone of Roseboro.

"My mom named me Wynn. But who wants to be called Wynn? Sure, it sounds all nice, until I explain it's spelled with a *y* and two *n*'s. It's an old family name. Goes back to God knows where. I've been Roseboro since I learned I could talk back. I'd rather go with a last name than a first if the last name is the thing I want to hear."

"I've always been Lucien."

"So they call you that. Nice name. If I were Lucien Roseboro, maybe I would've just been a Lucien. I like that more than Wynn, at least."

"How much farther is the wall going?"

"Farther?"

Lucien looked to the grass that still led to the woods, where his clearing to Gabrielle waited. There was still room to walk there. The wall had consumed almost everything else.

"I mean, how and where—what's going to happen?"

Roseboro leaned down toward Lucien. "The wall's going all around, of course."

"The whole House of Earth."

"Those are our instructions. We always do our job, as told. That's how we get paid, Lucien. I've got a boy at home, a little younger than you. I do the job for him."

"I won't be able to go into the woods."

"You used to go in there?"

"I liked to walk there. That clearing"—he gestured to where the gap still lay, the freedom that was now temporary—"and now it's going away."

"They tell me it's for your own good."

"Who does?"

Roseboro wasn't smiling anymore. "The boss, of course. Your boss. It's a nice little school up here. Maybe one day, I will send my boy."

"He can join House of Earth," Lucien said, his voice dropping as he looked back toward the wall, a hard and brilliant white sun burning without clouds.

"Should he choose to?"

The question stopped Lucien. Roseboro, this strange and large and new man, was asking him what to do. It was a question that could never have occurred in his own life because he had never made that choice. The word itself existed as theory, like God or the planets beyond the night sky. He knew, by now, he had known it only from a distance, on a television screen or in one of Jack's fables. He had not chosen House of Earth, just as he had not chosen to be alive. He was simply here. Always here, with Mama and Jack.

Choice. When he mouthed the word, it broke off weakly, against his front teeth.

"Excuse me?"

"Sorry, Roseboro. I was just saying, I didn't have a choice. To go here."

"Your mother or father, then, made the choice?"

"My mom did."

"So answer me then, Lucien. If you didn't choose, would you choose it now? For my son? For yourself?"

"I don't know."

For the next week, he followed Roseboro's progress. He moved with the wall. On the day the cinder block was laid to block the clearing, Lucien dashed over to Roseboro, his breath short. It was recreation hour. He couldn't see his trees anymore. The paint was still not dry.

"You've blocked the clearing."

"These are orders, Lucien."

"But, but—"

"We all have people we serve, don't we? I grew up in church, the fire-breathing Pentecostal stuff. Do you know what I'm talking about? Probably not."

"I don't know."

"It's just the way it is. You follow orders. I have to finish this wall. It's my paycheck."

"If I had money, I'd pay you to stop."

"I know you would, Lucien. Did you give any more thought to my question?"

"Which one?"

"If my boy should come here."

"Your boy . . ." Lucien turned to the wall, now so wide and high, the paint so white. "He's safe?"

"That's a question. I suppose, yes, he's safe."

"Where is he now?"

"He's safe at school."

"Is it a school like mine?"

"Public school."

Public school was where Gabrielle went.

"He should stay."

"Then he'll stay where is. But you, Lucien. Are you okay?"

"Don't tell anyone . . ."

"Tell anyone what?"

"I said I didn't want the wall. Just don't tell anyone."

"I'm not going to tell anyone, Lucien. I appreciate you telling me what you think."

Roseboro put down his brush in the bucket. He had more hair on his face than last week, Lucien noticed, and rings had darkened under his eyes. With the back of his hand, he wiped sweat from his forehead.

The rest of the Meadows were at play on the field, racing against one another. Out of the corner of his eye, he could see Jack, watching the race, beginning to walk toward him.

"Jack is coming," Lucien said.

"Is he one of your teachers?"

"He is, yes."

"I didn't realize he did that too. He's been my point of contact on this project here. I have to say this, Lucien: you remind me of my own boy. That's why I was asking. He's a little younger than you. He's got big eyes and that look about him, like he's known things, lived through worlds and lifetimes we can't imagine. You got it too. Like you're in real, deep thought. I come here, talk to you, and see him."

"Is he nice?"

"Yes, nicest kid you'd meet. Wouldn't hurt a fly. He doesn't do so well in school. Kids can be rough. Here, I was thinking, it'd be different."

Jack seemed to stop. He was halfway toward the wall, his hands in his pockets. He was smiling. Lucien didn't know what exactly he was smiling at. His gaze seemed to be aimed not at the wall but above, like an invisible creature was scampering across a precipice only Jack could see.

"It is different," Lucien said. "I should go. How long will you be here?"

"On the project?"

"Yes."

"Oh, at least two more weeks to get this wrapped. There's a little more fortifying that needs to get done."

Lucien saw that Jack was suddenly turning back and walking away from them, toward the building.

"Did Jack tell you what the wall is exactly for?"

"Now you're asking the tough questions. I like it."

"Did he?"

It was hard to tell what Roseboro knew and didn't know, what awareness churned inside him. Lucien was sure, until that moment, he was the one discussing House of Earth with a rare person on the outside, just as he had to explain Jack's teachings to Gabrielle. Roseboro's hand rested on Lucien's shoulder. He felt the ease of his strength, the power concealed in the fleshy bulbs of his forearms. Roseboro was not like anyone else he had ever met.

"He told me it was for your own protection."

"But you said it was peaceful outside. In town."

"It is, Lucien. I've got a fishing trip this weekend."

"Then there isn't a war."

"We're dropping bombs on Arabs. But those bombs ain't here."

"So why is there a wall?"

"I will tell you what they told me and my guys out here, doing the construction work we were hired to do. I was told it was a security project to protect you boys and girls. Sometimes, enemies show up that you don't expect. Sometimes you don't see them at all."

Roseboro turned back to the wall, whistling to himself.

"I want to see all my enemies," Lucien said, walking away.

———

During recreation hour the next day, the friends chose to play basketball. The teams were formed without him. It was as if they had all learned, at some unseen or unspoken-of time, who they would play with. None of them asked him to play. He went to the horseshoes to toss them, competing against himself. He saw that Maia had joined the basketball game.

The memory of the library returned to him, Mrs. Yelich and the scent of the aged paper and the duck pond behind the building, how the afternoon light bejeweled the surface of the still waters. He needed to go there one more time, take the familiar walk down Darling Drive to the waiting town, where Gabrielle would be. If there was a war there, if it was coming, if it had come, he would try to survive. There were no sounds of war beyond House of Earth. No guns, no bombs, no boot steps in the grass. The woods had not changed.

But they told him every day the war was coming. Roseboro said the enemies didn't have to be seen with your eyes.

The section of the wall blocking the clearing was now completely finished and painted. Roseboro had moved, with another man, to a new section on the far side, away from his familiar woods. With the friends in their game, Lucien had nothing else to do but wander over again, hoping to hear Roseboro's deep, rasping voice.

"Almost done now, Lucien," Roseboro said, mopping his brow. He had taken a break and was drinking from a soda can. It was poison water, Mama would say. Wherever Mama was now.

"You shouldn't look like that all the time," Roseboro added, finishing the can in one gulp. He wiped his damp lips.

"Like what?"

"You're young, go have fun. You got it made, right? House of Earth. I heard it's very selective, who gets in, who doesn't. You're here for a reason, I bet. A special kid. Special kids don't mope."

"This is how I look."

"Yeah? Change it."

"My mother is gone."

He had been afraid to say it out loud because saying it out loud would make it an inarguable fact, like the name of a flower or a species of bird. Mama was coming back; she could appear on the grass anytime and run toward him, her arms spread wide. It could happen. But until she did, she was as gone as all the others, those who never seemed to return. The only difference between Mama and the dead was the dead had no hope of return. That, though, was the solitary difference, and each moment that passed without her made her all the more indistinguishable from the dead. When he was younger, he imagined death as transformation. All he had seen in nature taught him that life merely changed form, that nothing could be extinguished. He nurtured this idea as long as he could. If Mama was away and not coming back, she was becoming something better, far beyond what he was ready to imagine.

This idea of death had slowly given way to another, one that clung to him with a new and heavy permanence. He wasn't sure exactly when this had happened—only that it had, and wouldn't go away. They were gone. It was a nightfall that never gave rise to day. There was no way to see through the dark.

"Do you know where she went?"

"No. I look and I wait."

"And I am guessing she didn't say where she was going?"

"No."

"That wasn't the easiest thing, I'm sure. But adults do things that are sometimes hard to understand. She'll come back to you. Your mom is an important person. A guy like Jack—he wouldn't let her slip through the cracks."

Roseboro knew Jack well enough to say something like that. Lucien didn't know Roseboro at all. He nodded at the painter, slowly backing away, realizing recreation was over and even if it wasn't, he didn't want to be outside right now, not anymore. Roseboro's expression was unchanged. His head was tilted slightly, one side of his face washed in sunlight. His mouth began to open, and Lucien turned to walk away, back inside.

"Come back tomorrow, all right?"

Lucien stopped in the grass. When the moment passed, his mouth still closed, Roseboro began to speak again.

"Listen, I think I can help you. Don't worry. There's a lot you understand that I don't. And there's some things I understand that maybe you don't."

When Lucien made it to the door, Antonio was leaning against the wall, looking up at a butterfly. Magnus was next to him, stretching his arms.

"Is he one of the mentors?" Antonio asked, his eyes still following the path of the butterfly.

"Who?"

"The man you are talking to."

"He's just a painter."

"Oh, okay. We should be careful who we talk to."

"Yes."

"Very careful," Magnus said.

———

Mama didn't come home that night or the next night or the night after that one. The room, once so filled, now seemed enormous. With the weather warming, he could sleep without swaddling himself in blankets and hoping the hiss of the pipe meant actual heat. He slept on top of his blankets, out of the sheets, his body exposed to the dark. His dreams were brittle, half-remembered, and he often found himself awake at hours in the morning he'd never known, his limbs shifting crab-like above his ruffled sheets.

Each day, Lucien checked for Roseboro. The workers were all there except him.

It happened sooner than expected. The wall, climbing ever higher, had already blocked the clearing, cutting him off from Gabrielle. He walked along it, hoping for an opening, any seam to slip back into the woods. The wall offered him none. Roseboro and his friends had done it. As he walked, his fingertips brushed against the cement, as if enough touching would turn the wall to sand. When he had walked the perimeter of House of Earth, which had begun and ended in what used to be his favorite spot, he fell to the ground. He'd known this was coming. He just hadn't known it would be now. There was no way to climb a wall as smooth and hard as this one. Trees had branches and grooves, convenient indentations for hands and feet. When he scaled a tree, he felt welcomed into it, as if his body were always meant to rise into its canopy.

The wall was not meant for him.

The evening was here and Gabrielle could be waiting for him, just behind the wall. She would know he was there, somewhere on the other side. He wanted to call out to her, to shout her name. Saying her name would not destroy the wall. Hearing his name from her lips would not destroy the wall.

His desire to see her would mean nothing against the cinder block that would not move.

"You like it?"

The voice behind him was familiar but rough, deeper than most. But it didn't rasp. Lucien's hand pressed the wall. Over his shoulder, he could see the voice belonged to Maia's father.

"I don't know."

"That's fresh concrete, Lucien. That's a special thing."

"It's hard."

"Very hard. If anybody tries to knock it down, they'll fail. There's a lot of bad shit behind that. People hating and hurting each other. And it won't get us."

"It won't."

"You stay out of trouble."

"I will. I do have a question about the new wall."

"Shoot."

"If I want to go to the woods—I like to walk there sometimes—how do I get there?"

"You don't need to go there, Lucien."

"Jack would take us to the woods."

"If your mentor or a parent wants to take you, they can find a way. But you can't go on your own, no. Too dangerous."

"I've gone before and been okay."

"World is changing," Maia's father said, walking away.

———

The next day, Lucien saw Roseboro by the wall. Mama hadn't come back, but he had. Lucien pulled inward, refusing to run toward him. He knew enough to walk slowly. The friends would comment if he ran. Jack would ask questions.

When he met Roseboro, it was always during recreation. And always by the wall. There was a rhythm, now, to what they did.

Without Mama and Gabrielle, this man with his paint bucket and tools was the person he could talk to in ways he couldn't with anyone else. And he had been gone a long time. As Lucien approached, Roseboro seemed to breathe in, his chest expanding. Dried paint flecked his overalls. He had even more hair on his face than before, patches clouding his cheeks.

Roseboro pointed straight at Lucien. "There you are," he said.

"You were gone."

"I was called to another site. They rotate us around. I'm back now. I've been waiting to see you."

"My mother is still gone."

"And your friends are beginning to disappear."

Lucien heard a flock of birds exploding from unseen brush on the other side of Roseboro's wall. Yes, it was Roseboro's too because he had helped to build it, cemented and painted the barrier between

Lucien and the lushness he'd so easily passed through before. Whether Roseboro had to serve his master or not, he had made a choice to build.

The birds were robins, Lucien saw, and they were fleeing up into the sky now visible from his vantage point on the other side of the wall. There had been a time when he'd dreamed of waking to a skeleton hollowed out, ready for takeoff. The birds flew with hollow bones. If he could shed his heavy bones, the dreadful human weight, he could soar above and find Mama and Gabrielle and Samantha and Evie. He could be wherever he wanted to be. He could outfly death.

"What do you mean?" It was all Lucien could manage to say. The sentence was choked at the back of his throat, almost lost. He wasn't sure whether Roseboro had even heard him.

"Let's go over toward the back and talk, as much as we can."

Lucien followed Roseboro as they walked the circumference of the wall, away from where his favorite clearing had been and toward a far side of the commons. There were no mentors and friends over there. His heart began to beat with a quickness that surprised him, as if he had been sprinting across the grass in a race with the friends. His walk was deliberate, three or four paces behind Roseboro, just beyond his wide shadow. Roseboro was larger than Jack and much shorter than O. C., but the mass of his body, the rolling flesh and swollen muscle, consumed far more space. Lucien felt, in that moment, like a falling meteorite in the crackling orbit of a planet.

Lucien kept pace as they continued their walk near the perimeter. Roseboro wasn't slowing and he wasn't turning.

How did he know about everyone who had disappeared?

When Roseboro stopped, Lucien readied to blurt out the question. He wasn't sure what stopped him, only that his mouth wouldn't move. Roseboro leaned back against the wall. No one, as far as Lucien could tell, was watching them.

"The project ends soon and I won't be here much longer," Roseboro said. "I can't say I understand everything that's happening here. Not even close. I've picked up information. I won't tell you how. And I can't tell you anything about your mother, if she's coming back or not. I wish I could. I like you, Lucien. Like I said, you remind me of my boy, and just as important, you're not like everyone else here. That I can tell, just from being around the block a few times. I took on this construction project, in part, because I knew I'd get inside here. House of Earth. The reputation is really growing in town."

"There's no war in town," Lucien said, his voice failing to rise in the manner of a question. He had delivered it with that intent, only to find the energy leaking out when he was done. He had spoken just above a whisper. Suddenly, he felt very tired.

"No, there isn't. Within these walls, though, starting with Jack and the man running this show, O. C. Leroux, there is something planned. A potentially dangerous thing. Like I said, I don't have all the facts yet, but what I have is leading me in a direction that I don't like, that you wouldn't like either. I work. I listen. I talk. I am learning more."

"I just want everyone to come back."

"It's possible they all will. It is. Your mother too. What I am starting to feel is that we won't get anything done—we don't get any answers, at least—staying here. Me and you, by this wall. I am going to try to help you, Lucien. When I was your age, I had a rough time, and I remember being a little like you. A lot smaller. A scared kid. And there was no lonelier feeling in the world, at that age, than wishing and hoping the adults would help you and watching as they failed you, again and again. That hope—that hope is the most dismal goddamn thing in the world. I used to wait at the window and ask God to stop my father from coming home to beat my mother. And then ask him to stop my mother, when she had time to herself, from turning around and beating me too, because she was so horrified with her own life, so ruined by it, that all she had was *me*. My bones, my flesh. I understood. I would stand there and let her do it. I was there for her. My bruises would come to match hers. I prayed for all kinds of things. Sometimes it was just for my mother to be possessed, somehow, so it would stop. So I could sit down and watch TV and drink a soda and not have to feel my father's big meaty hand taking me by the skull and throwing me against a dresser. I don't know. I am probably talking too much. I've been better about it until now."

"I've been hurt a few times."

"Yeah. I get that sense. House of Earth isn't what it should be. Or maybe it never was. People were here and now they aren't. I hope they can come back. I can't say much else. Not here, at least. But if we can get outside, out there, we can. We can figure it out. You have a friend out there, don't you?"

"I do."

Roseboro always knew more than Lucien thought he did. He could only begin to understand how this man knew of Gabrielle, if he had been watching for far longer, somehow, or was hidden in the woods where Lucien had gone. It was all possible. And within this possibility loomed a greater terror, one he didn't know how to distill into language. He didn't know what was coming anymore. He couldn't begin to guess. The future was the darkest of night skies, the stars vacuumed away, all light extinguished. The future was a void not unlike death. Within that absence he could pass through into something else, something more—he could be saved.

Or, in the vast and empty lightlessness, he could be lost forever.

"We can find her. There are possibilities. We will have to move quickly."

"I don't know."

"You want to find your mother?"

"I do."

"And live?"

"I want it to be like it was before."

"What was before?"

"Before we didn't have to live here and I got to be with my mother on Darling Drive and read my favorite books and we had a TV and no one left me . . ."

Years of memory unspooled. Mama whistling as she chopped vegetables. A woodpecker flying from the willow that drooped over Darling Drive. His own hands in the morning light, bending the faded cover of a book. In his head he could always collapse time and space. He could return. He needed only to stay there. When he went back to Darling Drive, there was no pit to be locked in, no swords to crush his bones, no gaping terror to swallow him. The future was not a void.

"We'll find a way to get you back," Roseboro said.

"Find a way," he said, trying to consider what that could mean. "Yes, I'd like to find a way."

"We'll go out tomorrow. You have to follow me and do as I say."

"What are we going to do?"

"I can tell you now that we are going to leave. And once we do, we are going to figure out how to help everyone here and help those who haven't come back yet. We are going to help everyone."

"Jack won't let me leave."

"I'll take care of that. Trust me."

Roseboro rubbed at his eye, his left hand balled into a reddened fist. That's what it came down to: he was trusting this man he didn't really know. He knew Jack. He knew Mama. He knew Gabrielle. But he couldn't see Gabrielle anymore without Roseboro's help—the wall had cut him off. Mama was gone. Jack was going to say he couldn't leave. Jack would come with a new punishment.

"I don't know if I want to leave my friends," he found himself saying, his gaze falling to a deadened patch of grass he had only just noticed, the grass beginning to brown. Had they forgotten to water here? Had the wall caused it? He allowed himself, momentarily, to wonder.

He would be leaving his friends. He hadn't liked how they'd left him. Now he would be doing the same.

"If we don't do this, I'm afraid, more of your friends may disappear. You have to think of it like this, Lucien—we will be doing this for them as well as you. It will be for everyone at House of Earth. It will be for their future too. We will have to move quickly."

"Will my mother find me?"

"We will find her." Roseboro rested a hand on Lucien's shoulder. "Find me tomorrow by the front oval. After your dinner. I have an agreement with the guard. He's a father of one of your friends, isn't he? He will let us by. I made him understand the importance of what we are going to do."

"Will we come back? Once we find my mother and my friends? My friend Maia . . ."

"We are going to try to help everyone."

"Where will we sleep?"

"The town. There's no war there, as I told you. It's safe enough for all kinds of things. There's still a lot I need to figure out. But you aren't going to be hurt anymore. Others won't be either. We will find a way to help them. That I promise—that effort. As I said, there's only so much I can say now. But meet at the oval after dinner tomorrow. You can't tell anyone else. If anyone else found out or accidentally told, even a friend, we could be in great trouble. Can you do this? Are you ready?"

It was a question, like many, he had no adequate answer for, nothing that could offer the certainty Roseboro wanted. House of Earth wasn't a choice. They lived this way to protect the planet. He still could believe this. And if he did, then leaving now would be an attack on the planet. It would be an attack on all he knew. That's what O. C. Leroux would say. He would be failing all that O. C. gave to him, this very world. It belonged to Lucien too—and would the world outside still be his? The library in town had once been his, with the pond to meet Gabrielle. But he had left it behind. The cottage had been left behind.

Darling Drive, the old way, before the attacks on the towers and the worst day and their move to House of Earth, all of it would have to be returned to, somehow, like inhabiting old skin that had already been shed during a transformation that was supposed to be radical and permanent. Roseboro was offering him the return. Could he go?

He could stay. He could not follow Roseboro. He could stay, eat his meals, sleep in his room alone. The wall was done and there would be no way of seeing Gabrielle again, not for a long time, not ever. And Mama. He would have to simply trust that she would return. He had her word and Jack's. Others still hadn't come back. He was afraid they never would, and he would never learn why. He was afraid—he could say it to himself now, in the cold churn of the interior mind—that he would be next. They could take him too. It could be another pit, another place of darkness, except morning would not come. They could keep him there. He could pound his fists against the wooden walls and cry and scream and no one would come. This too could happen. He could not disprove it, at least. He could not stare into the void that was his future and see something different.

He had the wall. He had his loneliness. He had the small tears that began to slip, one by one, down his cheek. They were warm when they met his tongue.

"I'll meet you tomorrow," Lucien said.

Roseboro smiled down at him. "Good, Lucien. Listen, we will get through this. It will be better. We will help everyone we can. We will find your mother. This is our best chance. Tomorrow, wait until it's dark. You'll see me at the front. Then we go."

"They won't stop you?"

"Not this time, no."

By the time Lucien dried his eyes, Roseboro had walked away.

———

Lucien couldn't sleep that night. He lay on his back with his eyes open in the empty room and strained to see all he could, the walls swimming in gray light. Minutes inched by. Each time he closed his eyes and pushed against this second layer of aqueous dark, he could feel his mind, this tenuous spool of memory, begin to splinter, broken images cutting him like shards of glass. Kisses from Mama, lectures from Jack, Evie's smile and Samantha's laugh and the friends, hand in hand, dashing across the bright grass. Tomorrow he would leave all of it. House of Earth, fading behind a hill, Roseboro leading him toward a new light. Leading him, he hoped, toward Mama. He knew it would be easier to stay. The fear had grown familiar, like an old animal lapping at his heels. Jack could devise new punishments, but they were in service to the planet, and it all had to be for the best. He whispered this and opened his eyes. The ceiling was unchanged. He closed them again. His chest and stomach burned. Sweat rolled from his forehead to his lips. In the night window, he could see the shadow of a bird passing in moonlight. When he closed his eyes again, he watched the bird continue its flight, all the way to the cooling lip of the exosphere, its beak outstretched at the stars.

He knew he would have to follow Roseboro. It was a feeling on the level of blood, too close to be denied. This was how he would find Mama and Evie and Samantha. Jack had lied about the war. Roseboro could lie, but Gabrielle wouldn't. Once in town, he'd find a way to her. He wouldn't always have to stay with Roseboro. Roseboro was a way past the gate, past the guard who was Maia's father. Roseboro had told him that he had been a boy once, frightened and alone. Roseboro's father had attacked Roseboro's mother. They'd both attacked him. He, too, may have spent time in his own pit, the darkness gobbling light. That was the understanding: Lucien and Roseboro had both reckoned with the kind of intimate terror that never could leave you, that clung like a virus. And that made them alike. That made them fit for this journey. Lucien continued to stare into the ceiling, his heartbeat finally easing. He had decided. Now all he needed to do was watch the sun rise. Each minute was a test he would have to pass.

The morning came like a dream. He couldn't be certain it had arrived, blinking heavily in the light. He rolled over, his eyes finding the blank wall near his bed. He would have to pass this day too. His last one in the life he had known.

At breakfast, he didn't talk. The friends had gathered without him, sitting down over their porridge, sipping at it slowly between sentences. Lucien ate so he wouldn't have to sit there. He didn't want to have to talk to Maia. By deciding to follow Roseboro, he had decided not to tell Maia. He ached with his knowledge. The only way to soothe it, as he left her at the table and walked to wait in the room for instruction to begin, was with the hope that he and Roseboro would come back for her. He didn't know what this would look like or how it would happen, only that it had to, and he wouldn't have made this decision without the belief that it would. What he couldn't argue anymore was the reality of the wall. Roseboro had helped build it; that was inarguable too. It was like the jailer freeing the jailed. But House of Earth couldn't be a jail— Mama wouldn't have kept him in such a place, where bad people went to rot for the bad crimes they committed. None of them had committed crimes. It was those on the outside, the destroyers of the planet, who were guilty. Roseboro was taking Lucien out there.

His head began to throb. Now he was at his desk, his hands clutching the hard edges. If he was afraid to go, he had to remember the wall. He could see the wall from the window. Every day, it seemed to grow. The land had been absorbed into it.

"Good morning, Lucien," Jack said, entering the room.

"Good morning, Jack."

"We have a wonderful lesson planned for today."

The friends trickled in, all taking their seats. This would be his last lesson from Jack, at least the last one for a long time. He would miss the transfer of knowledge, the new words bestowed to make order of the universe. In the new world, beyond House of Earth, he would return to the library. Mrs. Yelich could give him more books. He wouldn't need Jack to make sense of them. When he found Mama, Mama could teach him again.

He didn't listen to Jack's last lesson, which was on butterflies: how they migrate, how they transform, why they are how they are.

"Butterflies are insects in the macrolepidopteran clade Rhopalocera from the order Lepidoptera, which also includes moths," Jack said. "They have a four-stage insect life cycle."

There were still workers at the wall during recreation. Roseboro was among them. Lucien considered approaching, but there wouldn't be much else to say. They had a plan to meet tonight. Speaking to Roseboro again could, in some way, risk it. He tried to join the friends in a game of horseshoes. After the first round, he stopped, sitting down in the grass. For the first time, he felt weary from not sleeping last night. The sun disappeared behind a veil of cloud cover and he fell backward, his head soft in the thick grass. He closed his eyes and waited.

For what, he wasn't sure.

"Hi, Lucien."

It was Maia's voice above him. He looked up, finding her face against the slate-colored sky. He rose slowly, stifling a small yawn.

"Hey."

"Taking a rest?"

"I didn't sleep much last night."

"Oh. Did you have a bad dream?"

"I never went to sleep. A dream couldn't wake me."

"That's hard. I hate the feeling of trying to sleep, of lying in bed and waiting for it to take you. I wish there was a countdown in my head that could tell me when, exactly, sleep was coming."

"Dreams just have to swallow you, like a whale eating plankton. I waited and watched the wall. Now I want to sleep. I could sleep right here."

"The grass is a nice place to sleep."

"Jack wouldn't allow it, though. The habitation facilities. That's where we sleep."

"There's a lot that's not allowed."

"There is," Lucien said, standing up. "I wish the wall would fall down."

"You shouldn't say that."

"It's what I think."

"They did it for our protection, Lucien."

"I don't know why they did it."

He could see that Maia's lower lip was beginning to shake. Whatever else he wanted to say to her, he couldn't say it today. From now until he saw Roseboro again, he would have to keep it to himself. He wouldn't say anything more.

Before they went inside, he took one last look at the wall. Each day, it seemed to shine brighter with a new coat of paint, though he knew that was an optical illusion. It wasn't getting painted anew every day. The coats had been applied. They had dried. The wall was there for him, in its bare and overwhelming breadth, far taller than he was. There was no way to run through it or climb it. It was everywhere.

The wall had made the decision for him. A column of heat shot up his chest. It was not the ordinary fear. He was walking faster, almost running, his feet light beneath him. He was excited. This was it. Tomorrow, he would be running somewhere else. Tomorrow, he would be beyond the wall. He caught a glimpse of Roseboro and fought the urge to wave. In a few hours, he would see him by the oval.

"They did it for a good reason, I'm sure," Maia called from behind.

Jack continued teaching about the butterflies. This time, Lucien could sweep aside the afternoon. Time was moving at his tempo again. Or finally moving at it—he tried to recall a feeling exactly like this one. He was sorry for Maia, and he would come back for her. She deserved to get to the other side of the wall too. Once he found Mama, Evie, and Samantha, he would be back. Maybe Roseboro would let him go to the library tomorrow. It had been so long since he'd walked among his books, run his finger along the endless spines and pulled one out from the stacks without thinking. He could sit by the pond again. If he was there long enough, Gabrielle could find him.

At dinner, he ate silently. This wasn't as hard as it used to be because the friends had each other, and they didn't attempt conversation in the same way. Since the beating with the wooden swords, they had shied away from him, as if he were still bruised and bleeding. They still smiled at him and spoke back. He was not a ghost—not yet, at least. Antonio would pass him salt and pepper if asked. Cavan would play horseshoes. What they offered him was the bareness of their language, a gesture sanded down to its forgettable essence. A head nod, a hand wave, a shrug. He accepted the reduction. Tonight, Antonio's father served peas and carrots. Paired with a glass of water, it would do. Maia sat near him.

"You really don't believe the wall is there to help us," she said quietly.

"I hope it is."

"But you don't believe."

"It won't let me go where I need to go."

"House of Earth is where we need to go. We're here."

Lucien stood up. It was almost time.

"I'll see you soon," he said.

———

To get to the oval at the front, to reach the guard booth, he needed to pass across the commons. Night had come. He eased his way through the darkness, all of it too familiar now. It was close to him. It wouldn't frighten him anymore, he told himself. He walked on. No one was outside. At the guard booth, a small light illuminated the way forward, a new electric light to help whomever was coming see where they were going. The light was like a small eye winking, and he almost, in his fresh excitement, wanted to wink back. Soon he would be past the wall. Tomorrow, the first thing he would do was have Roseboro take him to Gabrielle. Roseboro was from the town too. He knew Mater, and that meant, if Lucien gave him a name, he could probably locate her. Then they could come together to find Mama, Evie, and Samantha. None of them drove cars, so they could only be so far. Maybe they were all waiting in the woods for him, just outside the wall. He could believe it. They could be planning to gather. Or Mama was on her own. Evie, perhaps, had started over in town, free of Sebastian. She was certainly free. He believed in Evie.

Dinner was done and he was where he needed to be. He had walked to the oval. He was nearing the front. If he got much closer, Maia's father would come out and warn him. Not too far. He needed Roseboro. Roseboro was going to appear.

He stopped and waited. Roseboro was nowhere.

This could happen. Roseboro might be late. He was a busy man, with painting and projects to do. He worked. He even knew Jack and maybe O. C. Leroux himself. Adults always had more worlds to retreat to, layering themselves with unnameable obligations, burdens of aging. He would get there soon. Now all Lucien had to do was wait for Roseboro. Roseboro was coming.

Only a matter of waiting.

The electric light was not winking at him. No, it was more steady than that, a stare that wouldn't relent, not even when he looked away. A new creature watching him. He dug his shoe into the soil. Soon, he told himself. Roseboro would have to come. He checked his watch. Only ten minutes had passed. It was not significant time. Roseboro had also not specified a time. *After dinner.* It was after dinner. He would have to come.

Lucien crossed his arms. A gust of wind blew at him, sending a chill down his back. It would be like when he waited for morning to come, just one night ago. Eventually, through the crawl of darkness, it came.

And Roseboro would. He was ready now. Only Roseboro could get him over the wall. O. C. Leroux shouldn't have told Roseboro to build the wall. Lucien didn't need it to be safe. He had always been safe. The war wasn't coming, not yet, and he had two people now who came from town and were unharmed. The wall wasn't right and the wall wasn't fair, and he was ready to shout this, lean back and cry at the sky glittering with his favorite stars.

Twenty minutes, thirty minutes. Another wind gust almost knocked him backward, on his rear end.

Time, it seemed, would always be his enemy, after all. It limped ceaselessly forward, uncaring of what happened to him or anyone around him. Time would not give him Roseboro in front of him. It would not give him Mama's return. He was guaranteed nothing. The electric light continued to pierce the night. He turned from it, gazing toward the wall, now distant in the dark. It was almost an invitation. He could dash at it and try, against the will of gravity, to climb and leap it. In books he had read before coming to live at House of Earth, heroes were always devising the means to obliterate an unacceptable reality and reconfigure it on the terms they required for survival. A new power was discovered, a talisman procured, a magical visitor arrived to announce a destiny. He supposed that was Roseboro. Then where was Roseboro? He was coming.

One hour was gone.

He didn't know why he expected the electric light over the guard booth to turn off. It would stay on all night. That was its purpose. But he shut his eyes and strained to will it off. He concentrated as hard as he could, locking his bones into place. He wasn't going to move. When he opened his eyes, he decided, the light would be off and Roseboro would be here.

The light was still on.

For one minute, he held his eyes on his digital watch. If he stared long enough and didn't allow himself to blink, the numbers could lose their rigidity and take on a new form. They could melt like water. Their very meaning could be rejected for something else, whatever he decided in that pocket of darkness. They weren't symbols of time. They could become what he wanted them to become. In this moment, he could assume a new kind of power. Time, he decided, would limp forward only when he decided. He would hold it still until Roseboro showed up.

But he blinked. More minutes had fled. Roseboro hadn't appeared. He wasn't coming from any direction Lucien looked. The wall was unmoved. He shut his eyes one more time, though he wasn't sure exactly what he hoped to see when he opened them again. He knew he would see the electric light and the guard booth and maybe the shadowed outline of Maia's father, standing guard.

Roseboro still wasn't here.

He began to walk. First he started toward the far edge of the oval, nearing the guard booth. If he got any closer, Maia's father would see him. He turned in the direction of the habitation facilities. An emptiness had opened up in his stomach. His forehead began to feel heavy. He was sinking, or would sink, and he imagined collapsing in the grass, sleeping there and living there and burying himself in soil until he was no longer ready to breathe. For the last time—he told himself this was it—he checked his watch. He wanted to rip it off and throw it at the wall. He would watch the shattering. At least he would have that sound, the rain of plastic shards on the earth. That would be his own.

He heard movement in the grass, a low crunching. One step, two steps, three steps. His heart sped up. He didn't want to turn yet. Roseboro wouldn't announce himself. They would have to be quiet. He continued to walk, expecting Roseboro to overtake him. Roseboro was a much bigger man, and his strides would catch him soon. All he had to do was keep walking. The sound was louder now. First, when he saw Roseboro, he would ask why he was late. Roseboro would have a good reason. He wanted to tell Roseboro he sometimes worried they would be gone and miss Mama if she suddenly returned to House of Earth.

There was a part of him that wasn't so confident that they would find Mama right away. Not on the first day. But he knew, still, they had to go, and he was glad Roseboro had shown up at last and they could walk past the guard booth and into the night beyond the new wall.

"Lucien."

He stopped hard in the grass, almost falling forward. His breath left him.

He heard one more footstep.

"Let's go inside, Lucien."

Jack was standing behind him; his hands rested on his hips. When Lucien turned, his mouth finally open, he saw that Jack was grinning at him, his front teeth flashing. They were the only two bodies in the dark.

"Jack."

"Come now, it's almost bedtime. You need to be inside."

Jack's touch was gentle, a light shove from the neck to the shoulder blade. They were walking toward the habitation facilities. He listened to the steadiness of Jack's breathing, how Jack easily moved him across the commons. Lucien kept expecting Jack to lift his hand from his shoulder. He only pressed harder, with the slightest pressure, just beyond the threshold for pain.

"You gave us all a fright," Jack said.

"I didn't mean to."

"You know you should go to the habitation facility after mealtime. It's understandable to want to be out here. It's quite peaceful at night. The stillness. I love it too. And the wondrous starlight. Like you, I enjoy this kind of activity. Your mind drifts, doesn't it? You begin to imagine all kinds of things."

They were near the door of Lucien's habitation facility. Jack was still smiling. He hadn't let Lucien go. With his free hand, he guided the door open. They walked together to Lucien's room, their footsteps echoing in the dark, vacant hallway.

The Night Burns Bright

"Here we go. Let's get a good night's rest, okay? It's very important to keep up your strength. You seem to be shaking a little. I hope you ate and drank enough at dinner. Did you?"

"I did."

"You need to be good. I see progress, Lucien. I only want to make sure you continue to make it, that you grow in the way you need to grow. Caterpillars need to become butterflies."

"I know," he replied weakly. They were in the room now. Jack had still not let go, even as Lucien began to sit on his empty, unmade bed.

"Now, you'll get the rest you need. I'll see you in the morning. We'll have more exciting lessons."

Lucien began to mouth the word *okay* before stopping himself, realizing he didn't have the strength for it. His head began to sag, his jaw slack, his mouth achingly dry. He was no longer looking at Jack. Jack's hand, dug deeper into his flesh now, began to slowly release him.

"After dinner, from now on, please go to your room, like the other friends. It's very important we do all of these things together. Is that clear, Lucien?"

"Yes."

Jack was in the threshold of the door now. His smile was unchanged, almost as if it had been sketched on in an earlier, unlikely time.

"Wynn Roseboro won't be meeting you. He never will," Jack said, closing the door and walking away.

———

Mama had been gone one week, then two, then three. On the morning of the three-week anniversary of her disappearance, Lucien went to breakfast, alone as he entered the nutritional hall. Several of the friends had taken their usual table. The other collectives were filing into the hall. Without thinking, he grabbed a tray and a bowl for his porridge.

He hadn't even noticed that Antonio's father was not in his typical position behind the steaming food. He was not there at all. Another man, whom he recognized as Magnus's father, was now scooping porridge.

"Good morning, Lucien."

"Good morning."

"This porridge is cinnamon. You'll really enjoy it. We just got a fresh batch."

"That's great."

The bowl landed on his tray, shaking with the weight of the porridge. Magnus's father had served him slightly more than he was used to.

"You're helping out Antonio's dad, Anders?"

"I'll be serving meals."

Sitting down, Lucien waited for the friends to ask about Antonio's father, how strange it was to have someone else serving them breakfast. Karthik was telling Jacinda about his favorite maypole dance. Magnus and Cavan were debating who could sprint faster on the commons. Antonio was sitting near Carlina, speaking with her about the Greenland shark, and how it could live hundreds of years.

"No one quite knows why," Carlina said.

"Wow."

"Imagine being in the water that long. Imagine," Antonio said.

"What do you think it thinks about?"

"I don't know—it's just amazing, that an animal like that could exist."

Maia sat next to him and she seemed to be waiting for it too, for the acknowledgment that another constant of their lives had been altered. She looked at him and he looked at her and they ate quietly. If anyone was going to say it, it would have to be Antonio.

They only continued to talk about Greenland sharks.

Lucien finished his bowl first. Maia was done soon after, wiping the corners of her mouth with a napkin. He drank a glass of water.

There was no talk of Antonio's father at instruction or at lunch or on the commons. When they broke into teams to play O. C., Lucien was not asked to play. Maia was chosen to be O. C. He listened to the shouts of *darkness* and *light*, the bodies ping-ponging on the grass, as he again tossed horseshoes and waited for the day to be over.

"You should play," Maia said, half out of breath after tagging Karthik.

"No."

"It will be okay."

"I'm fine here."

"Playing gets your mind off things."

"What if I don't want my mind *off*, Maia?"

The sound of his voice was harsher than he intended it to be, a hidden rage overtaking him. Maia backed away. He realized there was a chunk of grass in his hand and he had been pulling it from soil while talking to her.

———

Antonio was jogging past him, back to the instruction room. Recreation time was ending.

"Hi, Lucien," he said, mopping his brow.

"Antonio."

"Next time, you should play."

Lucien wasn't sure why Antonio suddenly wanted him to play again.

"Maybe."

"Listen . . ." Antonio was closer now, his shadow overlapping with Lucien's. "I know you're missing your mom. I'm not supposed to talk about it, but I'm missing my mom and dad too."

"They're both gone?"

"They had to, you know. O. C. called."

"They told you?"

"Kind of. Hinted."

"That's terrible."

"No, it's not! They're doing really important stuff for us, for House of Earth. This is it. They were chosen. Your mom too."

"We should be able to talk about them."

"We can't."

His days seemed to be emptying out. He tried to forget his night waiting for Roseboro. Without anyone in the room in the evening, time expanded in new, disorienting ways. He could draw as much as he wanted, until his pencils turned to nubs and the line disappeared like a distant memory. Opening Mama's drawer, he found two skirts she had left behind. If Mama had truly decided to leave, she would have taken every piece of clothing she could.

If she was forced to leave, it wouldn't have mattered.

When he dreamed, he saw the tombstones again. They would transform into the buildings and transform back. Fire sucked backward into the black stone, vanishing with a hiss. Airplanes fell from the sky like flaming teardrops. None of it meant anything to him, or anything he could put into words. Upon waking, he would sometimes scream, but even his fear felt like a waste with no one there to acknowledge it, to give it new form in daylight.

Roseboro was where Mama was or somewhere much worse.

On another day, with Mama still gone, he carefully removed his drawing of O. C. Leroux.

Magnus's father didn't smile as much behind the food counter. Lucien noticed this too, as he accepted his breakfast, lunch, and dinner each day. At breakfast, the porridge had been reduced, so it only halfway filled up his bowl. At lunch, carrots and string beans were parceled out carefully, as if Magnus's father were counting each one. At dinner, the hummus and lettuce were in noticeably smaller quantities, a half or even a quarter as much as he was used to eating.

The friends had less food too. Lucien, at least, could see he wasn't the only one not being served the portions he had always known.

It was Karthik who said out loud what they were all thinking. "There's been less the last few days, right?"

"I think so," Colt answered.

"Yeah," Maia said.

"My dad said it was O. C.'s orders, though I'm not sure I'm supposed to say that," Magnus said.

"Really?"

"He said we need to consume less. It's better for the planet that way."

"That makes total sense."

"Yes."

"Jack has said that."

"I'm still hungry," Lucien said, surprised to even hear himself speaking out loud.

They turned to him.

"You heard what Magnus said. We have to consume less now," Cavan said.

"Yeah. And I bet with the war, with all that's going on, we can't afford just to eat like we used to. Better safe than sorry," Antonio said, brushing a strand of hair from his eyes.

"Right—and Lucien, that all is more important than *your* hunger," Magnus said.

Lucien had nothing else to say. After dinner, he ignored the games on the commons and returned to his room for the long, silent hours until he could fall asleep. Sometimes he could dream while awake, watching the burning and hearing the screams as he sat up in bed, the towers-as-tombstones looming so high in the pale ceiling of sky he was sure they were built by the God he had never met to be destroyed when the time came.

The sun set. When he flicked the switch in the room, the overhead bulb remained dark. Electricity was increasingly a gamble, here one day and gone another. He was learning the dark. He could fear it less the more time he spent alone. He could mold it or let it mold him.

His hand suddenly twitched. He needed to draw.

The pencils were worn down. Soon he would have to go to the supply closet in the instruction room for more. This would mean asking Jack, something he no longer wanted to do. He wanted the pencils to appear in his hand. He wanted the ease he would never have.

Underneath the bunk bed, in a small pouch where he kept his supplies, was a red Crayola marker. He hardly used it because he didn't like to draw or color with markers. They were too thick, too wet, not nimble enough for the coloring and sketching he wanted to attempt on paper. He took the marker out this time, holding it in his hand.

He gripped the marker. His hand was shaking. He understood, on the level of the blood pumping hungrily through his heart, what he was about to do.

The marker found the wall before the urge could fully explode inside him.

He started where his O. C. Leroux drawing used to be, as well as the old drawings Mama had crumpled up on that day. His left hand stiffened to draw the thick, rigid line that would make up the first letter, a red he imagined so bright in the dark. He drew three horizontal lines that jutted out, like infant limbs, from the original hard line on the white wall.

The letter *E*.

In the same size as the first letter, he drew two sweeping diagonal lines that converged at the bottom, like wounded birds. He admired the *V* and quickly slashed an *I* next. The *E* was last, as bold as the first, and he stood back to see what he had done.

Her name was now on his wall.

He spun to the blank stretch of wall above his bunk bed. The marker trembled between his fingers, but he was more determined than ever to keep going. He was quicker now because the name was longer, a slithering *S* and a towering *A* and an *M* that reminded him of how he used to run up and down the small gulley in the middle of Darling Drive, when he still lived in the cottage and could leave to meet Gabrielle at the library. He pressed harder into the wall so the marker could bleed out every drop of color it held captive within its cylindrical casing.

He finished her name, the *ANTHA*, in all capital letters too.

If he couldn't speak their names, their names could speak from his wall. He lay back in bed, the marker rolling out of his palm and chattering against the floor. From his angle, he could stare directly at Evie's name, and when he turned his head, he saw Samantha's. He knew that if Mama or Jack saw what he had done, there would be another punishment. In his weariness, his arms going slack and his feet, still in sneakers, dropping to the side, he couldn't entirely ignore this fear. He could be the next to disappear. House of Earth didn't need him. No one did. Mama hadn't even told him she was leaving.

His eyelids flickered, open and closed and open and closed. In sleep, he would see their names too, bright red on a wall of black beyond any comprehension, including his own.

———

Antonio was not at breakfast. Lucien raced back, before instruction, to see if he was in his room. He pushed the door open and the emptiness immediately sickened him. The sheets had been pulled firmly over the mattress, the blankets folded over each bed. He last saw Antonio at dinner, turning away as he said *better safe than sorry*. Lucien had told the friends he was hungry. He wished he hadn't.

He was breathing hard as he hunted through the room for any sign of where Antonio had gone and why. His parents were helping House of Earth, just as Mama supposedly was, in a way Jack would never explain. He struggled to imagine what this help would mean: chopping wood, loading supplies, growing corn, laboring in a deep, dark place. Gabrielle had already told him the war had not engulfed Mater.

Even if he could prove that Jack was not telling the truth, what could he do with such information? Hold it close and hope? Roseboro wasn't coming back.

Even the word *hope* seemed too weak to Lucien.

He shut the door to Antonio's room, no closer to hunting out the clue that could tell him where the whole family had gone. Anders, Yolanda, Antonio. Two of them were branded. He had seen them on that night, ecstasy joined with raw pain.

At instruction, the conversations ranged everywhere else but Antonio. Lucien was conscious now of the empty desks, where Samantha and Evie and now Antonio used to sit. He could *hope* he would come back, just as he once hoped to see Evie again after the day Sebastian carried her away. The chairs were like bare memorials now, marking where voices once rang out and bodies once fidgeted during Jack's long lectures.

"Next week my mom is taking us on a hike," Colt said at lunch.

"That's awesome," Magnus said.

"I'd like to see the river," Karthik said.

"Me too," said Jacinda.

Maia sat next to Lucien. Each of them had one small cup of steamed carrots. Seeing the dwindling food served at lunch only reminded him of how hungry he was becoming.

"I wish they gave us more," Maia said.

"I don't think they will."

"It's for the best, I guess. We can't be consuming so much. The earth's survival comes first."

"It does."

He strained for a way to ask her about Antonio, to confirm he wasn't the only one who thought about his empty room, the sheets folded tightly against his hard mattress.

"Antonio is gone," Lucien said quietly.

Maia bent low, her lips closing in on his ear. "Don't talk about that," she whispered.

He turned to her. "Why?"

"We saw talking about them doesn't bring them back, and if they're doing better things or if they're bad, we just shouldn't say their names, either way."

"Antonio was just here."

"Let it go."

"Maia."

"I want to enjoy my carrots."

The next day, as if someone had heard his thoughts, the chairs that once held Evie, Samantha, and Antonio were gone from the instruction room. There were now exactly enough chairs and desks for all the friends. Jack stood at the center of the room and waved to them all. They waved back.

"Before we get into our lesson and workshop today—we're going to be carving and painting our own walking sticks for the upcoming hike—I wanted to just quickly talk about a change you may have noticed. I know it's been on your minds. It's been on mine too."

Was Jack going to talk about Evie? Samantha? Antonio? Mama? Lucien tried to see whether any of the friends betrayed the hope he held. If they cared, they wouldn't say. He held both ends of his desk. Jack was preparing to tell him, perhaps, what he longed to know.

"You've been served smaller portions at breakfast, lunch, and dinner. What you've noticed is true. This has been a conscious effort on our part to ensure we are living in a sustainable way that best helps us survive and thrive, especially if things beyond us grow worse. I know it's hard. I'm doing with less as well. Everyone sacrifices, together. It's important we recognize what harm we can do to the earth just by existing, and do whatever we can to make sure this harm doesn't continue to happen. Is this clear?"

They said that it was. It had to be. There was no altering the reality of less porridge, fewer carrots, a smaller glass of water. His hands relaxed on the desk. Jack wasn't going to tell him what he wanted to know.

"You remember our long lesson on the history of the earth. It's one I want you to keep with you as you grow. We've learned a lot together, so much, and sometimes facts and figures slip away. I want you to always remember Planet Earth is nearly five billion years old. For much of that time, for almost all of it, we were not here. We, the human race. If you imagine this time was a single day, we are less than a second. An eyeblink. There were single-celled organisms and then dinosaurs and then all kinds of creatures, other mammals too, before we arrived. For many billions of years, for so much of this time, there was a stability, a harmony, nature allowed to cycle onward. The humans were small at first. Only a few thousand, then a million. In less than an eyeblink's time, technology allowed the human race to grow rapidly in ways no one could have imagined. From millions to billions. Imagine your bowl of porridge, once empty, now overflowing to such a degree it pours over the rim, down the table, and begins to fill the floor. It's rising around your ankles. We have *filled* the planet. We eat, we drink. We absorb and destroy to build what we call a civilization. Some of you have seen the cities and the suburbs, the enormous houses and buildings, the energy gobbled and wasted. You have seen the destruction up close. Humans have been unleashed on the planet. If we weren't them—sitting right here in this room, with our eyes and ears and mouth—we would see them as a virus, a virus bent on exterminating all the earth has built over these billions of years. When you see a little less at lunch, fewer vegetables or fruit, you must consider what it meant when you had *more*. We've talked about infinity, what it means in math—nothing on the earth is infinite. Nothing. If human beings are a virus, *we*, here, must be something else. We must not live in such a destructive way. We must be the antidote. That is why O. C. Leroux has House of Earth for us. To give us a chance to be *more* than a virus."

This was the first time Lucien had heard Jack compare humans to a virus. He stared at his flesh, uncoiling his fingers, turning his forearm inward. He tried to see a virus. He tried to see how he was infecting the land, how they all were. If humans were a virus, why did they exist in the first place?

"More must live like us," Jack said.

Cavan raised his hand.

"Yes, Cavan?"

"How can we make sure the virus doesn't spread?"

Jack folded his arms gently in front of his chest, walking toward Cavan. "We're doing it right now."

"Really?"

"Yes."

———

Each passing week, Lucien tried to imagine what he would be discussing with Gabrielle, had Roseboro gotten him out. Her school, her summer vacation, her hardworking mother and troubled father. Noah. On the day and time when he would have met her, had the wall not separated them, Colt's mother came to the commons and told them it was time for a hike.

The friends gathered around her and cheered.

Lucien's first unspoken question was answered when they headed straight for the front, passing the guard booth, where Maia's father stood without uttering a word. They were beyond the gravel driveway, in a roadway Lucien had not seen in many months. The only way to the woods, then, was through the front gate, where all those who came and left were watched. If he ever wanted to see Gabrielle again, he would have to walk through here.

"Who's ready for some exploring?" Colt's mother asked.

They all cheered again.

Everyone, Lucien included, had their multicolored walking sticks, fashioned and painted during instruction. He didn't need a stick to walk. When he planted it in the soil, it seemed to get stuck. It was like a third leg his body had unnecessarily sprouted one night. They walked together on the outer perimeter of the wall, approaching the very same clearing where he once raced to meet Gabrielle. Colt's mother waved them on and they entered, descending the familiar slope, trying to avoid the indentations in the land he had learned so well.

Maia was ahead of him, Karthik to his side, Magnus behind.

He realized, surveying the other friends, who were all trailing Colt's mother, that Cavan was not with them at all.

Cavan had not been at breakfast. Cavan had not been at instruction. Since Cavan always sat behind him, he hadn't noticed.

"We are going to make our way to the river," Colt's mother said. "We'll enjoy the fresh air, appreciate our natural surroundings, and maybe, just maybe, I'll teach you some old songs I know."

They cheered for this too. Lucien was at least grateful for one time in the woods, reaching out and grazing as many tree trunks as he could, touching grass, silently identifying species of plants and flowers.

Lucien heard a loud crunch, feet sloshing through branches and leaves. He knew the approach wasn't any animal. It was too deliberate, too loud.

Colt's mother called out, "Natasha!" and the friends turned together toward the woman running straight at them.

"Kara," she said, breathing heavily.

Natasha surveyed the friends. "It's good to see all of you here, safe."

"Of course they're safe," Colt's mother said.

"We must go back now," Natasha said. "Come on, everyone."

"Wait—I was cleared for this hike. *You* cleared me."

"O. C. Leroux doesn't believe it's safe anymore. We're beyond the walls, and given the situation, we need to return."

"I just don't understand—"

"We must return now."

"We can, okay, it's just . . . we just left."

"Friends," Natasha said, turning toward them, briefly making eye contact with Lucien. "Why don't you go back up the hill now and return to House of Earth, where you can have so much fun on the commons, safe and sound? I'm just going to need a private moment with Kara."

They began the return, without Colt's mother. Lucien trailed the group, trying to hear what Natasha was about to say. But the two adults were walking deeper into the woods, Natasha's arm around the shoulder of Colt's mother. She was leading Kara away through the trees, growing smaller and smaller.

He wanted to run after them.

Magnus was leading the friends now, almost unseen at the top of the slope. Maia drifted back, ending up at Lucien's side.

"I wanted to go on the hike," she said.

"I did too."

"If it's dangerous, well, I suppose it's good we are going back."

"I don't see how it became dangerous."

"They saw something we didn't see."

"They always see things we don't see."

"That's good, though."

"I hope it is."

They were now the last two, straggling as the collective rounded the corner and followed the wall back toward the front gate. Magnus was at the front, joined by Colt and Jacinda.

"Cavan isn't here either," Lucien said to Maia.

"If he's not here, then maybe there's a reason."

"There's always one."

"I just don't know what good there is, you know, to *talk* about them."

"Antonio. Samantha. Cavan."

"Your mom. Their parents. If we talk about them, do they come back? And if we do—"

"You're afraid."

"That night we saw them all on the commons, with the fire and the branding . . ."

"I hated it too."

"Let's just—let's just not talk about it."

On the commons, he was no longer a participant in what once defined the fabric of his life, the stitching that connected one day to the next. He was not asked to play in any games. He was not asked about what he thought. Only Maia could be counted on to speak to him at breakfast, lunch, and dinner. If another friend did, it seemed accidental, like tripping over your shoelaces.

He sat alone, thinking about the hike that never was, Colt's mother shrinking in the distance. Nothing in the woods had betrayed the dangerousness of the hike. The war was still unseen, existing only in the words of the mentors who spoke of it often. He was tiring of asking questions inside his head that had no answers.

He was tired of asking himself where Roseboro had gone. It hurt him to wonder.

He could only recite the names of those who were missing, and go to bed under those he had scrawled, in his thick red marker, on the bedroom wall.

The next day Mama came home.

SUMMER

He woke to the strange sensation of human touch, picking through the webbing of a dream as his eyes opened to light. She was standing above him, and he knew it was real because he could feel all of it, his arms around her body, her lips on his forehead, the tears rolling down his cheeks. She held him and rocked him, whispering his name.

He murmured into her body. *Mama.*

"I'm here, honey."

He wanted to tell her so much. How the friends were vanishing, how long his nights were, what Jack said about viruses. She held him and then let go, her eyes roving to the walls where he had written their names in his bright red marker.

"We are going to have to clean these walls," she said quietly.

"I'm sorry, Mama."

"It will be okay. We all get sick sometimes. But we can get better."

She was staring at the names. *Evie. Samantha.* Her finger ran along the wall.

"We will wash these out. I'm disappointed in you, Lucien, but I know this hasn't been easy either."

When she left the room, his heart sank. She was going again. He needed to make sure she would come back this time, that she wouldn't disappear like all the others. He hurried after her, down the hallway to the bathroom door. She was inside, washing her hands in the sink. In her hand was a cloth napkin he hadn't seen before.

"I'm just wetting it with warm water and some soap. I'm going to clean the walls. Okay?"

"Okay."

He watched her scrub hard, the names vanishing. She started with Samantha, her forearm tensing as she slowly erased the *S* and the *A* and the looping *M*. It happened faster than he imagined it would. A faint smear remained, like the trace of blood, but nothing else.

She attacked the four letters next. *E, V, I, E*. He didn't expect to feel her loss again. It was as if she had returned to him, the way she had once been, before vanishing once more.

All that was left now was the name in his head he could no longer speak.

"You know not to write on the walls again. It was a bad thing to do."

"I won't."

"House of Earth can't be sustained if we continue to do bad things. We won't, though; I know that. I know you. I raised you to be good."

"I will be good."

"Let's go get breakfast."

Lucien sat with Mama at breakfast, a rarity. Magnus's father served oatmeal in a cup. Lucien ate as slowly as he could to savor what he had. The portion of oatmeal, like the portion of porridge he'd received yesterday, continued to shrink. There were no longer blueberries to sprinkle on top. Mama finished her oatmeal first. She asked him if he was enjoying his.

"I am enjoying it, yes."

"We're so lucky to have it."

The cup had only stray flecks of hardened oatmeal left, and he spooned out as much as he could, making sure no food was wasted. His stomach continued to grumble. He wished for the cup to be refilled, for the hot oatmeal to spill over the rim with abundance. He would eat slowly enough so he would always have some.

"Mama," he said, his spoon clinking against the cup, "have you seen the war?"

"I have."

"We went for a hike for a little yesterday and the woods looked the same."

"The war, unfortunately, is coming. And it doesn't always take the forms we imagine."

"Really?"

"It's not guns and tanks and missiles. It is much more than that."

"Someone told me there wasn't a war in town."

"Who told you that?"

"A person I knew."

"Lucien, who?"

"Her name . . ." He was afraid to say it, hoping somehow the syllables would dissolve in his throat and Mama would be satisfied with a gurgle. "Her name, it was Gabrielle."

"This is the girl from town, I take it. I remember. The one you used to see all those times?"

Gabrielle was his secret, the one part of him he had always kept from Mama. He had mentioned, only once, a girl from the library, but he'd never used her name. Had Mama watched him at the library the whole time? Had Mama watched him in the woods? Mama did always know. Even when she was missing, he always had the sense she could see him, that her presence in his mind was enough to ensure her eye never left him. She was in the grass, in the trees, traveling through the air.

His first and last words, he thought then, would be *Mama*.

"Yes."

"The people from town can't be trusted. They will lie to you because they know their way of life is doomed. Do you understand?"

"I do, Mama."

"They will keep lying to you because they don't want what's best for you, like I do. They want to destroy us. They are destroying each other, and then they will destroy us."

"Jack said we were a virus."

"We are human beings, yes, and we are a virus, honey. But we can also choose a different path. We don't have to destroy. We can live differently, live better, and *atone*—do you understand that word?"

"I've heard it."

"We can atone. We can do it. House of Earth, Lucien, is atonement."

"There are less people here than there used to be."

"Those that leave, they leave for a reason. And those that remain, remain for a reason."

At instruction, Cavan was still gone. Lucien recited their names in his head: *Evie, Samantha, Antonio, Cavan.* That's all he could do.

When he wasn't at instruction, he tried to follow Mama. He wanted to make sure she stayed at House of Earth. He waited for her, ate dinner with her, and asked her, please, to be in the room when he went to sleep.

"Don't go away."

The heat came. A thermometer in the bathroom read one hundred degrees. His room, like the habitation facility itself, was like what he imagined the inside of a stomach to be—a small, dark, broiling place. On the commons, the friends hid in the shade of what trees had not been walled off, inventing games that were not for him. A film of sweat covered his eyes when the sun hung, dead and bright, in the sky, and he sucked water out of a small tin canteen Mama had given him. The heat dulled his hunger. When Jack spoke, the language dripped away before it could reach his ears.

When he slept at night, he dreamed he hadn't slept at all.

Colt's absence only occurred to him on the second day. Jacinda, Karthik, and Magnus were clustered together on the commons, and he was used to seeing Colt with them. Colt was not at breakfast. He had not been at dinner the previous day either.

"There are less people," he said to Maia.

"Yes," was all she could say.

Colt's mother and father were gone too. Their room was clean and empty. The sheets had been made. The Sunflowers, the younger collective, seemed smaller. Several tables in the nutritional hall were empty.

Colt's chair and desk were soon gone.

Where are they going? He could howl the question each day, from morning to night. He could break through the heat choking him. He could rip the film from his eyes. He could suck the sweat back into him.

As the sun set, between dinner and bed, he walked across the commons alone. Mama had eaten dinner with him and said she needed to speak with Jack for a few minutes. She told him to wait for her. He remembered the flagpole that was once at the oval, how he had liked to lean his back against it and watch the birds wheeling above. Years ago, it had been removed. One day there, the next gone.

As Lucien stood, sweat dampening the hollow of his chest, he remembered the anguish of waiting. Once he had waited like this for Roseboro, hoping he would emerge from the dark to take him away. He never told Mama about Roseboro. It was possible that Jack had told her, that she already knew, or that it was some kind of original knowledge that could not be easily explained. For so long, he had told Mama everything. His day would simply be her day. He could feel, at times, that he was little more than her shadow, with breath and flesh and light. He followed her and it was enough.

But now, even as Lucien hoped to never lose her again, he would withhold some of himself from her. He knew this change was permanent. She'd been gone when he met Roseboro, and whatever she learned—about Roseboro's appearance and disappearance—would not be from him. Memories were secrets too. He wiped sweat from his eyes and thought about sitting in the grass. It was always coolest in that first moment you collapsed into it.

He saw, suddenly, that Magnus was walking toward him. He remained standing.

"Hey," Magnus said.

A jagged sweat stain covered the upper half of his white cotton T-shirt. He was leaning forward, his hands pressed to his knees. A rosy sunburn covered his wet, sloping forehead.

"Hi, Magnus."

"Can I, um, talk to you?"

"Sure."

"Between us. Quietly."

"Yes."

"No one else—"

"What is it?"

"I don't like that everyone's been gone lately."

Lucien could only nod.

"Cavan, his parents. And Samantha and even Evie, even if she was bad—are they coming back? They should get to come back."

"I don't know."

"Colt and his parents. His mom was going to be a mentor. I went by their room. Did you see their room?"

"I did."

"Empty. Like they weren't there. I've accepted it, you know, and it's all for the best, and I think about what Jack said and how this is really the only way. I just wish I knew where everyone was going. It would be easier."

"It would be."

"We never see them when they leave. It must happen at night."

"I've wondered that."

"Your mom came back, though. She was gone and came back. So they all might. They're probably doing something very important. Did your mom tell you anything?"

"No."

"Yeah, I just—well, it was good just to say it. Speak it. I'm sure it will be fine. I'm gonna go to bed soon. It's so hot."

"I'll see you tomorrow."

Mama walked up soon after. She took his hand in hers.

"Are you staying cool?" she asked.

"It's pretty hot still. I'm trying."

"Drink plenty of water."

They walked together, across the bend of grass and toward the habitation facilities. Mama hummed a tune he didn't recognize.

"Mama, I have a question."

"Yes, what is it?"

"Where did you go? When you were gone?"

"Lucien, that's something you'll understand when you're a little bit older. Just not tonight."

"When I'm older?"

"Yes."

"How old?"

"It will depend, honey. You'll be an adult before you know it."

She didn't say anything else. They walked together back to their habitation facility, night falling around them. When they got inside the room, she told him she was going to go to bed early.

"It's been a long day. Both of us need rest."

"Yes, Mama."

———

Jack stood behind the breakfast counter, scooping out cinnamon porridge.

"Good morning, Lucien."

"Good morning, Jack."

He knew better than to ask about Magnus's father. At their table, long stretches of the bench now empty, there was no Magnus. He knew. They always left in the night. Only Evie had appeared the day she vanished, and she'd been covered in blood.

He remembered Magnus, sweating, telling him that he didn't like everyone going away.

The conversations were thinning. Most of the friends ate in silence or remarked about the heat, which had dipped slightly from yesterday. The habitation-facility thermometer read ninety-two.

"I'm glad the porridge is cinnamon," Maia said.

"It's a good flavor," agreed Karthik.

"Cinnamon," Lucien said, as if testing the strength of its syllables on his teeth.

They turned back to their bowls. Lucien noticed how hushed the nutritional hall seemed now, devoid of the echoing voices that he'd assumed would always layer the background of this place.

He was done with his cup of porridge. There was so little to begin with, even less than yesterday. Hunger no longer left him. It followed him morning, noon, and night, like a stray wolf after blood, like the furious White Fang of his memories. He sat and waited for breakfast to be over.

He decided, before instruction began once again, he would take a walk around House of Earth.

"Where are you going?" Maia asked when he stood up.

"A walk."

"Can I come?"

"Yes."

Maia was done with her breakfast. He didn't ask her about the hunger but sensed its unremarked-upon presence. They pushed through the doors and entered the grass field in the back. He led her, unsure where exactly he wanted to walk. Without the woods, his only choice was to circle the perimeter, keeping the wall in the corner of his eye. The sky was cloudless, a cornflower blue he could once lose himself in. Maia was silent. He walked because he could, because he hadn't yet disappeared like all the others.

They were near the shed where they had once spent that night of the blizzard, the coldest he'd ever been. The same shed where Jack kept the shinai, the bamboo swords that had beaten him, wielded by bodies he no longer saw.

"Do you remember the night we spent there?" he asked.

"In the shed?"

"Yes."

"When we did the sled race."

"We were learning about the Iditarod."

"You were the musher."

"I didn't know where we were going."

"None of us did."

"He took the markers away on purpose. There were never markers when we started."

"It was to teach us a lesson."

"To that point in my life, I had never been so cold and so scared. I didn't understand what was happening."

"I like to think it made us stronger."

"I don't know if it did. Right now, standing here, I don't know."

"What's that on the side of the shed?"

"What?"

"That color. Here, let's go around the corner."

He saw what she was pointing at: a small streak of red paint on the corner of the white shed. As they approached, they could see that the streak continued on to the other side on the long wall. The streak was more than a streak—it belonged to something much larger, a whirl of bright-red paint hurrying elsewhere. He sped ahead of Maia, coming to the wall where the streak led.

The streak joined a letter, which joined another and another, forming two enormous words on the side of the shed. The paint was still dripping at the edges. It had the color of flesh, freshly ripped and bleeding. Maia stood next to him, her mouth opening. The words could have been painted hours or even minutes ago.

He heard the screaming in his head, Evie's scream, the memory so radical and piercing he could almost be certain Evie was screaming again, from the unknown place she had gone.

It was Maia who read the words and spoke them out loud. "Blood Earth."

He imagined the paint burning beneath skin, the painter tearing open a wound to pour it onto the palette, a brush swirling through the vicious red to make the letters as large as they could be. Each one spilling from a dream.

He took a step closer and touched the paint with his finger. "It's still wet," he said.

Maia stared at the paint on his fingertip, glittering in the sunlight. "It is. Who do you think did this?"

"It could be anyone."

"One of the friends?"

"Anyone."

"Jack?"

"Even him."

"Let's go to instruction. We'll be late. Do we tell Jack?"

"By the time we get there, he'll already know."

———

Jack did not talk about Blood Earth. He did not talk about the friends he used to teach who no longer sat in the room, the desks and chairs missing, the silences that now measured out the stretch of time between instruction and lunch. In their absence, Lucien saw what they had been, the subtle and boisterous ways they had filled static space. Maia no longer answered questions unless Jack directly called on her. Lucien had given up the habit long ago, but he was still sad, in ways he could not describe, to see her doing it too.

Jack talked increasingly about viruses. Viruses could be spread any-where at any time. People were the most malignant, he said. That's the word that stuck with Lucien through the day. *Malignant.*

Mal, he had once been told, meant *bad* in other languages.

The basketball court was empty. Karthik and Jacinda sat by the archery range but didn't shoot any arrows. No one suggested they play O. C. Maia found a red rubber ball and started tossing it to Lucien. Lucien caught the ball and tossed it back. He did this without thinking, letting his hand perform repetitive actions without his mind's approval. The more they caught and tossed the ball, the more determined they were not to drop it, to keep the game going as long as they could. Each time, Maia secured the ball with two hands. Lucien, who had been casually catching it with one, began to mimic her, cupping the ball every time it dropped from the air. The ball would not touch the grass.

He heard the words inside him.

Blood Earth. Blood Earth. Blood Earth.

The more he questioned the words, the meaning buried within, the louder they became. They beat at a furious rhythm he could no longer recognize, faster and faster as the ball rose and fell from the sky.

Blood Earth. Blood Earth. Blood Earth.

Maia tossed the ball into the air, and both hands closed too early, his fingers smacking together as the ball bounced off them and fell to the grass. He couldn't understand why he had tried to close his hands like that, why his timing had been so wrong. He had been right dozens and dozens of times. He stared at the ball, quiet at his feet, and bent slowly to pick it up.

"I didn't want to drop it," he said.

"It's okay. We can start again."

"I think that's it for me."

Mama sat with him at dinner. They ate hummus and nothing else. Jack had scooped only one large spoonful of hummus and smiled at him.

"Enjoy, Lucien," he said.

Maia ate with her mother and father, who had taken a rare break from the guard booth. As adults, they were entitled to pieces of broccoli to eat with the hummus. Their broccoli was mixed with the hummus and promptly consumed. Eating now was merely a reminder of how hungry he was and how hungry he would later be. He couldn't look forward to meals, even if his stomach begged for food. Once he was done, he always wanted more, and he knew, if he ever went up to request another scoop of hummus, Jack would tell him that it wasn't possible.

"I'm hungry," he whispered to Mama, surprised he was even saying this out loud.

"Here, I have a little hummus left. Take some."

"No, it's okay."

"You can have it, Lucien. Here."

With her spoon, she scooped the remaining hummus from her plate and put it on his. He ate it quickly, hardly breathing. He was immediately sorry he hadn't waited longer to eat the hummus. It was gone now and he was still hungry.

The day always ended with an empty plate.

"Was it good?"

"It was good, Mama."

"You know Jack prepares the best for you."

"He makes the food?"

"He does now."

"It used to be Magnus's father."

"Lucien."

"And Antonio's father."

"Lucien, stop it."

He saw how angry she was, the way her face had tightened, her eyes, smaller and browner than he remembered, failing to reflect the sunlight from the window. Her hand fell on his.

"You don't say those names. We discussed this."

"I know."

"Yet you said them."

"It was a mistake."

"You are getting too old, honey, to make such mistakes." Her hand remained over his, like a hard, curved shell. Their hands were almost the same size. "Jack is serving your food. That's all you have to worry about."

"Yes, Mama."

"Jack cares about you. I care about you. Natasha and Sebastian too."

"I don't see Sebastian very much."

"He is busy. Like I am, sometimes. Everything we do, we do for all of you. You are our future."

"Mama, did you see the shed today?"

"I did."

"Who did it?"

"It's gone now."

"Okay."

After dinner, Mama told him she was going to bed early again. He had an hour before bed, the sun still burning in the sky, his shadow looming as a second self just ahead of him on the grass. It was one of the longest days of the year.

Mama was right. The shed's walls were white again, as if no one had ever painted the words in the first place. The white paint even seemed to be dry.

"They got rid of it," Maia said, approaching from behind.

"They did. My mom said, and I wanted to see."

"That was fast."

"The words were upsetting."

"They were."

"I decided I don't want to know what they meant. Whatever they meant, it couldn't have been good. I'm glad they're gone."

They walked together to the habitation facility. He began to hear the words beating inside him.

Blood Earth.

He wanted to fall to his knees and rip them out of his head.

"Do you hear them?"

"What?"

"The words. The words written on the shed."

"Hear them from where?"

"I just hear them in my head."

Blood Earth.

"I don't know, Lucien."

Blood Earth.

Blood Earth.

"I'm going to bed."

Only when he slept, his dreams devoid of light and color, did the words leave him.

———

He woke to Mama standing above him.

"Let's get breakfast."

The nutritional hall was nearly empty. He saw Karthik, Jacinda, Jayson, and Carlina huddled together at one table. Jack was behind the counter to tell him and Mama good morning. The porridge was plain, no cinnamon.

"Why don't you eat with the friends? I need to have a word with Jack and Natasha," Mama said.

Now that he was awake, the two words were loud inside him. They were like a signal on a new, savage frequency, crackling through his head. He could hear little else. The friends were creating sounds with their mouths that formed language, but none of it mattered when all he could hear were the two words.

They struck like heat lightning.

Blood Earth.

Louder now.

Blood Earth.

His lips moved with their shape, his tongue pressing the back of his two front teeth to unleash the first sound, the blunt force a warning. He wanted it to stop.

Blood.

The porridge was stale, lacking the remnant of any flavor, and he finished it without looking up.

Each time, the words were louder.

Earth.

He begged for a thought, any thought, to drown them.

Who had painted them? When? Why?

Maia still hadn't walked through the doors.

He had hoped she was simply late. Sometimes she liked to sleep in. Breakfast would be halfway done and there came Maia, easing her way to the line for food. She had never been punished like Lucien was.

Now breakfast was over. The friends were standing up. Jack was done serving porridge. Mama was gone.

The clock said it was almost time for instruction.

By the time he arrived at the instruction room, Maia's chair and desk were gone. Jack was writing on the board. Lucien didn't know he was still standing until Jack turned around, a slight smile on his face, and asked him to please sit down.

"We have a lot to get through before the end of the summer," he said.

Maia was not at lunch and not on the commons. Lucien wandered to the guard booth. Inside sat Sebastian.

He wanted to do to Sebastian what Sebastian had done to Evie.

"Yes?" Sebastian said, when Lucien realized he had been staring too long.

"Nothing."

"You shouldn't be at the perimeter."

"It's dangerous?"

"For all of us."

Drifting back to the commons, he saw the red rubber ball lying in the grass. Maia had left it there yesterday.

He tossed it up into the sky and caught it. The ball felt heavier in his hands, like an object from another world.

The words rushed to him again, and he wanted to run into the trees, if he could reach them through the wall, if he could smash through it.

"This will be the most important summer of your lives," Jack said in the afternoon, when they returned to instruction.

Lucien couldn't remember much else. At dinner, Mama was with him again.

In the morning, Maia would have been gone a full day.

———

The day after Maia vanished, Lucien didn't talk to anyone but Mama. Even his words for Mama were few, just enough to ensure she had answers to her questions. Are you hungry? Yes. Thirsty? Yes. How did you sleep? Okay. I'll see you at lunch. Okay.

The two words taunted him from the front and back of his mind. The rhythm was fiercer, surrounding him, devouring his heartbeat and pulse. They were the beat of his life now. He sat on the grass and waited for the sun to disappear. Please, he said.

Please stop.

Blood Earth.

Jack was teaching just a few of them now, the room enlarged with the desks and chairs removed. The walls gained a faint echo. Today, Jack wanted to begin a unit on twentieth-century history.

"Never had there been so much mass death," he said.

As the morning bled into afternoon and then the long, quiet nightfall, Lucien's chest tightened. His breaths were short. If they were gone, almost all of them, soon he would be gone. It was only a matter of days, hours, minutes. Would Mama be gone too? He could warn her. The parents left with the children. She must know.

If she knew, why wasn't she worried?

Jack had told him that Mama was coming back, and she did. Jack never talked about the others.

Lucien would be one of those they never talked about.

Dinner was a plate of sliced carrots. He was done shortly after he set his plate down on the table. The fork shook in his hand. He looked up and Mama had sat down next to him.

"Hi, Mama."

"How were the carrots?"

"They were good."

"You know I'm proud of you? Do I tell you that enough?"

"You do, Mama."

"I'm so proud of you. We all are."

She ate her carrots quickly, finishing not long after him. Her wrists and forearms were thinner, the bones pushing against her skin, beginning to reveal themselves.

"I wanted to tell you that tonight I may have to go run an errand. I should be back by morning."

"You're going?"

"Only a few hours, Lucien. It won't be like last time."

"Can—can I come?"

"I'm sorry. Not tonight. When you're older."

"Please."

"It's not allowed. Not tonight." She took his head in her hands. When she released him, he wanted to cry. "Just a few hours. Okay?"

"Yes, Mama."

They walked together to the habitation facility. He was now used to the building's emptiness, the way sound echoed in the absence of others, room after room without bodies, only sheets made tightly on beds with blankets folded and creased on top. They reached Room 8, and Mama said she just wanted to lie down for a few minutes, to take a quick nap before tonight.

"If you want to close your eyes now too, you should."

It was still bright outside, sunlight playing on the curtains. He settled onto his bed, staring at the blank spaces where the names were once written in his Crayola marker. Before the names, his drawings, the baseball player of the book he was never allowed to finish.

He watched as the window darkened, the sun disappearing. Mama was on her back, her eyes closed. He no longer had the urge to draw. He would lie and wait for the physical world to dissolve around him, for a dream to reach him. It was dark and he was forgetting who he was.

His eyes began to close. He had nothing else to do but sleep.

———

The creak of the bed woke Lucien. His back was to the noise, his eyes opening to take in the empty wall. He heard Mama rise, her feet touching the floor. She quietly cleared her throat. He had been asleep for minutes or hours, he couldn't be sure. He held still, listening as her feet padded across the floor.

Once the door closed, he made his decision.

He climbed down from the bunk bed as gently as he could. He slipped on his sneakers, put on his watch, and inched the door open.

Peering down the hall, he caught Mama leaving, her back through an open door.

He knew he had to follow.

The night was warm, its silence given over to the crickets beyond the wall. He recognized the starlight, his constellations taking form, the sky like the bottom of an ocean. Dew was already forming on the grass. Mama was walking in a direction he wasn't familiar with—not toward the front gate or the nutritional hall or the instruction room. She was veering away from the commons. He knew he couldn't come too close, but he also couldn't lose her. He watched her turn a corner and hurried to where she had been.

She was rounding another corner, on a path that ran near the shed. The whiteness of the outer walls was dulled in the night, the paint no longer seeming fresh. He couldn't see a trace of the words.

He began to hear the words in his head.

Mama paused at the perimeter. The wall was at least ten feet high, much larger than either of them. He leaned back against the shed, hoping he was out of her view. She stood and stood, doing nothing. He tried to hold his breath. He hoped to disappear.

She walked two steps to her right, placed her hand on the wall, and pushed.

The wall began to move.

It was inching forward, then right, opening up a small slot. She glanced behind her and ahead. Pushing for another moment longer, she slid sideways into the slot.

Mama was gone.

He waited another beat, long enough to hear the two words ring through him again. He needed to forget them. But he didn't know how to forget.

When he thought she was gone, he moved toward the wall. He was surprised to see that the slot had remained open, that she had slipped through without it closing after her. Feeling his heart almost pushing out of his chest, he angled his shoulder and entered where she had been.

Wherever she went tonight, he would know.

It was strange to be on the other side. Once, before the wall had been put up, he had considered the woods as much House of Earth as the instruction room or the nutritional hall. Before the wall was built, before Mama told him he had to leave the cottage, he believed this would always be true. This was one of the great and dreadful misunderstandings of his life, he knew now, drifting into the very woods Mama was walking into, her back between two trees. If he thought too much about the darkness, he would have to stop. He would have to fall to the ground. Moonlight meant nothing here. It was too weak, always too weak, to light the way.

The trees loomed like a single, cresting wave, black water suspended above him.

He dived in.

He knew he had not lost Mama because he could hear her feet cracking over branches, sliding over leaves. He had to trust the sound. House of Earth receded, lost to the trees circling him, the darkness nearly total. The starlight was impotent too. All he had was the sound, her feet taking her deeper, wherever she needed to be.

The light was like an orange raindrop in the dark. It came suddenly, in the direction of Mama's sound. She was walking toward it. He strained to keep his footsteps low, to glide as much as he could across the unseen forest bed. He stopped. His foot had cracked a branch. He waited for the sound of Mama to draw closer, for her to discover him and punish him for leaving House of Earth without her permission.

A second light, as bright and orange as the first, opened up the darkness. It was a flame.

Two fires were suspended in the air, ahead of him.

The crunching of Mama's feet disappeared. He heard another voice, a whisper that joined hers. He leaned against a tree trunk, his breath short.

His hands, beginning to shake, pressed the bark. Two torches rose from soil. The outline of Mama neared one.

Another figure, immense in the firelight, waited for her.

Lucien's back slid down the tree, his position low. He could see them now. In the quiver of light, they were half-human, emerging out of shadow. He knew Mama from the shape of her nose and the curve of her forehead.

He knew O. C. Leroux from only his height.

They spoke in whispers he could not hear, O. C. Leroux's head bending toward Mama's ear. He rested both hands on her shoulders. She held his waist.

Lucien sat in a patch of grass, his heart thudding low in his chest. He could not say why he was here anymore. He had wanted to know, and now he did.

She had come to meet O. C. Leroux.

He would have to leave without them hearing or seeing him. It was possible, if he edged sideways and slid upward against the tree, if he fled as lightly as he had followed. He was ready to go back to bed.

Mama let go of O. C. Leroux, turning from him. She began to walk again. O. C. Leroux was at her side. They walked slowly away, their whispers tangling together. Lucien strained to hear what they were saying to each other. He would have to come closer.

He dashed to a new tree, hoping they couldn't hear him.

Mama and O. C. Leroux halted. They were staring toward the ground. She stepped to the side, her arm bending low. She was reaching.

Reaching—

Lucien saw a long wooden handle in her hand, stretching to the ground. She gripped the back, where there was a curvature for her hand. Her back curled. She aimed downward.

Mama was shoveling.

He watched, transfixed. O. C. Leroux stood near her, unmoving. The soil she had shoveled already dipped downward, the crater visible in the whipping torchlight.

She had started to shovel at another time, perhaps another night, when he would have been in his room, fast asleep. She shoveled deeper into the rectangular crater.

When had it begun? When had she first come here?

He bit down on his lower lip, hoping he could will himself to vanish.

Mama was shoveling quickly, her forearms firing back and forth in a rhythm he no longer recognized. Soil flew in rabid chunks over her shoulder.

O. C. Leroux, his hands behind his back, watched her too.

Each of them—Lucien and O. C.—did not move.

Mama stopped, her back still stooped. He could not tell how long she had shoveled for. Two minutes? Ten? Twenty? He had no understanding of time here. Mama peered into the crater.

She spoke, for the first time, above a whisper. "This should do it," she said.

O. C. Leroux did not respond. Mama gently dropped the shovel.

"Tomorrow," she said.

"Yes," he replied.

Lucien backed away from his tree. He was ready now. He knew Mama came out to the woods at night, and that was enough. Enough, at least, for tonight. The familiar fear, frozen deeper within him, returned. It was unthawing. He didn't want to be in the dark anymore.

In the morning, Mama would wake him with a kiss.

Turning, he broke into a jog, hoping he was moving in the direction he'd come. He wasn't sure anymore. He had no way to remember. He'd left no markers behind.

He was running until his right foot fell forward into a void, his left foot still firm on flat rock until that foot slipped too. His body was screaming, every part of him, but he swallowed the sound as hard as he could, tumbling in silence. He dropped until his feet thudded against another surface, softer and stranger, almost pliable.

He was leaning in some kind of pit, his left hand pressing against a crumbling edge for balance. Whatever was beneath him was not rock, dirt, or refuse from the woods.

Bending now, he tried to see. His sneakers pressed down on canvas material, a sack of some kind. His eyes were adjusting to the darkness, new shapes and details revealing themselves to him. He bent lower.

He had to see. He was so close he could smell it now.

At the top of the sack, lying flat in the pit, was an unmistakable shape and scent. The toe of his sneaker touched the flesh first, the hardness of a chin and the rounded softness of a cheek. He retched, trying to choke the sound as much as he could, to stay quiet as a new cry threatened to punch its way out of his throat.

Magnus's eyes were closed beneath him. The body did not move.

Lucien was scrambling backward out of the pit, straining to look away from Magnus bound in a sack.

The face drained, the color absent, a shadow gray.

He was sprinting now, tears clouding his eyes, until his feet again fell forward into darkness.

He stopped himself this time, not falling all the way. He told himself not to look and kept telling himself this as he did, as he found another sack in another pit below his sneakers, brushing canvas and brushing canvas and then touching, gently now, the silent face.

Her bluish lips were shut, almost in a smile, like an upturned incision in the skin. She was the same color as Magnus. He blinked through his tears, rubbing them away as hard as he could, his eyes beginning to burn.

Maia's body was gray and cold.

He climbed out of the pit and ran as fast as he could, until he could see the ground below him give way to many more pits, one after another, deeper still into the woods.

All of them filled with bodies.

The faces were like clay masks, frozen and colorless. He could almost tell himself they were unreal, simulacra of a memory he was prepared to lose.

Colt was between both of his parents. Cavan was between both of his. Samantha, and then Samantha's mother. Antonio, in a pit with his father, his mother nearby.

And Roseboro. There he was, crumpled at the end, the white paint of the wall he had built long dried on his denim pants.

Lucien smelled the flesh rotting away.

The torchlight grew closer. It was coming toward him, one from each side, and he ran until he heard her softly call his name, as if she only wanted him to sit down for breakfast.

"Lucien," Mama said.

The torchlight illuminated her face from the bottom up, her chin and mouth blazing bright while her nose and eyes were dissolved in darkness. Behind her came O. C. Leroux, his chest reaching beyond the top of her head. He held his own small torch.

Lucien realized the torches he had seen before, the ones put into the ground, were still burning. These two were separate, belonging to Mama and O. C. Leroux.

"How are you, honey?"

He couldn't speak, fear filling his throat. His saw Maia's face and Magnus's face, and he heard the two red words scrawled on the shed, each one crying out from the pits where the corpses now waited.

He could almost say them out loud now.

Blood.

"Come here. I know it's been a long night."

Earth.

She had closed the distance between them. Her arms wrapped around his back, and she pulled him close, his head into her shoulder. She hugged him, whispering in his ear, "Come here, Lucien. Come here. We love you."

No other words would form within him. He could only listen to the scream inside and Mama outside, his eyes in the darkness of her dress. She rubbed his back slowly, her voice softer.

"We didn't want you to see them first. We're sorry for that."

He tried to push off from her, to weaken her embrace, but he found she was holding him with a sudden strength he hadn't anticipated. He tried again, and this time, only because she let go, was he able to stumble back and away.

"Maia," he said. "Maia and Magnus and Samantha and—"

"Hush, honey."

"You are almost old enough to understand," O. C. Leroux said. "Perhaps, well, now you are."

He found that his legs were still moving, backing him farther into a tree. The bark was sharp and rough on the thin, sweat-drenched T-shirt he wore.

"They're in the ground," he said to Mama.

"It's my fault. I should have told you right away I knew you were following. You didn't need to see all of it. Not yet, at least."

"You knew I was following?"

"Lucien, of course. The opening in the wall was there for you. I've known about all your explorations. You are my son. I watch you; I care about you; I love you. I've loved you since the day you were born. We believe in letting you explore, making mistakes and learning from them. You were getting curious. You were always a smart boy."

She turned to O. C. Leroux, who looked toward him without any emotion that Lucien could discern. "Isn't he a smart boy?"

"He is," O. C. Leroux said.

Lucien found himself beginning to cry again.

"Don't do that, Lucien. There's no need. They are doing more for the earth now than they could ever do before. You learned about the life cycle. Jack taught you well."

"Are all of them—"

"All of them who?"

"Are they all . . ."

It was O. C. Leroux, advancing now, who cleared his throat. "Your mother and yourself are very important, valuable people."

"You were always going to be spared, honey."

"There must be some who carry on into the future, who must be there to lead us when the war ends, and the earth—once it has cleansed itself of the human infestation—begins to replenish itself."

The backs of Lucien's hands, scraping the bark, were trembling deeply. "There isn't a war," he said.

O. C. Leroux's smile revealed itself to him. The torchlight flickered just above his chin, his skin whitened by the flame.

"Please," Mama said.

"It's okay. Skepticism is reasonable. I was a skeptic once. I lived my life in such a way."

"All of them, you . . ." He could say it now, *just say it*, a voice cried, *say their names*. "You killed them all. I found them."

"I was going to explain it to you when you were ready," Mama said.

"He's ready now," O. C. Leroux said. "But I sense he's known it all along. Some are born with the awareness. Some know, from intuition and dreams. Maybe he is that kind of boy."

"It was never going to be you, honey. Never you."

Each time Mama inched closer, he slid his body farther around the large trunk of the tree.

"Jack was going to give you the final lesson," O. C. Leroux said. "But I can deliver it."

Blood Earth, Lucien almost sobbed. *Blood Earth.*

"Let's start from what you know, what you've learned. None of this is sustainable. Our planet is being murdered. It was slow at first, and now it's quick. The climate is unstable. The resources are dwindling. You're a child of the twenty-first century, and you'll be living through the worst one yet. There is nothing natural about any of this. It is human-made. It is our doing. We are false gods and destroyers."

O. C. was now next to him. He smiled and blew out his torch.

"House of Earth was created to atone for this destruction. We cannot simply live in a sustainable way—no meat, no plastics—and hope for the best. We are beyond that. Our planet cannot survive with human beings multiplying like rodents and insects. At least those detested species play a role in the ecosystem. Insects are a mediator. Rodents are prey. *They* have a purpose. But us? What do we do? We are egoists. We dream and build and dream and build. We invent ingenious ways to steal territory, murder the land, and keep killing. We offer nothing to the ecosystem. We simply *take*, Lucien. You are a smart boy. I know you see this. There will be justice for nature, for all we have wounded and destroyed. There will be justice for the planet. We will atone. You know what that word means now. It was taught to you. *Atonement* is the first order of business."

Even in the dark, Lucien could see him, how his torso seemed to expand with his words, stretch higher into a waiting canopy.

"You saw the graves tonight. Your mother allowed you to tag along. That was her decision. If it were up to me, you wouldn't have seen them until much later. You may ask how we can atone. We start here. We start in our backyard. These lives are atonement. They have given to House of Earth. Now they will give back in the ultimate way. They are pioneers. Many millions and billions will have to die like them."

Mama was near Lucien. "Do you understand, honey? They had to die. Humans like us have caused so much pain. When there are less of us, the earth can be strong again."

"In the new era, after the die-off, those who are left will know their place," O. C. Leroux said. "They will never put themselves ahead of nature. Only those who are enlightened enough—who descend from our movement—will be fit. Otherwise, the human disease will spread again. In a few centuries, we will encounter the same problems."

"They gave their lives," Mama said. "But they will be giving *back* once they are in the ground. They are of the planet now, doing more now than they did alive. They will replenish the soil. They will contribute to our biodiversity."

"They didn't want to go," Lucien said, his voice weaker. He hated the taste of his tears.

"*Want* versus *not wanting*—more human ego, unfortunately. The planet is on fire. We are the arsonists. The arsonist is not a priority. We do not worry about him after he has torched his own house. We worry about those inside, crying out. And we dedicate ourselves to making sure there aren't *more* arsonists."

Mama and O. C. Leroux stood next to him. She touched him on the side of his arm, rubbing gently. "Let's go home. You can sleep late tomorrow. I will tell Jack you are going to be late for breakfast. I will save you oatmeal."

"I hear it will be cinnamon," O. C. Leroux said.

"Everyone will die except you," Lucien said.

"Your mother has been chosen to help lead us. As have you."

"Lucien, I was always making sure you would never be like the others. You will be needed."

"She is right. You are one of the few."

"What happened to Evie?"

Mama gripped his arm. "Please, not this."

"It's okay. He can ask that question. Evie was like you, Lucien. She was chosen; she was special; she was given so much. Her father died at a young age. Sebastian raised her and loved her. She could not accept his love. There are people like this."

"What happened to her?"

"Lucien, *enough.*"

"Evie went away, like the others. We filled up her plot several weeks ago."

"She was always *bad*," Mama said. "That's the truth."

"Not always. But in the end, there was no choice. We needed to move quickly. Now, Lucien, you will be good. I know you will. Let's all walk home through the woods together. It can be difficult to navigate if you don't know the way."

"I can save you extra oatmeal for tomorrow," Mama said.

"Who—" Lucien's tongue was thick and strange in his mouth, the creep of language suddenly unfamiliar. His back was still hard against the tree trunk. "Who is next?"

"Not you," O. C. Leroux said.

"Let's go home, Lucien."

"All of them . . ."

Mama touched his cheek. "No more crying. Time to go, okay?"

"Everyone, all of them, you killed . . ."

"Enough of this."

"They're all dead."

"Stop it, now."

"Mama, all of them, dead."

"You stop it!"

She held him tight, her fingernails digging into his skin. He felt flash points of pain, her nails pushing harder.

"Let's go home," she said, quieter this time.

O. C. Leroux started to walk. Mama held Lucien as she trailed, one hand at her side, one clutching at his shoulder. He knew he had stopped crying because he could see clearly now, how the night, once so shapeless, had as much definition as the world of day. The trees and leaves were sharp in their grayness, the sky like glossy film. The word *home* slashed at him, the single syllable dropping like a stone down a well, settling within him, at his core.

She thought this was home.

"Lucien, what are you—"

He was running, faster than he had ever gone, his breath shooting from him as the tears dried on his skin. He ran in whatever direction was opposite Mama and O. C., dashing between trees, knowing only he had to go deeper. He could hear them in the distance, Mama's quick steps and O. C. Leroux's ranging gait, three steps for every one she took.

"Honey, come back. We need you!"

He heard this as he stumbled over a hidden root, his body pitching forward into a tree. His arm slammed the trunk first, then his head, warm blood racing down broken skin. He was curled, his skull aching. They were closer. Mama was first. He could almost smell her.

"Lucien, you shouldn't run like that in the dark. You'll trip and hurt yourself."

"He can't run like this."

"He'll be okay—won't you? You're my boy. You're my shining star."

He stumbled upward. He could feel O. C. Leroux touching him, then Mama, both her hands pressing him.

"Let's go home. It's time."

He pushed down on her foot, hearing her cry out in pain for the first time in his life. He ran with the cry inside him, falling through the darkness. Blood trickled into his left eye. His skull throbbed. His breaths were ragged, his lips wet with his own saliva, fatigue gripping him.

He remembered Gabrielle, how she'd once told him she would help him.

They were behind him again, their voices louder. He would have to keep running. He knew they would be angry, that their patience would go only so far. Mama wouldn't keep protecting him from O. C. Leroux.

The woods descended. He was on a sharp slope, bounding off jagged land. He swerved between trees, tasting his blood. He would run until he didn't hear them anymore.

Lucien. Lucien. Lucien.

He heard the river before he saw it. The churn welcomed him. He listened for the waters wrapping around the riverbed, the silver hiss as they passed him by. He broke through a bedding of leaves and branches that crisscrossed in front of him. They cut at him too and he shoved through, his feet sliding toward the craggy bank.

"Lucien!"

When he saw the first glimmer of torchlight, he knew there was no longer a choice. The river was shallow as he waded in, the water cool around his ankles. His sneakers began to fill with silt. The water was at his waist and then his armpits, and he could stand no longer, floating in the current that was sweeping him downstream. He had swum years ago, in the pool of a motel, and he remembered Mama had told him how to turn his arms and kick his legs and glide through the water.

Mama was shouting from the riverbank. Her torchlight winked at him.

He was drifting, too tired to swim. The waters bore and then overtook him, and he opened his eyes to their murky depth, the lightless gray-green whirling all around. He was coughing, choking, trying to stay up.

The river was faster than he had imagined.

Drowning was when you could no longer breathe. If he kept his head above water, if his arms and legs flailed enough, he would have air.

His bones and muscles burned. They were begging him to sink.

We are tired.

The blood was drying over his eyelid. He saw the moon, nearly full, so chalky and vacant in a sky that offered him nothing.

We are tired.

He slipped below the water's surface, the foam spraying in his face. Each time he slipped, he fought his way to air. He swallowed fresh water and heaved it back up.

We are tired.

As he sank, he saw all their faces, Magnus and Cavan and Samantha and Maia and Evie, all the masks shattering on the shore of a lightless beach. He was swimming nowhere, the waters closing over his head. His feet thrashed, slowing as he sank. He could feel the water filling him. He couldn't hear Mama or O. C. Leroux or anyone else. He was below, the river tugging him farther down, the last air bubbles escaping his mouth.

He heard himself breathing until he didn't. The voice was first, distant and low, until it joined a body and another voice and another body and the light was so bright, so full, all of it shining above.

Kid.

The voices continued.

Kid, c'mon.

His first feeling was water tumbling out of him. Each cough was loud and painful, tearing at him from the stomach to the throat. He bent over, heaving, his bones like putty.

There we go.

He wasn't in the river. He opened and closed his hand. He was here, wherever *here* was.

The voices belonged to three men he didn't recognize.

"Todd went to call the police. We don't bring our cell phones on the fishing trips, but you're lucky we like to start here. Good spot for bass. You okay?"

"You was just sleeping here on this bank when we came down."

"You was swimming or what, kid?"

"You're as pale as a ghost."

"Here, you want a sandwich?"

He shook his head slowly.

"Well, suit yourself. Maybe you'll be hungry later."

The police officer was named Officer Berger. She asked him questions in the car and again when they arrived in the police station. At first, he couldn't summon words. They had all gone elsewhere.

When he said his first name, she asked him to spell it.

She was larger and older than Mama. Her radio chirped with staticky commands he didn't understand.

"C'mon, let's get you some food and water."

The station was colored a sour beige, the walls painted unlike any he had seen at House of Earth. Dull, buttery lights hung above him. Officer Berger, sitting him on a bench, offered him a peanut butter–and-jelly sandwich. This time he ate, and it was gone before he could remember just how hungry he was.

"You were found passed out on a riverbank, Lucien. Where do you live? How did you get there?"

The blood had dried in his mouth. A bandage, at an indeterminable time, had been placed on the wound over his forehead.

"We'll take it slow."

She was holding a pen and pad. His tongue began to move behind his teeth.

"There's a phone number I'd like to call," he said.

———

No one picked up, but he heard a woman's voice on the answering machine. He guessed it was Gabrielle's mother. He said who he was, he wanted to see Gabrielle, and he was at the police station in Mater.

"You're in Stockport," Officer Berger said as he spoke into the phone.

He stopped, apologized, corrected himself.

It was a town he didn't know.

"Was that a relative?" Officer Berger asked.

"Kind of."

301

"So you're from Mater. Quaint town. My ex-husband lives there."

"Yes."

"Where do you go to school, Lucien?"

———

Officer Berger offered him another bottle of water after he finished his first. It was in plastic, a material that hurt the earth, and he considered telling her this.

He was more surprised he was getting a second bottle. The nutritional hall didn't offer more water after he finished his cup.

"Take your time," she said.

Gabrielle referred to it as a *school* too. But he never thought of it as that. He knew what school was, from when he watched TV.

House of Earth was much more.

"House of Earth."

"Oh, that strange little private school up from Mater. I know it."

"I lived there."

"I didn't know it was a boarding school."

"*Boarding?*"

"A place with dorms. Where you live."

"Then it was, I guess."

"You need to tell me how you ended up passed out on a riverbank, discovered by these fishermen. Their alibis checked out. Why were you there?"

His eyelids felt heavy. He was ready for a long, deep sleep.

———

"Tell me about your mother and father."

"I don't know my father."

"But you know your mother."

"She's . . ."

"She was the one you were running from?"

"There were others."

"You need to tell me, Lucien."

"Can I have more water?"

"You can always have more water. You jumped in the river."

"I was running."

"From your mother? We need to know her name, Lucien."

"No, it wasn't her. Not just her. It was House of Earth," he said quietly.

———

There was a commotion at the front desk. An older woman with long, dark hair asked about a boy at the police station. Behind her, peering around the station house, was Gabrielle.

He saw her before she saw him.

Officer Berger was writing in her pad. "Don't run in here," she said.

Gabrielle saw him running and ran too, meeting him where the hallway opened to the front desk. He hugged her, his eyes tight with tears.

"You hurt your head," she said.

"Yes."

"You got out."

"I ran."

"My mom said you sounded like, shaken on the voice mail."

"I don't know."

"It's Friday. We'll get lunch. We'll hang out."

Gabrielle's mother approached. "Were you being abused?"

Officer Berger had asked the same question. He didn't know how to respond.

"You need to answer more questions before you can leave," Officer Berger said.

"House of Earth is crazy," Gabrielle jumped in.

"He'll need to tell me."

"He told *me*. They locked you in a dark chamber if you were late for dinner. They made you sit outside all night if you painted things black. Nobody got to leave."

"Let Lucien speak."

Lucien, not looking at any of them, spoke into the ground. "They wanted to kill everyone."

———

That evening, Gabrielle and her mother took Lucien to a place called a diner. He had been to one like it many years ago, when he still lived in the cottage. He asked for a plate of carrots.

"Just carrots? You want, uh, a salad?" the waitress asked.

"The Greek salad here is good," Gabrielle said.

"I'll get that, then."

"You want large or small?"

"Small."

"You can stay with us until everything gets sorted out," Gabrielle's mother said.

"You take my room. I'll have the couch."

"No, that's okay."

"Trust me, you're doing *me* a favor. Couch is next to the TV. I'm gonna watch all the naughty channels while Mom sleeps."

Gabrielle's mother laughed, shaking her head. "I see that TV on at midnight, you're grounded until Halloween."

"Ah, fine."

"I'm going shopping tomorrow. What would you like, Lucien, for the fridge?"

"Carrots and string beans."

"You're the only twelve-year-old in America not asking for Mountain Dew and Doritos."

"Lucien is healthy, Mom."

Gabrielle, by either talking to him or invoking him, tried to pull him directly into as many conversations as she could. The energy for speech, on the consistent level he'd once enjoyed with her, had not returned to him. He wanted to curl up in the darkness and sleep, letting his thoughts dribble out of him. He did not want to dream.

Gabrielle's hamburger and fries arrived. Her mother had a taco salad. Lucien picked at his Greek salad, avoiding the feta chunks, his fingers feeling weak around the metal fork.

"How is the salad?" Gabrielle's mother asked.

Lucien wasn't sure what to say. "It's good."

"Next time, the hamburger," Gabrielle said, biting down.

"It's meat," he replied.

"Right, right—you are vegetarian, totally forgot. That's fair."

"We're going to get you off red meat when you're older," Gabrielle's mother said.

"You had a steak like, last week."

"We'll both quit, together!"

None of it was like how he spoke to Mama. This comforted him as much as it unsettled him.

———

There was a single photo of Noah in Gabrielle's room. It was on her dresser, in a golden frame. He was smiling, in a dark-blue gown and cap Lucien recognized from the kind of graduation ceremonies that would never be held at House of Earth. He could see her face in his, the same bend in his nose, the soft dimples and light-brown eyes.

She caught him looking at the picture on the first night.

"He couldn't wait to get out of school," she said.

He could only nod.

"He wanted to see the world. He was so restless. He believed very deeply, Lucien. You would've liked him. He would've been excited to have you here, if he stayed."

"I would've liked to have met him."

"I'll be in the den, watching TV for a bit, if you want to come out. I can't really sleep."

"I thought I was going to sleep. I was ready to, even at dinner, but now I'm up."

They sat on the couch, the TV blinking on. Gabrielle had a remote control to change channels, something Mama never had at the cottage. One image after another flashed by. There were many more channels than he had ever seen, dozens, countless lives passing before him in an incomprehensible whirl of color.

Gabrielle stopped at an image of police cars and sirens.

"Local news," she said. "This looks serious."

He understood, then. The graphics were secondary, unneeded, because he knew the grass, the wall, the commons, and the oval, and the very tall man and woman being led away, silently, by police. A war had come, another kind, and he felt a deep well of sickness opening up inside him.

"Lucien, it's House of Earth."

She turned to him, expecting him to say something. He was looking away, his fingers digging deeply into the sofa cushion.

The faces of his friends, silent and cold and colorless, came to him, one after another after another. He should have joined them. He should have been one of them.

Evie was dead. Maia was dead. Samantha was dead.

Not him.

"It's justice," she said. "They're bringing justice. You're safe."

He was grasping the couch, his cheeks warm with blood, the air leaving him. He could feel Gabrielle hugging him, whispering, telling him it was okay, it was all okay, he was here he was here he was *home* and somewhere a telephone rang and there were footsteps and the voice of Gabrielle's mother shaking from the room, *No he does not live here please do not call again* and then *Fucking journalists* as the phone rattled against the wall. The TV was turned off and he was still in her arms, his eyes crushed shut.

"I see all of them. Every one of them."

"Tell me about them."

He started to tell a story.

EVER AFTER

Thunderheads blackened the western sky. Lightning, vertical and unhinged, slashed the horizon.

He drove on, faster than before, hoping to outgun the coming downpour. In West Virginia, he had already been caught in one, his windshield silver with heavy rain.

He had Route 64 almost to himself. A lonely tractor trailer muddled ahead.

He preferred driving, still, to flying. He didn't board an airplane until he was twenty-two, a college graduate, and he could remember the warnings of his youth, the flying machines that poisoned the sky. Automobiles were no better, of course, but he appreciated their smallness, the way he could control his destiny on an open roadway.

When he crossed into Kentucky, he stopped at a McDonald's. Three years ago, he had finally tried a cheeseburger, and he felt he understood, at last, something fundamentally American, the taste bright and strangely electrifying in his mouth, seductive self-destruction in every bite. It was in his mouth and gone, and he immediately felt sick.

At the McDonald's on the Kentucky border, he asked for a small order of chicken nuggets. He ate them in his car, the crumbs falling like little brown stars from his fingertips.

When he called, he didn't say exactly when he was coming. He said only he would be on his way. Only later, when he was on his way, did he confirm. The voice, while familiar, was weaker, thinned by the years locked away. They had two and a half minutes. He used to want those minutes to last, to expand into the safety of a life unlike the one he was living, like the one he had once known before it had all gone so horribly wrong.

"I'll come," he finally said.

How many letters had gone unanswered? At his last count, twenty-six. He always opened them all. He wished he could stop himself.

It was the handwriting that drew him this time, as much as the words formed on the lined paper. The letter arrived with the familiar Bureau of Prisons postage, his name printed rather than scrawled. He opened it up and saw how carefully she'd printed each letter, the pencil fading as her sentences trailed on, every letter rendered sharply, without ambiguity, for him to read. She had spent time on this.

She told him she thought she was dying.

Not even during the pandemic did she write that. She didn't write with any fear. She never got sick during that time. The prison wouldn't just let her die. She was a star inmate, the most famous, by leagues, in the women's Federal Correctional Institution, Heed. She was not yet fifty, and as his friend Zed once reminded him, swiping through his phone, she was the subject of one of the more popular docudramas in Netflix's history.

Lucien promised never to watch it, just as he hid from all media coverage—the news stories, the magazine features, the first TV special, the books. Hundreds of times, if not thousands, he had ignored phone calls and email requests, always surprised when some journalist or seeker of information found his latest address, each one more obscure than the last. Writers wanted his cooperation on books. A studio wanted the same for a movie that, as far as he could tell, wasn't produced. There were women who declared their love for him, men who did the same, and the occasional death threats, because whatever burned so bright would have to die.

In time, it began to fade. It couldn't be 2002 forever.

He was twenty miles from Heed, a three- or four-stoplight town in Kentucky that drew its withered vitality from the medium-security prison in its wake. He had visited before, but not once in the last five years. Last time he was there, he had eaten alone at an Arby's on an otherwise vacant strip, wondering how it remained open.

The radio crackled with Christian rock. Sometime, just as he crossed the border, the news had changed to hard rock about the life of Jesus Christ. The melodies soothed him, the thrashing pop hooks, the bearded men he imagined calling for God's grace. He had no use for God, Christian or otherwise, but there was a simplicity in the longing.

Gabrielle, and even Gabrielle's mother, couldn't quite understand why he didn't want all of them in prison forever. They cheered the police raid until they saw that he was not cheering with them and never would. He could say it was my mother, it was Mama, but that wasn't the whole truth. It wasn't just her. The yellow tape corralling House of Earth, the images of Jack and Sebastian and Natasha with their wrists locked in handcuffs, the suddenly ubiquitous face of O. C. Leroux, a photograph taken years before, when his beard was trimmer and he was serving in the navy—none of it could ease what was inside him, a yawning despair that would not be soothed by the mechanisms of a criminal justice system he could hardly understand. He was a foreigner, the customs and signifiers and in-jokes that, together, knitted a tapestry of an existence lost to him. All he had was the English language and the books he had found in the library and the TV he watched before Mama left it on the side of the road.

At fifteen, he would seethe. She was always Mama. Even locked away, a life sentence like Jack, Natasha, Sebastian, and O. C. Leroux, he could only call her that.

Before he learned to ignore the coverage, he learned everything. His life unraveled in a public machine he barely knew existed—it was like, he decided, discovering an enormous mountain in a shallow forest, the peak looming so large he somehow forgot it was even there.

Mama, the newspapers and TV stations and radio stations and magazines and internet articles said, was born in a part of New York City called Bensonhurst, a neighborhood in another part called Brooklyn. She was pregnant with him, *the boy*, at age sixteen, and never graduated high school. The newspaper taught him her birthday, which she never celebrated: September 1. Not long before his. Sometime around his birth, she turned to drinking and pills before sobering up and answering a job opening for a new school in Mater, New York, run by a man named O. C. Leroux. She was his first hire.

All this he never knew.

How she sobered up couldn't be ascertained, just as no one report could tell him who his father was. This was lost to history. They called her "resourceful" and "cunning" and "vicious" and "lost" and a "ringleader" and "O. C.'s girl." A newspaper in a 7-Eleven one day told him, in large, blocky letters, that O. C. had sex with his mother many times. Another newspaper told him she was the one who, with her slim fingers, had put poison capsules into the mouths of the boys and girls and men and women chosen for death.

They wrote and talked and filmed much more about O. C. Leroux, the charismatic leader of the "murder cult next door."

The facts crashed upon Lucien as he tried to hide from them all.

His real name wasn't O. C. Leroux. He was born Oliver Ralph Wilkinson in Albany County, raised in a suburb, his parents absent. He played high school basketball. He joined the navy and was dishonorably discharged for punching an ensign. After that, he drifted. He was a bartender, a bouncer, a delivery driver. He lived in Georgia, Alabama, and Wisconsin before moving back to New York. O. C. was an alias, short for Oliver Cromwell, the English military leader who killed the king. At various points, he self-identified as a libertarian, a socialist, a conservative.

No one knew where Leroux came from. It was French and he chose it.

Over time, he could believe many different things and be many things to many people.

House of Earth was a fantasy of his, first noted in a 1990s online tract. Everyone who knew him—those who grew up with him, worked with him, lent him money to make his fantasy real—remarked on his "charisma," an "intensity" and "dominance" of personality that was difficult to ignore.

At the foundation of House of Earth, when Mama first worked there, it was advertised as an alternative school with nature-based independent learning. In the aftermath, when the bodies were discovered, each with exotic poisons in the blood, and the count eventually passed into the high double digits, there were questions about how the authorities could not know what was really happening at the secluded private school in the woods. The boys and girls, and even their parents, were slowly being starved before they were led to their deaths. Theories were posited that Lucien didn't pay attention to. Many times, he would see and hear his own name and look away. *If the boy hadn't escaped . . .*

The cabin in the woods where O. C. hid with his mother, the cabin that was never seen, was found and defaced and eventually, under the cover of night, burned down.

No one could conceive the logic of it all. The press coverage strained against it. O. C. Leroux believed humanity was the ultimate contagion. If enough people died, if enough bodies stopped making demands of the planet, there could be a renewal. He dreamed in a scale of billions, the sort of ultimate culling that could not have been accomplished with a hundred Hitlers and Stalins working in concert. It was not sustainable death.

What had O. C. hoped for in the end? For House of Earth to indefinitely attract families and silently murder them, only to attract more? Yes, the federal investigators had concluded, that was the directive. The court transcripts spoke of hope. Like any deeply ambitious entrepreneur of the new century, O. C. sold a dream to himself and others. With each passing day, the delusion grew grander. The body count would grow until the earth was saved. And for a long time, he had been succeeding. The deaths passed easily. Those who died believed in him until the very end. Cataclysm doesn't end faith in a god. As O. C. took more from his followers—their comforts, their friends, their food—they only reached for him with greater love and desperation. Was there a difference between the two, really? They loved desperately. When they shut their eyes, they saw only him, golden beneath their eyelids.

What still staggered Lucien was the discovery of the bodies. As the trial dragged on, the public—and even the prosecutors, salivating at the absurdity of the not-guilty pleas—became hungrier for a systemic understanding of them all. Why were these particular children chosen to die? Who was Wynn Roseboro? The more that was revealed, the more the logic wilted, the berserk thrown into disorienting daylight. The children died because it was their time to die. There was no superstructure, no greater logic. O. C. picked them in dreams. There were survivors, like Karthik and Jacinda, and no one could explain why. Had House of Earth lasted longer, the survivors would have died too. If O. C. didn't immediately choose a child, requests could be made. Sebastian, rejected by Evie, asked for her to die. Roseboro was the lone death of someone who did not live at House of Earth. This was tied to the help he apparently offered. The plot to escape. None of that was surprising. By letting Roseboro try to help him—by believing in Roseboro—Lucien had given O. C. reason to act. Jack killed Roseboro on O. C.'s orders, the trial revealed. Eventually, Jack testified, he expected O. C. to kill him too. It was only right, Jack said calmly. He was a human virus.

There had been another media flurry over *Blood Earth*. What did it mean? What *could* it mean? It had been scrawled everywhere. For a time, the phrase had bled into the minds of the thousands, and then millions, transfixed daily by O. C. Leroux's mission and his slaughter. There were debates, exegeses, even panels convened. They speculated that someone on the inside had written it—one of the kids or one of the adults. The documentary strained and failed to produce an answer.

Lucien thought he knew, or was beginning to understand as he aged, his time as an object of public fascination was fading away. The words were the logic of his childhood with Mama. They were the beating of his heart. The blood of the people who poisoned the earth would soak it, not in drops but in waves, whole oceans of death to atone for the species. All would be gone except O. C. Leroux and those chosen to stand with him at the dawn of a rejuvenated planet. On top of blood, the plants would grow, the fauna lush, the animals once driven to extinction returning to a planet emptied of its malignant intelligence.

Had a lone being been able to view this all from outer space, in the first moment after O. C. Leroux's vision had been made real and everlasting, the being would have seen the blood everywhere, washing every city and forest and plain and desert, wherever the people had been, their cries echoing all the way up to where oxygen, finally, left the planet.

Blood Earth. Mama would roam the reborn world with O. C. Leroux. And Mama could choose to have someone walk with her. Mama, no matter what, wanted her son. He stayed alive, perhaps, only because of her.

Long drives like these to the prison, the rain drowning his windshield, forced him to confront how unlike everyone else he was, how his life, through more than three decades, had diverged from whatever was supposed to be an ordinary American childhood, with Little League games and ice cream for dessert and the permanence of friendship. He was like a superhero absent a superpower, utterly alien, without any ability to impress or protect others, to inspire hope or worship.

He knew, early on, he was famous. It was a word he learned—a word he considered in all its savage enormity—only when he heard it at Mater Middle School, the whispers following him in the hallway. His picture had been in the news, a photograph taken when he left the police station. It was the only photograph the news possessed, but they showed it again and again, his face turning up in surprise at the lens pointed like a gun, his eyes flashed open, his small mouth rounded with shock. He was talked about, but rarely talked to. Eighth graders didn't know how to befriend him, and neither did ninth graders, tenth graders, eleventh graders, or twelfth graders.

School was a reminder of what he never knew. A parallel world of education had been unfurling beyond the walls of House of Earth, and now that he had escaped them, slowly understanding that *this* was regarded as the default, the bedrock, and he was what they called in statistics the *outlier*, he could confront the paucity of what he possessed, the abilities to fashion wood into a bird feeder or identify wildflowers of no use here, in a school of comparatively little color and sunlight, concepts like algebra and chemistry landing like inscrutable tablets in his wake, a person—a *teacher*—who demanded the honorific *mister* urging him to decode the language as quickly as he could.

On the day Mama was sentenced, again a national news event, a boy named Brock met him outside the gym and started laughing. "Your mom is going to jail," he said. Boys surrounded him, echoing Brock, creating a chant: "Your mom is going to jail! Your mom is going to jail!" Lucien punched without thinking, the idea of his fingers folding inward to project his sharp knuckles outward at others no more than an impractical theory until he was doing it, smashing Brock in the face, and it felt good, he could admit to himself later, sitting in the principal's office as Gabrielle's mother, who had become the closest thing to a mother he had now, arrived to reckon with the news he would be suspended. He held his hand up, Brock's dried blood still faint on his skin.

"You can't hit people, Lucien, no matter how terrible the things are that they say about you."

Gabrielle protected him when she could. She was two grades ahead, rededicating herself to her studies, trying to get her grades up for college. When he started living with her, she began to care again about attending classes, digesting information, and repeating it back correctly for teachers. He was in summer school, extra help after school, scrambling to absorb as much as he could about the parallel universe he had now entered and would forever inhabit. The portal had been closed. House of Earth was a crime scene, soon to be demolished.

All the friends were dead or scattered elsewhere.

Gabrielle's house was covered in graffiti and egged. It happened when they took a two-day vacation to Niagara Falls, Gabrielle's mother driving, both of them in the back seat. The graffiti was light-red spray paint, the yolk smeared and dried on the windows and siding. He said nothing, hoping he could soon disappear, vanish into the wind. It was all for him.

The graffiti was simple. SON OF A KILLER. How could he argue? Gabrielle's mother, shaking her head, said the town was very sick and she hoped to move soon.

For a week, the TV remained off. Gabrielle and her mother would not discuss the trial, the verdict, the sentence.

Envelopes arrived that were left unopened. He couldn't even try. He knew they were from Mama.

He hated, driving through the slashing rain, how memory worked this way—how images and scents and moods could return to him, unsummoned, like insects roving a countertop. He wanted nothing of it anymore, yet it was all he could really think about once an idle moment presented itself. Mama in handcuffs, blank-faced, leaving the courthouse in the city. Despite his best efforts, TV history always found him, in the late nights and early mornings tucked between wherever he was supposed to be.

The prison was Exit 36. He was ten exits away.

Gabrielle left for Hunter College in Manhattan. She would live among friends, four crammed into a two-bedroom across the river in Brooklyn. He had a cell phone and they texted daily, more about her than about him because he never knew what to say.

She was the one who alerted him about O. C. Leroux. Did you see? He was a senior, leaving European History, and hurried to the computer lab to confirm.

One year into his 150-year sentence, the "charismatic cult leader" had killed himself in a federal prison. He was forty-three. Never on suicide watch, he hanged himself with a bedsheet. It was over in two minutes. Again, the news erupted, and Lucien found it inescapable, the websites and newspapers and TV shows writing and speaking of nothing else, his nascent Facebook account, begun on a lark, filling with articles and conspiracies about what really happened. An obituary in the *New York Times* went a quarter read.

> Wilkinson, described as both an idiosyncratic loner and a captivator of crowds, grew obsessed with the belief that to save the earth, human beings must have their population severely reduced.

It was after his high school graduation, with a vacant summer looming, that he made the decision, confiding first in Gabrielle and then her mother. They each hesitated, but understood.

"Shouldn't you have thought of this *before* they printed your name on the diploma?" Gabrielle asked.

He wanted it done after school was over. High school had been dreamlike, not like a daydream or a nightmare but an interlude between what his reality had been and what was still to come, the uncategorizable and unfathomable future without Gabrielle near him. She had been the only reason to endure school, with its rituals fantastically untethered from all he once learned, the knowledge amassed in the before time rendered more useless each day. Gabrielle was going to New York City. Her mother wanted to move out of Mater.

He decided, three days after graduation, to change his name.

In the fall, he would enroll at Mater Community College. The high school guidance counselor, a bespectacled man with sagging jowls and a voice that always seemed to dip into apology, told him he was a bright boy who needed to strengthen his grades before attempting a four-year school.

"You've been through a lot, son," he said. "You'll get there."

On a late spring day, hunched over a desk that had once belonged to Noah, he heard the name. It came to him, first and last, and he scrawled it on a piece of lined paper he ripped from his notebook.

Salvatore Lux.

He knew no one in existence with such a name, and it would become his. *Lux*, Latin for "light." Salvatore, a name he had seen in a book about an immigrant boy who tries to make good in the gritty streets of Brooklyn. Apart, they made little sense, and together, they would have to.

Gabrielle made a spitting sound. "I have to call you *that?*"

"You could call me Lucien. But everyone else will call me that."

"That'll be their problem."

He practiced signing his name. He belatedly learned cursive, and he came to enjoy looping and connecting his letters more than printing them. The sentences were his to tame.

Mater Community College, a series of brown block-shaped buildings with darkened windows, was not like high school. There were no Brocks to bully him. Students much older than he was fled class to pick up children or work evening shifts. Several spoke halting English. The professors were younger, more hurried, arriving with sweat beading their foreheads. One smoked when she wasn't supposed to. Another said he was paid just enough to "afford the gas to get here." Yet another cared tremendously for all her students, telling them they would succeed with enough hard work, her smile flashing white.

318

All of it, for reasons he couldn't explain, comforted him.

He began working while in community college. After school and on weekends, while still living with Gabrielle's mother, he started as a cashier at a local hardware store, Lawson's. He was paid the minimum wage in cash and sometimes less. He liked the smell of rubber in the place and nothing else. Gabrielle's mother paid his community-college tuition, though he insisted on contributing what he could. Most of his money at that time accumulated, untouched, in a local credit union.

The rain surged as he approached Exit 36. It was a summer storm, unconnected to the changing of the climate, but the news station, before bleeding into Christian rock, had warned of another devastating hurricane bearing down upon Florida, a Category 5. Another storm, a month before he moved, drowned Fourth Avenue in Brooklyn. Record heat waves tore through Europe. Forest fires consumed the Amazon.

The earth seemed to be dying. Hadn't Jack said it would?

Though it had been years since he'd driven here, well before the pandemic, he remembered every inch of the coming freeway and the service road, how the asphalt dipped and the bumps lightly shook his vehicle, a smattering of gravel waiting at the entrance gate. The women's prison was the only significant feature of the landscape for fifty miles, rising out of the parched earth as a range of muddy cinder block and razor wire, now electrified to foil escapes. Four solitary towers, dark against the sky, watched the people in chains. He had the urge to flip his car in reverse and drive away as fast as he possibly could.

When he first came, he learned of the point system—eight points per month, one deducted for each Friday visit, two points for each Saturday and Sunday visit, none for federal holidays—and how it eventually grew to be meaningless because he stopped coming. He had his points.

Instead, he would put money on her books. She could buy her coffee, toothpaste, and whatever else she might need, staying in the same place until she died.

Other inmates had more than one visitor. A brother and sister, a mother and father, a friend referencing another friend on the way. If he didn't come for her, no one did. This fact, in all its bareness and solemnity, lent him actual power over her, which he had never had before and didn't want now. She had fame, actresses portraying her and commentators attempting to analyze and rationalize her sickness, but fame didn't visit her. It wrote letters and found its way into the magazines, weeks or months out of date, that ended up in her hands. He alone could be what he had always been to her, the outpouring of a world, and he answered, at last, when she wrote the words *I think I'm dying*.

What he didn't want to do was provide updates on his life. He didn't want to talk about the decades gone since they'd sat in front of the little TV in the little cottage and she'd told him, in a whisper, that O. C. was right. She would have to make do with what was in front of her: a man in his thirties in a dark-blue L.L.Bean button-down, wisps of black hair threatening, in a few days, to take the form of a beard. The past would stay locked within him, his own private amusement and torment. He was not going to share.

When Jan broke up with him, six months ago, she advised him to visit his mother. This was before the letter came. "You carry her everywhere. The less you speak to her, the less you visit her, the bigger she looms inside of you."

"I don't think that's true."

He'd been smoking, a habit picked up at twenty-five, and they were sitting apart on the couch of her Queens apartment.

"In absence, people take on the level and power of myth. That is what she is to you. It weighs you down every day. You've become a very sad, private person."

When was he not private? When was he not sad? He wanted to genuinely ask her. They had met two years earlier, as low-level associates in a very large public relations firm. She wanted to be an artist. He simply wanted to quit. No job fit. After transferring from the community college to Stony Brook, a state university on Long Island, he chose biology as a major, took out student loans, and scribbled strange short stories and poems in his free time, unsure where they would go or why he did it. With his new name, no one asked questions. He resembled, each day, less of the boy he had been: he slashed his hair short, clouded his cheeks with an attempt at a beard, and adapted, as much as he could, to the culture sloshing around him, the politics and bands and athletics and drinking, so much of it, the thirsty Thursdays and, occasionally, cocaine Fridays and Saturdays. He could be anyone he wanted to be. He had no past there. He was the kid from upstate—a little weird, a little quiet, willing to do whatever. He kissed his first girl, then had sex with his first girl, their bodies groaning together on the third-floor couch of the common area on a Saturday afternoon, blocking the door with another couch. On the night of Obama's election, he danced with everyone else on the quad, hoping that through their performative joy, he could understand the profundity of the moment, what it meant to elect a new leader of a country he hardly knew, a leader unlike any other.

———

Gabrielle was different from him. He was happy she was. She told him to fly to Kentucky, not drive, and he said he didn't like to be in airplanes. This summer was her busiest yet. After her internship in the governor's office, her communications and then chief-of-staff jobs for a city councilman in Brooklyn, she was running for office herself, and expected to win. The Gabrielle he'd lived with would not have done these things, but she was able to adapt to where she was, to make the frenetic city machine her own. She mastered it. He was proud.

Her mother had moved closer to her, to an apartment in the city. Gabrielle would never have to visit her mother in a federal prison.

At the entryway, he filled out his visitor forms, emptied his pockets of his cell phone, wallet, change, and keys, and walked through the metal detector. The machine didn't beep, but the guard stopped to pat him anyway, before sleepily sending him through. He was stamped on the back side of his left hand with the invisible ink that would later be inspected under the black light before he left. It was a ritual he never quite understood, though he had come to see that a federal prison, like House of Earth, was determined to control every breath within its walls.

When he removed his driver's license to show the guard and complete yet another form-filling, check-in ritual, it struck him that not only was Mama's birthday in two days, but he was older, by several years, than she had been when she was last free. When he followed her into the woods, she was not yet thirty years old. He had never had a concept of her age at any point he lived with her. If he could never do as Mama did—so blindly follow a madman to ruin—he could also never summon the strength to raise a child as a teenager and then spend the subsequent decade ascending to power in any kind of organization. He could love her or hate her or ignore her, but he could not deny this. She, at one point, perhaps even behind bars, knew who she was.

He was ten minutes early. The visiting room, like everything else, was unchanged, dimly lit and windowless, filled with a row of dark tables welded to the ground, four flat seats per table attached at the base. Guards milled in the corner, staring straight ahead. Several inmates were there already, sitting in orange jumpsuits, one talking to a woman alone, another to a man and woman together. He sat at an empty table, prepared to wait.

In the early years, he would visit with questions. *Why* did you— and Mama could only say she was trying to get better, she wasn't well, she was doing her best, it was a complicated time, you will understand when you are older. That was one lie she told the most: that age would somehow help him better understand. He was no more ready to *understand*, to reckon with, to comprehend and analyze and explain to *himself*, let alone to other human beings, where he had come from and what, exactly, he would attempt to do for the remainder of his life, other than rent the first floor of a house five miles from downtown Mater and smoke cigarettes on the sagging porch. He had called Jan once after moving, to tell her he had found a place and settled, and she said she hoped this could be *regenerative* for him, to be close to home. After trying to teach biology to kids in charter schools and eventually edit press releases one cubicle away from Jan, he was trying to make money painting houses in Columbia County.

He bought his paints at Lawson's, where he used to work. He was making less money working on houses than he had at the public relations or teaching jobs, but he could paint without talking to anyone. He painted the walls of houses like Roseboro had painted the wall of House of Earth.

"It's all I want to know," he said to Jan.

In one of his last visits before today, he had asked Mama why she threw the book out. She told him it interfered with what needed to be done.

He had been fourteen when he, by accident, found a TV station showing *The Natural*. By then, he was aware the movie existed but knew little else about it. A few months before, he had rediscovered another copy of the book in the library and finished it. His hero, Roy, is offered money to throw the game. He accepts the money but decides, for the sake of a pregnant Iris, he will try to win. A young, promising pitcher, a boy not so different from what he used to be, rears back and strikes him out. In the final pages, a newspaper report appears about Hobbs's bribe-taking. The baseball commissioner says Hobbs will be kicked out of baseball and his records forever destroyed.

"Say it ain't true, Roy," a boy says to him. Roy can't tell him it isn't. He brings his hands to his face and begins to weep.

The ending was never what Lucien had imagined for Roy, who had existed as a prodigious hero in all his thoughts and dreams in the years after Mama forbade him from reading the book. That Roy was much more, a troubled man who also attempted to do good, saddened him when he closed the book, and he spent the night and early morn-ing in a despairing haze, unable to think of much else. As the book's conclusion settled within him, he began to see more of Roy in himself and wondered how differently he would have acted were he thrust into Roy's existence. In his failure, Roy was wholly real to him. Roy could have attended his high school. Roy could have been one of the friends, stolen in the night, bound and poisoned, tossed into a shallow grave.

On TV, Roy was golden. He looked nothing like Roy. He was still a New York Knight, still trying to win a pennant, but he was not Roy. As the movie built to the climax, Lucien wondered how they would depict the strikeout, how this actor, so golden, would summon the anguish of a career lost. What he found instead was a betrayal: Roy, blood staining his jersey, smashing a baseball in slow motion into the lights above the stadium, explosions raining glass on the field, Roy jogging elegantly around the bases, his future with Iris secure.

The unreality disgusted him. He shut the TV off.

Sitting now in the visiting room, drumming his fingers on the bare table, he felt the old indignation return. He would meet people who considered this the only fitting conclusion for Roy's life. Most of them were unaware there had been another reality, an original one, where there are only tears instead of explosions. They didn't understand the divergence. They didn't understand why this offended him.

When he wasn't looking, she entered the room. A guard was nearby, escorting her soundlessly. No one in the room betrayed any awareness of who she was, as they used to, and perhaps this was the advantage of time, he thought, the distance it always created between cataclysm and the present. Her face had grown pinched, almost shrunken, wrinkles dug into her forehead and cheeks, gray streaking the hair she had pulled tightly into a bun. When he was a child, she'd been titanic to him, and even when he had reached her height in that final year, she still tow-ered over him. He was still unused to her this way, a small woman in a jumpsuit uneasily approaching the table. When she smiled, he could see that her teeth had yellowed and one, near the front, was badly chipped.

"How are you?" she asked, sitting down across from him, her movements more deliberate than he recalled.

He remembered then he had no idea what to say to her. "I'm fine. I know it's been a while."

"You answered me. That's what counts."

He had answered her. The letter rendered with obscene precision, the *k* almost chiseled in front of the *y*. He tried, for just a moment, to imagine twenty years in this place, a generation passing in rural Kentucky. He came away with little, only Mama's face in front of him, waiting for him to answer her.

"How are you feeling?"

"It's been rougher of late. There's a bitch in here who hit me. She thought I was someone else. Now I have some pain in the side of my face."

He assumed this was the reason for the tooth.

"I'm sorry to hear that."

"You look—you look well. A little thin, honey. It's been so long. Are you still in the city?"

"I left. I moved back up, actually, not far from where we lived."

"It's very quiet there. Very lovely. I'm glad you left the city. It's a godforsaken place."

"I just thought it was time."

"It was. The country is much more agreeable. It's how we should be living, anyway."

"Well, the density of a city isn't necessarily bad either. It can be energy efficient."

"It's all going to be underwater soon," she said, lightly flipping her hand.

"Maybe."

"Are you enjoying your time in Mater?"

"I paint houses. It's enough to cover my rent."

"You were always very resourceful."

"I suppose."

"You must enjoy the fresh air, when you're out. I always loved the smell of the woods in the summer."

"I didn't know that."

"It's so important to preserve what we have."

"Yeah."

"Honey, you should really be concerned. The storms, the droughts, the melting ice. It's good you moved. You would've been drowned."

"If I stayed, I would've learned to swim."

"That's some sense of humor you have."

"I've needed it."

He had no concept of what she thought of every day, how she acted behind bars, if she had befriended fellow inmates, become a leader, started fights, finished fights, mentored new arrivals, exploited new arrivals, if the guards liked her, if she was still famous to all of them, if she ever thought about getting out. It was true what Jan said: in front of him, she was entirely reduced, a woman in middle age nursing pain in her face. This woman was his mother. This fact could stagger him.

"Lucien, how is that girlfriend of yours?"

"That's not my name."

"That's right—well, I don't so much like the other one."

"Well, Lucien is not my name. Legally, or anywhere."

"I'm sorry. It's just hard for me. You were my little Lucien."

"I—I just can't do this."

"It's hard for me, that's all, I wish you'd understand—"

"It's hard for *me*, okay? For me. Are you really dying?"

He was quietly shaking, both hands on the table now. His voice had jumped just enough for one of the guards to fidget in the corner, his fleshy face turning toward them.

"I don't always feel well."

"You're fine, aren't you? You aren't dying at all."

"You come so little, and I miss you."

"I come when I can. And now I'm going to leave."

"Everyone else, they have people come, sons and daughters and friends, and me, I don't have—"

"You never said you were sorry, you know that? Even at the trial. Not once. Not in a statement, not to me, not to anyone."

"That was a very tough time."

"All of my friends . . . I still think about them, do you know that? I can still hear Evie, Samantha, even Roseboro—I can't believe I'm even telling you, *you* of all people. I didn't even tell Jan."

"It was a very tough time."

"Stop fucking saying that."

"Then what do you want me to say?"

"Well, there is nothing to say to unwind more than twenty years, to bring us back somewhere else, is there? If I didn't follow you in the woods, who knows how long it would've gone on. I'd be dead."

"You were always safe, honey. You were. You were never going to die."

She always told him this, and he'd had more than two decades to consider whether it was actually true, whether O. C. Leroux, when the time came, wouldn't have decided he needed to die too. He didn't know. And if that decision had been made, Mama would have had her own choice to face.

"But what about them? All the others? All these years, all this time, and it doesn't even occur to you."

"It all occurs to me. Every single day. Did you come here just to tell me this? I wrote so many letters to you."

"You told me you were dying."

She looked away. "I said I don't feel well."

"You don't *feel* well. Okay. I can't remember when I felt well."

"Everything I did, honey, everything, I did it for you."

"You did it for a sick man."

"You don't understand."

"I don't want to. I don't know why I'm here. I don't know why I drove here. I'm going to go."

"Please don't go. It's good to see you, to be near you. I used to see you so much."

"Mama, you always left me. You were always gone. Don't you understand? I would look for you, wait for you, beg for you to come home."

"When I was gone, it was always for you."

"You were helping him kill people."

"We were trying, honey—"

"Trying for what? Murder, torture, God knows what that sick fuck Sebastian did to Evie. I wish he killed himself too, all of them."

Her eyes fell to her own veined hands laid flat on the table. She was not speaking, not moving. The guards were peering. She could always do this, withdraw from him, letting rage silently build. She could still inspire fear. Two decades in a cage, her body shrinking, and she had not lost that power.

Her lips began to move. "Lucien, dear, you follow the news, don't you?"

"I told you, that's not my—"

"Listen to me." She was still not looking at him. "I read what they bring us. I know the facts. I have so much time to learn them. Don't you know the facts?"

"The facts?"

"The National Oceanic and Atmospheric Administration recorded this past July as the hottest month in Earth's history. Nearly fifty thousand square miles of Arctic sea ice lost each day. And soil is being lost one hundred times faster than it's forming. The permafrost is disappearing. The global food supply is shrinking. The climate is rebelling. The oceans will rise. When the pandemic came, there was a pause, wasn't there? For a moment, the climate breathed. But now it's faded. We have returned to our old ways. We are the contagion. It's just as he said."

"He was a psychopath."

"O. C. Leroux loved you. He loved all of us."

"I can't stay here and listen to this."

"He wanted to build a new world. He wanted to save us. He understood it couldn't go on this way."

"You really don't get it, do you? All these years later—I know we fucked up. Humans fucked up. It's bad. One murderer in the woods, killing children, wasn't saving Earth; he was just killing people, killing and killing and killing . . ."

He was pounding the table, his voice cracking, his vision beginning to warp as he shot up to leave her. The guards were circling now, hands edging near their batons. Mama was smiling up at him. She made no move to stand up.

"We all did so much for you. He was going to spare you. You were special, honey. You always were. And you still are. He was never going to kill you. O. C. had Jack punish you because he believed in you. He knew you could handle it, that you needed to grow. I made sure it was never going to kill you. You were never going to be like the others. I protected you. I love you. I was always watching over you. Why don't you stay just a little while longer?"

But he was turning from her, walking as quickly as he could without breaking into a sprint, the double doors of the visiting room in arm's reach. When he turned, one final time, to look at her in the room, alone at her table, he could hear her speaking to no one, her lips forming the two words he knew now in only his dreams, when the lights went out and the night closed like a fist over everything he ever wanted to see.

Blood Earth.

But he wasn't going to hear that forever. He was here; he was alive; he was free. Yes, he repeated to himself: I am free. Gabrielle met him when he got into the city. He'd told her she didn't have to, that he knew how busy she was, that she was going places.

"You're going places too, Lucien," she said.

She drove with one hand on the wheel, a smile hanging on her face. They were in Queens now, stalled in traffic on the Grand Central Parkway. She was the last person to still call him Lucien, and he let her do it, allowed himself to be what he was to her all those years ago.

"I just don't know what to do."

"None of us do. None of us truly know."

"You know, Gabrielle."

"I'm only guessing."

He briefly looked out the window, catching a flock of birds in a V pattern escaping toward the bay.

"When we get back, can I introduce you to someone? She's a friend of mine. She's quiet, like you. She has your intensity and purpose. I think you'll be a good fit."

"Who is she?"

"Her name is Miranda. She volunteers on my campaign and is fairly new to the city. She came here for work. Like you, she avoids the dating apps. She doesn't do social media. No grid for her, other than a cell phone."

"I don't know. I think I need to be alone for a while."

"No one *needs* to be alone."

"I hear her voice in my head too much."

He was in the room with her, with Mama. *He was going to spare you.* On the flight home, in the car with Gabrielle, this was all he heard. His mother speaking to him in the prison, through walls, across air currents. He looked down, trying to stop his hand from shaking.

"You don't need to hear it anymore. You did what you had to do. Now you should rest."

At her apartment, he slept on the couch. His dreams were blank, so unlike what they once were, his mind bleeding into and out of a void. In the early morning, as Gabrielle made eggs, he drank a glass of orange juice and tried to imagine what he could possibly do next.

"We're going out later, so get ready," Gabrielle said.

"I don't know."

She sat down across from him. "You saw her in prison, but she's not *you*. You have to remember that. I get it—the past is eating you, and these scenes and sounds and images play on in your head, like a bad movie. You get to turn it off. You're allowed to do that. You did a brave thing by going to visit her. You saw her again. Now you live."

"I don't know," he said again, more quietly this time.

"But you do know! You don't have to live a shadow existence anymore. You don't have to retreat, curl inward. I know you. I know, like me, you become afraid. This parasitic fear. I hate it so much. You can think, sometimes, that's all there is—"

"Can we not talk for a bit? I'm sorry. I just need to lie down. I didn't sleep well."

"In the afternoon, we're going out."

Gabrielle had said he was living a shadow existence, which implied, in his own mind at least, that he was slight, without weight, seeking a space where light would not go. This wasn't wrong, but it wasn't right. He felt unbearably heavy. Not long after he fled House of Earth, Gabrielle's mother had taken them both to the aquarium in New York City, a day trip far beyond what he had known. Now it was ordinary, this city, but then its colossal breadth had staggered him, the way thousands of lives could pass before you in a single breath. He had pressed his nose against the car window to watch them go by, one and two and three and a thousand, dizzy with their mass. At the aquarium, he watched a nurse shark sink to the sandy floor, lying in wait. In that moment, drawing closer to the glass, he wanted to become the shark, to carry onward toward death in such a way—as a creature, confined and silenced, safe in the murk. Schools of fish created silver streaks around the nurse shark's body as it began to rise, inching up from the sand. It would be on the move. This was a life, rising and falling.

Gabrielle didn't want to make it easy on him, because that would mean abandoning him, letting him fall away from her and everyone else. He had done it and could continue to do it. It was like entering a liminal state, waking death, here just long enough to taunt his body and mind—you can be someone else if you want to, somewhere else. You can divide yourself further, into smaller and smaller pieces, invisible strands of soul that disappear in the wind.

He still loved Mama—that *still*, when it was all finished, was what made it so debilitating. He answered her letter and entered that prison. He listened as she spoke. He heard her again, was young again, the shadows creeping over his shoulder. Even in the memory of blood and death, the reeking bodies, he wanted to be near her.

Awaking from a brief nap, his dreams silent, he saw Gabrielle sitting at the edge of the bed.

"I've felt too, sometimes, it'd be nice to be able to destroy memory. To really will it away. Imagine, going in there like a surgeon, *this* memory gone, now this one too."

He didn't know what to say back. As he sat upright, his mouth had a cottony taste and he felt light-headed. Gabrielle continued to talk.

"I wanted it like you wanted it. Never as badly as you—no one could, Lucien—but I understood. You changed your name, and I said it was stupid, but that was me being me, playing a little role, you know? I respected it. You had to move on. We all do. We can't destroy memory, and forgetting only gets us so far, but we can isolate it, quarantine it a bit, push it away . . ."

She was playing with a small gold ring on her pinkie finger.

"I've tried all of it," he finally said. "I thought going there to see her, it would somehow—I don't know. I don't know what I thought."

"You don't have to think anything. We're going out."

They walked together out of the apartment, down three flights of stairs. It had rained an hour or two ago, he realized, and the sidewalk had been dampened, a scent he couldn't place now in the air. A man jogged by, then a small woman with a stroller, the sidewalk shrinking with this human life. He almost wanted to touch them, ask them how they were, how they did it—how they rushed, so easily, into the future. Gabrielle was one of them, walking one pace ahead, her eyes trained on an indeterminate point beyond them. She turned down one block, then another. He didn't know where they were.

"You're fine with diner food, right?"

"I'll take that, yeah."

"I texted Miranda. She's inside already."

"I don't know . . ."

"You'll know."

The diner was smaller than the ones he had eaten in upstate, a corner restaurant with one row of booths and a counter where a couple of older men sat, sipping coffee and staring up at a television showing a basketball game. His body propelled him forward as his mind fell back elsewhere, to the woods shrouded in darkness, the soil crushed beneath his feet. He was running as fast as he could, his breath cracking in his throat. Trees shot up to block his path. Voices he knew called for him, the familiar voices from deep in the woods, telling him, urging him.

Come home, come home.

"Miranda, this is my friend Salvatore Lux—"

"Lucien," he blurted out. "Salvatore is my full name, but Lucien— people call me that."

He didn't know why he had just said that, hot blood pumping in his temples, through his heart, the beads of sweat inching down his back. They were in a ruby-red booth, his legs tucked in tight. When he looked up, he saw her.

A small woman with brown eyes and a large, inviting smile. She was offering her hand. "It's a pleasure to meet you, Lucien."

The name was his again. Lucien, Lucien, Lucien. He hadn't spoken it out loud in years. Paperwork with the state of New York had excised it from history. A glass of water with ice was placed in front of him, and he began to drink.

He knew people, in these situations, asked what you did for a living. An occupation established stasis, rooted identities in an exchange. He didn't know how to ask the question. Instead, somehow, he began to talk.

"I actually haven't gone by Lucien in a while."

"Oh, really?"

"It was my birth name. Then I changed it. I wanted to forget myself. Now, I don't know why, I saw you—I felt compelled to say it."

"I've been Miranda since birth, so I can't say I've experienced quite the same thing. But while I order coffee, why don't you tell me why you decided to do this?"

Miranda sat back and spoke to the waiter. He asked for an iced tea. The waiter gone, Miranda turned back to him. He decided he needed to keep speaking to her.

"Gabrielle must have told you."

"I didn't," Gabrielle said. "That was for us. But you can tell her, Lucien. Sometimes that's the best thing to do."

"I grew up in a place that was quite wonderful and quite terrible, that I believed was all life could be. I never knew people could die until I saw so many die."

These words, he was surprised to find, were his own. When had he last spoken like this to anyone other than Gabrielle? When had he not been afraid to?

"Tell me where that was."

"House of Earth."

He waited for her to react. Everyone over a certain age would. He, along with the dead bodies, belonged to the discourse, pulsed there in a kind of cultural eternity that everyone who wasn't him could reference almost cheerfully. *Remember that cult in the woods? And that guy who wanted to kill everyone? Remember? The kid who escaped? Remember?*

"You were that boy."

"I was."

"You've grown up."

"I have."

"Into someone who is here, in this diner, willing to talk about it."

"They were strange times," Gabrielle said.

"The truth is, well, what I've seen—" He stopped short, unsure how to proceed. They were waiting for him. He cleared his throat and allowed the words to bubble up, coalescing into the sentences he needed. "Well, it's the universe. We all learn about it at some point, how it just expands and expands, how infinite it is. We accept it. This is our planet, our universe, there are the laws of reality. House of Earth was like that. People would wonder how it could go on. Why did they do it? Why did they listen? Why did it take one little boy, running for his life in the dark, to change everything? It's almost like asking, Why don't you defy the laws of physics right now? Why don't you swim through that wall, fly through the sky? Why not? My mother was a part of it, at the center of it, and I can't believe I'm saying this out loud, but I still love her."

"That's understandable, Lucien," Miranda said, reaching her hand out across the table. He took it. "She was everything to you. And you were in such a confusing place."

"It didn't become confusing until later on. That's the thing. There was such a beautiful simplicity to it, beautiful to people who were inside the walls. It didn't matter that your friends were disappearing."

"Growing up in an abusive home can be a little like that."

"How did you grow up?"

"With my mother. Just my mother. My father died when I was young. He slept around a lot, from what my mother said, and one day got so drunk he smashed his car into a telephone pole. I was maybe four at the time. I was sad, but I also didn't know what to think. It was me and Mom after that."

"I never knew my father."

"Well, there's something we have in common!" She smiled again and sipped from her coffee cup. "Mothers. Mine was a terror, but she was what I had. You'd watch for her moods like watching for weather, checking in on the sky, trying to figure out just when the rain would come. You never knew what it was. It could be something as simple as pouring a glass of milk. Playing in the yard. Asking her where the extra paper towels were. The rages, Lucien—those rages, they were down-right biblical. And you learn to think they're ordinary. It all feels *right*, almost."

"Yeah."

"You were right about one thing: it was like a universe. These were the laws you did not defy, could not dream of defying. It was a three-stoplight town in Indiana. They all knew her, knew me. The London kid. Archie's kid, even though Archie, my father, was dead. I didn't think I'd ever leave."

"But you did. We did."

"We did, didn't we? My mother used the belt. Your mother didn't seem like the type who'd hit, right?"

"She never hit me, no."

"I bet she was a quiet, raging type. Well, with my mother, it was the belt, it was take your pants down, turn around, five strikes with the buckle. She once wrapped the belt around her fist and she—well, you can imagine. But that's enough of that, right?"

They ordered. He got a turkey-and-American cheese sandwich. Miranda had a Greek salad. Gabrielle went for a chicken wrap. When the food came, they ate quietly, and every time he glanced up, he could see, just for a moment, that Miranda was looking at him too.

"What we have to remember is that we aren't those people any-more," Miranda said, wiping her mouth. "We keep the memory, but the memory isn't only us. We aren't *just* an accumulation of bad memories. For a long time, I really thought so. I teach now, fifth- and sixth-grade social studies, and see how my kids are. At that age, you don't have enough of the past to weigh on you. Or if you do, you aren't quite aware of it, how it swells, how it constricts. But we are more than that."

He heard a faint buzz and Gabrielle pulled out her phone. "Oh, it's my campaign manager," she said, smiling slightly. "Let me step outside for a bit. She wants to talk about something important."

"No problem at all," Miranda said. "You hop to it."

He watched Gabrielle walk out of the diner and pull out her phone again, confidently leaning against a lamppost. Her lips began to move.

"So what's next for you?" Miranda asked.

"I don't know. That's the thing. I stare into the future and I don't know what I see. On one hand, it's empty, vacant, nothing—on the other, well, it's like staring into the sun. I'm blinded. There's so much, and I'm just bent over and crouching there, in the light."

"You know, I felt that way too, for a long time," she said. She looked up toward the window, nodding in Gabrielle's direction. "And believe it or not, even that woman, with her wonderful nerve, did too. Sometimes, Lucien, we think we are the weakest people, the most alone, the most crushed, but we aren't. We never are."

"I want to believe that."

"You're going to."

He gazed up at her, tentatively at first. He realized he was afraid to look into her eyes. This fear was a fresh kind, unsettling at first, taking full bloom in his body. But he was unsettled because he wanted more of it, because he did not know what to expect—it was like that blinding light, except he needed to keep walking toward it, tilting his face upward to drink its heat. He couldn't stop looking at her, and he understood, with a hidden thrill, that she hadn't stopped looking at him either, that they were looking at each other and would continue to as long as they wanted, until day turned to night and they were two bodies walking down the street, melting together in shadow. He was not there yet, though. The sun still beat down on the pavement, and Miranda was taking his hand now, her fingers kneading his own.

"I believe you," he said.

"Do you want to go for a walk? I think Gabrielle will be a little while on her call. Then she can catch up to us."

"I'd like that."

They waved to Gabrielle, who waved at them, and they went out together into the daylight of the city, the sun warm on them both.

ABOUT THE AUTHOR

Photo © 2017 Vanessa Ogle

Ross Barkan is a novelist and journalist from New York City. He has published two previous books, *Demolition Night* and *The Prince*, and his journalism and essays have appeared in a wide variety of outlets, including the *New York Times*, the *Nation*, the *Guardian*, and the *New Yorker*.